THE
TATTERED BANNER

Duncan M. Hamilton

ISBN-10: 148101322X
EAN-13: 9781481013222

PROLOGUE

The heavy wooden door slammed shut and the booming sound reverberated in Soren's ears. He was plunged into a darkness like none other he had ever experienced. He could hear the scratchy metallic sound of the lock being turned and then nothing. No sound, no light, nothing. It felt as though he had been blindfolded and his ears had been stuffed with cotton. He retreated further into the cell, vainly probing into the darkness in front of him with his hands. His foot stubbed against something on the ground and he fell flat on his face against the cold stone flags of the floor. It had been a long time since he had lain on cold stone, but the faint familiarity offered no comfort.

His wrists and ankles burned from the rubbing of the shackles that had only just been removed, but the cold floor seemed to suck the rest of the heat and energy from his body. Despite this discomfort there was nothing in him that could motivate him to stand, so he lay there, blinded by the dark, deafened by the quiet and utterly robbed of hope.

PART I

Chapter 1

FIGHT OR FLIGHT

He waited until he was near the end of the alleyway before he slowed to a walk and then with a final backward glance, a halt. The bustle of the city seemed to disappear allowing him this brief moment of privacy. His hands trembled slightly as he tugged at the strings on the small purse that he had just stolen. It was a good, clean lift, he thought as he slowly teased the purse open. The excitement began to drain from his body to be replaced with the hollow ache of disappointment as he peered inside. He had known from the weight that it was a modest prize, but he had hoped that it would be enough to keep him in honestly purchased food for a few days. It wasn't.

'I thought I told you to stay off our turf, you little rat-shit!'

Soren knew the voice, which sent a shiver down his spine. Disappointment was replaced by fear. 'It's not your turf,' he replied.

'You had your chance the last time. We let you off light, but we won't be so easy this time! Now hand over the purse and take your beating.'

Soren scanned the alley as he slowly turned around. There was nothing he could use to defend himself. Not even a rock to throw at them. Them, because he knew Hetha would not be here alone. He always talked tough in front of his cronies, but on his own he didn't tend to sound quite so sure of himself. Faced with the inevitability of confrontation, the fear seemed to fade. He was sick of being pushed around by Hetha and his gang.

There were four of them. More than he expected. Hetha seemed to have managed to recruit another moron to his gang.

This changed things. Two he might have managed. Three he might have managed to run from. Four meant he was trapped. Why did he have to have run down a dead end? This was not his usual hunting ground, but he ought to have known the streets better than to have made this mistake. His complacency had compounded it. When there was no shout after he took the purse, he did not worry about changing direction and had just continued on into the alleyway to count his spoils. Greed and stupidity. He was angry with himself for having made the mistake, and he was angry for having been frightened by Hetha's voice. He weighed the purse in his hand. It was a shame, but such was life.

He flung the purse at Hetha with as much force as he could muster. The leather clad metal thumped into Hetha's face with a satisfying crunch and Soren could not help but smile. Hetha let out a screech of pain as his cronies raced past him, blocking off any chance of escape as Soren had expected they would. One of them swung at him, but he ducked underneath and rolled forward as he dropped. He knocked into the legs of another boy, tripping him with the unexpected move. Hetha had regained his senses by now, and squinting the tears from his eyes he rewarded Soren's little flourish with a hard kick in the stomach. Soren managed to squirm away from the blow just enough to reduce the impact, but it still knocked the air from his lungs.

Struggling to his feet, he stumbled on, trying to suck in some air and inch ever closer to the open end of the alley. A kick to the backside knocked him flat on his face, but he quickly rolled out of the way of another kick from the fourth attacker. Scrabbling in the rubbish in which he found himself, his hand closed on something solid. He rolled onto his back, pulling a lump of wood with him. A boot closed in on his face, but a hard crack across the shin with the piece of wood diverted the kick and gave Soren enough time to roll back to his feet. He was still a little dazed; he must have hit his head harder than he had thought when he fell.

Hetha came towards him, his face caked in blood. The purse must have broken his nose and the thought made Soren smile. Without thinking he lashed out at Hetha with the stick. Hetha's cronies paused for thought, surprised by Soren's sudden aggression and the vicious blow that their leader had received. Soren was surprised also. He had intended to give Hetha a stinging crack to the head with the stick, but not to hit him nearly as hard as it seemed that he had. Hetha let out a whimpering gasp as he fell to his knees. His eyes glazed over as he slumped the rest of the way to the ground, revealing a dent on the side of his head and a clump of hair matted with blood.

Had he killed him? Soren's surprise was genuine, but it didn't matter. He couldn't care less whether Hetha lived or died; he had beaten Soren too many times for him to have any concerns for his safety, but if he hoped to escape unharmed himself, he would have to capitalise on the situation.

He turned his fearsome gaze on the others. He wanted to make it clear that same fate awaited them if they tried to avenge Hetha. 'Come any closer and I'll fucking kill you too!'

One of the Hetha's gang shouted to run, and they all did, leaving Soren alone in the alleyway with his freshly stolen purse and Hetha's even fresher corpse. He looked at the bloodied face but felt no remorse. Fate had discerned against Hetha that day and had favoured Soren, but perhaps tomorrow it would not.

Chapter 2

THE SHOWMAN

The crowd roared as the wounded man was helped from the sandy arena floor, but the roars were not for the victor of the duel. Soren strained to get a view of the Bannerets' Enclosure, nearly losing his grip on the beam on which he sat and thought better of it. He would see the man the crowd were cheering for long before most others. It made him smile to think that the best seat in the Amphitheatre was also the cheapest; free to be exact, but probably also the most dangerous, for Soren sat perched on one of the massive wooden sun awning beams that jutted out over the arena.

He had spent two hours that morning sneaking through the Amphitheatre building after having slipped in through a goods entrance while no one was looking and then carefully worked his way up to the roof before precariously crawling out along the beam to the position he now occupied. He had a clear view of all below him, the crowd, the arena and the food vendors that moved around the stands. His stomach rumbled and he closed his eyes for a moment, hoping to catch scent of the treats they carried on the warm afternoon air.

Tens of thousands were packed into the Amphitheatre, all hungry to be entertained by the duellists, some famous, some less so, who would ply their trade in the arena that day. The citizens of the city were passionate about their duelling as was often evidenced by the devoted and emotion filled support and hate they had for different swordsmen. Each week this huge stadium, as well as many smaller arenas around the city would be packed to capacity. This stadium, 'the Amphitheatre', was the largest and where the very best, the Bannerets, came to duel.

Dismayed by the lack of regard the crowd had for him, the victor of the most recent duel made his way from the centre of the arena and disappeared into the Bannerets' Enclosure, leaving the arena empty save for the spattering of blood left on the sand by his wounded opponent.

The next pairing walked out and the audience became animated with excitement once again. The man walking out in front was perhaps the most famous swordsman in all of the states of the Middle Sea and certainly the most famous swordsman in Ostia. His name was Amero, also known as Amero the Magnificent, the Swift, the Dashing, the Brave. He was known by many names, all were flattering and in Soren's opinion, all were well deserved. Soren didn't know Amero's opponent's name. He doubted if anyone did and didn't imagine anyone particularly cared. All he represented was the foil against which Amero would ply his magnificent craft. He was the city's darling and his appearance sent the audience wild.

The day began to go from warm to hot, and as it did, the crowd began to stink. Slowly but surely the smell of thousands of sweaty bodies began to fill the air, giving it a pungent tang, which added a further layer of depth to the spectacle about to unfold beneath.

The Master of Arms joined the two combatants in the centre of the arena at a black mark that had become all but obscured by the golden sand of the arena floor. A bead of sweat itched as it trickled down the bridge of Soren's nose but he forced himself to ignore it. Just don't forget to hold tight, he reminded himself.

Amero and his opponent saluted and took their guards. The Master of Arms quickly moved back, and the two swordsmen went at each other. The unknown swordsman thrust, and Amero exploded into movement. Parry, riposte, balestra, seamlessly followed by a fleche. Soren knew the names for all of the moves and tried to identify each one as it happened, difficult as it was considering the speed at which they were executed.

The first touch was scored in that blindingly fast exchange. It had happened so quickly that Amero was already walking back to his side of the black mark before Soren had registered it in his mind.

The Master of Arms acknowledged the scoring touch and reset the duel. He gave the signal to restart and Amero attacked again without wasting a second, flourishing his blade in a style that Soren had never seen before. The crowd gasped and his opponent stumbled backwards as he was caught off-guard by the unorthodox attack. It was one of the many reasons Amero was so loved by the crowd. So many of the top duellists stuck rigidly to the tried and tested techniques. Amero on the other hand was an innovator. The swordplay he used today would be mimicked by children on the streets by the afternoon, and by other duellists on the next arena day.

The chink of metal, the occasional shout and the stamping of boots on the sand were the only sounds that could be heard now, for the crowd was utterly silenced, awed by the magnificent dance in front of them. For each graceful and flamboyant attack, Amero's opponent managed to block, dodge or dive away. After what seemed an age, Amero's blade hit true once again and this time a red stripe appeared around a slash in his opponent's white shirt. The crowd roared in appreciation.

The duellists in the arena did not use sharpened blades. The edges of their rapiers were dulled, but they still met at a pointed tip that was capable of drawing blood, which they often did, or killing, which was not an unknown occurrence.

Amero had killed in the arena once before, and the city mob was never squeamish, always eager to see the ultimate victory. Bannerets in the arena never intended to kill; it was not in their interests. Duelling in the arena was a career choice for many less wealthy bannerets and they all desired lengthy careers. Their sole aim was to win the fame and fortune for which they crossed blades, but as everyone knew, the more intense the fight and the more closely matched the duellists, the more likely one of them was to be seriously wounded or killed. Amero looked to the Master of Arms who acknowledged the touch and then returned his wolfish gaze to his opponent, who by now must have known that the result of the duel was inevitable.

Soren shuffled forward on his beam, his palms sweaty from the heat and the exertion of clinging on. He was holding his breath now, without realising it, as the opponent finally showed signs of tiring, whether from the loss of blood, the heat or the exertion. No one really cared, but the rise in excitement in the crowd was palpable as it was obvious that the end was near.

A scrape of metal, a sharp cry of frustration and the opponent was on his knees. Amero followed up with two more attacks but his opponent valiantly swatted them away. The crowd oohed and ahhed, expecting each blow to be the last, but each time they were wrong.

Then he was up again and Amero shrugged his shoulders. This unknown young man was proving far more of a test for the greatest blade in the State than anyone, least of all Amero, had expected.

He stepped back two paces and circled around to his left before commencing his attack once again. He stepped up the intensity, stamping hard with his front foot as he pressed in attack after relentless attack. The two blades flashed in the sun so brilliantly that at times it was painful to watch. There was another cry, but this time of pain and then a gasp from the crowd as Amero spun around in his follow-through. His opponent held a hand to his abdomen, and, unsteady on his feet, threw down his sword. A third touch and the fight was over. There would be no kill today. The crowd let out a somewhat disappointed sigh followed by lacklustre applause.

Usually protocol dictated that the duellists bowed and left the arena without a word, either under their own power or with assistance from the stewards if they were injured. Today, however, Amero walked back into the centre of the arena, his sword held in his right hand, triumphantly above his head.

'Good citizens of Ostenheim!' he called out.

The stewards and the Master of Arms looked to one another unsure of what to do. Anyone else's victory-drunken ramblings would lead to them unceremoniously being dragged from the arena, but this was Amero the Magnificent. To treat him so was unthinkable. The crowd began to hush as they realised he intended to address them, and Amero spoke again.

'Good citizens, my regards to my noble opponent.' He gestured toward the man who was being helped to his feet by the confused stewards and saluted with his sword. 'It is fitting that today was one of the most hard fought victories of my career, against a more than worthy banneret, for I have a sad announcement to make.'

Amero paused, masterfully teasing the audience, every one of whom was now teetering on the edge of their seat. Soren felt his heart drop.

'First of all, I wish to thank you for your continued support during my years of duelling, it has given me great encouragement. I must now, and not without regret, announce my retirement from this most noble of pursuits. My responsibilities to our great city and Duchy have made themselves known to me and it is to her service that I shall devote myself henceforth. Once again, thank you, and farewell!'

Soren nearly fell from his beam in shock. After a flourishing bow in which he swept his sword in a wide circle, Amero left the arena. At first everyone was quiet, then a hum of muttering grew with a sound like an approaching stampede until it was impossible for Soren to even think and begin to come to terms with what he had just heard. The people spoke in disbelief, disappointment and pride that the city's favourite son was sacrificing a life of fame and glory for a dull and invisible existence in civil service. The conversations differed, but the opinions were all the same, Amero, Count of Moreno was a great and selfless man.

Chapter 3

THE BUNGLING THIEF

Soren walked away from the Amphitheatre with a hollow feeling inside. He felt a sense of personal loss that seemed to him to be irrational, but he could not shake it off. He hoped some food would alleviate it. It had been a particularly bad year for begging though; he could remember being hungry more often than not lately. Scavenging hadn't been much better. The end result was that Soren was skinnier than he had ever been. The previous night he had passed the time counting his ribs. Counting was the one thing all of the street children were good at. There were probably reasons for the times being particularly hard, but they were beyond Soren, and he wouldn't have even wondered at them had they not had an impact on his belly. Nevertheless, he was hungry and despondent, and food was always the best way to cheer himself up.

Begging was prohibited everywhere in the city, but in the market square, known as Crossways, the City Watch made sure that rule was applied in the harshest possible way. A boy he had talked to from time to time, Piero, had died soon after the beating they gave him when he had been caught begging there and he knew of many more stories like that. It was thieving that brought Soren to the market though, not begging. It was a far more effective method to fill one's belly and you had less chance of making yourself known to the City Watch if it was done properly.

Crossways was a great open square in the middle of the city, bisected by two roads that ran east-west and north-south. From dawn until dusk every day, the square was packed with buyers and sellers. Everything was for sale there; spices and silks from the south, food, slaves and luxuries from across the Middle Sea, furs, metals and precious stones from the north, and every other type of item imaginable from places that Soren had never even heard of. Wagons and fat bellied merchant ships entered the city day and night, providing the city with its lifeblood.

If trade was the city's religion, then the merchants were its priests. They were jealously protected and it was death to impede their trade. Stealing in Crossways was treated as severely as murder. The death penalty was not such a frightening thing to someone who was starving though. Despite this, Soren was no fool and had no desire to meet a swift end on a watchman's pike. So he waited and watched for the perfect moment. A loaf of bread, a slab of beef, it didn't matter so long as it was food.

He had waited most of the afternoon, hoping that the traders would be fatigued and have let their guard down by the early evening. He had also limited himself to the poorer side of the market; the stalls here were smaller, belonging to the lesser merchants, often one-man operations and not so heavily policed by the City Watch. One trader in particular seemed to be paying less attention to his wares than trying to attract customers to his stall. When one finally stopped, Soren saw his opportunity.

The customer was well dressed, not as well dressed as a noble or a wealthier merchant, but neat, clean and tidy. A servant perhaps. Shrewd though, he was haggling hard and this was creating Soren's chance. The haggling was intense and the opportunity was growing greater by the moment. With as much nonchalance as he could muster with the smell of the different foods all around nearly driving him to madness, he walked quickly, but not too quickly, past the customer and into arm's reach of a beautifully shaped, golden loaf of bread. A series of inviting diagonal grooves were cut across its back, betraying its crusty shell and no doubt hiding delicious fluffy bread underneath.

His hand was shaking; the thought of the bread set his mouth awash and his heart was racing. The bread was firm to the touch, but yielded to the slight pressure of his hand. Then he had it, clutched to his chest. Keep walking, he thought, slow and steady, it is as easy as anything. The weight of anticipation was beginning to lift from his shoulders when disaster struck.

'Stop there! Thief!'

For a moment Soren hoped that the shout had been directed at someone else, but a glance over his shoulder proved that it had not. The merchant had pulled a long thin club from underneath his counter and was striding purposefully toward him. One of the smaller side alleys that ran off the square was his best chance; they led to the warren of tight twisting alleys that riddled the city like veins, a web that anyone who had grown up on the streets was intimately familiar with.

With eighteen years under his belt, Soren had found over the last couple of years that his body had become inconveniently large. The small spaces between adults at leg level that had once provided free passage when he was younger were now closed to him. Instead he had to use his size to try to bash people out of his way to clear a path ahead. It was not the most economical of escapes, knocking from person to person.

With each bump and curse, the merchant got a little closer. Just as one of the laneways came into sight and with only a few heads bobbing between him and it, he felt a firm hand grab a handful of his shirt between his shoulder blades. He spun around, and the first swing of the merchant's club cracked him on the back of the hand and knocked the precious loaf of bread from his grasp. He watched with agonising hunger as the loaf hit the smoothly cobbled ground and was quickly trampled into oblivion.

Recovering quickly from this setback, Soren pushed backward as hard as he could, driving with his legs and forcing his way past the last few people and into the free space at the entrance to the alley. Unfortunately the merchant had followed swiftly through the void he had left in his wake. Throwing himself backward to avoid the swing of the merchant's club, he fell into a pile of rubbish; various junk heaped there by the nearby traders. Luck smiled upon him as his hand came upon a piece of wooden doweling rod, which he quickly raised to parry off the next blow.

'You'll pay for that loaf, you little shit!' said the merchant.

'Fuck off, you fat pig!' said Soren. The merchant could easily afford to lose a loaf of bread. Its value to Soren was ten times what it was to him.

The merchant didn't reply. Soren's backchat just infuriated him. He bellowed in rage and kept furiously hitting down at Soren with his club. Soren scrambled to his feet, fending off each attack with his rough wooden rod. He consciously mirrored the stance of the swordsmen in the arena, his feet planted wide apart and his knees slightly bent. The contact of the two pieces of wood made a satisfying 'thwock' and Soren found that he was almost enjoying himself, or would have been if it were not for the painful hollowness in his belly and the disappointment at having lost the loaf of bread, which he was still feeling keenly. The merchant swung at him from left and right, the club swishing through the air. Some strikes Soren ducked, others he sidestepped, but the most pleasurable were those where wood struck wood, and Soren effortlessly deflected the club up, down, left or right; to any direction of his choosing. The merchant's attacks seemed to come at him at a snail's pace and Soren felt as though he could do as he liked.

The merchant, on the other hand, was not enjoying himself. Each spoiled attack was enraging him further. Instead of the satisfaction of beating the daylights out of a street urchin who had just robbed him, he was presented with the smiling face of a filthy gutter rat who he could not seem to lay a single blow upon. Furthermore, a chase that he had expected to take but a moment was requiring considerably more time, and his stall was unattended and inviting further theft. Finally reason overcame rage, and he paused, his face red as he gasped for breath. Soren remained in a crouch, gently swaying his weight from foot to foot, his piece of wood held out in front of him, the tip deadly still. With a curse at both Soren and the conspicuously absent City Watch, he flung his club at Soren, which Soren easily dodged, turned and walked back toward his stall. Soren put one hand on his hip and with the other raised his club high, in the salute that Amero had always made after easily defeating an opponent.

As he stood and straightened himself, the bitter disappointment at having lost the loaf struck him, and his empty belly with renewed force, but he was quickly distracted by a slow clapping sound. It was not the sharp sound of bare skin against skin, but that of soft, thick leather on leather drumming out behind him.

'Bravo, young man, bravo! I particularly liked the salute!'

Soren turned to face the source of the sound and was greeted by the fine figure of a gentleman and his servant. The gentleman stood in front of his servant, who had a suspicious look on his face. He was finely dressed, his breeches crisp and swash topped boots gleaming. He wore a fine dark doublet with puffed shoulders and sleeves, with only the collar and cuffs of a white silk shirt visible beneath. His hand rested on the beautifully shaped hilt of a rapier. A long black cloak with fine silver trim was slung casually back over his shoulders and a wide brimmed, feathered hat sat slightly askew atop his head. His countenance was cocky, and he seemed to be leaning on the pommel of his sword with perfect balance.

Soren wondered what a gentleman was doing in an alley like this until he spotted the red mage lamp of a brothel hanging above a doorway some way behind him.

'Where did you learn to wield a stick like that, boy?' the gentleman asked.

'I don't know, my Lord,' said Soren.

'Really. That's very interesting. Do me a favour, boy, and there's a crown in it for you.'

A crown was more money than Soren had ever had before, a veritable fortune, but nonetheless he hesitated a moment. The gentleman sensed this and laughed out loud.

'Fear not, boy, I just wish to see another demonstration of your skills with a stick! Spar with Emeric here for a few moments.' He gestured to his servant who, with a look of resentment on his face stepped forward and picked up the wooden club that the merchant had discarded. He adopted a low pose with the club held well out in front of him. Soren dropped back into the easy stance he had used against the merchant.

'Go!' said the noble, his voice a mixture of amusement and curiosity.

The man called Emeric shrugged his cloak back over his shoulders and jabbed forward quickly, the tip of the club shooting forward in a smooth motion with far more control than the merchant had ever exhibited. It jabbed Soren hard in the chest and left a stinging welt that sucked the breath from his lungs. He had only just regained his balance in time to slap the next attack to the side and was not able to linger over the pleasant sound it made. Unlike the merchant though, Emeric was not long knocked out of his rhythm by the parry and recovered almost instantly, countering with a swipe that nearly caught Soren in the midsection.

He danced out of the way, spinning as he did, swishing the chair leg through the air until it satisfyingly connected with cloth and flesh.

'Enough!'

Soren was breathing heavily and feeling light headed with hunger by the time they stopped. His arms and legs burned and he was not at all certain that he would not be sick.

'You say you've never had any training at all?' asked the gentleman.

'No, my Lord, none,' replied Soren.

'Tell me then, what is your name?'

'Soren, sir.'

The gentleman remained silent for a moment and then conferred with his servant Emeric for several more. He turned back to Soren and scrutinised him for a moment longer before speaking again.

'Well, Soren, my retainer disagrees with me, but I am feeling in a generous mood this evening. How would you like to learn how to use a sword properly?' he asked.

Seeing opportunity, Soren grabbed at it with both hands. 'Very much, sir!' he said. 'I'd like a hot meal also,' he added more in hope than expectation.

The brazen request drew a laugh from the noble. 'I'm sure we can manage a hot meal as well. You are now under my patronage. I am Banneret of the Blue Amero, Count of Moreno. Emeric here will see to your needs.'

The name sent a shiver through Soren's body. The gentleman had seemed vaguely familiar, something about his bearing, his

voice, but in the shadows of the alleyway, Soren had not recognised him. He had only ever seen Amero from a distance anyway.

Amero gestured to Emeric who discarded the wooden club
and turned back to Soren.

'Well, lad, you've had a stroke of luck today. Let's see about
getting you that meal,' said Emeric.

Chapter 4

THE OPPORTUNITY

O stenheim was a city of many different coloured buildings with roofs of burnt sienna or grey-blue slate. The
city sat on a natural harbour in the lee of a hill that
became a cliff at the water's edge. Atop this hill sat the castle,
which watched out over both the surrounding countryside and
the sea approaches to the city. The Duke's palace was nestled
behind it on the landward side. On the remainder of the hill,
which sloped gently down to the city, was Highgarden, where
the wealthy citizens of Ostenheim made their homes. It was surrounded by leafy squares and parks, and the air was clean and
fresh; a world far removed from the warren of tight twisting
streets and houses built virtually on top of one another in the
city below. Also sitting on this hill was the Academy of Swordsmen, known simply as the Academy. Ever since the Mage Wars
that saw the final break up of the ties of the Saludorian Empire,
those who earned the right to carry a sword had been revered
above all others in the states lining the Middle Sea, even above
the sea captains and merchant princes whose skills ensured the
prosperity of the mercantile nations.

Unlike the other buildings in the city, the Academy was built
from a pale, creamy stone that had been brought from far away by
the mages who built it many hundreds of years before to serve as
their headquarters in the city. The architecture was a testament
to their power and wealth, but even this power and wealth had
not saved them. They and their society had long since been scattered to the wind by the swordsmen known as bannerets. It was

something of an irony that their vanquishers adopted their former residences.

The Academy was responsible for the training of swordsmen in Ostenheim, who, once graduated, were granted the title 'Banneret'. It carried with it the right to carry a sword within the city walls and to go to war under your own banner, but the benefits for graduates were many. Access to the Academy was, in theory available to everyone from all levels of society, but attendance was expensive and entry was competitive, which meant that its student numbers were dominated by the wealthy, with a minority being those lucky enough to have attracted the attention of a wealthy patron that would sponsor them for their time there. It meant that a homeless orphan like Soren could find himself elevated to the highest and most respected level of society if he could just manage to complete his training there.

It was to this campus that Emeric now took Soren. The consequences of this life-altering stroke of luck were still far from fully settling in his mind. Soren had never before in his life come to this part of the city; the Watch didn't like people in rags disturbing the serenity of Highgarden for the inhabitants. As the streets began to broaden and become leafier, Soren felt ever more out of place. Were it not for Emeric constantly pushing him on with a firm hand, he would have turned and run, golden opportunity or not. He had tasted the clubs of the Watch before, and had no desire to repeat the experience.

The night was drawing in and the boulevards were quiet, but not empty. The occasional gentleman passed by, often drawing with him the bittersweet stench of alcohol. Soren and Emeric were attracting the odd glance but Soren was somewhat comforted by the fact that Emeric was attracting just as many as he was. The Count's retainer had a completely bald head and a wicked scar that ran down the right side of his face, turning his scowling mouth into something more like a sneer. Were it not for a doublet bearing the arms of his employer, Soren was certain the Watch would be making themselves known.

The Academy overlooked a square, or more correctly a triangle, a small cobbled courtyard with trees in each corner and a small fountain in the centre. Lining two sides were grandly built five story buildings, luxury goods shops on the ground floors, with apartments, no doubt also the height of luxury, above them. On the longest side of the courtyard sat the façade of the Academy.

With broad columns, graceful lines and windows along its length, it was an austere yet strong statement and, like all the other Libraries of Mages in the cities of the former Empire, had architectural designs that had been copied but never since improved upon. Emeric walked confidently up to the large, dark wooden doors recessed in the archway in the middle of the façade. He pounded on the door with his fist, ignoring the knocker and stepped back to wait. It was a moment before they could finally hear some shuffling from behind it. A small panel opened and a face illuminated in the pale yellow glow of a mage lamp could be seen behind it.

'What do you want? The Academy is closed for the night,' said the man. His voice was rough, suggesting he had just been woken from his sleep. A pair of sleepy eyes surveyed Emeric for a moment and then Soren. His voice took on an even less pleasant tone, if such was possible. 'Trade entrance is around the back anyhow. Now clear off and come back in the morning. The back gate mind!'

Emeric took a step back so the doorman could see his doublet.

'I'm here on the business of Count Amero dal Moreno. Open the door or I'll have the hide off your back!' said Emeric, with menace in his voice.

The doorman instantly took on a more formal and less dismissive approach. 'What business do you have at this hour of the night?' he asked.

'I have a new student for admission,' Emeric said.

'Term started a week ago. His lordship should know that,' said the doorman. 'That boy is far too old to start here anyway,' he added, nodding toward Soren.

'Enough of your impudence.' Emeric's voice was calm and level, if anything a little quieter than usual, but it was far more frightening than any roar of anger Soren had heard. 'The Count requests that this boy be admitted to the Academy right away.

Neither one of us wants for him to have to come down here and see to it himself.'

The doorman remained silent for a moment, then the panel was slammed shut and a clank of metal rang out from behind the door. The main doors remained shut, but a smaller wicket door opened in the centre of one of them. The doorman stood behind it, mage lamp in hand with a dark cloak covering his nightclothes.

'Well, be quick about it then,' he said impatiently.

Soren looked at Emeric, who remained motionless. He smiled for the first time.

'Well, on you go, lad, I've taken you as far as I can.' He paused abruptly, as though he had stopped himself from saying something, but then continued. 'Don't let where you've come from hold you back. This place isn't everything, but it's as much as the likes of us can hope for. Just make the best you can out of this opportunity, another one this good ain't likely to come along again.'

With that he took a step back, turned, and paced away into the night. Soren walked hesitantly through the door to be greeted by the grimacing doorman. He slammed the door, bolted it shut, and turned to Soren.

'You're filthy, and you stink. It's the stables for you tonight, m'lad. The Master can decide what he wants to do with you in the morning,' he said. He beckoned for Soren to follow him and walked off into the darkness, his mage lamp creating a soft bubble of warm light around them.

The stable was, compared to what Soren was used to, palatial. He couldn't even guess at how many horses it housed, but it must have run into the hundreds. When he had asked the doorman, he had been ignored. The doorman had led him to an empty stall, told him that someone would be there for him in the morning and left him to the darkness and the sound of hundreds of restless horses. Soren didn't mind however; the straw was fresh and deep, the stall a perfect shelter.

As he sat down on the hay, he found it hard to believe what had occurred that day. The sponsorship of promising young men of humble backgrounds into the Academy was a well known tradition in the city, and a source of popular pride. Even the most lowly man could reach beyond what he had been born into and achieve virtually anything if he was lucky enough to have the opportunity to attend the Academy. When Soren was a boy at his orphanage, both he and all of the other boys dreamed of being spotted by a wealthy benefactor and trained for entry to the Academy. It was probably the dream of every boy of a modest background. As he had gotten older and the dream ever less likely, he had forgotten it, along with all of the other dreams of childhood as life became a daily struggle just to survive. Now, it seemed, the dream was coming true. He was almost too afraid to go to sleep in case he awoke to discover this day had all in fact been a dream of the dream coming true. Nevertheless, eventually he lay back on the fresh straw and had the best night's sleep that he could remember.

———◆◆◆◆———

He awoke to beams of sunlight piercing down through ventilation slats in the roof. They illuminated the countless particles of dust drifting through the air, which made it seem chokingly thick. There were two men standing over him, silhouetted in the contrasting murk and brilliant illumination of the stables. Soren's heart raced until he remembered that he was in safe surroundings. They were talking, clearly unaware that he was awake.

'He's too tall, and far too old to be starting off his training. What was Amero thinking? He must have been drunk again,' said the taller of the two men.

'Hmm, I agree. Too tall by far,' said the other, standing with his arms akimbo.

'And it looks as though he has just been dragged out of the gutter,' uttered the taller one.

'He probably has, but there's many more than him here that have been dragged out of the gutter. Be that as it may, Amero's man handed over a purse of crowns this morning that will more than cover his fee, lodging and expenses for two years, so he must have seen something in the lad.'

'Maybe he's taken a fancy to him!' said the taller man.

'Ha! I don't like the man any more than you do, Bryn, but I like unfounded speculation even less. Amero is a Banneret of the Blue and has the right to nominate one student every year. This is the first time he has ever done so, so we must give the lad a chance. Wake him up.'

The taller man, the one who had been called Bryn, stepped forward and nudged Soren with his boot. Soren made his best attempt to seem startled and sleepy.

'I am Dornish, Banneret of the Blue and Master of the Academy,' said the shorter man, his arms still akimbo and his features still hidden in the dark. 'What is your name, boy?'

'Soren, sir.' He added the sir as an afterthought as he got to his feet. Standing, he was taller than both men. He had assumed himself to be over six feet, but didn't really know for certain.

Dornish gave him an appraising and not particularly encouraging look.

'A bloody giant, and scrawny as a starving rat. I expect you're as clumsy as an ox, lad! Still, you'll have reach and strength if we can put some muscle on you,' said Dornish. He stared at Soren with a look of uncertainty on his face. 'You will have a chance here, lad. I don't have high hopes, I'll be honest, but you'll be given a fair run. If you aren't up to it, having the Count of Moreno as sponsor won't do an ounce of good.' He turned back to the taller man. 'See that he's washed, fed and given proper clothes. We'll have a look at him this afternoon, and if he isn't up to it we shall send him on his way.'

Chapter 5

THE ACADEMY OF SWORDSMEN

After being pushed into an ablutions block with a towel and a bar of soap, Soren was taken to the Academy supply shop, where he was given a new set of clothes, the uniform of a student at the Academy. Having been used to loose rags, the fitted clothes he was given felt restricting. He conceded that they fit well and allowed him a full range of movement, it was just that being fully enclosed in cloth was a new experience. After washing he had looked at himself in a mirror, and had to acknowledge how thin he was. With the muck washed off there was more bone than flesh and next to the people around him, he looked like a walking skeleton. With the new clothes he looked like an entirely different person; perhaps even one that might fit in there. He hoped they let him at least keep them if they threw him out, as they most certainly would. They would come in very handy in winter, if they weren't stolen first.

When taken to the canteen, referred to simply as the 'Dining Hall', it became clear to him that his emaciated look would soon change if he managed to stay at the Academy. The hall was a long, high ceilinged room, with dark and ancient looking roof timbers. At the end opposite the doors, there was a long table upon which was placed great silver serving dishes full of food. Porridges, stews, soups, potatoes, vegetables, fruits, meats and breads of all description. The hall was open all day and you could eat as much as you wanted, he was told. It sounded too good to be true, but then everything he had heard so far that morning had. The only other place he had seen this much food was in the Crossways, and access to that fare was considerably harder to come by.

He loaded up his tray with a little of everything that caught his eye, which amounted to an awful lot, and picked a seat on the end of one of the long tables as far away from anyone else as he could get. In the deepest recess of his mind he feared that the food would be stolen, and his natural reaction to it was defensive even though he knew that this would not happen. What was this strange place, and how did he end up there?

The steward who had shown him to the dining hall had told him that he would be back in twenty minutes or so to take him to class, so he tucked into his food with ravenous intent. As he ate, he surveyed his surroundings in more detail. The walls were lined with great portraits of distinguished looking men. They could all have been great heroes of Ostia, but the images meant nothing to Soren. He might have heard of their names, but he had never seen paintings like that before. In the centre of the long, wood panelled walls on both sides of the hall, great marble fireplaces housed roaring fires. The heat they gave out kept the massive hall comfortably warm.

There weren't that many people there and Soren supposed most of the students would be in a class of some sort. There were a few small groups huddled together around the hall though, eating and talking intently. They were all dressed identically in their uniform of white shirt, beige britches and sleeveless white waistcoat, with their dark blue doublets hanging over the back of their chairs. They paid Soren little interest. He supposed he didn't stand out all that much anymore now that he was clean and wearing the same uniform as them. He had not yet been given a doublet, but was told that he would be in due course. There was a black, brimless felt hat also, but he was told that it was only worn for assemblies and reviews and such like. He was glad that this was the case as he thought the hat looked ridiculous, and it made him feel ridiculous when he had tried it on.

By the time he was finished, he was beyond completely full. His stomach felt tight and ready to split, but he had not left behind a single morsel of what had been on his tray. He thought about getting some more and putting it in his pockets for later. It felt as though it would be an act of madness to allow the opportunity to go by, but as he was about to do so the instructor named Bryn entered the hall and after scanning the room quickly made his way over to him.

'I hope you are done eating, Master Dornish is in the training hall and wishes to see you,' he said.

Soren nodded and got up to follow him. They walked out of the dining hall into the cobbled courtyard outside. Bryn led him through courtyards and around corners until they eventually reached a larger square flanked on all sides by tall buildings of the same pale stone and lined with windows. Bryn led him along the side of the square to the building on the opposite side.

As was the style of all the buildings that he had so far been in, this building was entered through massive double doors slightly recessed into the long side of the building that faced out onto the square.

'This is the Tyro Training Hall,' said Bryn, as he reached for the door handle. 'If Master Dornish chooses to allow you to remain, you will get to know this hall very well.'

They entered it and any questions Soren had about why the campus seemed so quiet were answered. There were hundreds of young men, about his age or younger training all around the hall. They were running, lifting weights, climbing ropes, doing all kinds of exercises. They were fencing against each other, against stationary dummies, or against dummies that moved and attacked by themselves. This wonder seized hold of Soren's attention for some time as he walked across the hall notionally following Bryn.

'Master, here is the boy,' Bryn said.

The man turned around. It was the first time Soren had seen him clearly. Master Dornish was quite a bit shorter than Soren. He could in fact see clear over the Master's head. His hair was long and had once been black but was now liberally streaked with grey and was tied back in a tight, neat ponytail. He had a thick moustache the same colour as his hair, and a neat pointed tuft of hair growing from his chin. On closer inspection Soren realised the moustache was concealing part of a scar that ran from his cheek down to his lip. Bryn had a scar on his face also, and he recalled that Emeric had one also. It seemed to be an identifying mark for men in this trade.

'I'll match you against one of the tyros. They are about the same age as you, some a little older perhaps, but have already been studying the sword for at least a decade and have completed two years of study here. They are your peers and the students you must ultimately prove yourself against. If you do passably well you can stay. No one can expect much more than that from you at this point,' he said, as they walked across the hall's floor. 'Ranph! Bring an extra sword.'

A boy with dark brown hair instantly stopped what he was doing and ran to one of the sword racks from which he extracted two rapiers and ran to Soren and Dornish.

'Ranph dal Bragadin, meet Tyro Applicant Soren,' said Master Dornish.

Other students began to gather around, followed by more as they became aware that something was going on. They formed a wide circle around Soren, Ranph and Dornish, their boots shuffling on the wooden floor. Their whispers were both irritating Soren, and intimidating him at the same time. He didn't like being the centre of attention. They were all watching every move he made. He had always lived in the shadows, surviving by never being noticed. He could feel beads of sweat form on his brow and tried to focus his attention on the boy in front of him. He was shorter than Soren, but well built. Fit and strong in comparison to Soren's scrawny and malnourished. His hair was of the fashionable shoulder length, held back in a ponytail more carelessly tied than Master Dornish's, which gave him a rakish, carefree look.

Despite his attempt to concentrate, the whispers, chuckles and slights gnawed at the back of Soren's mind. Ranph handed him a sword and then stepped back.

'Ready? Duel,' said Dornish.

Soren had just registered the words when Ranph lunged forward, the button tip of his rapier a blinding flash of light as it tore through the air toward him and stabbed into his chest. Guffaws of laughter, applause and cheers consumed the dull murmur of voices that had existed before. Soren felt embarrassed and angry.

If he was to be thrown out of the Academy, it would not be to the sounds of the jeering laughter.

'A touch! Excellent form, Bragadin. Again! Duel,' said Dornish.

Soren dropped into a crouch and sprang backwards, his body moving clear of the path of Ranph's sword not a moment too soon. Expecting another quick scoring touch Ranph committed too much weight to his otherwise perfectly executed thrust and paused a moment too long on his front foot as he pushed back to a balanced stance. Angered by the constant muttering Soren lashed out, sweeping his rapier back in an arc, twisting his body into it as he did. Ranph let out a yelp as the length of the rounded blade lashed across his back. Gasps replaced the laughter and cheering of the previous touch. There was more muttering, but now of disbelief, which made Soren smile to himself. This boy was fast, but he was faster.

'A touch! All even. One more touch to be scored,' said Dornish. There was a note of surprise in his voice. 'Ready? Duel!'

Ranph was angry, both at the shame of having conceded a touch in front of his peers and at the hot red welt that was forming across his back, but he was not stupid and this time he approached with more caution. Soren had not really expected another swift attack, but had moved quickly just in case. Sword out in front, he took two quick steps to the left and brushed aside the testing feints Ranph fired in quickly but without the conviction of a proper attack.

The mocking voices in the background seemed to fade into oblivion, as Soren was only aware of his opponent, the sound of their boots scratching on the dull wooden floor and above all, the hammering of blood through his ears. Ranph lunged again, faster this time, his eyes not locked on Soren's any more. Why not? They were locked on his target! Soren stepped to the side and twisted his torso, the blade passing a hair's breadth away. Soren tried his fast counter again but somehow Ranph got his blade back in time and swatted away Soren's with ease. The gathered audience gasped with the same excited tension that Soren had seen at the Amphitheatre. The thought that his actions could elicit the effect that Amero had on people filled him with an enormous sense of something he couldn't quite describe, but the momentary lapse in concentration nearly cost him dearly. Ranph came back again, thrust after thrust, his front foot hammering down on the floor with each attack, breath hissing out of his mouth with exertion.

Eventually Ranph gave up the flurry as fury gave way to fatigue. The duellists circled one another for what felt like an age; all the while Soren waited for the next series of attacks. The tension was building to a point where Soren felt as though he could no longer bear it. He did the only thing he could think of to break the impasse. He lashed out with all the speed, strength and energy he could muster. As his body lunged forward, his arm outstretched, Ranph's movement seemed to slow. However, as had been the case with Soren's previous attack, this one was wild and uncontrolled. As fast as he was, his strike was not on target. Ranph ducked out of the way and fired in a counter thrust of his own.

'A touch!' said Dornish.

Soren held his breath, his eyes squeezed shut, his chest stinging from where he had just been struck. Had he done enough to remain?

'Thank you, Tyro dal Bragadin, you may return to your class,' said Dornish. When Ranph had gone and the crowd had dispersed and returned to their classes, Dornish turned to Soren.

'That was some of the ugliest sword play I have ever seen, young man, but by the Gods you are fast! It seems the popinjay was right!' He muttered the last words, as though he was thinking out loud. 'I don't know if I have ever seen anyone move quite that quickly, especially not someone your size. There are not many here that can put a touch on dal Bragadin even on a bad day; he really is very good. You can stay. I'll have a steward find you a bunk in the Under Cadet Dormitory for now.'

He was in. Soren did not know whether to be pleased or worried. Perhaps feeling both was most appropriate. A doorway to a completely different life had been opened to him and the swift and drastic change in his circumstances left him feeling lightheaded. He was suddenly very tired, no doubt due to it being the most tumultuous day of his life, but at least he wouldn't have to worry about where his next meal would come from anymore.

Chapter 6

A JUMBLE OF LETTERS

O ne of the Academy stewards took him from the training hall to the Under Cadet dormitory. Those in their first year at the Academy were referred to as 'Under Cadets', or 'Unders' and they lived in this building. The porter had said that all four hundred of the first year students had their rooms here. This was one of the years that Soren had been skipped past, but as a newcomer there were many formalities, such as membership of a house of residence, that had yet to be addressed, so for the time being he was being given a room here.

Those that matriculated from the Under Cadet year were allotted to one of the four houses of residence on the campus, Stornado, Ancelot, New and River, when they became students of the Academy proper and began their Cadet year. Soren had also been skipped past this year to place him in a class with students closer to his age. The matriculating under cadets were offered a place in a house by the class that were graduating from the Academy, which was usually done by names being balloted on by those senior students. Those who were not invited to join a house were assigned to one and had to be content with where they were sent. The result was that the makeup of the residents in any particular house tended to be along the lines of familial alliances outside of the Academy. Aside from the Campanile, the large round tower in the front square of the Academy, the Under Cadet Dormitory was also the tallest building on the campus.

Soren had been given a room on the top floor of the building. Rooms on the higher floors were unpopular, as despite having a magnificent view over the Academy grounds, the Citadel, the city itself and the harbour below, the tight spiral staircase was a misery to climb for six floors, particularly after a hard training session. Not to mention that each floor up was also one further from the ablutions block on the ground level.

His room was tiny and designed to be shared with one other student. It was painted plain white with a cot bed on either side of a narrow space running from the door to the dormer window which jutted out from the roof that sloped sharply down from mid-way along the ceiling of the room. Two small closets and two foot-lockers were jammed into the small remaining spaces left by the beds on either side of the room. In the time it took him to survey his new home, the steward had disappeared.

He went in and sat on one of the vacant cots. The other cot and closet appeared unused, so it didn't seem as though he was to have a roommate. A folded blanket and pillow were stacked at one end of the bed he sat on. Soren idly opened the footlocker and closet on his side of the room, not really expecting to find anything, but was still oddly disappointed when they indeed proved to be empty.

So this was his new home. His home. A smile broke out across his face.

***

There was to be no time afforded to Soren to settle into his new surroundings, nor to come to terms with the abrupt change to his life. His attendance at class would be expected on the following morning, and as the porter had indicated on the night he had arrived, term had begun a week before. Soren was also aware of the fact that he had many years of training to catch up on.

He encountered his first major obstacle almost right away. A steward knocked on his door and left a pile of papers for him. Soren took them and returned to his cot, sitting with them on his lap. He looked at the sheet on top and felt a wave of panic run through his insides. He stared at the markings on the page with all of the concentration he could muster, but nothing would cause them to make sense to him. He looked at the next sheet, but with the grim certainty that it too would be completely unintelligible. He had never needed to read anything while living on the street, and wouldn't have been able to find anyone to teach him even if he had. There were cursory lessons given in the cathedral orphanage he had lived in as a child, but little if any had stuck as it had just never seemed that important.

It was difficult to suppress the feeling of desperation that was welling within him. For a large portion of the day at the Academy he would be entirely unable to function. As soon as he was found out, he was certain that he would be thrown out on the street. He could not allow this opportunity to be taken from him so easily.

What was worse was that he had no one to go to for help. Anyone at the Academy would surely make it known that he was illiterate, and that would achieve the exact result that he was trying to avoid. As despair became realisation that his first day at the Academy could also be his last, it occurred to him that perhaps he did have someone he could ask.

It was not particularly difficult to find where Amero dal Moreno lived. All Soren had to do was wander around Highgarden for a little while until he spotted a servant wearing the arms of the House of Moreno, an emblem that was familiar to any fan of the arena. His plan was not quite as efficient as he had hoped however; the servant he chose to follow was on his way out on an errand rather than returning from one, but he eventually led Soren back to the mansion that was the Count of Moreno's town house.

He didn't bother going up to the front door, going instead directly for the staff entrance to the side. He knocked and waited for a moment before a middle-aged man in the same navy and gold coloured waistcoat that the servant he had followed had been wearing opened the door.

'How may I help you, sir?' asked the servant. Soren was somewhat taken aback by this. In particularly hard winters he had begged door to door, but the reception had usually been harsh and unpleasant. He had never been called 'sir' before. The clothes. It was the clothes. What a difference they made!

'Emeric, I need to see Emeric,' Soren said. 'Please,' he added as an after thought.

'Might I ask who is calling on him?'

'Yes. Soren. My name is Soren.'

'Very good, sir, I shall fetch him. For future reference, gentlemen usually call at the main door, to the front of the building. If you wouldn't mind waiting a moment.' The servant went back into the building and Soren felt his nerves mounting up as he waited. Would Emeric be able to help him? Would he even be bothered to? He certainly had no reason to, although he had been kind to Soren thus far despite his gruff appearance. It wasn't long before he appeared at the door, a quizzical expression on his hard face.

As soon as he saw him, Soren blurted out what he had been trying conceal up to that point. 'I can't read,' he said, feeling ashamed of the fact for the first time in his life.

Emeric nodded and remained in contemplative silence for a moment. 'Should've thought of that I suppose, can't rightly expect a lad off the streets to be able to read. I gather you're not too keen on them finding that out at the Academy though?'

Soren shook his head. 'I don't want to miss out on this chance over something as stupid as reading.'

Emeric smiled, which made his face even less congenial, if possible. 'Well, we can't have that, but you'll learn soon enough that reading ain't stupid. Come in and we'll have a think about how we can fix this.'

Emeric led him into the house, at first passing through narrow, undecorated corridors, then into wider, high ceilinged ones that were lavishly decorated. He brought him into a room of plush wooden framed sofas that were intricately carved and upholstered with the softest material Soren had ever felt.

'His Lordship is out, so if you wait here, I'll see what we can organise,' said Emeric. He left Soren alone in the room for some time before returning.

'Come back here tomorrow and every day after at four bells. Tell your masters that the Count needs you on house business for an hour a day; they shouldn't have a problem with that.

'For the time being, pick out someone you recognise and follow them to all their classes, you shouldn't go too far wrong doing that. Keep your mouth shut and try to stay invisible in class. If you're asked anything, just say you don't know. You'll look like a thicko for a while, but better that than the alternative, and hopefully you'll sort the reading out quickly enough. Now off with you, and don't forget, four bells sharp. I'll tan your hide if you're even a minute late,' said Emeric.

———◆·●·◆———

Soren's first proper day at the Academy began shortly before dawn. A horn sounded somewhere on the campus and Soren could hear movement beginning on the floors below his room. As he had been instructed the previous day, he made his way straight to the training hall. He was among the first of the students to arrive, although three masters stood in the centre of the room talking quietly. Almost empty of people, even the slightest sound made an echo in the enormous hall. Soren tried not to draw any attention to himself as he entered the room, but each step on the polished floorboards boomed out like a bass drum.

By the time he had gone a few steps, all of the masters were looking at him. He recognised one of them as Banneret of the Blue, Bryn. All of the instructors were graduates of the highest level of the Academy, the Collegium, which was reserved for only the very best. Being asked to teach at the Academy was a mark of honour that was almost impossible to match anywhere else in the Duchy, at least in times of peace.

'I'm glad to see you here so punctually, Tyro Soren. You can begin your day with twenty laps of the hall. Run!' shouted Bryn, giving Soren a start. His body responded to the command before his sleepy brain had even fully registered it and he found himself breaking into a slow run before he even realised what he was doing. The other instructors chuckled amongst themselves as they watched Soren make his way to the wall and begin his laps.

Five laps in, he was beginning to wonder if this was some sort of punishment for being the new boy. However, when what appeared to be the full complement of the class had arrived, they too were sent off on a run. Bryn's sending him off as soon as he had arrived made sense to him now, as the other students seemed to be able to maintain a much quicker pace than Soren. So much so that most of them had finished their twenty laps before he had his, despite his earlier start.

With the laps completed, one of the other instructors had them file out across the floor for what seemed to be some form of torture. Press-ups, jumps, sprinting on the spot, handstands and dozens of other exercises were repeated in sets of twenty until every joint in his body ached and his muscles burned. Sweat poured down the bridge of his nose, dripping off onto the floor each time he reached the bottom part of an exercise. By the time they finished, he had created an impressively large stain of sweat on the wooden floor.

The relief he felt when the instructor called an end to the exercises was overwhelming. He had never before understood how relaxing it could be just to stand normally. The respite was not to last long however. They were broken up into smaller groups, each group being assigned an instructor and a different task. The first task assigned to Soren's group was rope climbing. A dozen thick ropes were suspended from the beams of the roof above, but how anyone had gotten up there to attach them was beyond Soren. The challenge was for the tyros to race one another to the top and back down in smaller groups of four, each rest lasting until the other three members of the group had completed their climb and the exercise was repeated.

By the time it came to actually getting a sword in his hand, Soren did not think he would be able to lift his arms. He had been concerned that the other boys would show him a cold shoulder, but thus far they had all been far too busy for any kind of social interaction beyond the shouts of encouragement during the rope climbing races. As before with the exercises, all of the students lined up in file, but this time with a blunted rapier in their hands. Master Bryn stood at the head of the assembled class and guided them through a series of moves, both attacks and defences. Soren felt like a clumsy idiot at first, but soon found that he was able to follow the movements well enough. For the first time that day, he began to feel as though he was capable of keeping his place there.

Another hour was spent on this exercise, 'doing the positions' as it was called. At one point Soren was even rewarded with an approving nod from one of the instructors. Soren was amazed at the effect such a small mark of recognition had on his morale. Once that was finished, and all of the swords were returned to the weapon racks, they were released from the class to go for breakfast.

As he walked toward the dining hall, Soren found himself questioning how he could go on. He had never been more exhausted in his life, and it was still morning. His stomach rumbled, which was something he was very used to. What he was not used to however, was having the prospect of a near limitless supply of delicious food only a few steps away. The thought filled him with a little excitement that gave him the energy to pick up his pace enough to get into the dining hall ahead of the crowd.

He loaded his tray with porridge, toasted bread and fruit jams, as well as a full plate of sausages, eggs and bacon. To wash it down he had a large tumbler full of orange juice and a mug of something dark and steaming that he was not able to readily identify.

As he turned away from the food counter, the question of where to sit cropped up. It occurred to him that there would probably be some kind of hierarchy in terms of where students sat when they ate. It had certainly been present during the exercises; the students who appeared to be the best all lined up at the front, and the weaker students were towards the back. Needless to say Soren had been right at the back, and although he would grudgingly admit that his performance during the physical exercises warranted it, he was determined that his sword play would have him to the front in short order.

Nonetheless, it did not answer the question of where he should sit. It was ridiculous to be standing there with a tray loaded with hot food growing colder and not being able to eat it for not knowing where to sit. He hovered awkwardly until he saw some of the tyros from his morning training session sit and then went over to the long table that they were at. He sat next to one of the tyros who had not been too far ahead of him in the training line, but his welcome was less than warm. In fact, Soren doubted he would have been made any less welcome had he jumped up on the table and urinated in the other boy's porridge. Never one to miss a subtle hint, Soren slid down the bench to the end of the table, where he sat and ate his breakfast alone.

After breakfast, he left the dining hall before the others and waited outside for someone he recognised. As chance would have it, Ranph, the student he had sparred against on the previous day and who took pride of place at the front during all of their training exercises, came out not too long afterward and walked briskly back to his house, Stornado. Soren assumed that he was returning to collect materials for class. Soren tried to remain unseen as he waited for him and when he emerged, with conspiratorial glee, Soren followed him to his first class.

All of the academic classes were held in two buildings that abutted either end of the front building of the Academy. Students dashed between the two in the break between each class to get to the next. In the bustle, it was difficult for Soren to keep track of his classmates, but somehow, he just about managed it. A further complication was that it seemed his year was broken up into smaller academic groups of twenty-five students. He had to be careful not to follow the first face that he recognised as opposed to someone on the class schedule that he was following. He supposed that it did not matter too much as Ranph might not have even been in the group that he was assigned to and he could be going to the wrong classes anyway, but at least there was some consistency in his method.

Emeric's plan was successful for the better part of the day. He had taken desks at the back of the lecture rooms, and hunched down as much as he could behind those in front of him, which was made difficult by the fact that he was taller than all of them. When the lecturer was speaking, he listened intently without ever making eye contact, and when they were directed to their books, he scrutinised the text furiously, without ever being able to understand a single word.

Soren was surprised to discover that he found the classes fascinating. He had been disheartened when he had first learned that nearly half of the tuition at the Academy was in classrooms. He had the misconception in his head that it would be all swordplay and physical exercise, but it was clear that almost as much time was devoted to the mental faculties as was to the physical.

The first class had been History. The lecturer, Master Terhorst, had spent almost a full hour speaking on the execution, successes and failings of a cavalry charge during a battle hundreds of years before. Despite seeming tedious at first glance, the analytical way the lecturer approached the subject matter caught Soren's attention. Instead of merely outlining what had happened, one boring step after another, he broke it down into causes and effects; how an action of the enemy commander had caused the Ostian commander to react. Then he considered whether the commander's reaction was justifiable both with the benefit of hindsight, and subjectively under the conditions of the battle and then to whether or not he made the correct decision. He then examined how that decision was acted upon, and if those actions had been executed effectively. The class was over before Soren had realised more than ten minutes had passed.

The second class had been Politics and Diplomacy. Soren had not found this quite as interesting, as it had not centred on combat. However, he could see that it would have its uses, not just on the wider scale, but also in how he survived society with his fellow students. As he left that class, the professor had called him over and told him not to forget that he had to have submitted the form with his chosen elective courses by the end of the week. He had no idea what the professor meant, but he just nodded and said that he would not forget. The final class of the day was Etiquette.

<hr />

'New boy!' said the Master.

It took Soren a moment to realise that it was he who was being referred to.

'Answer, boy, we don't have all day.'

'I, well I don't know, Master Rilid,' Soren replied.

'Did you read the required materials? You were given your requirements in the papers supplied to you yesterday. I know this because I helped to prepare them.'

'No I didn't. I mean to say, no I didn't, Master Rilid, I'm sorry,' Soren replied. He was still having difficulty adjusting to the formality of the Academy. Speaking with deference was not something to which he was accustomed. 'I'm still settling in, Master, I haven't had the chance to find the library yet.' It was a lie of course; he passed by the library to get to and from the dormitory. Knowing where it was wasn't much use to him though, considering the fact that there was not a single word contained within that he could read.

Master Rilid frowned at the lack of a textbook in front of Soren. He flung his copy at Soren and seemed disappointed by the ease with which Soren caught it. He had a petulant face, black hair cut shorter than was the common style and heavily oiled giving it a slick sheen. It was showing the first signs of greying and he had a perpetual shadow of dark stubble beneath his smooth face. Rilid continued to glare at him, and Soren could feel his face heat with embarrassment. Most of the other boys in the class were looking at him.

'Find the answer, I will be coming back to you,' said Rilid.

Soren opened the book, his face down to hide the red shame glowing from it. There were sniggers from around the room, one from Ranph who had turned around to watch him in his discomfort. Soren flipped through the pages, his eyes scanning the jumble of squiggles on the paper, a hope somewhere deep within him that he might find the answer here by some divinely inspired miracle.

It had never occurred to him that there would be more to the Academy than learning the use of weapons. He had no idea how he would survive classes such as this.

'As Tyro Soren here has failed to realise, etiquette is as important for a swordsman as prancing about with a length of steel spilling blood. I was as fine a swordsman as you could hope to find in my youth,' he said, smiling at his self-flattery. He looked around the class for support, but finding none, he continued. 'As I have said, it is all well and good to wander around slaughtering all comers,' he made an ape at a thrusting motion with his chalk stick, still impressed by his own notions of grandeur, 'but for a swordsman to truly make his way in the world, particularly for one of humble origins, one must know the workings of princely courts, of embassies and of polite society. I feel confident in saying that when you venture out from this great Academy into the world, it is the lessons that you learn in my class that you will feel serve you the best. Hearts and minds cannot be won with steel alone. Tyro Soren!' He turned his attention back to Soren. 'Do you have my answer yet?'

'No, Master Rilid, I'm sorry, I don't,' said Soren. There were more sniggers from his classmates.

'Don't be sorry, boy, be competent! Well, gentlemen, it appears that we have a dunce in our midst!' Rilid said, with satisfaction.

The bell in the Campanile rang out signalling the end of the class and Rilid sighed dramatically. Soren felt a wave of relief at this lucky timing.

'You may all go.' Rilid made a spiralling gesture with his hand and returned to his desk. 'The next chapter of the text for next lesson,' he added as they began to file out. All of the boys left, glad to be finished with classroom lessons for the day. As Soren passed Rilid's desk he spoke again.

'Wait!'

Soren stopped, a feeling of exasperation washing over him. Had this prick not chided him enough already?

'My text please, Tyro Soren,' he said, holding out his hand.

As Soren handed the book over Rilid scrutinized him carefully. 'You can't even read, can you?' he said.

Soren cringed as he realised his secret was out. He hadn't even managed to bluff his way through one day. He remained silent and glared at Rilid.

'You will find the academic requirements of your studies rather difficult to pass if that is the case,' he said. 'I will be interested to see how long you last here. I expect it won't be long at all, and then it will be back to the gutter. You may go.'

Chapter 7

NEMESIS

S oren was relieved to be done with academics for the day. His encounter with Master Rilid had left him a little shaken, and he was confident that he had not heard the last about the discovery of his inability to read. It would not be long before one of the other masters came to the same conclusion that Rilid had. He could only hope that whatever solution Emeric had come up with would be effective and fast.

There was more fencing practice in the afternoon, after which the students were left to their own devices, the intention being that they would train further, study, or work on assignments for their academic classes. This free time would allow Soren to get out to see Emeric at four bells. Before that happened however, there was lunch, and one more training session.

Lunch had been an enjoyable experience, even if he had been given the cold shoulder by all of his classmates. It didn't bother him though, as he found the thought of conversation quite unappealing when faced with so much food, and he had to admit that he was finding it difficult to stop himself from over eating. Having access to that much food was still a novelty to him and he hoped that once this had worn off he would be able to moderate his attitude to the dining hall.

The afternoon training was duelling. After a morning of classes where he had to either hide in the back, or look like an idiot, the chance to assert himself over the other students was a welcome opportunity. He was still smarting over the humiliation he had experienced in Rilid's class, and he was looking forward to returning the favour to his sniggering classmates.

Pairs were assigned to duel against each other with respect to position in class. Each odd numbered tyro duelled against the even numbered student ranked below him. Each duel was the best of three touches and a win moved you up a place in class, while a loss would see you paired against the student beneath you who was hoping to keep moving upward. As Soren was the newcomer, he was starting at the very back of the class.

The scoring was based on the honour code system that all students were expected to follow. It was assumed that they were honourable enough to acknowledge a hit against them fairly. By and large, the system worked well, but the instructors did maintain a vigilant watch to ensure it was abided by.

The session started easily enough. While everyone who had reached this level of the Academy had proved themselves and there were no poor swordsmen there, the comparatively weaker students resided at the back of the hall where Soren found himself during the duelling class. Because of this, the first few duels were not difficult for Soren. His speed allowed him to exploit weaknesses that would be inaccessible to others. He progressed steadily over the course of the session only conceding one scoring touch over the course of five duels.

Toward the end of the session he was matched with a stocky student only an inch or two shorter than he.

'Tyro Soren,' he said, by way of greeting. The masters had instructed him to introduce himself to each of his opponents as a way of getting to know them.

'Tyro dal Dardi,' said his opponent.

Another aristocrat. Soren was beginning to wonder if he was in fact the only commoner student in the year.

They saluted and took their guard. Dal Dardi came at Soren fast and hard, determined to stop his swift advance through the ranks. Soren was able to swat his attack out of the way but dal Dardi's elbow struck him on the follow through, which Soren had not been expecting. It knocked him off balance and coupled with the surprise, allowed the other student to put a touch on him.

It rankled Soren to concede another touch, but he supposed that he must accept the fact as he moved up through the ranks and faced opposition of greater skill, conceding the occasional point would be difficult to avoid. Despite his speed he had much to learn and had to accept he was well behind the other students in all other areas of swordsmanship. As such, this once he was willing to pass the elbow strike off as an accident. He acknowledged the touch against him and they reset the duel.

Dal Dardi came at him hard again, but once more Soren was able to parry his attack, which in truth was not that skilfully executed. As Soren had suspected might happen, an elbow followed, but this time he was prepared for it. With any doubt as to the other student's intention in the previous point now cleared, Soren decided to send a blunt message in response. He easily ducked out of the way of the elbow and slashed back with his own sword, whipping painfully across dal Dardi's shoulder. He let out a gasp in pain as Soren stepped back.

'One touch each, I believe,' said Soren, as menacingly as he could. He wanted to make it clear to everyone there that he was no fool and would brook no disrespect. If he was shoved, he would shove back.

Dal Dardi was poor at concealing his emotions and there was a flash of anger across his face that he quickly tried to supress. Despite this, Soren knew his next attack would be fuelled by anger, rather than cunning or finesse. He was correct and dal Dardi came at him furiously with as much force behind his attacks as he could muster. Rather than being intended to skilfully score a touch, these hacks were intended to cause pain.

As Soren toyed with the attacks, parrying them away with little difficulty, it was evident to him that dal Dardi based his technique around intimidation and bullying rather than skill. He could see how this tactic could be brutishly effective and had encountered similar demeanours on the street many times, but it surprised him a little that the instructors had not steered dal Dardi away from it, as it was unlikely to take him far in the company he was in.

Dal Dardi left many openings to counter attack, and when one was so glaringly obvious that Soren was certain he could not fail to score, he took it. He threaded the tip of his sword past steel and limb to strike dal Dardi squarely on the chest. He stepped back and lowered his sword as he did. He only narrowly dodged dal Dardi's continued attack. He pounced back a pace and regained his guard. Dal Dardi continued to come at him furiously. Soren parried the strikes away but found it difficult to see the duel as a practice bout any longer. Their duel had gained the attention of one of the roving masters, but he did not intervene. It appeared that Soren would have to take matters into his own hands.

He stepped inside dal Dardi's reach and shoved him backward, then took another step forward to follow up the push with something a little more strenuous.

'Stop that!' came a shout.

Soren lowered his raised fist. The master who had been watching had evidently seen enough.

'There is no physical contact in these duels. It is a pure test of swordsmanship. You should both know that. Save the brawling for your unarmed fighting lessons. Tyro dal Dardi, step down. Tyro Soren, step up. Shake hands and await your next duel,' said the master.

Soren was being given the match, which was of some small consolation. However, he wasn't satisfied at allowing treatment like that to go unanswered. He put out his hand to shake, which dal Dardi did grudgingly. Soren could see clearly in his eyes that the matter was not done with. That suited him quite nicely.

⸺⬥⸺

Soren sat in the library of Amero's house, at a large table at one end of the bookshelf lined room. A sheaf of paper and a pile of pencils had been left out for him. He tapped one end of a pencil against the table as he waited and wondered what was to come.

It had not been difficult to get out of the Academy for a few hours. Many of the older students seemed to leave for various reasons during their free time in the afternoon. In particular it seemed expected that those at the Academy on patronage would be required to attend to the matters of their patrons from time to time. When seeking permission to leave, he was told that the only rule was that they were back by eight bells in the evening. After this they would be considered absent without permission, which was a serious offence. The steward that had outlined the regulations explained that the rule was an old one that stemmed from students going into the city at night, getting drunk, and starting fights that had very often ended in deaths, of citizens rather than students. This did nothing for the reputation of the Academy, nor the popularity of students in the city, so strict rules had to be applied. As a result, all students, except those in the Collegium were essentially confined to the campus every night.

A few minutes passed by before Emeric came into the room with another man in tow. The man was slight of build with a mop of grey hair and a short, neat beard. He wore a pair of wire spectacles, and from his body language, he was clearly terrified of Emeric. Emeric gestured to the table and the man bustled forward clutching a bulging leather satchel. He looked back to Emeric, and Soren thought he was actually shaking.

'Sit,' said Emeric, in exasperation. 'The boy has two hours, make the best of the time.' With that he left Soren alone with the extremely awkward man.

He sat down and took some books and papers from his satchel. 'My name is Eluard Frerr. I'm a professor of Imperial at the University. I understand you are a tyro at the Academy.'

'Yes, I am,' replied Soren, with more than a hint of pride.

'Ah, so next year, if we get you properly taught, you will be an adeptus. Tyro means a novice, or beginner, in Old Imperial you know, while adeptus means to have obtained, or attained,' said Frerr. He relaxed a little now that he was on familiar territory. 'But I digress, I am told that you have some difficulty reading.'

'More than difficulty. I can't read at all,' said Soren.

'I see, I see,' he said. 'Such a pity that a lad of your age is igno-
rant of the written word. Still, we shall remedy that. The Count's
retainer has made it clear to me that you are to be taught to read
in the shortest possible time. In view of that, I would suggest at least
one hour of study in addition to the time you spend with me each
afternoon. I expect you will be able to read to good standard of liter-
acy in six months of regular tuition, although I would hope that you
will be at a functional level in a much shorter time. Now, to begin.'

———————

Frerr had given Soren a number of books to take away with him.
They contained only the most elementary things, as Frerr had
gone to pains to point out how important it was that he had a firm
grasp of the foundations before he try to move on to other things.
He spent each night in his room poring over the book, copying
out letters while sounding them out at the same time. It made him
feel like an idiot, but at least there was no one else to see it, and
after only a few days of lessons, Frerr had him reading simple passages and this progress was enough to convince Soren to place his
trust in Frerr's method. Nonetheless, Soren's eyes ached each evening when he finally went to bed, which he thought was somehow
appropriate, as with all the training, they had been the only part
of him not to beforehand.

Chapter 8

UNEXPECTED ALLIES

T he first week went by quickly, with the routine of training and classes quickly ingraining itself into his life. At first it had felt odd having somewhere that he had to be at a particular time, but now he found that he enjoyed the sense of purpose that it brought. When he awoke one morning toward the end of that week to find his blue doublet waiting outside his door in a brown paper parcel, it felt as though he had reached a watershed moment. Until that point he had not been able to shake off the feeling that at any time this dream scenario that he found himself in would come crashing down around him. Now, with the finely tailored doublet with its expensive crest embroidered with silver thread sitting across his lap, the dream seemed to solidify into reality. This was now his life, and what went before was the dream, or perhaps more fittingly, the nightmare.

He had not encountered dal Dardi for the remainder of that week. He had kept progressing through the ranks of the duelling ladder whilst dal Dardi had remained much where he had been on the day Soren duelled against him. Even in the dining hall their paths had not crossed. Soren was not sure how he would deal with the situation when they did inevitably encounter one another again, but he was still tempted to seek him out and thrash him just to be done with the matter. He knew that if he wasn't seen to respond aggressively to disrespect, that treatment would become the norm.

He wore the doublet to the dining hall that morning; the weight of it across his shoulders lifted his spirits in some way, instilling a sense of something that he had not experienced before. Pride.

He was minding his own business, trying to decide between honeyed figs or peaches, a process he took particular delight in, considering how ridiculous it would have seemed to him only a few weeks before, when dal Dardi walked straight up to Soren and slapped his tray from his hands. He only had a couple of items on it at that stage, but they went spilling across the floor.

'Watch where you're going, street rat,' dal Dardi said, as he began to walk away, eliciting laughter from a group of the other tyros standing behind him.

The laughter stopped abruptly with Soren's response. He may only have been learning swordsmanship for the past few days, but he had been learning to defend himself, often at the peril of his life, for as long as he could remember. He grabbed dal Dardi by the shoulder before he could get out of arm's reach and spun him back around. Their eyes met and for an instant Soren saw fear in them. He smiled and with an open right hand, he slammed his palm into dal Dardi's face three times in quick succession. On the final strike, he could feel dal Dardi's nose break with a satisfying crunch.

He let go of dal Dardi's shoulder, allowing him to drop to the ground. Soren smiled viciously and looked around to see if anyone else wanted to pick a fight with him. At first there was no one, which was what he expected, but then he spotted three students headed his way, Ranph dal Bragadin leading them. By the time they got to Soren however, two prefects, Blades they were called, had arrived on the scene to break things up. Soren noticed that Ranph was wearing the same badge as the prefects. He was also a prefect, it seemed. They spoke to him quietly for a moment, and the look of anger on Ranph's face dissipated a little as he stared at Soren with steely eyes.

He directed his two hangers-on to take dal Dardi to the infirmary, and then stepped forward to Soren, still carefully watched by the other two prefects.

'You've struck a Stornado, and it will not be quickly forgotten,' said Ranph. He meant it to be threatening, but Soren was unmoved.

'Perhaps you should bring more lackeys next time; swords and fists don't seem to be the strong suit of Stornados,' Soren replied.

Anger flashed in Ranph's face again, but he cast a glance to the other two prefects who were still standing there. He composed himself again and smiled at Soren before walking away. It occurred to Soren that he should perhaps start applying himself more in Diplomacy class.

The incident had done nothing to dissipate his appetite and he reloaded his tray and then attacked his breakfast with vigour. He sat alone, as he always did in the dining hall. He had spent most of his time alone when he lived on the street, and it had not bothered him. It was safer not to rely on anyone, and it was certainly easier not having to worry about anyone else. However, in the short time he had been at the Academy, he had started to feel isolated, something that he had never felt before. On the street, it had always appeared to him that in reality everyone was alone and that anything else was merely an illusion. Here though, everyday all he saw were groups of friends laughing and joking together, and also supporting one another when necessary. In seeing this every day, he began to notice its absence in his own life.

He was very surprised when two tyros that he vaguely recognised came over and sat beside him. They nodded to him in acknowledgement and started into their own breakfasts.

'You didn't do yourself any favours beating Reitz dal Dardi like that,' said one of the tyros after a moment, between bites of bread and jam. 'I'm Henn dal Raffio by the way. This is Jost dal Dreuss.'

For them to sit next to him had been surprise enough, but actually engaging him in conversation was a complete shock. He wasn't sure how to respond. Only moments before he had been in a fight and it felt as though he was staring down everyone in the Academy, but now two of his contemporaries were being quite friendly.

'I don't mean to be rude, but why are you talking to me? I thought everyone here hates me,' Soren said.

They both started to chuckle.

'A lot do. You seem to have a particular knack for making friends! You knock the stuffing out of Reitz today and on your first day you made Ranph look like an Under Cadet. Everyone knows he was caught off-guard, but even still, he wasn't happy about having a touch put on him by a blow-in, no offense. I wouldn't bother applying for a room in Stornado House anytime soon. You've also skipped two years of study, the first of which was hell and nearly half the class get thrown out of the Academy after it. The second wasn't much easier, but at least by that point we knew there wasn't as much chance of getting chucked out. Not having to go through all of that is bound to generate a bit of resentment!' said Jost. 'To tell the truth, Ranph isn't the worst of fellows, but you really embarrassed him. He's the best in our year and only one or two people have been able to put a touch on him in all the time we've been here. For someone fresh off the street to put a touch on him, well let's just say he was less than pleased. As a result, all of his friends are less than pleased, and anyone who wants to be his friend is less than pleased.'

'And you two aren't in either of those groups?' Soren asked suspiciously.

'Nope,' replied Henn, this time over a mouthful of porridge. Soren waited for him to continue, but when he didn't Soren raised his eyebrow quizzically.

'Don't get me wrong; we don't have any problem with him. Like I said, he's not that bad once you get to know him a little, but our fathers' baronies are in the county of Moreno,' Henn added finally.

Now it was beginning to make sense to Soren. Friendships and house memberships in the Academy seemed to run along similar lines to family alliances outside of it. That was not to say that friendships did not form outside of these lines, often they did and would ultimately lead to future familial alliances when those boys became heads of their respective households.

'You are here on the Count of Moreno's sponsorship, which means we're friends, more or less,' Jost said.

'So I take it most friendships here work that way?' Soren asked.

'Pretty much, although most chaps here are pretty easy going about things. Tensions outside of the Academy don't tend to find their way in here. There's enough competition here as it is without that adding to things, but at the end of the day, we all have to know where our loyalties lie,' said Jost.

'I wouldn't worry too much about Ranph. He might try and see to it that you get a few thumps when you aren't expecting it, but he'll have forgotten about it before too long. Reitz is another matter though, he's a nasty little shit. You would be well advised to keep an eye out for him,' added Jost.

'I hear that you are still rooming in the Under Cadet dormitory,' said Henn. 'You should petition River House to take you in. That's where most of the students from Moreno families are. Ancelot is okay too, but we're in River so don't tell anyone I said that. Obviously you can forget about Stornado, and New House is full of royalists. Amero and the Duke's supporters have never been on the best of terms, so with him as your patron I doubt you'd fit in too well there! I don't think you'd have any problem getting in to River though. Some of the lads will be jealous that you got to skip two years and are still able to thrash most of them after being here for only a few days, but someone who can put a touch on Ranph dal Bragadin is always going to be welcome enough.'

'Bragadin? As in the county of Bragadin?' Soren asked.

'It is indeed. He's the oldest son, and will one day be one of the richest men in the Duchy,' said Jost.

Bragadin was a county that sat a couple of day's ride to the northwest of the city. It was best known for the large lake there, Lake Blackwater. Its name came from its dark murky water and it was the source of the Westway River that ran through the city. Miles of dense forest lined one side of the lake, the trees from which produced a particularly strong and hardwearing timber, known as steelwood. The trees were cut and the logs were floated down the river to Ostenheim, where they were either exported around the Middle Sea at a premium price, or used by the city's shipyards to keep its merchant and military fleets supplied with ships. As if this wasn't enough, vast vineyards lined the other side of the lake, producing some of the finest and most expensive wines in the world. The county was a comparatively small one, but it was extremely wealthy, and the Count of Bragadin was one of the most powerful men in the Duchy, not to mention he was also one of the Electors of Ostia, eligible to vote in Ducal elections, and also eligible to be elected. So far, Soren didn't seem to be doing well in his choice of who he rubbed the wrong way.

Chapter 9

THE DRONES

Once the masters were confident that Soren could tell one end of a sword from the other, he was given the chance to train against the drones. He had seen them on his first day in the training hall, but had so far not been allowed anywhere near them. They were hideous, marvellous things. Ugly and ungainly to look at, their smooth movement was almost creepy. They were ancient too, a leftover from the time of mages, who built them to train their soldiers. There were all centuries old, perhaps even over a thousand years in some cases. Such was the quality and skill of their construction that they still functioned perfectly. Perhaps the magic had something to do with their longevity. They were cylindrical and as tall as Soren was, but floated half a metre off the ground when they were activated. They were thicker than an average man and had four appendages at what would be shoulder height when they were activated. Each drone had a number stitched into its brown leather covering and could attack with four different weapons at a time, through a range of three hundred and sixty degrees.

He watched them put student after student through their paces, moving faster and with more precision than most human attackers would be able to. One after another, they scored a hit on the student who was fencing against them, which signalled that their turn was over. A hit was considered to be a kill, and all students were given time to think that over before they were allowed to try again. Soren was tingling with excitement when his turn came. Its massive physical presence created a huge psychological challenge, far more so than when squaring up to a human opponent. Its monstrousness represented the childhood bogeyman he had often dreamt of defeating in battle. What made the challenge all the more appealing was that it had bested all of his peers.

The drone held four individual blunted rapiers, one in each of its hands. They were articulated in such a way that it could attack with all four at the same time if required, which made it like fighting two or more men. There were a number of heavily scuffed patches on the brown leather surface of its body, the leather here both worn but newer than the rest, having been replaced over time. These were deactivation, or kill points. A strike to one of these would turn the drone off. To increase the challenge to the student, the drone could be set to not deactivate until it had been struck cleanly on more than one of the different kill points, up to the full six that were on it.

Master Bryn called the drone by its number and it came to life. For a moment Soren thought he saw a faint blue glow around it, but then dismissed it as a figment of his imagination. Bryn barked out a command and Soren jumped to respond before realising that it had been directed at the drone. They functioned entirely by voice command. It moved forward, gliding silently across the wooden floor toward Soren. Floating as it did, it towered over him. Its ominous advance placed a momentary seed of doubt in Soren's stomach, but as soon as it engaged him his nerves subsided.

Its attacks were precise and relentless. Unlike a person, it did not slow. It did not need to pause to catch its breath after a particularly intense series of attacks and Soren could see for the first time the value of the intense physical training they were subjected to. In his present condition, still scrawny, weak and unfit, not to mention stiff and sore, the drone would wear him down and strike him even more quickly than it had with his peers.

He knew he could not last long, as the drone did not yet seem to have reached its full speed and he did not expect to be able to keep up with it when it did. When he had watched it attacking the other students it had seemed to be far faster. He began to wonder if Master Bryn was going easy on him, but surely if he was holding his own Bryn would increase the intensity to an appropriate level.

Perhaps it was just deceptively fast and it was his apprehension that had increased its apparent speed.

His confusion turned to impatience before long, so he decided to end it. If Master Bryn was underestimating him, he would highlight the mistake Bryn was making to ensure he realised it. As he fended off the attacks, he made his plan. He had seen Amero win a duel in the arena with a flashy strike from behind his back. It began with a quick straight thrust, followed by a twist when he made a second strike with the sword behind his back. He waited for the drone to attack, parried and then quickly stepped inside its reach, thrusting the button at the end of his training rapier into a kill patch on the drone's left side, before twisting and flicking his sword around behind his back, using the force of the twist of his body to drive the tip home onto another patch on the drone's left side.

The instant the tip touched the second kill patch, the drone's arms went slack and it slowly dropped back to the floor. He turned to face Master Bryn and saluted him with his rapier. Bryn had a bemused expression on his face, and waved Soren to the back of the queue without a word.

⸻

Soren petitioned River House as Henn and Jost had suggested and was pleased to find that he was quickly accepted. He felt a little sad leaving his small, lonely room at the top of the Under Cadet Dormitory as it had been the first proper home he had ever known, even if only for a brief time. However, life in River was far more enjoyable than the isolation of his attic room had been. For a start his new room was larger, as was his bed. The number of steps he had to climb to get to it were far fewer also, which after a tough training session was a blessing. There was also a sense of camaraderie there that he was quickly included in, purely by virtue of his membership of the house.

Life at River centred around a large common room on the ground floor. The pecking order of the Academy was at its most apparent here, confusing as it was to a newcomer like Soren. Generally speaking the oldest students, the adepti, had seniority over the tyros. That meant if a tyro was relaxing on one of the sofas in the common room, and an adeptus wished to sit there, the tyro had to move. There was another layer to it however. The best students of the Academy were members of the Society of Blades, the name given to the Academy's prefects, and they were senior to all others irrespective of the year they were in. Membership was attained in one of two ways. The most usual way was when a Blade graduated and either left the Academy or moved to the Collegium to continue his studies, his place became vacant. Students who wished to become a Blade put their name forward and would have to duel for the spot. The winner would be admitted to the Society, and the variety of privileges that this entailed.

The other method was a direct challenge. If a student was ranked highly enough within his class, he could directly challenge a Blade for his place. This was rarely done however, more of a left over from older times than a rule that was in practice. Although any student was eligible to try for membership, in reality, most Blades were adepti, with only an occasional tyro managing to get in, Ranph being the sole example in the Academy at that time, and it was unheard of for cadets to get in. The prospect of being a Blade, and all of the benefits that came with it was immediately attractive to Soren.

Chapter 10

EQUINE COMPLICATIONS

All graduates of the Academy were expected to be competent horsemen. While Soren had seen many horses during his life, he had never been on one and he felt a certain amount of trepidation as he sat on a bench outside the stables, which overlooked the manoeuvres field at the back of the Academy campus. He felt somewhat resentful at having to take part in the class as he felt it was pointless for him. The expense to outfit a heavy cavalryman was far beyond the means of a jobbing swordsman. His future, if not in the service of Amero, as it would most likely be, would be as an infantry officer, or perhaps as a duellist in the arena. He thought it extremely unlikely that he would ever be called upon to perform as a cavalry officer. Nonetheless, being able to ride a little for transportation purposes alone would be necessary, so however grudgingly, he did attend the class.

The first thing that intimidated him was how big the horses were up close. They seemed far larger than the horses he could recall seeing around the city, although he supposed that these were war horses, while those he had seen before would have been riding or work horses. These were proud and haughty beasts with personalities and attitudes that further intimidated Soren. He had no idea how he was supposed to impose his will on one of them.

He was handed the reins of a grey, dappled horse that was very nice to look at, but that towered over him, and regarded him with suspicious disdain. While his speed and agility made up for his raw swordplay, he was completely out of his depth with a horse. He couldn't see how any of the ability that had so far kept him at the Academy would have any bearing on controlling one.

When handing him the reins, the Master of Horse, Master Thadeo had let Soren know that he was aware of his recent arrival and would come back to him once all the others were ready to go. This did little to quell Soren's nerves as he watched all of the others check their equipment and mount their horses with ease and familiarity. Master Thadeo returned to him once he had checked that all the others had properly fastened their saddles and bridles and were ready to go.

'Am I to take it that this is your first time on a horse?' he asked.

Soren just nodded in reply.

'Ok, we'll take it very easy today then. I won't have you join in with the others, as that would just be a disaster! You've seen the others mount, so just do as they did, and I will hold the bridle to make sure nothing unexpected happens!' said Master Thadeo.

Soren nodded again, and somewhat daunted, turned to the horse. He put his left foot into the stirrup and, taking a deep breath, pushed down on it and swung his body up onto the back of the horse and his right leg over the other side. This left him lying forward on the horse's neck, so he very unsteadily sat straight up. He could feel the horse moving ever so slightly beneath him and he realised that his knuckles were white on the reins and his thighs were clamped to the saddle.

'Very good!' said Master Thadeo, as he moved to adjust the stirrups. 'Now, today, it will just be the basics. I want you to get used to the feeling of sitting in the saddle and the balance that is required. I'll have you walk the horse around the field, getting used to the controls. The Academy horses, yours is called "Barto" by the way, are well trained and quite biddable. If you treat him well, he'll do the same for you.

'Now, when sitting at a halt, maintain some tension on the reins. When you want to move off, say "walk on" and release some of that tension. To stop him, say "whoa" and gently put some tension on the reins again. Also, smooth and gentle movements, they are more than enough. Don't yank at the reins. Now try that for yourself. Walk Barto forward a few paces and then stop him. And remember to breath!'

Soren nodded again nervously, trying to make sense of everything that he had been told.

'Walk on!' said Soren, and on the command Barto moved off.
There was a gentle and slight bouncing movement as the horse
walked. Soren felt a giddy excitement overcome him at the novelty
of the new experience. In that instant, heroic images of armoured
cavalrymen charging to battle flashed into his head. It was a sight
far removed from a tense, wobbly and scrawny youth taking his
first riding lesson, but one that was not beyond the limits of his
imagination nonetheless.

'Excellent,' said Master Thadeo. 'Now stop.'

'Whoa!' said Soren, as he tentatively pulled back on the reins.
Barto stopped abruptly, and in a way that made Soren wonder if
he was doing it because he knew that was what he was intended to
do, rather than down to Soren's command.

'Good,' said Master Thadeo. 'Now, to turn him you increase
the tension on the rein on the side you want to turn to, while
easing the tension on the other side. I want you to ride back and
forward across the field, no faster than a walking pace, starting
and stopping Barto every so often, and turning to both directions.
I will send one of the other students to keep an eye on you, but it's
not so hard once you get a feel for it!'

Master Thadeo mounted his own horse with the smooth and
practiced efficiency of an expert and galloped off toward the rest
of the class who were in a group at the far side of the field, cantering along. Soren pulled on the left rein and eased off on the right
one as instructed, and Barto turned to the left without moving
forward. His hooves clacked and scraped on the solid cobbles of
the stable yard, and Soren wondered what it would feel like on the
softer turf of the field.

In spite of his initial anxiety, he found that he was enjoying the
experience tremendously. He urged Barto forward at a walk, the
clip-clop of his hooves silencing to dull thuds as he moved onto
the grass. He had just reached the far side of the manoeuvres field
and begun to turn around when he noticed a rider break away
from his group of classmates at the opposite end of the field and
head in his direction. He kept Barto walking forward as he watched

the group cantering as one cohesive unit, wheeling left and right, speeding up and slowing down. It was an impressive sight to watch but he tried to shut it out and concentrate on the task at hand. As the student sent to assist him drew closer, his heart sank however and his rising concerns made concentration impossible.

'Well, well. I don't think I've ever seen a rat on a horse before. Perhaps a large dog would be a more appropriate mount for you!' said dal Dardi.

Soren wasn't sure if he was just a victim of circumstance, or if dal Dardi had volunteered to supervise him. He suspected the latter, but he was certain that the situation would not end well. He wished Master Thadeo had taught him how to make Barto back up, but as it was, forward, left and right were the only options available to him.

'I'm glad to see your face is healing,' said Soren. He just couldn't stop himself from baiting dal Dardi. 'It's just a shame that with the swelling gone everyone can see what an ugly sack of shit you are again!'

Dal Dardi started circling his horse around Soren and Barto, but Soren's balance was still precarious at best and he could not twist in his saddle to watch him when he went around behind him. He felt a shiver run down his spine as dal Dardi circled around out of view, and his entire body tensed. He almost breathed a sigh of relief when dal Dardi came back into his line of sight.

'Hmm, not bad for a gutter rat,' he said. 'But your bridle is all wrong. Let me help you with it.' He reached forward and undid the noseband and pulled the bit from Barto's mouth.

'There, much better,' he said. 'You'll find the control a little different when you gallop, but I think you'll like it,' he added, with mock sincerity.

It was all that Soren could do to remain still and try to ensure he did not fall from Barto's back. Reaching forward to fix the bridle was a challenge too great for him. Dal Dardi backed his horse up, once more out of Soren's view. There was a loud slapping noise, and Barto reared up before breaking into a bucking gallop.

Soren did his best to hang on but the reins were ineffectual and did not provide any resistance for him to be able to pull against. He roared at the horse to stop as he dropped the reins and clung desperately to the edge of his saddle. He managed to hold on for a few moments, but with each stride Barto took, Soren was bounced further out of the saddle until he lost contact with it altogether. As he flew through the air it felt like the world was slowing all around him. He could see Barto galloping off across the field, and all of his classmates watching in bewilderment. Above all, he could hear dal Dardi's laughter. There was a bright flash behind his eyes, and then darkness.

———◆◆◆◆◆———

Soren woke up later that afternoon in the infirmary. At first he was not able to remember what had happened, but even at that point dal Dardi's laughter echoed in his ears. Gradually, as his memory of the events returned, anger twisted in his stomach.

His first visitor was Master Thadeo, who felt obligated to check on Soren's recovery. He said that dal Dardi had claimed the incident had occurred without his involvement, but he was clearly of the opinion that this was a lie. He had fitted the bridle himself and did not believe that it could have come loose without interference. Once he had confirmed that Soren had not tried to adjust it himself, he seemed satisfied with his belief. Soren's second visitor was more of a surprise.

Ranph dal Bragadin appeared with a somewhat sheepish expression at the end of Soren's bed.

'How are you feeling?' he asked.

'I've been better,' said Soren guardedly. He didn't see what Ranph was there for, as he didn't seem the type to gloat, or to try to make out that Soren had gotten what was coming to him for breaking dal Dardi's nose.

'Look, I'll come right to the point,' said Ranph. 'We all know what Reitz did, and it was a stupid, dangerous and low thing to do to someone who has never been on a horse before. He's brought dishonour on Stornado House, and both I and the other Stornados want you to know that should you choose to call him out over it, you will be entirely within your rights.' With that he left.

Soren was left bemused. It struck him as having been an apology of sorts, but he didn't really have a clue what Ranph had meant by 'call him out'.

He was allowed to rest in the infirmary for the remainder of the day before being sent back to River House in the evening.

Chapter 11

THE DIKTAT OF HONOUR

As sore as he had felt the day before, a night's sleep did little to improve things. All of his joints ached, every muscle was stiff and to top it all there was a large purple bruise running from his backside to half way down his left thigh that screamed at him every time he put any pressure on it or brushed against something, even gently.

He sat in the dining hall seeking the comforting solace that food usually brought him, but was so uncomfortable sitting awkwardly on his right side that the food was little help in lifting his spirits. It didn't stop him from making short work of it, but he could not get past the fact that dal Dardi had gotten the better of him and that twisted his insides with a mixture of anger and impuissance.

He was just contemplating a second plate when Henn and Jost appeared in the hall. Soren had been woken every time he had rolled onto his bruised side and eventually gave up on sleeping, so he had arrived far earlier than necessary for breakfast, when the hall was still empty and the staff were only beginning to put things out. The main crowd was only beginning to arrive as he finished. He asked Jost to bring him another glass of orange juice as they passed. They collected their breakfasts and then joined him.

Jost slid the orange juice across the table, regarding Soren closely as he did.

'You know your little spill on the manoeuvres field is the talk of the Academy,' he said.

Soren groaned inwardly. He disliked being the centre of attention when the event that drew the attention was not of his design.

'I can't say I'm surprised,' said Soren, 'but I'd really rather that wasn't the case.'

'He's never been popular, dal Dardi, but what he did could have gotten you killed, and that's just beyond anyone's opinion of what's acceptable. Most people expect you to call him out,' said Henn.

'Yeah, Ranph said something about calling him out. What does that even mean?' asked Soren.

'To call him out. For a duel. Things have gotten to the point where it's the only acceptable way to settle the matter. It's against the Academy rules of course; duelling between students is strictly forbidden, but it does go on, more often than you might think,' said Henn. 'Just so long as you don't kill or maim him, everyone will look the other way. If you do kill or maim him, well, let's not even consider that!'

'You're talking like it's already settled that I will duel him,' said Soren. 'Until a moment ago, I hadn't even thought of it!'

'Well, look at the alternative,' said Jost. 'Dal Dardi and everyone else expects you to now. It's part of the unwritten honour code. If you don't, it will be difficult for you to get any respect from anyone, and dal Dardi will take it as an invitation to run roughshod over you for the rest of your time here.'

'I don't like being dictated to, least of all by some bloody honour code that isn't even permitted by the Academy. Maybe it's different for you two; you have nice little estates to run home to in Moreno if anything goes wrong here. It won't make much of a difference to your life if you get thrown out. If I cock up here and get thrown out, I'm done. I'm back on the street and have nothing. For me, being here is everything. I'm not going to risk that for your honour code or anything else,' said Soren.

Henn just looked to Jost, who shrugged his shoulders.

'There are just certain ways that things have to be done Soren, like it or not. You know what the alternative is; if you're ok with that...' said Jost.

Soren found that he was actively avoiding company over the next several days. Gradually the pain and stiffness from his fall from the horse faded and he had been trying to avoid thinking about dal Dardi and the expectations that 'honour' seemed to be placing on him, but on a number of occasions he had seen others looking at him and whispering. He was beginning to become concerned that the whispers were no longer about if he would duel dal Dardi, but rather saying that he was a coward, and it was difficult to keep the issue from the forefront of his mind.

It was easy for the privileged aristocrats to make such judgements on honour, but Soren had not exaggerated when he had told Henn and Jost that being at the Academy was everything to him. Honour alone would not fill his belly. The whole matter was playing on his mind far more than he would have liked. He had hoped the matter would blow over and he would be able to exact an appropriate but more discreet revenge on dal Dardi, but even that seemed as though it would be impossible. Any action that he took would be viewed as dishonourable and carried out because he was too craven to face dal Dardi in a duel.

He sat in Hoplology class, usually one of his favourites, and not down to the fact that it involved little reading or writing, which was the case, but because he found the study of different weapons fascinating. For him the rapier, or the rapier paired with a dagger would always be the ultimate. He had spent far too many years sneaking into the Amphitheatre to watch them being used to perfection and imagining himself doing the same, to be tempted away to a preference for something else. A hand and a half, or perhaps a two handed sword would have been more appropriate to his large and rapidly strengthening frame, but despite encouragement to focus on them by the master, he steadfastly refused and maintained the rapier as his primary weapon of study.

Despite his interest in the subject, he found that he could not concentrate. His mind was too occupied by dal Dardi, and the whispers that were being exchanged with him as the subject matter. His attention was pulled back to the class every time the master removed a new object from the glass display cabinet at the back of the lecture theatre, but the diversion was only temporary, as he felt the need to deal with dal Dardi to be ever more pressing. What fools these pampered aristocrats were, to risk so much for something as intangible as honour.

Soren was not in any way worried by the prospect of facing dal Dardi in a duel. On the one occasion in which they had crossed swords, Soren had found him to be only a middling swordsman who relied on underhand tactics and cheap shots to cover his shortcomings. These things were not an issue for Soren. Perhaps had he been steeped in the rigidity of a formal training since childhood it may have been different, but for him, a kick, punch or elbow intermixed with swordplay seemed to be no more than a common sense approach. It took considerable concentration to ensure he did not incorporate any of this into his own swordplay during sparring, as it was explicitly against the rules. Dal Dardi seemed to have no compunction about it however, which made Soren smile bitterly when he compared dal Dardi's behaviour to the lofty notions of honour that were so hypocritically espoused in the Academy. It seemed to him that honour was a shoe that fit many feet.

However angry it made him, he knew that anger would not bring him any closer to a solution. Henn and Jost had outlined how honour duels were fought. All the usual rules of the Academy applied, except that sharp blades were used and the fight was to first blood. Once blood had been drawn, it was considered that honour on all sides was satisfied and life would return to normal as though the duel, and all matters leading to it, had never happened. It seemed to be a bizarre way to do things, but then he could not profess to understand how the aristocratic mind functioned.

Soren's only concern about a duel was the potential impact it might have on his presence at the Academy. He didn't give a damn if he killed dal Dardi. In his estimation Soren had met few that deserved it more, but this would be devastating to any hope he might have to remain at the Academy. Not only would he be expelled, he would more than likely be handed over to the Watch and from there dumped in a dungeon cell, with the release of the headsman's block being the only thing to look forward to. Maiming would have much the same result, perhaps only with the omission of the headsman's block.

As long as he was careful, he saw no reason for either of these eventualities to occur. He knew that dal Dardi would happily utilise whatever dirty trick he could come up with, so he felt his best plan of action was to utilise his speed to score a quick cut to a non-vital part of the body and be done with the whole thing.

He realised that he had started planning how to deal with the duel before ever acknowledging even in his own mind that he would actually fight it. It seemed that the duel was always a foregone conclusion, even in his own head. He still disliked the way he felt as though he had been left with no option but to take this course, but if he wished to remain at the Academy and to thrive there, it seemed he would have to tread a narrow line between doing what was expected of him and what was required to ensure his own advancement.

With his course of action settled upon, he found it was far easier to return his attention to his classwork, and the gnawing sense of anxiety he had been feeling seemed to have disappeared.

———◆◆◆◆◆———

Alien as it was to him, Soren's next step was to discuss with Henn and Jost how exactly he would go about calling dal Dardi out. As everything else seemed to be dictated by the honour code, he expected that the method of initiating a duel would be also. The whole matter made Soren quite uncomfortable. It was not the way he would have chosen to deal with matters.

He did not want the fact that he now intended to fight a duel to put the issues with dal Dardi behind him to become common knowledge. He accepted that once the challenge was made it would be the gossip of the Academy and there was little that could be done about that. Up until that point however, he wanted as few people to know of his intentions as possible.

He arranged to meet Henn and Jost in one of the private reading rooms in the library. He made sure that he was there well before them, but felt faintly ridiculous about the surreptitious way he was going about things.

Henn and Jost arrived together and sat down with Soren around the single table in the room.

'How does this work?' asked Soren.

'The duel you mean?' said Henn.

'Yes, of course the duel. What else?'

'Well, you have to call him out. I think that means a challenge to him in public,' said Jost. 'I've never actually seen it being done though. Striking him in front of others and demanding satisfaction is the traditional way I think.'

'And won't making a public challenge bring the whole thing to the attention of the masters?' said Soren.

'Yes and no,' said Jost. 'As we told you before, as long as there isn't a death or serious injury, there isn't a problem. I assume you've seen the scars on Master Dornish and Master Bryn's faces?'

Soren nodded. He thought also of the scar on Emeric's face.

'Well,' continued Jost, 'how do you think they got them? A blind eye will be turned so long as the duel is limited to first blood. Just make sure that it is. There will be others there to make sure tempers don't flare and cause things to get out of hand. Which brings me to the other thing. You'll need a second to take care of all the details once the challenge is made. I'm happy to do that for you, or Henn said he would either; it really doesn't matter. All the seconds do is arrange the time and venue and inspect the weapons before the duel and ensure that the rules are complied with.'

'All right,' said Soren. 'Tomorrow then, in the dining hall at breakfast. Since you offered, Jost, I'd like you to be my second.'

Jost nodded. 'Tomorrow then.'

Chapter 12

THE CHALLENGE

While he wasn't worried by the prospect of duelling dal Dardi, he felt a sense of foreboding about the whole situation. His ambivalence about having to fight the duel at all, according to someone else's rules had not subsided. Events had overtaken him and taken on a life of their own. Even on the street he had, to a certain extent, been the master of his own destiny. He was quickly learning that this was no longer the case.

He was full of nervous energy that he knew would keep him from sleeping, so instead he slipped out of River House after lights out and made his way to the training hall. He was hoping to kill two birds with one stone, the extra training would tire him out enough to sleep and the extra practice certainly would not hurt either.

He called out two drones, which like biddable animals came out from their storage area and hovered, waiting for further instructions. Soren equipped each of the four arms on both drones with practice rapiers. He had only ever been allowed spar against one at a time previously, but he had never found a single drone to be a particular challenge before, and his state of anxiety was such that he wanted as demanding a session as he could take without being hurt in the process. Despite the practice rapiers being blunt, button tipped and slightly more flexible than a real sword, being struck hard by one was still painful, and if that strike was in the wrong place, it could cause injury.

'Drone one, all arms, two against one, random patterns. Drone two, all arms, two against one, random patterns,' said Soren. With the commands given the previously lifeless arms lifted their weapons and prepared to attack.

The four arms were spaced equally around the body of the drones, which allowed them to attack no matter which way they were oriented. There was no benefit to be gained by attacking them from behind, nor any respite to be found by hiding there.

By some trick of the magic used to create them, when a drone was informed that it was working in connection with another, they would be able to coordinate their movements, rather than just bumping around independently. They came at him, one first with the other moving forward in a supporting role. Blades clashed and Soren twisted and turned between them, dancing to the sound of metal clashing against metal.

He knew the drones were fast; he had seen as much when watching others train with them from the sidelines. They just did not seem as fast when he used them. After several minutes he began to feel a little light headed. He ignored the feeling and kept pushing himself, but the light headedness became a piercing headache, and then he began to feel nauseous. He persisted a little longer, refusing to give in to discomfort but he found it difficult to concentrate and maintain his focus. His mental clarity became so confused that it seemed the drones were even slower now than they had been before. He must have pushed too hard and needed to stop. He ordered the drones to a halt and then back to their storage area. He quickly disarmed them and made his way back to River House, concerned now for the first time about the challenge he had set upon making in the morning. He hoped the sudden ailment would subside with a good night's sleep. The last thing he wanted was for an illness to seem like fear to the others in the dining hall.

He had been awake for some time when the morning bell rang to wake all of students. Happily his nausea and headache from the night before had subsided. He got up, dressed and washed quickly. When he got down to the common room, Jost was already there, waiting for him. He bore such a solemn expression that Soren almost laughed.

'Come on then,' said Soren cheerfully. 'I'm starving!' Now that he was set on a course of action that was in motion, he found that his spirits, which had been flagging over previous days, lifted considerably.

It was obvious to Soren as soon as they entered the dining hall that Henn and Jost had both remained silent about Soren's intentions, as the atmosphere in there was perfectly normal. There was no air of tense expectation, which Soren had feared there might be. There was no sign of dal Dardi when they arrived, so Soren and Jost went about things normally, collecting their breakfast and sitting down to start it as they ordinarily would.

Soren sat facing the doorway, his heart speeding up a little each time the door opened as he waited for dal Dardi to arrive. Several students entered, pushing Soren's anxiety levels up a little each time. Henn arrived also, but he sat with a different group, giving Soren and Jost an encouraging nod as he passed by. Eventually dal Dardi stepped into the hall.

'I'm just going to get right to it,' said Soren. 'No point in dragging this out any longer than is needed.'

As dal Dardi made his way down the central aisle between the tables toward the food counter, Soren stood and stepped out in front of him. Jost had taken his place reassuringly behind Soren's left shoulder, which he was grateful for. As soon as dal Dardi noticed Soren, his usual smug, arrogant expression deserted him. Soren stepped forward and slapped him hard across the face. The crack of the open handed strike rang out over the sounds of morning chatter in the hall, and silenced the room almost instantly.

'My honour demands satisfaction,' said Soren, before walking back to his breakfast. It was customary to address one's opponent as 'sir' when making the challenge, but Soren refused to be completely dictated to by the requirements of the honour code, and in any event did not wish to afford dal Dardi the respect addressing him as 'sir' conveyed. Jost stepped into the place in front of dal Dardi that Soren had just vacated.

'Have your second call on me at River House to arrange the particulars,' he said, before also returning to his breakfast.

———◆◈◆———

News of the challenge spread around the Academy like wildfire. Soren was instantly uncomfortable with his new found celebrity, as he immediately became the subject of conversation wherever he went on campus.

For the time being, his participation in the duelling process was not required. Jost and whoever stood as second for dal Dardi would make all the arrangements and inform the principals of when and where the duel would occur. Soren had no intention of allowing it to dominate his thoughts and so instead threw himself into his studies, particularly on working at his reading and writing, which was improving quickly, to his great satisfaction.

He distanced himself from everything to do with the duel all of that day, until the evening, when he met with Jost in the common room of River House. Jost explained to him that the duel would be fought the following morning outside of the city walls at ten bells, in a field near the Blackwater Road that was often used for such purposes. Soren was a little surprised at the detail that went into the organisation. Soren and Jost would leave the Academy shortly after eight bells and leave the city by the Blackwater Gate. Dal Dardi and his second would leave a little earlier and exit the city via the North Gate, so as to ensure the opposing parties would not encounter one another before the duel.

Jost had also organised a physician to attend on them at the duel. It was the mention of the physician that really brought home to Soren the seriousness of the whole matter. He had been so pre-occupied with the danger of killing or injuring dal Dardi and the consequences that would have had for him that he had not considered the possibility of being injured or killed himself.

Being killed didn't bother him all that much. He had already lived longer than he had ever expected that he would, but living with a serious injury did concern him. It would mean the end of his chance at the Academy. Amero would most certainly not want a half trained, crippled retainer, which meant a return to the streets, but as a cripple. He had seen crippled former soldiers begging around the city. They never lasted long. Death would be a better result for him. What made matters worse was the realisation that unless he was careful, in terms of consequences, there would be little difference between defeat or victory.

Chapter 13

THE DUEL

T he field chosen for the duel was a short distance from the
road and was screened from passing traffic by a row of squat
trees. Soren and Jost arrived first despite leaving later; dal
Dardi had a slightly longer distance to travel. The physician was
already there. He had arrived in a small cart and had a medicine
chest open at the back, displaying bottles, bandages and a number
of metal surgical instruments. The experience felt surreal. Surely
giving dal Dardi a few punches at an opportune moment would
have been a far better way to deal with this.

Rapier and dagger were the weapons that had been chosen by
dal Dardi. Jost had obtained a reasonable pair from his family's
house in the city, and it occurred to Soren that it was the first time
that he had ever held a real, sharpened sword. He disliked waiting
but used the time to familiarise himself with the balance of the
sword. He had not spent very much time training with a dagger in
addition to the rapier, but he thought he might as well have it as
not and did not see how it could get in the way.

The sword felt good and Soren appreciated Jost having lent
it to him. The alternative would have been to break into a weapons locker in the Academy to get at one of the sharp rapiers contained within. While perfectly functional, they would have lacked
the craftsmanship and attention to detail that Jost's family would
demand from a weapon. He went through a few practice positions to loosen up and develop a feeling for the sword and dagger.
While he was doing so, Reitz dal Dardi, his second and a third man
arrived on horseback. Dal Dardi's second was Ranph dal Bragadin.

Soren did not recognise the third man, who dismounted first and took the reins from the other two as they also dismounted.

They stood together and talked as dal Dardi unbuckled his cloak and handed it to the third man who Soren took to be a servant. Dal Dardi was wearing a fitted leather duellist's doublet, similar to the ones that were worn in the arena. It would provide some protection to the torso, but only against a glancing blow. Nonetheless it would reduce the chance of blood being drawn by a deflected attack. Soren wore only his white cotton shirt; he had nothing else. Jost had made it abundantly clear that he could not wear his blue academy doublet for fear of bringing the Academy into disrepute. The extra protection was certainly an advantage in dal Dardi's favour, but Soren did not intend for the matter to be decided by a lucky strike.

Soren and Jost stood together by the rear of the physician's cart when Ranph approached them. He carried with him a sword and dagger.

'I'd like to inspect your sword and dagger, if I may,' said Ranph.

Soren handed him both, and Ranph handed the pair of blades he was carrying to Jost.

'I wanted to let you know that I am here as Reitz's second purely because no one else would stand with him.' He gave both weapons a looking over and exchanged them for dal Dardi's, to which Jost had been doing likewise. 'Good luck. I'll signal when we're ready,' he said, before returning to dal Dardi.

'Well,' said Jost, 'from here it's just like duelling class. Except the pointy bit will hurt more if he hits you.' He let out a forced laugh, and handed Soren the blades.

While Soren appreciated his attempted levity, it was unnecessary. He had felt the tension leading up to this moment; all of the expectation and having his choices dictated to him by a code that he thought ridiculous. Now however, he was in more comfortable territory. He could directly influence the events that would follow, one way or the other.

Ranph nodded to Jost, who acknowledged the signal.

'Time to go,' said Jost. 'Remember, just like duelling class. Good luck.'

Soren walked forward to meet dal Dardi, but the two exchanged no words. Jost and Ranph stood to the side with the physician behind them. Part of Soren hoped that the physician's services would not be needed, but he was confident that they would.

'As agreed, the duel is to first blood,' said Ranph. 'Both combatants are duty bound by honour to cease fencing as soon as they become aware of a wound to either party drawing blood. I will call out the presence of a wound drawing blood as soon as I become aware of it, and if combat has not ceased already by that point, it is to cease instantly on my word. Are the rules understood?'

Soren said that he understood, dal Dardi did likewise.

'Very good,' said Ranph. 'Begin.'

Dal Dardi came at Soren right away. His attack indicated the complete contempt with which he considered Soren. He was a little better than Soren remembered, but perhaps he had unintentionally been playing down dal Dardi's ability in his own mind in order to boost his confidence. He settled into a nice flow of defensive strokes, alternating between rapier and dagger smoothly and Soren was content to continue defending until he had a better measure of him.

He had always been taken by flights of imaginative fancy and he found himself wondering what the scene must have looked like, the clashing of blades in a tree lined field before the morning haze had fully lifted. His wandering imagination nearly cost him as dal Dardi's dagger passed perilously close to his midsection.

He focussed and took the initiative. He directed most of his attacks through his rapier, as he was not confident enough with the dagger to use it for anything other than defence. He forced dal Dardi back several paces before dal Dardi countered back hard, cutting low at Soren with his dagger and forcing him to jump back out of the way. It put him off balance, which was not something that had been done to him often. He recovered his balance quickly but his legs and arms felt heavy and slow.

Dal Dardi came at him again, and for the first time Soren began to feel unsettled. He did not seem to have his usual speed and the loss of that edge rapidly exposed his less polished technique. Soren allowed himself to be driven back as he attempted to rally.

He focussed hard and gradually it felt as though his body was coming back to life. His reactions seemed a little quicker and his body responded to his commands at the speed he expected of it. Dal Dardi had grown more confident as a result of his promising start and continued to come at Soren, seeking out a gap in his defence. It took Soren several counters before he regained the initiative, but he was beginning to feel back to normal. As the ease with which he usually moved returned, it seemed as though it had just required a little more concentration than was ordinarily needed. He did not want for the duel to go on any longer than necessary and risk another slump into weakness and possibly even the headache and nausea he had suffered two nights before, which still played on his mind.

Soren pushed in with a fast thrust that he followed up with his dagger. He had expected the dagger to strike dal Dardi on his right shoulder and put an end to the duel, but somehow he parried the secondary strike and countered. Soren's surprise at the failure of the attack must have shown on his face as dal Dardi sneered and pressed forward with his own attack.

The sneer infuriated Soren and with a sudden burst of effort he deflected dal Dardi's rapier with his dagger and thrust forward with his own sword, directly at dal Dardi's sneering face. The sneer quickly changed to apprehension, and Soren's heart leapt, as he feared that he was on the verge of delivering a killing blow. All the luck that had come his way, and all the hard work he had done to capitalise on it would count for naught.

He released a sigh of relief as dal Dardi managed to move his head out of the way enough to avoid the tip, but not the edge. He shrieked in pain and recoiled as Soren's blade cut a deep slit across his left cheek and on past his hairline.

Soren heard both Ranph and Jost call out to signal the duel was over. Dal Dardi dropped his dagger and held his hand up to his face as he staggered backward, blinded by tears. The physician rushed forward to inspect the wound and Soren lowered his weapons, utterly drained by the whole experience. He had won.

Chapter 14

ACCEPTANCE

There was something ignominious about walking back to the Academy after the duel, even if it was in victory. However he could not afford the price of renting two horses or a carriage and he had already prevailed upon Jost's generosity twice in imposing on him to be his second and then again to borrow his sword and dagger. What made it worse was that Soren was completely exhausted. As soon as the duel had ended, weariness hit him like a hammer and each step closer to home felt like a thousand.

Dal Dardi had still been at the duelling field when they had left having the cut to his face treated. Ranph had confirmed that the duel had been fairly fought and Soren had confirmed that honour was satisfied, even if he had never given any thought to there being a slight on it. Dal Dardi had not made any eye contact with him, but Ranph had assured him that he would ensure the matter ended there and that life would be made very difficult for dal Dardi if he did anything to renew the hostility.

When they finally returned to River House, Soren was surprised to see that the entire house were waiting in the common room. Jost gave the assembly a nod of his head and a smile and they burst into a round of applause. The regard they were showing him came as a shock. While membership of River House had eased the isolation and sense of not belonging that he had felt when he had arrived at the Academy, he had been accepted by virtue of his sponsorship by the Count of Moreno rather than in his own right.

Now they applauded him for his own deeds. It was one of the best feelings that he had ever experienced.

———— ◦•◦◦•◦ ————

It seemed that dal Dardi had a reputation as a notorious bully. Many of the students in the lower years, and in particular the under cadets, had suffered his constant torment. Soren facing him down and beating him in a duel was something many of the other students had wanted to do themselves and went some way to explaining why dal Dardi had so much difficulty in finding someone to stand second for him. His victory in the duel had won Soren not only his honour, but also a great deal of regard amongst the other students, who would now cheerily greet him whenever they passed. He had gone from barely tolerated to popular in the space of one duel. Despite enjoying the acceptance he was experiencing, it was difficult to reconcile just how fickle his fellow students were. From being a pariah one day to fêted the next, he wondered if movement in the other direction could be as swift.

The duel, despite his success, had alarmed Soren in a number of ways. His first concern was that the speed which he had come to take for granted had seemed for a while at the start of the duel at least, to have deserted him. He couldn't understand why but perhaps feeling unwell a couple of nights previously had something to do with it. Nonetheless, that had exposed his second concern. Stripped of his speed advantage, he was at best a below average swordsman. Dal Dardi, for whom Soren had no great regard, had shown himself to be more technically proficient. This was a matter that Soren needed to address quickly. He could not allow himself to remain completely dependent on something that he could not be certain of when he needed it most.

There was only one way he could see to achieve this. Hard work. He wasted no time, beginning with a trip to the library. His reading was coming along well, but was still far from the point where he could make sense of everything he came across. It was not of great importance for his current task however, as most of what he needed came in the form of diagrams and basic explanations of attacks and guards. He took a notebook with him and tried to make rough drawings of each of the forms and positions to help him fasten them in his memory, but also to have something to refer to when he was in the training hall, as it was forbidden to remove books from the library unless you were a member of the Collegium.

He went through a number of volumes, picking out positions, movements and treatises that caught his eye. As he read, it struck him that fencing was very much like reading, writing, and in a sense, speaking. The books contained, in their diagrams, all of the different words and phrases needed for a swordsman, who could pick from them to make a sentence. Like real words, they would not make sense unless placed in a proper order. Like real words, the same meaning could be conveyed in many different ways, but some would be more eloquent than others.

As with learning new words to read, by expanding his vocabulary of positions, strikes and defences, he would become a far more fluent swordsman. The realisation of how this learning could impact on his training seemed daunting at first, as though he had just built himself a mountain that he would now have to climb.

In that first study session in the library he made dozens of diagrams and added his own crude notes. It was late when he finished and he had to force himself away from the desk. Each book that he opened and each page that he turned seemed to reveal some new and intriguing perspective and only served to increase his hunger for more. Eventually, when he felt his eyes could take no more, he returned to River House, resisting the urge to pay a visit to the training hall to try some of the new material in his notebook.

Enduring classes the next day was torture, as all he could think about was starting his new training regime.

Autumn had given way to winter and the end of Soren's first term at the Academy was approaching when he was told to report to Master Dornish's office. Soren did not know how to react to this and if it might mean trouble for him. There was no reason that he could think of to precipitate the meeting, other than the duel, but as several weeks had passed since then he didn't expect that anything more would come from that.

The office was on the top floor of the front building of the Academy and overlooked Old Square, the main quadrangle of the campus. Master Dornish's adjutant showed Soren in. The man was little more than a secretary, but such a job description would not fit in very well with the martial nature of the Academy, so he was called an adjutant instead.

Dornish instructed Soren to sit and then proceeded to study him, his fingers arched in front of his face, for what felt like an age. A very uncomfortable age.

'I've had some reports back from your masters. As we are at the end of your first term, I thought I might take the chance to discuss them with you,' he said slowly.

It was Rilid. He knew it the second the word report had left Dornish's mouth. His face flushed with anger. If he was expelled over this, the man would never again be safe to set foot outside the walls of the Academy, Soren would make very sure of that. Dornish continued.

'Master Bryn's reports are of the most interest to me. Particularly in light of something I thought I might have glimpsed myself when I've seen you spar, but more of that shortly. Master Bryn is of the opinion that you are the fastest swordsman that he has ever seen. Praise like that from a man like him is not to be dismissed. He tells me that in the weeks that you have been here, you have caught up with your peers in terms of technique, and that if your development continues at its current rate, he expects you to have surpassed them before this academic year ends. He also pays tribute to what he describes as an awe inspiring work ethic and goes on to say that he is aware that you've been spending quite a bit of extra time in the training hall.

'I don't want to swell your head though. I should also point out that there have been some less than glowing reports. Master Terhorst applauds your diligence and attentiveness in class, but thinks you to be a halfwit, and Master Rilid seems to be convinced that you are completely illiterate. Happily for you, however, Master Bryn's is the opinion that counts for most. Our duty as instructors is to ensure that you can use the sword that graduating from this institution entitles you to wear. Our responsibility to the city is to produce men who can fight, longer, better and smarter than any of our enemies. It is helpful if they have as good a brain as they do an arm though, so I would encourage you to persevere with the academics, and to get as much out of this opportunity for education as you can. It will serve you well in the future, wherever your career may take you.'

'I understand, sir,' Soren replied. 'I will work hard at it.'

'Good, good,' said Dornish. 'Now, to the other thing I mentioned. I could be completely wrong, as I've never before actually seen what I want to talk to you about, and there isn't much more than a few mentions of it in books, with not much in the way of explanations being given even then. Despite this, I doubt if there is a swordsman alive who has not heard of it, and dreamt of having it. What I am talking about was called the "Gift of Grace". It was something all the bannerets of the olden days could call upon, but sadly it has been lost to us for generations. It imbued them with great speed and strength, and is credited as being what allowed them to overthrow the mages and defeat them in the old wars. I have watched you spar and fight a drone, and I'm certain I've never seen anyone move with the speed that seems to come to you effortlessly. At first I was not sure, and even now I feel a little foolish just mentioning it, but from what I have seen and from what your instructors have been saying, I can't shake off the thought that perhaps you have this gift.' He leaned forward over his desk and fixed his gaze on Soren. 'Is what I am saying to you making any sense?'

'I don't really know, sir. I hadn't thought there was anything unusual about it. I mean, I know I am fast, but I hadn't thought there was anything more to it than that,' said Soren.

'Perhaps there isn't,' said Dornish, leaning back into his chair. 'It could well just be me looking for an explanation where none is necessary. It may be worth keeping an eye on though, so bear in mind what I've said. You may go now. If you continue working the way you are, Soren, you will do very well here. Keep that in mind also!'

Chapter 15

A BRAVE DEED

While most of the other students returned to their family estates for the break between terms, Soren remained at the Academy. He had partly expected the Count of Moreno to call on him for some purpose or another, but he had not, so apart from the lack of formal tuition, life continued on very much the same for Soren.

He took the opportunity to redouble the effort he was putting into his personal training regime. Master Dornish's conversation with him had proven that he had made a good impression during his first term, and he was determined to continue in that vein. Each evening he spent in the library and the following day he spent in the training hall, putting all of his studies to practice.

As with the effort he had put into reading, his extra effort in the training hall began to show through. His economy of movement improved and he found he required less and less thought to execute complex attacks and reacted to attacks ever more effectively. Where once his sword cuts had been wild and ill disciplined, they were now precise and tight, no more than was necessary with the tip moving perfectly as Soren intended.

The Academy was quiet, as was River House, as there were only a handful of students still on campus. It would have felt lonely once again were it not for the fact that he kept himself busy all day, and each night, Soren collapsed into bed.

With the hectic schedule he imposed on himself and the constant sense of urgency he felt with regard to it, the few days between the two terms went by quickly and River House began to fill with noise and laughter again as quickly as it had emptied.

———◆◆◆◆———

The new term felt like easing back into an old and comfortable pair of shoes. The routine was now familiar to Soren and the fear he had felt over the potential of the between term holiday becoming dead time, where, through laziness, he might allow his progress to come to a halt, subsided and the feeling of purpose and of achieving something each day returned.

His lessons with Eluard Frerr also recommenced, which he was somewhat apprehensive about. He had neglected specifically working on reading and writing, in the hope that the effort he was putting in to digest as many fencing treatises as he could would make up for this.

While his duel with dal Dardi had seemed to make him accepted at the Academy, he was still concerned about something similar occurring in the future. With his rapid advance, and the many obstacles that he had not had to pass, there were still those that resented him. There were also those that continued to harbour distaste at the fact that a blow-in from the street could better them despite their generations of aristocratic breeding.

The best way to ensure that he did not have to address this resentment with steel, in his mind at least, was to become a Blade. While duelling was forbidden in the Academy, as he had found out, a blind eye was turned so long as the consequences were superficial. A blind eye would not be turned for a Blade, who was supposed to be setting a better example. As a result there was an understanding among the students that Blades could not and would not duel under any circumstances. Any slight to a Blade by a student would be dealt with harshly by the Blades as a whole, but within the rules of the Academy. To cause insult to the honour of one who could not call for satisfaction was considered to be a cowardly act.

He felt quite ruthless in setting out the things he wanted to achieve in the coming term, but after his run in with dal Dardi, the precariousness of his position had become ever more present in his mind. Membership of the Blades was the first item on his list. This would solidify his position beyond interference from other students. The second aim was to reach the front rank in duelling class. He felt that the additional work he had already put in had improved his ability immeasurably, and if continued would make this goal a realistic possibility.

—◆◆◆—

Despite spending two hours each afternoon at the Moreno town house for his reading and writing lessons, he almost never saw Emeric and never saw Amero, even though he was wintering in the city.

Not long after his second term began, Soren had discovered a shortcut of alleys that allowed him to take a more direct route between Amero's townhouse and the Academy. It led him out onto the square in front of the Academy, where it twisted between the dense concentration of buildings around the square and on to the leafy boulevards where the wealthy kept their city mansions. One evening, as he took this route back to the Academy after darkness had fallen, he heard a commotion in one of the alleys that led off from his shortcut.

His natural inclination was to continue on and ignore it. During his time on the streets he would not have even contemplated stopping to investigate. Someone was always being done over, and to interfere was only to invite injury to oneself. Things were different now though; he was a student of the Academy, a gentleman in training, and this was Highgarden. He had never heard of a mugging or street crime being committed here. Out of some high sense of duty and dignity, he decided to investigate.

He turned down three or four corners in the alleyway to reach a dead end containing five people. He could only see four of them, but presumably the fifth, their victim, was on the ground in front of them.

He took a deep breath and cleared his throat. One of the assailants turned to look at Soren.

'Piss off and mind your own business. You don't know what you're getting yourself into!' he said.

His accent surprised Soren. It was not the accent of a street thug, but one considerably more refined. It was not quite upper class, but this man was not a common thug.

'I'd say the same to you, be off with you,' Soren said, in his most superior tone.

'Oh for fuck sake,' said the man, with a sigh. 'Finish off here and I'll take care of this "young gentleman".' As he stepped forward he caught sight of Soren's blue doublet. 'Bloody Academy brats,' he muttered, as he approached.

Soren noticed, however, that he had dropped the casual air he had a moment before, and was approaching more carefully. Soren carried a small dagger on his belt beneath his cloak, but decided not to use it unless absolutely necessary. He was well aware the trouble an Academy student killing a man on a city street would bring him.

The man carried a club and moved well. He was certainly used to fighting, and in a more trained way than Soren would expect from a thug.

'Last chance,' he said.

Soren just smiled. The man sighed again and swung the club at Soren. It was not a wild, uncalculated swing, but a well constructed attack. It was aimed for Soren's face, and it did not put the man off balance. His surprise was palpable when Soren's hands shot out from beneath his cloak and seized him by the wrist. Soren quickly twisted his arm before the man could react to stop it, and pulled it back sharply, doubling the man over.

'Lads!' he managed to gasp. Soren brought his elbow down on the back of the man's shoulder as he had been taught in class, while holding the arm straight, twisted and high. Soren felt the tension across it give way as the man's shoulder popped out of its joint. He gasped again as Soren hammered his fist down on the back of the man's neck, dropping him to the ground.

One of the others had reacted to the now unconscious man's gasp and grabbed Soren from behind. Soren pinned the man's hands to his chest with one hand and shifted to the side, slapping back between the man's legs with his other hand. The man jumped back to protect himself, giving Soren the space he needed to twist out of the hold and pull one of the man's arms into a lock similar to the one he had used on the unconscious man. In a swift and well-practiced movement, he dislocated the man's shoulder, and pulled him into a knockout hold. He dropped the body as soon as he felt it go limp and turned to the other two.

The victim had taken full advantage of his change in circumstances, and it seemed he did not have the same compunction about killing the attackers as Soren did. One of the other assailants was staring glassy eyed at the stars with his hands clutched around his neck. His blood appeared black in the darkness as it flowed from between his fingers. The final man had backed up and drawn a short bladed weapon. He stood crouched before the now standing victim. He had taken no notice of Soren, who stepped up behind him quickly and grabbed two handfuls of the man's hair. He bashed his head off the alley wall until he felt the body go limp and then dropped it. Only then did he have the chance to take a proper look at the victim.

Like Soren, he was wearing the blue doublet of the Academy. His face had been so badly beaten that he was hard to recognise though. It was only when he spoke that Soren realised that it was Ranph. His words were slurred by the swelling, but the voice was unmistakable.

'You're the last person I expected to see,' he said, his swollen mouth twisting into a smile. 'Thank you, you've done me a great service. I won't forget it. I hope we can put that other business well and truly behind us!'

'I do too,' Soren replied. Perhaps Jost and Henn had been right about him after all.

Their nocturnal adventure was not over yet however. By the time they made their way out of the alleys, it had passed eight bells. They could hear the chimes of the bell in the Cathedral tower echo out through the cold air over the city. There was no way that they could get in through the front gate of the Academy without being spotted. They paused on the square for a moment, their breath clouding in the air before Ranph had an idea.

'Follow me, there is a place we can get in over the fence that I know about,' he said, heading off in what Soren assumed was the correct direction.

How he knew about it, Soren didn't ask. He suspected that it was the route taken by some of the students to sneak in and out of the Academy at night. Drinking, gambling and whoring were all popular diversions with the students and none of them could be indulged on the campus. Soren had heard some of the adepti in River House, drunkenly trying to sneak back into their rooms at all hours of the morning on more than one occasion. Soren had never felt any reason to try sneaking out. Other than his reading lessons, his entire world was contained within the walls of the Academy.

An alley ran along the eastern wall of the campus that provided access to the rears of the houses that fronted onto the next street over. A pile of rubble had accumulated, or had been intentionally left there for this very purpose, next to the wall a few hundred yards down this alley. It was high enough to allow them to get up onto the top of the stone wall, which was surmounted by thick, black iron railings. Just by the spot where the rubble was piled, two of the bars seemed wider at their base. It was perfectly sized to let a man of normal build squeeze through, but Soren was taller than average and with all the food and training, had finally begun to fill out. He was concerned that he would not fit, but after Ranph slipped through and turned to wait for him, he knew he had to try.

It all seemed to be going well until he got to his hips. In the position that he had squeezed his head and shoulders through, he had no leverage to twist his hips to get them through as well. When it became apparent that he was stuck fast, Ranph shuffled along the ledge toward him and grabbed him. He grimaced in pain as he twisted Soren and pulled him through. They both tumbled off the wall and into a bush below, with far more noise than either of them would have liked.

After they crawled out and dusted themselves off, Soren took stock of his surroundings. Ranph seemed quite familiar with where they were, but it took Soren a moment to realise that they were behind the dining hall. Ranph had a reasonably short journey to get to Stornado House, but Soren would have to make it all the way across campus to get to River House, without being caught by a steward.

'So I suppose we wish each other good luck now and make our separate ways,' Soren said.

'Not a chance,' replied Ranph. 'You'll never manage to get to River without being spotted by a steward; there's too much open ground between here and there. There are usually a dozen of them patrolling the grounds all night. No, we'll go to the infirmary. I'll need to pay a visit there anyway, and it's about half way. If we get spotted we can tell them I had a training accident and you're helping me to the infirmary, which isn't too far from the truth. Once we get there the doctor will give you a pass to get back to River. Now, let's get going.'

Although obviously injured, Ranph was well able to make his own way, or could have waited until morning. Soren recognised the gesture for what it was. As soon as they got out of the cover of the dining hall, Ranph draped his arm over Soren's shoulder and began to feign a pronounced limp. It was well that he did for they were barely half way across Dining Hall Square when the warm orange-yellow glow of a mage lamp appeared around the corner with the shadowy figure of a steward attached to it.

At one time, the nocturnal misdeeds of Academy students had made it a danger for them to move about the city alone. The Academy was being brought into such disrepute that harsh measures were enacted. The curfew was imposed, and it was made an expellable offence to be out after dark. What angered wronged citizens even more was the fact that students enjoyed immunity from the City Watch and the laws of the city. They led a privileged life, raised hell in the city and had the ability to maim or kill almost anyone who tried to stop them. All the Watch could do was arrest them and deliver them to the Master, which once would have amounted to nothing more than an irritated telling off, but now would be far worse. Dishonourable expulsion from the Academy was a shameful stain that a man would never be able to wash from his character so long as he remained in the Duchy of Ostia.

'Well, gentlemen, out a bit late aren't we?' said the steward. He was careful to remain polite.

Ranph groaned as though he was dazed, giving Soren his queue.

'My friend was injured training. A drone caught him a bad one in the face,' Soren said. It was a well-delivered lie, but the steward seemed well used to tall tales.

'I assume neither you nor your friend has a pass to be out this late?' the steward asked.

'No, steward, we don't,' Soren replied.

The steward let out a long 'hmmmm'

'Got hit more than once, by the looks of 'im,' he said slowly, stepping closer and holding his lamp up for a better look. He scratched his chin thoughtfully for a moment before moving his head closer to Ranph's and inhaled deeply through his nose. 'Well, no smell of booze anyway. Not so sure I believe your story, but I don't reckon the young gentleman's been drinking. Get 'im to the infirmary as quick as you can and don't let me catch you out again after hours.' With that, the steward shuffled off, the glow of his lamp bobbing around in the darkness.

Ranph painfully stifled a laugh as they made their way to the infirmary.

Chapter 16

THE GIRL

It tended to only be the wealthier and more senior students that sneaked into the city at night regularly, although most students did at some point or another. Since Soren's steady rise in popularity had begun after defeating dal Dardi in the duel, he had been getting occasional requests to accompany the group sneaking out of the campus and finally decided to go along. While the idea had never really appealed to him before, he eventually relented to Henn and Jost's entreaties and agreed to go once they had assured him that there was another way over the wall that was closer to River House that Soren would fit through without difficulty.

The Sail and Sword was a large tavern in Docks, the warehouse district of the city that fronted onto the harbour. The tavern was a favourite with the Academy students and had been for some time. The long history of custom that they brought to the tavern meant that the owner turned a blind eye to some of their drunken excesses and would provide an easy escape for them on the rare occasion of the tavern being raided by the Watch, who would happily hand over what they viewed as the spoiled Academy students to the Academy Provost.

The tavern was large but not particularly full, although it was early in the week and Soren expected it would be fuller when the stevedores and other dockworkers received their wages. There was a mixed crowd there, with the Academy students occupying the tables and booths near the fireplace away from the rest of the patrons, who were a mix of merchants, sailors, off duty watchmen and a variety of other difficult to pin down denizens of the city.

Soren sat quietly in a corner of the booth while the other students chatted. House divisions seemed to be present here as well as on campus, as students tended to congregate at tables according to their houses. As he sat sipping at a glass of ale, a girl working behind the bar caught his eye. She was cleaning glasses with a cloth before returning them to the shelf behind the bar and worked with the practised nature of one who had done the job many times before and no longer needs to give it any thought. She was slender and of average height, with long curly, dark brown hair and pale skin. She was quite simply the most beautiful girl Soren had ever seen.

As though she sensed his stare, she turned abruptly and looked in the direction of the booth in which Soren sat with a slightly bemused look on her face. She paused her cleaning and Soren looked away quickly, feeling his face flush slightly with embarrassment.

'Would you consider entering for it?'

Jost was speaking, but it took Soren a moment to realise that he was speaking to him. Eager for the distraction, he asked Jost what he had meant.

'The Competition of course. The thing I've been talking about for the last ten minutes. Are you going to enter it?' asked Jost.

'I hadn't really given it any thought,' Soren replied. 'I don't really know very much about it. I thought you had to be in the Collegium to enter for it.'

'No, usually someone from the Collegium represents the Academy, but it isn't a requirement. They just tend to be the best, but with your speed and another year of training, you'll easily be up to that level by then,' said Jost.

Each of the cities of the old Saludorian Empire had an Academy of Swordsmanship. The Competition was one of the few ties that still held them all together. After the Mage Wars, the Empire had dissolved and each city went out on its own, becoming a duchy or principality in its own right. For a few decades they had remained in a confederation, but that too had fallen apart. Each city claimed to have the finest swordsmen, and each year, the finest student from each city's Academy was selected to compete against the others for the honour of that title.

'Perhaps I will, then,' Soren said thoughtfully. Winning the Competition was a quick route to celebrity status in the arena. Ostenheim had won the Competition a few times during his lifetime, and each of the winners had gone on to great careers in the arena, each of them becoming wealthy and famous. It was an appealing thought. Even winning selection would be a feather in his cap.

A tap on the arm and a nod from Jost broke his contemplation. He was nodding toward the bar girl, who was now moving about the tavern collecting glasses and wiping down tables. She moved with ease and confidence, but with none of the haughtiness that Soren had seen beautiful women comport themselves with in the past. She was beautiful, but did not seem to realise it.

'A Competition winner would be sure to catch the eye of a girl like her,' Jost said, with a grin. 'Most of us have tried, but she'll be saving herself for some wealthy merchant I dare say, to whisk her off to a life of luxury. Getting knocked up by an Academy brat with no intention of marrying her isn't likely to be high on her list of things to do!'

Soren flushed again a little. She approached their table and Soren could feel his heart begin to race.

'Can I get anything else for you, lads?' she asked.

'Two pitchers of ale and a kiss!' Henn said.

'The ale I can get you, but it will take more than a cheeky grin to get the rest!' she said good-naturedly.

She left them and came back a few moments later with the two large pottery jugs of ale.

'That's two shillings, lads!' she said. As she took the money her gaze seemed to linger on Soren for a moment longer than necessary. His heart raced. She had the same quizzical look on her face that she had had when she caught him staring at her before.

Jost caught Soren's expression.

'This new face is Soren. He's the talk of the Academy. I think he will be the next great swordsman. Greater than Amero even!' said Henn, who Soren was beginning to realise was prone to exaggeration.

Soren flushed again. He was pleased that he was being thought of that way, but being the centre of attention made him uncomfortable.

'Hello, Soren,' she said, smiling as she gathered up the two empty pitchers and wiped away the wet rings they had left on the wooden table. 'My name's Alessandra. I hope you don't spend too much time with these drunken reprobates, they can drag any good man down!'

The other tyros roared with mock indignation, and then she was gone.

As the night wore on the house divisions melted away and the students mingled freely. There were so many of them there that they took up half of the room. With so many missing from the Academy, Soren found it hard to believe that their absence would go unnoticed by the staff. It seemed that so long as everyone paid lip service to the rules and did not draw any unwanted attention in breaking them, a blind eye would be turned. Eventually Soren found himself talking to Ranph, with the conversation naturally turning to a discussion of technique, and Soren was eager to impress with his new and expanding knowledge.

They had not spoken since the night of the fight in the alley-way and neither of them brought it up. The memory of having experienced what seemed to Soren to have been something far more than a random mugging must have been troubling for him, although it was impossible to tell what was going on beyond his calm countenance.

Soren did not reveal the fact that he had been spending most, if not every evening in the training hall experimenting with, and, he hoped, perfecting new techniques. Despite this Ranph pointed out that he had noticed the dramatic improvement in Soren's technique and also his progression through the class, and by the end of the conversation, Soren found himself agreeing to train with Ranph outside of class hours.

———◆◆◆———

Drones were excellent training tools, but were no match for the unpredictability of a person. The strength of the drones lay in their technical perfection and their ability to continue relentlessly and without tiring. A person however, could benefit from imperfect technique and the other creatures of chance that would not be exploited by a drone. Training with Ranph was also a good opportunity for Soren to measure his own improvement, having sparred against Ranph on his first day at the Academy. Ranph was still far superior to him, but the gap had narrowed considerably proving to Soren that his extra efforts were worthwhile, and enforcing his belief that he could rise to the head of his class if he continued.

Each evening, as they tidied up after themselves, they tended to discuss the session, and how they might both improve upon certain aspects of their swordplay and tactical approach. It bolstered Soren's confidence for Ranph to discuss these things with him, confirming that Ranph saw him as having a worthwhile opinion on swordplay, rather than as being nothing more than a capable workhorse useful only for sparring.

As they were putting away the swords they had been using one evening, Ranph steered the conversation in a different direction.

'You know there is a vacancy coming up in the Blades,' he said.

'Really?' replied Soren. He tried to sound casual about it, but in fact it was an opportunity he had been waiting for. Being a Blade would preclude the repeat of an episode like that with dal Dardi, but he had to admit his motivation was driven as much by this as it was by the status alone of being a Blade.

'Yes,' said Ranph. 'Carter dal Galasin's father died a few days ago and he is being graduated early so he can go home and take over his barony. Applications for his place will be taken from next week. I wanted to let you know that if you decide to put your name forward I will endorse your application.'

'That's kind of you,' said Soren, 'but I have to admit that I'm a little surprised. Surely there are others in Stornado that will be going for it.'

'Yes, but none of them pulled me out of an alleyway and an attempted assassination. I always try to repay my debts, and being a Blade will bring you a lot of benefits. I can't promise anything, but my endorsement should carry some weight!'

———•◦•◦•———

Soren found himself thinking of the Sail and Sword, or more particularly the serving girl, Alessandra, as often as he thought of his studies. It was a week before they went there again. As usual, Soren had trained with Ranph after dinner and by the time they had finished everyone else had already gone on ahead of them. They sneaked out together and then continued on to the Sail and Sword, chatting and joking as they went.

Soren had put in an application for the Blades as Ranph had suggested, but had yet to hear anything more about it. He had found that as the evenings spent in the training hall continued, he was spending more time with Ranph than with either Henn or Jost and Soren was beginning to think of him as a friend rather than just a training partner.

When they arrived at the Sail and Sword, the night was already going strong. The bar girl, Alessandra, was worked off her feet but just the sight of her was enough to make Soren's day. He joined in with the others, Jost and Henn among them, but was always hoping that Alessandra would stop for long enough for him to talk to her. While he was scanning the crowd for her, he noticed a man by the bar that was watching them. He was stocky with a weather beaten face and hair pulled back into a short ponytail. He had the look of a sailor about him, but there was something else too, something sharp and calculating.

After a little while, he made his way over to the table.

'Evening, lads. Can I stand you a round of drinks?' he asked.

The students were never ones to turn down drinks, so they accepted and made polite and idle conversation with the man, who introduced himself as Braggock. The name went some way to explaining his slightly unusual appearance. It was a barbarian name, so he was not an Ostian, but would originally have come from the plains to the east.

It was clear from the get go that the man was working his way to something in particular, and his redundant chit chat was not hiding the fact. Eventually he got to his point.

'I expect some of you lads could use a little spare cash every now and then. On occasion I find myself in need of people who can handle a sword, just for appearances you understand. If you're ever in need of a little coin, search me out as I may have something that needs doing. I'm here most nights, but you can ask for me at the bar if I'm not. Enjoy your drinks.' He raised his cup to them and returned to his place at the bar, this time with his back to them.

'I'll gladly drink his ale, but I wouldn't sully my blade for a thug like him. Anyway, what do we look like, paupers?' said Jost indignantly, before casting a glance at Soren and flushing slightly. It occurred to Soren that he was the only one of them around the table without a title.

As the second term progressed, Soren found himself increasingly busy with all of the demands on his time. There was the regular coursework to keep up with as well as his continuing efforts with reading and writing, although this now took less time and energy than it once had. Matriculation tests were looming in the near future, and the Competition was also occupying his thoughts, distant though it was. All of these things filled him with a frustration at how few hours there seemed to be in the day, and also at the fact that he was being kept from the Sail and Sword and any chance to talk to Alessandra.

Despite his desire to loiter around the tavern for any and every opportunity to speak to her, he fought to maintain his focus and if anything poured more effort into training and study. He also kept in mind what Master Dornish had said to him before the end of the previous term, about this ancient ability he had called the 'Gift of Grace'. He had looked out for anything unusual, but it was difficult to know what was unusual, as he did not feel any different, or notice any behaviour that was different, to the rest of his life. How could he identify something when this was all he knew, and even Master Dornish had not been able to tell him specifically what to look for?

Chapter 17

THE EXAMINATION

S oren sat outside one of the fencing salons on the first floor
of the front building of the Academy. There was a slight flutter of nerves in his chest, although he knew that he had no
reason to be concerned about what awaited him during the exam
he was about to take. It was more the uncertainty of what would be
asked of him that gave him pause for thought.

Only the previous week he had finally made it to the front row
of the class, and had not even taken a touch in a sparring match in
several weeks. While his technique still left something to be desired
it was far more functional than it had been, and might even be
described as competent. Alone it was nothing to set him apart
from his classmates, but when combined with the speed that came
naturally to him, which had not let him down since that one occasion fighting dal Dardi in the field outside of the city, he was easily
among the more exceptional members of his class. He also took
pride in his large and growing knowledge of the theory of swordsmanship that he felt was now superior to that of his classmates.

The door latch clicked and the door opened. Henn stepped
out, his face covered in a sheen of sweat. He raised his eyebrows to
Soren when he spotted him sitting there.

'Good luck!' he said. 'It's not all that bad actually; you shouldn't
have any problem with it!'

Soren nodded and went in. Master Bryn was standing at the far
end of the salon. The room was lined with windows looking down into
the front square of the Academy along one side and mirrors along the
other. It made the room seem far larger than it actually was.

'Take a sword and start with the positions please, Tyro,' he said.

Soren nodded and took a sword from the open locker by the door and began. Master Bryn watched him with a sideways glance as he filled a glass with water from a pitcher on a side table and drank. He had a sheen of sweat on his face also, so it appeared that sparring would form part of the examination.

Soren began to go through the positions, which at this point he had practiced so many times, repeating them required no thought whatsoever.

'That will do,' said Bryn, once he had finished his glass of water. 'Take your guard.'

He walked forward purposefully and launched into his attack without pause or salute. Soren parried the initial barrage but was forced to take several steps backward. Bryn's class showed through in his swordplay. In every way he was superior to the students Soren was accustomed to sparring against, even Ranph who many of his classmates would have considered to be of a similar ability level to an instructor.

He attacked again, with an angry intensity that startled Soren. It was almost as though he viewed the sparring as being for real. The hesitation caused Soren to execute a parry an instant too slowly and all he could do was deflect the point of Bryn's blade away from its intended target, Soren's heart, and into his shoulder instead.

'A touch!' said Bryn, through gritted teeth. 'This is not just about defending!' He launched into another combination of attacks. As Soren parried, he smiled to himself as he recognised the combination from one of the manuals he had studied. Bryn executed it perfectly but Soren was able to duck out of the way and move to his blind side. He made an economical thrust to Bryn's midsection and evened the score.

'Excellent!' said Bryn. 'Truly excellent. Well done. That will be all.'

With one night of the regular term remaining, there was little for Soren to do. Most of the other students had gone home as soon as they had completed their matriculation tests, but as Soren had nowhere else to go, he had remained. Once again River House was empty of its usual sounds of life, which was something that made him feel uncomfortable. It wasn't that the silence was particularly eerie, it was just something that prevented him from being completely at ease. The solution that came to him most readily was the same one that always did, to train.

———◆◆◆◆———

He wheeled between the drones as they hacked and slashed at him. A blade passed so close to his face that he could feel the rush of air against his skin. Other students always complained about how they hated the drones, but Soren had never found them to be much of a challenge. Beyond being a moving opponent and providing a tough physical training session, Soren did not especially rate them. They always seemed to be much faster when he watched them than they actually were when he trained against them.

He had continued to give thought to what Master Dornish had said to him about the 'Gift of Grace' but still could not identify anything specifically out of the ordinary, but then it was unlikely that he would have; he knew no different.

When he deactivated the final drone, he was swallowed whole by a wave of exhaustion that forced him to one knee. As he fought to catch his breath he felt a nauseous ache in his stomach and his head throbbed. Despite the improvement in his fitness and physical condition over the course of the academic year, training against the drones always brought him past the point of exhaustion. No matter how skilled an opponent he sparred against, he could never push himself to that level of physical distress any other way.

'Exceptional physical fitness was the only solution the old bannerets ever found to the exhaustion, but even that was lacking. It seems that exhaustion and even nausea were common side effects of the Gift of Grace.'

The voice startled Soren, and he turned to see that Master Dornish had entered the hall.

'The gift seems to have come in two parts. The first part was simply the gift. This aspect seems to have been enjoyed by bannerets most of the time, to varying levels of intensity. I'm not sure how or why the intensity varied; perhaps they could control it to some degree. This state was a lesser manifestation of what was called "the Moment", which seems to have been the very highest expression of their powers and appears to have occurred far more rarely. Only in the most extreme times of peril to the banneret or the mage he guarded. That was the original purpose of the bannerets you see, to provide physical protection for mages. The side effects for the Moment seem to have been far more severe than the exhaustion and nausea that could be caused by the Gift. I did a little research, but that is the sum total reward for my labours,' Dornish said.

'After the Mage Wars, all writings pertaining to the use of magic were destroyed, and I suspect almost all mentions of the Gift of Grace were also. The only mentions of it that I did find were from books that would have been written decades after the last of the old bannerets had died. But it is something to go on. If you can contemplate on the way you feel when in training and combat, perhaps you can identify if you have the Gift, and if you can identify the extreme effect of the Moment, but be careful! There is a more pressing matter however, which is the reason I am here.' He clutched several oddly shaped swords loosely wrapped in oilcloth in his hands. He handed them to Soren.

'They are properly known as "storta", but they are more often called Ruripathian backswords due to only having a single sharp edge and the fact that it is mainly the Ruripathians who use them. Usually we don't train students in the use of and defence against foreign swords until they are adepti, but I think you ought to become accustomed to them rather sooner. The Count of Moreno has notified me that he will be here to pick you up tomorrow so that you can accompany him on a diplomatic mission north. He wants to give you a taste of your future duties with him no doubt,' said Dornish.

Soren nodded, still too tired to make conversation and took the items from Dornish, his arms shaking with fatigue.

'While we place a broadly even emphasis on cut and thrust, these swords are primarily used for cutting, although they can be used for a thrust also. The drones will know how to use them, but to look at you I would be inclined to recommend some rest over more training this evening!' said Dornish.

Soren nodded again. Sweat dripped from his face with the movement of his head. It was all he could do to stay standing and he fought to control his breathing.

'In case you are wondering, you did well in your exams, and have again impressed Master Bryn. Well, I'll leave you to it,' he said.

Soren nodded a final time, the fact that it would be the first time he had ever gone beyond sight of Ostenheim's great walls sinking in and filling him with excitement and uncertainty.

Chapter 18

JOURNEY NORTH

Soren had spent the morning packing and was quite surprised by the luggage all around him. In the course of one academic year at the Academy, he had gone from owning nothing but the rags on his back to having several cases of clothing. A ceremonial uniform, a mess uniform, several sets of training clothing and various other accoutrements required for daily life at the Academy sat neatly folded in his cases. He was waiting in front of the Academy to be collected by Amero, and was quite taken aback when his patron finally did arrive.

A great black carriage drawn by a team of six horses pulled up outside the Academy gates, followed by one other smaller carriage that stopped behind it. Two men sat on the seat at the front, one of whom he recognised as Emeric. Emeric hopped down from the carriage, and made a quick hand gesture to the men on the second carriage.

He walked up to Soren and was followed by two liveried servants from the other carriage.

'Well, Tyro, I hope you've enjoyed your year so far. I dare say you'll be earning your keep in the weeks to come,' said Emeric, as a matter of fact. He cast a glance back into the Academy and for the briefest of moments his face darkened. The two servants gathered up Soren's baggage and Emeric gestured for him to get into the main carriage.

He stepped up into it. Getting into a carriage was another first in a long list of firsts for him that year. He had to check his balance as it rocked gently under his weight. The interior was something of a surprise to him. Pale blue silk upholstery lined its entirety, with two plush couches facing each other front and back. Amero, Count of Moreno looked up at him from a bunch of papers that he had been reviewing. He caught Soren's inquisitive gaze.

'Ah yes, the powder blue. Not really to my taste, but my mother had it done and I haven't been bothered to change it. Still, it could be worse I suppose. Please, sit,' he said. He gestured to the couch opposite him. 'How have you been enjoying the Academy?'

'Very well, my Lord,' Soren said respectfully.

Amero smiled broadly.

'Well, I see that old prick Rilid's etiquette lessons are still good for something. Master Dornish tells me you are something of a phenomenon. From scrawny wretch to near top of your class in only a year. I knew you would be good when I first saw you, but that really is quite an achievement. Nonetheless it is gratifying to hear from someone as tight with compliments as Dornish that I haven't pissed away eight hundred crowns on tuition,' said Amero.

'I'm very grateful for the opportunity you have given me, my Lord,' Soren replied, balking at the size of his tuition fee. It was more than an ordinary worker would earn in years, perhaps even a lifetime.

'I only expect to be called "my lord", "count", or any of that other rubbish in front of others, Soren. In private Amero will more than suffice. And there is no need for gratitude, be very assured that I will have full value from my investment in you in the full passage of time!' he said, with a wolfish smile that Soren had seen so many times in the arena just before Amero made his winning strike.

The carriage jolted to a start and clattered away from the Academy and down the cobbled road.

'It's down to the docks where we will take a ship north to Baelin. It's the most northerly port in the Duchy and the powers that be want me to call in and deliver some dispatches seeing as we're passing that way anyway. Regardless, we couldn't get any further north by sea at this time of the year. It will still be iced up any farther north. We will overland from there to Brixen. I hear that they call it the "Mirrored City", because of the lake it overlooks.

I've never been there myself but it's meant to be beautiful, as are their women, which I have to admit I'm a damn sight more interested in seeing!' said Amero.

The door to the carriage opened, and Soren made as to close it, thinking he had not pulled it shut behind him properly, but as he reached over Emeric swung in. He took a seat next to Soren and nodded to them in greeting.

'Ah, Emeric! So, what was it like being back at the Academy?'

Emeric glowered at Amero for a moment, before turning his head to look out of the window without giving a response. Amero continued.

'Emeric here was my father's protégé, as you are mine. He was expelled though. He killed another student in a duel. It caused quite a fuss at the time. I was still an under cadet, but I'll never forget it. By rights he shouldn't even be carrying swords, but he was booted out only a few weeks shy of graduating, so I suppose it doesn't do any harm. At least not so long as you're on the right side of him!'

Emeric continued to look out of the window, as though to hide embarrassment, but he did not strike Soren as the kind of man who was embarrassed so easily.

'He had it coming,' said Emeric. His hand involuntarily went to the scar that ran down the right side of his face. 'Being able to call yourself Banneret isn't the be all and end all. You'd do well to remember that, lad.' He returned his gaze out of the window, at the city passing by.

'I don't know how much Dornish told you about what you'd be doing on this trip, but it won't be a holiday. I don't know how well you cope with refinement now, passably well by the look of you, but you will certainly be tested on this trip. There will be plenty of formality and ceremony, so it should be a worthwhile experience for you.

'The Duke has determined that I should go north to renew and reaffirm the treaty of peace between the Ruripathians and us. Every few years, factions up there start agitating for a warm water port. All of theirs become completely iced up in the winter. Can't get any shipping in and out, so they want one of ours, by treaty or by force, but we don't want them to get their paws on one. If it weren't for all the metals and gems they dig out of their mountains, I dare say the entire principality would be back to eating raw meat and using stone tools by now. As it is, with a limited trading season, it puts a bit of a choke on their wealth, which suits us very nicely. Ostenheim isn't quite the crossroads of trade between east and west that it was in the days of the Empire. If Ruripathia were to grow too wealthy and powerful, they would be in a position to challenge us for dominance in the eastern Middle Sea, and we can't have that.

'Usually this kind of job would be given to a more seasoned diplomat, but with my reputation, they thought I would be a better choice, a better statement of our strength and also our sincerity in maintaining the peace. I've brought you and Emeric along as my two toughs!' he added, with a smile.

'Sending three of the most dangerous swordsmen in Ostia should be a clear enough message if it comes to that, which I doubt it will. Although with these Northern types you never know when a show of strength will be needed. A demonstration duel or something like that. I'd rather like to see you measured against one of them myself, truth be told! There may be other little tasks for you along the way too, so keep on your toes!' said Amero.

The carriage pulled up at the docks where Emeric jumped out and walked briskly down one of the wooden jetties that stretched into the inner harbour from the stone quays. He chatted with a man in a naval uniform before returning to the carriages and barking orders at the servants.

'They're ready to take us on board whenever you want,' said Emeric when he arrived at the window of the carriage. They got out and Soren cast an eye over the harbour. He had always liked it there, the bustle and crowds of workers created an energy about the place that he enjoyed. There were so many strange faces, accents, tongues and smells that it never ceased to pique his curiosity.

There were only three large ships, Oceanmen, warped to the jetties in the inner harbour. It was large enough to accommodate more, but the empty space allowed more freedom of movement for the smaller merchant vessels and coasters. Out in the bay, past the two towers that guarded either side of the entrance to the harbour, a half dozen or so more Oceanmen sat at anchor waiting for their turn to enter.

The vessel they were to board, the *Paryso*, was significantly smaller than the behemoth Oceanmen, and was of a sleeker design than one would expect of a merchantman. It wasn't rigged for fighting either, so Soren assumed it was one of the Duchy's dispatch ships. Fast, well enough armed for a fight, but also able to take more cargo than a warship.

———◆◆◆———

When he lived on the street, violent sickness had often followed eating a suspect piece of food, usually fowl or rancid meat of some description, but often the hunger had over ridden any concerns he might have had and he had chanced a suspect morsel. The reward was a full belly for a few hours, a few hours of violent vomiting and then the ever-present problem of an empty belly once more. It had not been an issue ever since he had started at the Academy and he had almost forgotten what it felt like to be physically ill. The sea voyage was reacquainting him though.

The master's mate, Ensign Phenning, a young man about Soren's age and a student at the city's Naval Academy on his second practical posting, had told him that it would not likely last past the first twelve to twenty four hours, but each minute seemed like a lifetime as he clung to the bulwark of the ship, doubled over, his empty stomach trying to eject non existent contents. Occasionally a little fluid came up, but for the most part the violent contractions in his chest and belly produced nothing but pain.

While Amero and Emeric drank, ate and gambled in the captain's stateroom, Soren swore that he would never set foot on a ship again if it could be avoided. The prospect of the return journey would doubtless haunt him for the duration of their stay in the north.

Ensign Phenning's first prediction had proved to be incorrect. Soren remained violently ill for the duration of the six day voyage. After what had seemed an eternity at sea, Soren was delighted to put foot on land, only to discover with dismay that Ensign Phenning's second prediction was completely correct. Land sickness. Six days at sea had made him become accustomed to the constant pitching, moving and angle of the deck of the ship. Now that he was on firm, dry land, he could not adjust, and the movement continued, the solid ground pitching, never being where his foot expected it to be when he took a step.

Baelin was a small and bustling harbour town that benefitted from Ruripathia's lack of a port that did not ice up during the winter. The buildings were a mix of designs, betraying the fact that it had changed ownership on more than one occasion since the fragmentation of the Empire. The air was far cooler than in Ostenheim. The temperature had steadily dropped since they had left on their voyage north, although Phenning had told him that a few weeks earlier it had been far colder.

Baelin was the most northerly port on the east coast of the Middle Sea that was not susceptible to winter ice, which explained why the Ruripathians had been so eager in the past to have control of it. It was sheltered on the southern lip of the headland that formed the bay to the north, which suffered the full force of the winter wind, the Niepar, which blew down from the Telastrian Mountains to the northeast. Everything north of that headland spent nearly half of the year frozen, ice as far as the eye could see. Then, when the Niepar was spent a second airflow prevailed over the north, this one from the deserts to the south. This wind was called the Nistra, and was hot, causing a rapid thaw and hot summers. In autumn this airflow stalled, and the Niepar returned, the cycle repeating each year.

The ships were all smaller here than they had been in Ostenheim and the harbour was not big enough to accommodate an Oceanman, but the air was fresh and everything was so new that Soren felt incredibly excited. All the time at the Academy there was an overbearing sense that everything was just a dream that could end at any moment and that he would be plucked from the fragrant air of Highgarden and dropped back in the cess and filth of the backstreets in the city slums. Now he was having his eyes opened to how much more there was to the world than just Ostenheim.

He stood on the dock, arms akimbo in the fashion he had seen Dornish adopt with an air of authority, and struggled to maintain his balance. He wondered how long it would be before the feeling that the ground was moving beneath him would go. He thought it unlikely that he managed much authority, swaying like a drunk as he surveyed the small but bustling port town. He was hundreds of miles from anything he knew, in this strange and foreign place, but wearing the blue doublet of a banneret in training, even this far from Ostenheim, he was recognised for what he was by everyone that passed. It was not as a street urchin, but as a man of importance, position and danger. It was empowering and for the first time in his life he felt as though he actually represented these things, rather than merely being a gutter rat trying to eke out an existence, or an imposter in fancy cloths.

He felt a firm hand on his back and turned to see Amero, his blue banneret's doublet standing out among the crowds on the dock. It was trimmed with silver and gold embroidery, which differentiated it from an ordinary banneret's doublet that was trimmed with white, and denoted Amero as a Banneret of the Blue, a master swordsman of the highest level. It bore the arms of the Academy and the city on the sleeves and chest. In his hands he carried a long slender wooden box.

'They aren't exactly a work of art, but they are as good a pair of working blades as you could want. I dare say you will need them sooner than you might think, or than either of us might like. Don't thank me for them though. They are less a gift than a necessity. You're wearing the blue of Ostenheim and the insignia of the Academy, so you are permitted to bear arms while within the town limits. I suggest you put them on now,' said Amero.

He handed Soren the box and went back to confer with one of his servants as to the loading of the two carriages that would be taking them the rest of the way north. Soren opened the box, to reveal dark wine coloured felt, a sword, dagger and their scabbards and baldrics pressed into its mouldings. He took the dagger out and fastened its baldric around his waist, and then, scarcely able to contain his excitement did the same with the sword, its steel wire guard forming a loose basket around the hilt inviting his hand to sit neatly in it.

Unable to contain himself any longer, he drew the sword from its scabbard, and revelled in the smooth dark sheen of the unmarked blade. It was an inch wide at the hilt and tapered into a spear point tip. It measured about thirty inches long and it was sharp down the full length of both edges. The blade was thick for strength with a narrow fuller running down the centre and the balance felt so much more natural than any blade he had held at the Academy.

'Excuse me, sir.'

It took Soren a moment to realise that the voice was directed at him, and then for an instant his old instincts set his pulse racing. He remembered who and where he was, and turned to the voice.

'Yes?' Soren asked in response. It was a member of the Town Watch. The town crest was embroidered in gold thread on the left breast of his black leather gambeson.

'If you wouldn't mind re-sheathing your blade, sir, makes people nervous,' he said. He was polite and deferential.

The last time Soren had a run in with a member of the City Watch in Ostenheim he had been given a thorough beating.

'Oh, yes, of course, I'm terribly sorry,' Soren replied. He re-sheathed it with a satisfying hiss of the metal against the leather and felt that lined the scabbard.

'Quite all right, sir, enjoy your time in Baelin,' he said, and with that he moved on.

Soren watched him wander off into the crowd and then became aware of a presence beside him. Wearing a long black coat with a high collar that almost completely hid his face and a wide brimmed hat, Emeric was standing beside him.

'We are a long way from home now, lad, and swords aren't for play and impressing young ladies. When the time comes you will have to use it like it's meant to be used and not think twice about it. All our lives might depend on it. Understand?'

Soren nodded, the solemnity of what Emeric had said bringing his mood down. What questions would be asked of him in the days to come? Emeric continued, preventing Soren from reflecting more on what he had just said.

'We have been to war more times than I can count with the Ruripathians. There are enemies all around us. Keep an eye out and we'll be all right.' He gave Soren a slap on the back. 'The blades look good on you.'

Chapter 19

THE CITY OF ASH

Soren was somewhat disappointed that they did not spend any time in Baelin, but he supposed that there wasn't a great deal to see or do there by comparison with Ostenheim. After a quick meal while the carriages were loaded, they rolled out of the small walled town and headed toward Northmarch Castle that sat overlooking the border with Ruripathia.

The new carriages were not nearly as comfortable as Amero's personal one. These had been borrowed from the Baron of Northmarch. Amero was clearly not entirely pleased with the come down in luxury, but he was happier at not having to formally meet with the baron.

'These appointed barons are always such a bore,' he said. 'I know we need men with proven military records in the border marches, but they never seem to be able to fit in with the idea of nobility. They always seem to feel the need to go the extra mile to impress their superiors. The funny thing is, they all earned their positions and are twice the men that many of those that were born to a title are. Although you should take note, young Soren, appointment as a marcher baron is the prize for any landless banneret. And a very rewarding one it is too! Old Baron Calfax had squirreled away half the wealth of Southmarch for his heirs by the time he died. Timely thing too, with the new Duke being elected. It was said Valens had Calfax at the top of his chopping list.'

Soren suppressed a smirk at Amero's casual use of the Duke's first name. Such a short time ago, all of these things had seemed a world away. Now it appeared as though he was right at the centre of them.

'This fucking carriage smells awful! Who is Baron Northmarch anyway, I don't recall his name?' said Amero.

'Benciveni dal Orta,' replied Emeric. 'The mayor said he's off settling a border dispute between two of his knights.'

'Hmm. Ben Orta. I think I remember the name. Made a bit of a reputation for himself clearing the bandits out of the southern passes as I recall. Useful enough chap I expect. Still, at least we don't have to go through the rigmarole of being formally received. I'm going to sleep, wake me when we get to the castle,' said Amero.

◆━◆╳◆━◆

Northmarch Castle sat in a pass through some low-lying mountains and hills that ran from the coast to the Telastrian Mountains in the east. It was the main road between Ruripathia and Baelin, which had been a focus of the fighting each time that Ostia and Ruripathia had gone to war with one another. The route bore the scars of this clearly; none of the trees were more than a few decades old and the ancient Imperial road was marked by many more recent repairs. Were it not for the Ruripathians needing access to Baelin during the winter months, Soren suspected that the road would have been allowed to fall to ruin many years before.

The castle had been built to defend the pass not long after Baelin was retaken during the First Northern War. It had stood there ever since, under the control of whoever had control of Baelin. It struck Soren as odd how the borders had placed Baelin within the Duchy of Ostia considering its location, being connected to Ruripathia by land but only by sea to Ostia, but it had been under the Ostenheim's control for the greater part of the time since the Saludorian Empire came to an end, and the stranglehold that the Niepar placed on Ruripathian maritime trade helped Ostia to remain the dominant power on the eastern coast of the Middle Sea.

They did not halt at the castle however, even with its lord away. Amero was eager to make the fastest time possible, and it was not long before they crossed the border into Ruripathia, Soren's first time in a foreign land.

———— ◆━◈━◆ ————

The carriage jolted to a halt and Emeric hopped out. Soren followed him, and reluctantly, so too did Amero. They had stopped atop a rise that afforded a view over the plain below. Spread out in front of them was the ruin of a once enormous city, big enough to rival Ostenheim as it now was.

'Welcome to Rurip,' said Amero. 'The city of diamonds and sapphires, where the College of Mages made their final stand. In one hundred days of fighting, the city was ruined beyond repair, countless numbers were killed and the scourge of magery was finally put to an end.'

Soren was too awestricken to comment. To imagine Ostenheim reduced to rubble was beyond comprehension. This city would easily have been as large before its destruction and now it was nothing but a dead, grey scar on the landscape.

'We will ride on alone from here. The servants are too slack-bladdered to come with us. They say the city and its environs are haunted. Old women the lot of them, but I think they'd rather a good flogging than face the spectres of Rurip. They will take the carriages on the long way and meet in Brixen. Riding through the ruins will have us in a warm bath, a warm bed and if we can find one, a warm wench two days sooner!' said Amero.

Soren spotted him winking at Emeric. He expected that Amero was trying to scare him, but he was not bothered by it; there were far more frightening things in the dark than ghosts. He knew that from personal experience.

They made camp shortly before darkness fell in a semi-circular hollow formed by banks of rubble at the roadside. Emeric scavenged some dried and twisted pieces of wood from the ruins and lit a fire. The flickering flame cast ghostly shadows all around them as they sat and ate the food that had been packed for them by the servants before they had parted ways. Soren chewed idly at a piece of dried beef and stared into the flame waiting for sleep to come. A whistling howl drifted through the air imposing itself over the crackling sound of the fire. Soren looked to Amero, and then to Emeric when Amero shrugged his shoulders.

'Wolves, rats, who knows? Who cares?' said Emeric. He threw the remainder of the contents of the tin mug of coffee he had been sipping from into the fire with a boiling hiss before standing and stumbling into the darkness while wrestling with his britches.

There was another howl, and this one made even Amero splutter. Soren wondered if it was a ruse, if Amero had sent one of the servants into the city ahead of them just to add weight to his ghost stories. This thought was quickly put to rest however.

'I think I need my blades,' said Amero.

Soren pulled his sword from his bedroll as Emeric returned and removed his sword from his own. Soren had seen Emeric put them there earlier and had thought it an inspired idea. Another howl rang out which startled all three of them. This one came from behind and was far closer. The three stood, their swords drawn, the blades flashing in the firelight. It struck Soren as being rather heroic, like a scene from one of the paintings in the dining hall at the Academy. Three swordsmen staring bravely out into the unknown, lit only by the flickering campfire. He shook his head to empty it of such useless thoughts, but they bolstered his spirits nonetheless.

Another howl, even closer this time, but Amero merely chuckled.

'Perhaps this crumbling shit hole is haunted after all!' he said. His voice was animated with excitement.

Emeric merely shrugged, while Soren squinted out into the murk. Something large and black flew out of the darkness and landed squarely on the fire, smothering it and drenching them in darkness. There was silence for a long moment and Soren felt his pulse quicken as his eyes struggled to adjust to the sudden gloom.

Three howls, all at the same time. They were all around them. The howling became a constant now, one howl following another, never from the same place. Then the sounds of movement became audible, much closer, behind, in front, on both sides, scratching, shuffling and pattering. A screaming, howling, billowing shape fluttered between them, too quickly to make out what it was. Then another flashed past Soren, only inches away, leaving a stale, musty smell in its wake. He twisted quickly, tracking it with the tip of his sword, his boots crunching on the gravel beneath his feet, the weathered rubble of the once great city, but the shape disappeared into the inky blackness.

The howling continued, screeches, cackles, laughter, all around them, from many sources. Soren felt a shiver run down his spine, but it was the unknown rather than fear that caused it. He was excited, eagerly anticipating the opportunity to fight. His blood was hot and he could hear it pulsing in his ears. It had always been the way for him, when he was afraid or in danger, the urge to strike back with violence became his primary emotion. Emeric stepped forward into the darkness as the howling became relentless. Soren wanted to tell him to wait, but he knew the man would ignore him.

Another shape swept out of the darkness, moving in Emeric's direction. There was the sound of steel on cloth and a howl that was of a different sound to any of the others; it was a screech of pain. The shape disappeared back in to the darkness and Emeric walked back toward the others.

'If it feels pain, we can kill it. Ghosts my arse!' Emeric said firmly.

Soren kicked what turned out to be a mass of damp cloth from the fire, which started to sputter back to life. A black shape blustered into the faint circle of light, a flash of something metal in the midst of its amorphous shape. It brushed past Emeric, too fast for him to react, and then in to the darkness once more.

'Fucker!' said Emeric, as he clasped his right arm with his hand, blood seeping from between his fingers.

The howling continued unabated. It was only sound, but Soren quickly recognised the effect it was having on him. It overwhelmed one of his senses and made him edgy. If these were just men, then they were not fools, as it was an effective tool. From the corner of his eye, Soren spotted movement. He was determined not to go un-blooded on this night. He pivoted on his heel and lashed out toward it. He felt his sword connect, heard a screech of pain and pursued his attack, pressing his blade forward into whatever it had hit and stepping forward to follow up with his dagger. He felt it strike home, slipping into something soft, crunching against something harder. Both blades anchored in it, he stepped back toward the fire pulling it with him and dumped it down on the ground.

Bathed in the light of the small fire, it appeared to just be a mass of black cloth. Emeric stepped forward to it and knelt down, reaching a bloodied hand into the mass of cloth and pulling it back. He revealed a pale and dirty face, but one of a man nonetheless. He was dead.

'Just a man.' Emeric grunted. Then as an afterthought, 'your first?'

Soren nodded with hesitation. He hadn't killed a ghost or a demon, just a man. Amero smiled at him, with an amused and suspicious twinkle in his eye.

'Looters and grave robbers probably, taking a chance at live prey for a change,' Amero said, raising his voice to be heard over the incessant howling. 'Even after all this time there must still be a fortune in gems and precious metal buried beneath all of this rubble.'

Emeric pulled a wide bladed dagger from his belt and reached into the mass of cloth once more. There was a sickening squelching sound and then a crunch. Emeric stood, pulling the man's head out from the cloth with him. He held it up above his head by the hair and stared out into the darkness.

'If any of you fuckers want the same, you know where to get it!' he yelled.

He hurled the head out into the darkness, a dull thud returning from the darkness a moment later. It was only now that Soren realised the howling had stopped. When they turned back to deal with the headless corpse, it was gone.

They stoked up the fire and allotted watches, but none of them slept that night.

Chapter 20

THE JEWEL OF THE NORTH

It took another day's ride to get them out of the dead zone surrounding Rurip. They remained vigilant and stopped only when they had to. None of them wanted to spend another night there. They didn't encounter any more trouble, but Soren breathed a sigh of relief when finally they emerged from the ruin back into open countryside.

It took nearly a full day after that to get to the Brixensea, the great lake by which the city of Brixen sat. The lake's surface was like a mirror, perfectly reflecting the cloud scudded sky and the steel coloured, white-capped mountains that loomed on the horizon.

The sun seemed to be touching the surface of the lake as the city of Brixen came into view. Immediately Soren could see why the city had earned its name, the Jewel of the North. The crystal blue waters that stretched out in front of it mirrored its high towers and great domed roofs and in places it was hard to tell where the city ended and the water began.

They rode along the shore of the lake, with the city on the other side getting larger all the time for the remainder of the lighted hours. They reached an impressive gatehouse on the south bank of the river that fed the lake, which guarded the bridge across and into the city shortly after darkness fell.

The guards eyed them warily, but after reading a letter of safe passage that Emeric showed to them, they allowed them through, muttering directions to the Palace. It seemed southerners were not a regular, or welcome presence in Brixen. They rode slowly over the arched bridge. It was made of white stone and it was a magnificent piece of artistry, with a rail of perfectly shaped columns capped with an intricately carved lintel of twisting vines. Every five columns the lintel was topped with a magnificent statue holding a mage lamp up over the bridge. Once they had crossed the bridge and passed through another gatehouse, they arrived on a wide boulevard that ran along the shore of the lake. It was lined with trees and statues and paved with the white stone. Every building in view was constructed from this pure white stone. The stonework of the buildings was decorated with square columns that were topped with ornate carvings of foliage. The windows had triangular arches that lent the buildings an austere but elegant beauty. The verdigris roofs provided a strong contrast with the white walls. Everything about the city shouted out its wealth.

The boulevard was quiet, but much like Highgarden there were finely dressed couples walking along the bank enjoying the serene and peaceful surroundings. Soren and his two companions drew some curious glances, but not quite the same suspicion that Soren had felt the first time he had entered Highgarden. It seemed their clothes marked them out quite clearly as not being local, but also as not being undesirables.

As they rode along the boulevard toward the Palace, Soren could not help but admit that the city was the most beautiful place he had seen. He knew that he had only seen its exquisite façade and not the underbelly that he was sure was hidden away behind it, as was the case in Ostenheim, but still it truly was something to behold. The Palace itself was built on an island a short distance from the shore and was connected to the mainland by a bridge that was even more ornate than the one they had crossed to get into the city. Out on its own in the lake, it was mirrored perfectly by the still water and grabbed one's attention completely and utterly.

On the journey north Amero had told him that while Ostenheim had made its wealth as the trade hub between the empires in the east and all of the cities of the old Saludorian Empire that surrounded the Middle Sea, Ruripathia's wealth was solely based on the fortune in gems and precious metals that were extracted from the Telastrian Mountains to the east. Diamonds, emeralds, sapphires, telastars and the ore from which Telastrian steel was made, as well as platinum and silver were all mined in large quantities and exported around the Middle Sea.

Telastrian steel swords were one thing that Soren very much wanted to see while he was there. They were a rarity in the rest of the world, and fetched a king's ransom but Soren thought, perhaps naively, that there would be far more of them in Ruripathia, being as it was the source of Telastrian steel. Amero had one, but said it was far too valuable to bring on a dangerous mission such as this. The blade would be kept safely and passed on down the generations of his family. Soren had thought it a shame that such a sword would never be used for its intended purpose, and resolved that if he was ever lucky enough to own one he would use it properly.

The most famous of them were named, usually by the man that had first wielded it but sometimes with the older ones, the name had come afterward as the deeds that were carried out with it drifted from history to legend. The steel was said to be unbreakable, flexible yet also hard enough to retain a razor edge. It didn't rust and there were few things hard enough to chip the blade. The combined qualities created a peerless sword that would last for generations. Once it was forged however, it could never be re-forged, and the steel was notoriously difficult to work. Only the most skilled smiths would even attempt it.

While the city was magnificent, the Palace was truly awe-inspiring and ever more so the closer one got. It was constructed of white stone and its roof was a mix of blue-grey slate turrets and verdigris domes. It was beautiful, imposing and a firm statement of power and wealth.

'They certainly have a flair for the dramatic, these northerners,' said Amero disdainfully. 'And architecture,' he added, grudgingly. They trotted out onto the causeway leading to the Palace after again showing their letters of safe passage to the guards stationed at its shore end.

As they drew closer Soren could see that the walls were decorated with alcoves between the columns that contained bronze statues, looking grand and ancient, weathered as they were to a faded blue-green colour. Added to what was already an impressive building was the fact that there were lights on behind many of the windows. Their warm glow was also reflected in the water. In the centre of the front of the building was a great arch supported by massive ornate pillars. Recessed into this was a double door that entirely filled the space created by the arch.

A guard hidden in the shadow of the arch issued a challenge. He stepped forward out of the gloom to take the letters of safe passage from Emeric. He nodded to a second guard, who like the first was dressed in a livery of dark grey.

'Dismount and come with me please,' he said, in heavily accented Imperial. Language was conveniently the one remaining common feature in all of the states of the former Empire, although differences in accent and slang could on occasion make comprehension a little more difficult.

He banged three times on the door. A small hatch opened and then closed, and the door was opened. The arch continued underneath the building, opening onto a courtyard at its centre, flanked on all sides by the Palace itself. Their horses were taken by a stable boy and led away.

They waited there for a few minutes, Soren taking the opportunity to absorb his surroundings. The courtyard was paved with slabs slightly darker than the walls of the building. In the centre there was a magnificent marble fountain surrounded by neatly trimmed ornamental bushes and small, carefully shaped trees. Opposite the archway through which they had entered was the main door into the Palace itself, a grand affair at the top of several steps set amidst a mass of stone carvings of battle scenes. The walls were lined with windows and smaller doorways, and it was to one of these smaller doors that they were led.

A grey haired man in very fine clothes exited a door on the opposite side of the courtyard and walked briskly toward them.

'The city gate sent word of your arrival, but it came as something of a surprise as we weren't expecting you for another couple of days! I hope you had a safe journey,' said the man.

'We took a shortcut through the ruins of Rurip, not altogether the safest choice, but it saved us some time,' replied Amero.

'No, that road is very dangerous. Clearing the ruins of looters is high on the Prince's agenda, but with so many stories about the place it is difficult to generate any enthusiasm for the job, but that is neither here nor there. I am Varo, the Royal Steward. Allow me to formally welcome you to the court of Prince Siegar the Fourth. I shall take you to your apartments and the Prince will receive you in the morning.'

The step from a street corner to his small attic room in the Academy had been monumental. The step from there to the room he was presented with in the Palace was equally big. The accommodation assigned to him in the Palace was opulent, and, he noted with some slight embarrassment, far better than that assigned to Emeric, who had been given one of the several servant's rooms attached to Amero's apartment. He was a pupil at the Academy though, and it was one of the first occasions that he began to realise what this really meant.

There was a bedroom, a water closet with both hot and cold running water on tap, which was something he had never seen before, a lounge and a dressing room. There was also a small servant's room attached, although this would remain vacant. The whole apartment shouted a luxury that was entirely alien to Soren. He had thought his room in River House to be the height of luxury. Compared to this it was little better appointed than a stable.

The household had dined already that night, so a meal was served for the three in Amero's apartments. The food was not in the same quantity as Soren had experienced at the Academy, but the quality was far higher, something he had not believed possible. As he tucked into his second helping of a sweet, fluffy meringue, he decided that should he ever be wealthy enough, he would very much like a personal chef who could make them. He chuckled to himself at the thought. It certainly was a far cry from stolen, stale bread.

'As the diplomatic gifts aren't here yet, I expect the formalities will be dispensed with and we will cut straight to business. The Duke desires that the peace treaty between Ostia and Ruripathia be extended. He seems to think that the people do not have the stomach for another war so soon after the last one, but I wonder if perhaps it is he that does not have the stomach for such matters,' said Amero. He watched Soren closely as he made his comment about the Duke, but when Soren did not react in any way, he continued. 'Soren, you will join me for most of the meetings, it will be good for you to learn some diplomacy by seeing it rather than reading about it in a book. Some of the sessions will be closed however. I will let you know when you need to leave.'

The following morning Soren unpacked and dressed in the one set of clothes he had brought on the ride ahead. They were ones that he had not seen before, having been bought by Amero's servants in preparation for the trip north. There was an entire trunk of other clothes and accessories following on with the carriages that he had also not seen. It was all fine and fancy so as not to let down the great city-state of Ostia.

They weren't all that bad though, a navy colour with white trimmings, it seemed to go well enough with the blue Academy doublet he wore over it. On top went the wide brimmed hat. The whole ensemble made him look like one of the dandies he saw walking around Highgarden and made him feel like a peacock, but he did have to admit that he now looked the part, and didn't imagine he would attract many suspicious glances in the better parts of Brixen. At least the hat didn't have a plume, as seemed to be becoming more fashionable, but something he could not abide.

After they had enjoyed a delicious breakfast in Amero's apartment, a chamberlain came to collect them. He led them to the lowest floor of the Palace and down a series of plushly carpeted halls,

lined with busts and paintings. This hall brought them around the
inside of the building to a larger hallway that the main entrance
he had seen the night before led in to. At the end of this hallway open double doors with the royal arms of Ruripathia above
them led into what Soren assumed was the main hall of the Palace.
There were people hanging around in that hallway, many looking
nervous, pacing up and down or wringing their hands, clearly waiting for an audience with the Prince. There were also a number of
aristocratic looking types in martial clothing with heavy looking
steel coloured fur cloaks over their shoulders. Soren's party were
brought straight through and he caught several annoyed glances
being cast in their direction.

The next set of doors led to a small antechamber, which
accommodated two guards in impressive dress uniforms and
shining silver breastplates. The doors out of this room led finally
to the main hall of the Palace. The room was in keeping with the
rest of the building. The floors, the great ornate columns that
stretched up to the high ceiling and the statues that filled alcoves
along the room's sides were of white marble with a grey swirl
running through it. Furnishings of dark wood were decorated
with silver, and silver was inlaid in all the statues and decoration
on the marble. Swaths of fur lined with red cloth decorated the
room, the red warming the otherwise cold appearance, as did
two massive fireplaces on either side of the hall, which crackled
and spit as the massive logs within them were devoured by the
flames.

'Banneret of the Blue, Count Elector of Ostia, Amero, Lord of
the County of Moreno and his party,' announced the Chamberlain.

A few of the other people in the room turned to look at the visi-
tors from the south, the guards remained impassive as ever, and
the Prince, sitting in a chair on a raised platform at the other end
of the hall whispered with the steward, Varo for a moment before
Varo beckoned them to come forward.

'Your Serene Highness, it is an honour to present myself at
your court. I bring the warm greetings and regards of the Duke of
Ostia,' said Amero, bowing formally.

Soren copied Amero's bow and stepped back, watching the
formalities unfold. Emeric shifted uneasily beside him, uncomfortable in these surroundings. Soren, despite himself, found that
he was quite enjoying the new experience.

'I receive your mission from Ostia gracefully and in the spirit
of friendship. I hope our discussions may prove fruitful,' said the
Prince.

'The great state of Ostia also sends gifts, Highness, but sadly
they and our baggage have not yet arrived,' replied Amero.

'Yes, my chancellor tells me that you took the road through
Rurip to make better time. A courageous choice,' the Prince said
evenly.

The exchange was so formal it felt as though it was scripted,
and it continued for several minutes. There was a girl sitting in
front and to the right of the Prince. From the neat tiara she wore
he assumed she was Princess Alys, the widower Prince's only child,
his only legitimate child at any rate. She was not especially pretty,
handsome might be a more appropriate word, but attractive nonetheless and about the same age as Soren.

What was most striking about her was the combination of honey
coloured hair, fair skin and impossibly blue eyes. Women in Ostenheim tended to be dark of hair and complexion and although he
had seen some whores who dyed theirs, he had never seen a girl
with hair quite like hers. She had a disdainful, haughty look on her
face, but when she caught Soren's gaze, her expression became
unreadable. It was stern, but betrayed no information about what
she was thinking, despite the fact that she was clearly appraising
him. It reminded him that he was representing his Duchy now and
not just himself. He tried to adopt an equally unreadable expression. The last thing that he wanted to do was to reveal the fact
that he was a diplomatic novice and of how impressed with the
whole experience that he was. Disdainful boredom seemed to be
the appropriate demeanour.

The remainder of the morning was spent discussing a variety of
unimportant things, unimportant at least to Soren. Trade quotas
and tariffs were the main topic, with concessions for merchants
and similar economic topics featuring in the discussion. There was

nothing to do with a peace treaty, but perhaps Amero was setting the stage and tone for those negotiations. In the afternoon the session was closed. Emeric went back to his small room to read, leaving Soren at his own devices for the remainder of the day.

He sat by the fountain in the inner courtyard for a little while, wondering whether or not to venture into the city to explore. He was struck by how peaceful the little courtyard was, the babbling of the water in the fountain, and the way the surrounding Palace shut out all the noises of the world around it. The bench he sat on was in a little alcove of miniature trees with its back to the fountain. He was lost in his thoughts when he heard a voice.

'You are in my seat!'

He looked around to see the Princess standing in front of him.

'Your Highness, I apologise, I had no idea!' he stuttered, as he stood up.

'Don't panic, I'm only joking!' she said. 'You haven't brought the negotiations to a calamitous end.' She smiled in a tired, forced way and sat. 'Now sit, I never get to talk to people my own age.'

Soren sat and she continued.

'Your rooms? Are they to your satisfaction?' she asked.

'Yes, your Highness, they are quite simply magnificent. My room at the Academy is smaller than the dressing room!' he said.

She smiled and looked down at her feet.

'The steward said that you are a tyro. Have you visited our Academy yet, or the Bannerets' Hall?'

'No, your Highness, we only arrived in the city last night,' Soren replied carefully.

'Oh, they didn't tell me when you arrived. It's quite an important mission, you are lucky to have been taken along at such a young age!'

'Yes, the Count of Moreno is my patron at the Academy. He wanted to bring me along for the experience.'

'Ah, a patron. It is not a common practice at our Academy, but it happens occasionally. Some of the best swordsmen in the city were of common birth, though. Are you any good?' she asked, then added quickly, 'oh but of course you are going to say you are!'

'I am thought to be competent, your Highness,' Soren replied as diplomatically as possible.

'That's nice,' she said, her lips curled slightly hinting at sarcasm. 'Competent.' Her voice drifted with facetious contemplation for a moment as she made a poor attempt at suppressing a smile. 'It gets very warm in Ostenheim I understand. Does it ever snow there?'

'No, your Highness, it doesn't. It gets cold and wet in the winter, but I've never even seen snow!' said Soren.

'There is no need to say "your highness" every time you speak. I'm not likely to forget the fact any time soon! Never seen snow though? You should come to the Summer Palace in the mountains. At this time of the year there will still be lots of it! It only thawed here a couple of weeks ago. It's a shame you missed it.'

'Yes, I'd like to have seen some,' said Soren.

'So what do young people in Ostenheim do for fun?' she asked.

'Well, some of the students go to taverns, but mainly we just practice. Being at the Academy is too great an opportunity to squander,' he said. He realised that he had betrayed his humble origins, if she had not already worked it out for herself. 'I can't really speak for anyone not in the Academy,' he added, 'but I imagine it's balls and parties for the wealthy, and work for those not so.'

'Much like here then really!' she said, with a little disappointment. 'Occasionally I go sailing on the lake, but I don't get to do that often. I practice with a sword from time to time also. It's fun, but I'll never get to be particularly good. It isn't really seemly for a princess to spend all of her time at sword practice. Father says that when I am in charge I'll need to have some idea how to defend myself just in case!'

'It certainly couldn't hurt,' Soren said.

'Hmmm.' She laughed as she stood up. 'You'll have to sit next to me at the banquet tonight. I can't stand having to listen to some decrepit old lord who wants to marry me. You can tell me all about your journey and about Ostia.'

Soren only now noticed the two ladies who were standing by the door beckoning for Alys to go with them.

Chapter 21

DIPLOMACY IS DEAD

Soren was not surprised to find a card bearing his name at the place beside Alys at the top table that night. Amero sat with the Prince and his council of state while other nobles made up the numbers at that table, many of them middle aged, single and hoping to find the favour of their future ruler. Unlike Ostia, Ruripathia had become a hereditary principality after the fall of the Empire due to the popularity of the first Prince, who, then still only a baron, led the state back to power from the wreck left behind after the Mage Wars. The current Prince was the last in an unbroken line of fathers and sons that led back to the first. Alys's mother had died in childbirth, and the Prince had never remarried. This meant that for the first time in its history, Ruripathia would be ruled by a princess, and by the man lucky enough to wed her.

Soren was entirely unprepared for what exactly a royal banquet entailed. Ten courses were to be served in total, all washed down with expensive wines that were imported from all around the Middle Sea. On Alys's other side sat one of the younger residents at that part of the table. He was raven haired, but of the same light complexion that was prevalent among Ruripathians. He wore a black fitted coat, similar to the ones worn by the officers on board the ship that had brought them north.

'Tyro Soren, this is Captain Varrisher,' said Alys.

Varrisher looked at him appraisingly and nodded, not offering a hand. 'A pleasure to make your acquaintance, Tyro,' he said, his voice sharp and confident.

'Likewise,' replied Soren.

'Captain Varrisher has the accolade of having captained the first and last ships to run the ice for the last two years in a row. It marks him out as our premier captain! Great things will follow for him no doubt,' Alys said to Soren quietly.

'Run the ice?' Soren asked.

'Mmm yes,' she said, taking a sip of wine. 'The sea is frozen by the Niepar as far south as the border during the winter. Every year when the wind turns and the thaw begins, it is a race to see which captain will brave the melting ice flows first. The same happens at the end of the Nistra season, as the sea starts to freeze again, merchants take chances by sending out their ships as late as possible to bring out the last cargo of the year. They are the two shipments that will fetch the highest price, but many ships are lost each year trying. It's still worth the risk for them to try though.

'Captain Varrisher is the most successful at it, ever, as far as I know. They use smaller faster ships for the run than the normal Oceanmen, with crews of only twenty or thirty, but these cargos often fetch as much in foreign markets as a full sized shipment. Also, it has become something of a sport for the captains. Some of them become as famous as our best swordsmen. Captain Varrisher is one such captain.'

Soren nodded, not sure what he could say. Varrisher was clearly very good at what he did and from the disdainful way he carried himself it was clear that he knew it.

'I spent a year at the Academy in Brixen, you know,' said Varrisher, out of the blue half way through the dinner. Up until that point the conversations were split on either side of the Princess, she giving her attention to each of them as best she could. This time Varrisher spoke directly to Soren. 'I was able to take a year there during my studies at the Naval College. What with all the pirates around these days I thought it a prudent move. The instructors said I had a talent for it and that it was a shame that I had been sent to the Naval College. Still, I love the sea, so I am happy with the way things turned out. I still like to spar though. Perhaps we could have a few bouts before you leave; there is an excellent fencing hall here in the Palace.'

'Perhaps. Yes. I'd like that,' said Soren, remembering what Amero had said about displays of strength. He had no doubt that he could not only thrash Varrisher, but also show him up for the pompous popinjay that he was. For some reason he was feeling a growing rivalry with the man, but was not really sure why. 'When will you make your first run this year?' asked Soren.

'Ah!' He laughed. 'That is a secret between me and my crew. Not even my backers get that information, but you may rest assured I will be leaving as soon as the waters are navigable!'

His bravado was greeted by encouraging shouts from several of the other men at the table, many of whom wore military uniforms of dark grey with scarlet and white sashes.

Soren had taken an instant dislike to Varrisher, and he felt from the way the man spoke to him that the feelings were entirely mutual. At first he was not sure what the issue between them was, but then it occurred to him that every time Alys spent any length of time talking to Soren, Varrisher would interrupt with some interesting fact about a foreign culture, a foreign city or some other interesting and exotic fact. One thing that Soren had quickly realised about Alys was her hunger for information about foreign places and the world outside of the Palace in general.

As the meal progressed however, Alys spent more and more time talking to Soren, asking him about the city, the weather, and every other aspect of life in the south. The conversation flowed easily. Alys was open, witty and insatiably curious. He wasn't sure if it was to spite Varrisher or her engaging personality, but as time wore on he began to see an attractiveness in her that he had not initially.

Alys excused herself when the meal had finished, as did all the other women. The atmosphere grew rowdier and more drunken, but Soren did not find himself talking with Varrisher again.

By the time Soren's head hit the pillow in the early hours of the morning, the room was spinning around him.

Amero sat on a plush armchair on the balcony of his apartment looking out over the Brixensea, nursing a glass of tonic salts. Emeric came out and stood with him, taking in a deep lungful of the crisp air.

'Never tasted air so fresh; it feels like a glass of icy water,' said Emeric.

'Yes, it is quite refreshing, particularly after a night like last night, and I paced myself at one glass for every two our hosts had!' said Amero.

'Never had much of a thirst when in unfriendly lands,' replied Emeric.

'Well, the potential problem we discussed seems to have arisen,' said Amero, bringing matters back to business.

'Who?' said Emeric.

'The Chancellor; the portly old fellow with the red face. Marin is his name. He won't go for it at all. The others seem keen, but the Prince listens to Marin, over all the others. As long as he has the Prince's ear, there will be no deal,' said Amero.

'So, as we discussed then?' Emeric said solemnly.

'Yes, Ruripathia is the key to the plan, so I am not leaving here without an agreement. All of the others are biddable enough. Sweetening the deal a little will keep them all on board, but it is clear that Marin won't budge no matter what. It can't come back to us though, that would be the worst possible scenario. We'll need to find a way to do it that won't bring any suspicion to our door. I'd like to get home with my head still attached to my body,' said Amero.

'Understood. There won't be any problems,' replied Emeric.

'Have Soren kill the old bastard,' Amero said after a moment's consideration. 'I want to make certain he has the stomach for this type of work before I spend any more money on him.'

'Are you sure that's wise?' asked Emeric.

'Yes. He looked tasty enough in the ruins, and I don't believe for a second that was the first time he's killed someone. He's probably been knocking off rival gutter rats since he was weaned off the tit. It's the life he's accepted for himself and I want him to be made aware of it sooner rather than later. He doesn't need to know the real reason why,' said Amero. He returned to sipping his mineral salts and Emeric left, knowing his master well enough to be aware of when a conversation was over.

———◆◆◆———

Soren's head was throbbing that morning also, so he was glad that the negotiations were being held in closed session. He tried to sleep fitfully until just before lunchtime, when there was a knock on the door.

He got out of bed, wrapped himself in a gown and went to the door. Emeric walked straight in.

'There is something we need to talk about, lad,' he said.

This piqued Soren's interest, momentarily making him forget that his head felt like it was about to split open at any moment.

'Amero has a job for us. For you mainly,' he said.

Soren nodded. He had expected something like this sooner or later.

'The negotiations have hit a stumbling block. One of the Prince's more elderly advisors, Chancellor Marin, is a firebrand. He wants Baelin back as part of Ruripathia, and won't agree to any deal that gives them anything less. The Prince places a lot of faith on what he says. As long as he is around, the Count feels that a peace treaty is impossible,' said Emeric.

'He wants me to kill him?' Soren asked uncertainly.

'Not kill, assassinate. This is a political assassination and a necessary one at that. No less necessary a killing than the man you skewered in the ruins,' replied Emeric. 'This man is agitating for a war. Thousands would die. This is what you took upon yourself when you agreed to go to the Academy. You didn't think it would be all fancy uniforms and swooning ladies and banquets now did you? This is how men of our type earn our keep. This isn't some penny paid back alley killing, although more than one swordsman has ended up in that line. That's the bottom of the barrel for men like us, and I assure you that you are destined for greater things if you play your cards right. This is statesmanship. Our actions can help secure the future of Ostia. Us. Two nobodies from nowhere who've got somewhere. That is responsibility indeed, and as noble a purpose as you could look for. We won't be doing it for a night or two yet, so prepare yourself for it.'

Soren spent the rest of the day lazing around in his room thinking of the task ahead. He had killed before and it had not bothered him. That was in his own defence. Now he was being asked to kill on behalf of the city. It was the duty of a swordsman to kill, or indeed be killed for the defence of the city. Whether that was on the open battlefield or hidden by intrigue made little difference. Whatever the method or reason, it was better than living from moment to moment on the street. If that was what was required for him to be a swordsman, that was what he would do.

There was another knock at the door that pulled him from his thoughts.

'Like most of the other men, you seem to have kept to your bed chamber for an uncommonly long time today!' said Alys.

She had two of her ladies in waiting standing awkwardly behind her as she stood staring at Soren's bedraggled appearance.

'May we come in?' she inquired.

Soren stepped back and gestured for them to enter. She sat at one of the chairs by the small table at the window, while her ladies in waiting sat on a chaise longue near the door.

'My father has said that he will take a break in the negotiations for a few days to think on what has been said. By a few days he means a week or so, and I thought it might be the ideal opportunity to show you some snow!' she said.

Soren was taken aback. 'Where?' he asked.

'The Summer Palace. It's in the foothills of the mountains to the northeast, a little more than a day's journey away. The belek hunting season will have just started by then. It will be fantastic fun,' she said enthusiastically.

'I'll have to ask the Count of Moreno. I'm not sure what he will intend for me,' Soren replied.

'It's all been arranged; he is staying here but has said you may come. We will leave the day after tomorrow and spend four days there. A belek hunt is a right of passage for young Ruripathian noblemen. You may have noticed most of the nobles wearing grey fur cloaks?' she asked.

Soren had. They were the shimmering blued-steel and silver coloured cloaks of incredibly rich looking fur that were worn by many, but not all of the noblemen at the court.

'I have, they look very nice,' he said. 'Very warm!'

'Those cloaks are worn by noblemen who killed a belek before they turned twenty one years old. They are the only ones that are allowed. If you are lucky you might have one by the time you return south!' she said.

'Forgive my ignorance, my Lady, but what is a belek?'

'Do you not have them in Ostia?' she asked, somewhat puzzled.

'We might, but I have never seen, or heard of one before,' Soren said.

'Oh, well, they look a little like a cat I suppose, but are as big as a bear, sometimes bigger! I assume you have cats and bears in Ostia?'

'Yes, we do,' said Soren in amusement.

'Good, well, belek are incredibly intelligent and cunning, and very, very dangerous. Many young noblemen are killed or maimed hunting them every year,' she said.

It did not seem like a particularly attractive pursuit to Soren, but he would never claim to fully understand the ways of bored aristocrats.

'Anyway, I have much to prepare, so remember, the day after tomorrow. We leave early, so be ready!' she said.

It was clear that she would not accept any refusal to go on his part, so he acquiesced to her command. In any event, it would not be the done thing to refuse such an invitation from royalty. With that she and her two ladies breezed out of his room.

Amero was not altogether pleased at the prospect of the planned hunting trip, but he acknowledged that there was little that could be done about it. It would not look good for Soren to refuse the invitation when it was clear the young Princess considered his going a foregone conclusion, and had begun preparations.

It forced them to push their plan for Chancellor Marin forward. Thankfully, however, it appeared that Emeric was not one to wait for necessity to dictate his actions. Ever since they had arrived, he had been sneaking out of their room for an hour or two each night and exploring the Palace. For obvious reasons it was too risky for him to draw up maps, but he had made detailed observations and could recollect them accurately.

He knew the locations of all of the rooms belonging to the senior members of the Prince's council, which rooms were unused, and most importantly, the numbers and routes of the nocturnal guard patrols through the Palace. Soren had to admit that he was impressed by the thoroughness of Emeric's intelligence gathering and the unadorned practicality with which he approached the matter was far more enlightening than a year's instruction on the subject at the Academy.

Chancellor Marin was old and portly. He had been seen to have a vigorous appetite and a fondness for wine and ale at the formal dinners and as such was a prime candidate for a heart attack.

Killing a man of Marin's position was delicate. He exerted considerable influence over the Prince and was apparently alone among the Prince's ministers in opposing Amero's treaty. If the assassination were to go wrong, the consequences would be catastrophic. All three of them would be executed and in all likelihood the two countries would go to war. However he died, it must appear to have either been accidental beyond suspicion, or of natural causes. His dying at such an inopportune time would certainly give rise to questions, so there was no room for any error that could lead to further suspicions.

Amero decided that staging a heart attack was really the only option available to them considering the time frame. Murder by a jealous whore or mistress was always a convenient way to get an aristocrat out of the way Amero had said, but sadly there simply wasn't the time to set it up. Soren and Emeric would have to sneak into Chancellor Marin's apartments and administer a suitable poison that would precipitate a heart attack. They would then have to return to their own apartments undetected. It seemed a simple enough concept, but Soren knew there were many things that could go wrong.

A staged mugging on a night time street would have been far more to Soren's taste. He disliked using poison and had limited experience of it. It was considered a less than honourable way to kill, and certainly not one to be utilised by a banneret, so his lessons at the Academy had only given it the most cursory of appreciations. He knew what the major poisons were, and what they did, but the Academy had instilled in him a sense that a blade was the only acceptable way to dispatch someone in a clandestine fashion. Nonetheless, needs dictated otherwise.

The poison that was most suited to their purpose was simple and called the Queen of Poisons. It had many advantages as an assassin's poison. It was undetectable, was absorbed through the skin, and caused heart attacks. It was perfect for their purpose, and with great forethought, Emeric had included it in the secret case of poisons hidden in his trunk.

The greatest advantage it offered was that it did not have to be directly administered. They could apply it to his bed sheets or nightclothes at any time, and allow the poison to do its work while they were elsewhere, preferably in plain view of others. As if this was not enough, once exposed to the air, the poison began to break down. By morning, when the Chancellor's body was discovered, the poison would have degraded to a non-lethal form, and the servants handling the sheets and body would be unaffected.

This was the plan that was decided upon. Soren and Emeric would enter the Chancellor's apartments and liberally coat his nightshirt with poison. Before morning, he should have absorbed enough of it to cause heart failure. If everything went to plan, it would appear that an old, overweight man had died in his sleep.

Carrying out the assassination proved easy enough. For whatever reason, during the day there were very few patrols through the inside of the Palace; virtually all the guards were on the exterior. The Chancellor's apartments were empty and likewise unguarded. Emeric and Soren sneaked into the apartment. Soren carefully applied the poison on the nightshirt that had been left folded on the Chancellor's bed as Emeric had instructed, using a brush and thick leather gloves so as to ensure none of the lethal liquid came in contact with his skin.

In only a few minutes, they were done. Soren felt a giddy excitement but forced it down. They would have to wait until the following morning to discover if they were successful, but the danger of being discovered had passed. The sense of purpose and power that Soren felt afterward was almost overwhelming. That he, a former street urchin, could dictate the future of two countries with his actions was intoxicating. He wished he had been able to do it with his sword though, rather than in the less than honourable fashion with poison.

———◆◈◆———

News of the death of Chancellor Marin spread quickly about the Palace the following morning and was greeted with great sadness. While the hunting trip was to go ahead, the Prince and the senior members of the court would be remaining behind. Amero had congratulated Soren on a job well done at breakfast that morning, but he had not seen him since. There was great excitement surrounding the departure of the hunting party, coupled with mourning in some sections of the court. It appeared that Marin had been very popular with some, and resented by others. Either way, Soren had done his duty and successfully completed his mission. He was comfortable in the thought that the threat Chancellor Marin had represented to Ostia was now gone.

He awoke with a start in the carriage on the morning of their second day travelling north. As a foreign dignitary he had been given a carriage to himself, which he was grateful for as it allowed him to stretch out and sleep for most of the journey. He opened the shutter and window on the door to peer out, and was amazed to see the entire landscape covered in a blanket of white. His breath formed a cloud as it floated out of the window, while the fresh air coming in was freezing cold and dry. He coughed slightly at first until his lungs grew accustomed to the crisp bite, but his attention was completely monopolized by the fairy-tale landscape.

The wheels of the carriage made a 'shushing' sound as they ploughed through the churned up snow that had been left behind by the carriages and horses in front. Despite the cold, Soren could not stop himself from leaving the window open and revelling in the way the chilly air felt against his skin and in his lungs. He took in all the majesty of the snow covered scenery, as thick forest broke to allow craggy snow covered peaks burst through and reach up so high Soren had to stick his head out of the window and look almost directly up to see the sky.

After an hour or so more, the carriages bumped to a halt and Soren jumped out. His boots hit the snow and crunched and squeaked their way down until the snow had compressed to a solid base beneath them. He reached down and took a handful of the light powdery substance and was surprised to see how dry it was initially, until the warmth of his hand began to melt it.

'Well, what do you think?' Alys had gotten out of her carriage in front and her ladies were fussing over cloaks and fur wraps behind her.

'It's fantastic!' Soren shouted back, a smile splitting his face from ear to ear. He looked back at the handful of snow, which was now no more than a puddle of slush dripping between his fingers. He could not help but feel a childish excitement and curiosity at the alien environment.

He jumped as he was hit in the face with a slapping thud of snow. He cleared it from his face in bewilderment. The cold burned his skin in a strange but not entirely unpleasant way. As his vision cleared, he saw Alys standing a few yards away, laughing furiously, her hands red from the cold of the snow she had just been holding.

'I'm glad you like it!' she shouted back between laughs.

Soren continued to scoop snow from his ears, mouth and nose, noticing that the blanket of snow seemed to dull all ambient sound, giving the moment an incredible sense of peace and serenity. It was like nothing he had ever experienced, and he loved it.

Chapter 22

THE HUNT

The Summer Palace was true to Ruripathian fashion and was a magnificent building. It seemed to be an attempt to blend opulence with a rustic charm that gave it a different, more relaxed character to the buildings in the city, but that was not to say it was any less impressive. It blended into its forested and mountainous surroundings perfectly. It was hard to picture what it would look like in the summer though, with the snow blotting out most of the features around it.

The interior was warm and welcoming with great crackling fireplaces ensuring that the temperature inside was high enough so as to require one to quickly remove the heavy outer-garments they had been wearing in the cold outside.

They spent the rest of the day relaxing in there, drinking heavily sweetened tea that was laced with a fruit liquor that Soren could not identify and had at first found sickly, but gradually became accustomed to. He sat with Alys and her ladies and several gentlemen who had made the journey with them. Cards and dice seemed to be the pastime of choice. Others had been arriving over the course of the day, all heading there as soon as they had gotten word of a royal hunting party. Favour with the ruling elite was unsurprisingly a prized commodity, and impressing at a hunt was a sure way of gaining it. Banneret of the Grey, Captain Jarod, the Royal Hunt Master, was a prime example of this.

Soren had been introduced to him shortly after arriving. Alys had told him that he was the son of a minor and impoverished lord and had been taken along by his father's lord to a hunt as a favour. He had displayed great bravery when faced by a wounded and very angry belek, and had won himself a belek cloak, and a post as Master of the Royal Hunt for the remainder of his life. A barony would likely be the reward for his years of loyal service when the time came for him to retire.

He looked far older than his years, with a stern and serious countenance always present on a face that looked as though it had been hewn from the mountains of his birthplace. He was something of an enigma in the court, and set the hearts of many of the ladies fluttering with his commanding and dignified bearing. Many of the stories Soren heard about him came from their gossiping, and Soren had no doubt that they had been heavily embellished. Nonetheless, if they contained even a grain of truth, some of them were very impressive indeed.

His body, it was said, was criss-crossed with the scars left by belek teeth and claws. He was the saviour of many aristocrats, delivering a killing blow with deadly precision an instant before the belek was about to perform a similar deed on a Ruripathian nobleman. It seemed he had made himself into something of a legend in hunting circles, always dependable, stoical and distant. It didn't particularly impress Soren, but the ladies of court relished it.

Hunting clothes had been made for him, rushed along by royal decree, and they fit perfectly. Despite being thick and bulky they were well designed and did not restrict movement at all. However, in the heated interior of the palace, they were overly warm, and Soren found himself in a sweat by the time he stepped out into the not so fresh air of the stable courtyard.

He had difficulty recognising who was who as many were already wearing the hat that was part of the early season hunting uniform. It was fur lined with a perforated flap that fastened around the face, covering the mouth, but more importantly the nose. Jarod had given Soren a briefing the previous night, and had told him that at this time of the year it was important to keep it fastened to safe guard against the dangers of something called frost bite. Apparently one's nose could turn black and drop off from it, although the thought made Soren smile and he found it hard to believe. Perhaps the steely Jarod was capable of humour after all. Jarod was easily spotted though, from the crimson embroidery on the sleeves of his coat denoting him as the master of the hunt. Nevertheless, upon seeing so many others wearing it fastened, he resolved to do the same as soon as they got going.

'Your horse, and your spear. Can you use them?' asked Jarod.

The spear was a wicked thing, longer than he was tall with a stout wooden shaft. The tip was razor sharp, barbed and with a cross guard a few inches back from the tip. It was designed to do the maximum damage with one thrust and then to be easy to withdraw. With a belek it was rare that one would get the chance at a second strike though. Jarod mentioned that the cross guard also helped to prevent the beast from driving the spear through its body in order to get at its attacker. They sounded like truly fearsome prey.

'Yes, I've training with both. I'll be fine,' said Soren. He was glad that riding was a part of the training at the Academy, in addition to the hours of weapons drills. Despite the sword being the weapon of choice, all weapons were taught. One never knew what would be available to them on the battlefield.

He had been introduced to many of the other hunters the day before, but they all kept their distance. Some were like him, on their first hunt and were clearly quiet due to nerves, while others had casually breezed into the palace the day before wearing their belek cloaks with a confident and haughty air about them. The Princess was sulking in her chambers, after having been strictly forbidden from coming on the hunt by Jarod, on the instructions of her father. The Prince had one state funeral to attend to and had no interest in encouraging a second, he had said.

They trotted out of the stable courtyard in single file, twenty of them in total. There were twelve members of the Ruripathian nobility, himself and Jarod, and six huntsmen. The clip clop of the horses hooves was quickly replaced by a quieter crunching sound as they left the cobbles and reached the snow covered ground, although the peacefulness of the scene was broken intermittently when one of the hunters blew a note on their small, brass hunting horns.

They rode heavy Ruripathian horses, the type used by the old Imperial heavy cavalry that had won such fame in all corners of the world. They were giants by comparison to the swift and trim horses found in the south. He had been told that despite their size, they were deceptively quick, and that when properly trained, even without a rider they were fierce fighting machines that craved battle. Legend had it that in the early days, before the Empire, if a Ruripathian cavalryman's horse was killed in battle he would later commit suicide, such was the bond of friendship and trust between man and beast, which would have been gifted to him when he became an adult. It was harsh, but the horses really were magnificent creatures.

They rode for several hours, mostly in silence, along trails that ran through the forest and rocky outcrops. The scenery was magnificent, but so far there had been no sign of belek, and Soren was beginning to bore. Even with the heavy hunting clothes he could feel the cold start to penetrate. He was even beginning to struggle to stay awake in the saddle.

Eventually, after what had seemed like hours of drudgery in the freezing cold, there was some commotion up at the front of their column. He trotted forward to see what was going on. Jarod was on the ground, bent down inspecting a massive clawed paw print.

'It's crisply outlined. Still fresh. It isn't far ahead of us,' he said

'Why don't you use dogs to sniff them out?' Soren asked, knowing that dogs were used to hunt regularly in Ostia.

Jarod gave out a short, stifled laugh. 'We could send dogs after one I suppose, but we wouldn't see them again. I think you need to see a belek to understand what I mean. Now, we need to move quickly to catch up with it.'

The huntsmen broke into teams of two and trotted on ahead, moving away from the group in a fan shape, making as much noise as they could. At first Soren thought they were trying to scare the belek out of the undergrowth, but Jarod whispered to him that the belek was such an aggressive creature, it would attack the huntsmen, and that would be their opportunity to ambush it. It occurred to Soren that the job of a huntsman was not a particularly attractive one if the belek was as dangerous as Jarod was making out. It seemed that they were hunting a creature that was also hunting them.

They waited in the small clearing where the print had been found, until a howling roar that sent a shiver of panic through Soren's gut echoed between the trees. It made the howls from the ruins of Rurip seem like the mewling of kittens. It was swiftly followed by the metallic blast of a hunting horn. Jarod blew a long note from his in response and they were off, the massive horses thundering between the trees of the forest. While Soren was a competent rider, he had not the years of experience that the others had, and fell to the rear of the pack along with another rider, who was on a slightly smaller, and what Soren assumed was younger, horse.

There was another roar, closer now and then the scream of a horse beside him. The other horse, distracted by the roar, had put a foot wrong and stumbled, throwing its rider. Soren cast a glance over his shoulder, and spotted the prone form. The riders in front of him were so intent on their prey that they did not notice the fallen rider, and Soren's calls to them were lost beneath the pounding hooves of the heavy horses. Soren reined back hard, amazed by his horse's reluctance to stop. It wanted to go on; it wanted a fight.

After several paces it slowed back to a trot, shaking its head with irritation. Soren wheeled about and the horse snorted loudly with indignation. He walked the horse back to where the fallen rider was and slipped down out of his saddle, holding the horse by the reins. He had no doubt that if given half the chance it would charge after its friends in search of the belek. He knelt by the prone form, which let out a decidedly feminine groan. He pulled back the face warmer from her hat. It was Alys.

'What in three hells are you doing here?'

'Hunting belek, what did you think?' she replied.

'You shouldn't have come. I can only imagine how much trouble this will make for Jarod when your father finds out,' said Soren.

'How can I expect to win the loyalty of my nobles when I am Princess Regent if I have not hunted. I have to be able to show I can match them!' she said.

Soren shook his head. 'Come, let's get your horse back, and you on it.'

There was a particularly loud snort from his horse, and it jerked sharply, pulling the reins from his hand. Then there was a low, earthy, rumbling growl.

The belek was an incredible creature. It was like a cross between the bears and wolves and great cats he had seen in the menagerie in Ostenheim, large, sleek and powerful. Its coat shimmered in the pale winter sunlight like gleaming metal armour. It circled slowly around them, its large blue eyes flicking from Soren to Alys and back again, a raw, feral intelligence emanating from them. Its pointed ears flickered at any sound, as its large paws gently crunched on the snow. It had two wicked fangs, curving down out of its mouth from its top jaw, sharp and deadly looking.

Soren's horse stamped one of its hoofs against the ground and snorted aggressively. Alys's had bolted and was nowhere to be seen.

The belek let out another long, low growl and Soren's horse charged, no longer able to contain its boiling aggression. The belek screeched like a cat, pouncing out of the way of the horse's hooves as it attempted to stamp the evil looking creature to death. The horse was larger and stronger, but did not have the agility of the belek. It struggled to turn quickly enough as the belek dashed around behind it. It kicked out with its hind legs and the belek once again enjoyed a narrow escape. Soren and Alys looked on, stunned.

His spear was still attached to the saddle on the horse and there was no chance of retrieving it, so he drew his sword. The horse knocked the belek to one side with a ferocious kick that would have crushed a man, sending it rolling across the snow. It quickly found its feet and pounced back before the horse had a chance to react. The belek lashed out at the horse's leg with one paw, its large claws slashed through the muscle and tendon in the back of the horse's leg. The horse's leg gave way instantly and the horse fell to the ground, roaring in pain. He thrashed on the ground in agony, but the belek was no longer interested in him. Its focus was now purely on Soren.

Soren took a faltering step back toward Alys, who still lay on the ground, as he fought to ensure his courage would not fail him. Fear was not something he usually had to contend with. Death was commonplace on the streets and fearing it was of no benefit. One quickly learned to just get on with things. If you died, you died, if not, all the better. Death may be still waiting the next day. There was something about the belek that did inspire fear though, a deep, primal one that Soren could not control. It was the intelligent, predatory desire in its eyes. It not only wanted to kill him for food, it wanted to do it for the sheer enjoyment of the kill.

The belek prowled slowly forward, carefully placing each paw as it surveyed Soren; its eyes brimmed with calculating intelligence. Soren lashed forward, piercing the belek in the shoulder. The creature had not expected the attack and for an instant it was stunned. That instant did not lost long however, and with lightening speed it leapt back out of reach and let out a loud rasping roar. Soren felt calmed by having scored a hit; his wavering courage had now firmed up. The belek's blood glistening on the end of his sword filled him with determination. Emeric's words echoed in his ears. 'If it bleeds, you can kill it.'

The belek came at him again and Soren lunged to counter but it dodged to the side. He twisted and tried to catch the beast on the move, but it swatted his blade away with a paw, and pounced forward without missing a step. Soren slashed at it again, but missed. This massive beast was far larger, far quicker and far more agile than any man. No matter what way he considered it, survival seemed unlikely.

A blast from a hunting horn caught his attention, stealing a part of his concentration that was vitally needed against the belek. Alys had composed herself and was signalling the hunt for help. The belek took advantage of this lapse in concentration and swatted at Soren's sword, driving its tip down to the ground and into the snow covered mud. With a second swipe of its paw, it pressed down on the blade on its flat side. Soren watched in horror as the sword bent, and then snapped, only an inch from the hilt. Why couldn't he just have let go of it? He hurled the hilt at the beast's head, but it merely batted it away with a flash of its unnaturally fast paws. Perhaps he was imagining it, but he thought for a moment he saw the flicker of a smile on the belek's snarling face.

Help would be coming soon; it had to. The other hunters would heed the sound of the horn. All he had to do was draw the beast away from Alys and survive for just a few more seconds. He began shouting at the belek, anything and everything, all of the curses he could bring to mind. His face warmer had fallen open and flapped irritatingly about his face so he pulled his hat off and threw it at the belek who caught it in its mouth and then tossed it aside. He edged his way toward his now barely twitching horse, and away from Alys. Just as importantly, he was also edging toward his spear.

As he moved, Alys continued to back away, shuffling on her backside toward the tree behind her. Could beleks climb? Could she for that matter? The creature cast her a furtive glance, and then looked back to Soren, focussing its attention on him. He was far more interesting prey. The freezing air was filled with the steam and the metallic tang of the horse's blood. The red stain the blood had created on the snow painted the only colour on the otherwise black and white scene. Out of the corner of his eye, Soren could see the spear, intact in its fastenings on the horse's flank. He moved toward it, one step at a time, waving his arms and shouting abuse at the belek, which inched ever closer to him. It clearly enjoyed the anticipation of what was to come but it always maintained the caution that betrayed its superb intelligence.

The spear was only a few feet away. One or two more steps and he would be able to reach it. Alys was now at the base of the tree, quietly getting to her feet. Soren tried not to look at her, or the spear, not wanting to direct the belek's attention at anything other than him. The spear was closer now, so close he thought he could almost reach it. He put out his hand seeking it, his eyes locked on the belek's.

His head was filled with a blinding flash and he was on the ground, on his belly, his face full of mud, blood and snow. The horse had kicked at the wrong moment, hitting Soren at the base of the neck as he reached for the spear. As he rolled over, trying to regain his wits, a foul stench of rotted flesh and sourness filled his nostrils. His vision cleared to be greeted with the face of the belek no more than an inch from his own, saliva stringing between its teeth as it curled its lips back to bare them in preparation for the kill. For the first time he noticed the faintest of blue glows coruscating between the hairs of its fur and along its whiskers.

It took its time, placing a paw on each of Soren's shoulders as it regarded him carefully. Its claws dug deep into his shoulders, so painfully that it did not seem real. Its cold and merciless intelligence was never more obvious. From somewhere in a world that no longer appeared to exist, a female voice called out, harsh and desperate, but the belek ignored it. For now, there was only the two of them, locked in their own little world. The single voice was then joined by others, male voices, but these seemed to be even farther away. The hunters had arrived, but the belek ignored these also. It prodded his chest gently with his fangs and then slowly lifted its head back for what would be the killing strike. Then it slowed even more. Soren felt a wave of nausea wash over him, but it passed as quickly as it had come. It was only then that Soren realised everything seemed to be going at so much slower a pace than it had. A droplet of saliva falling from one of the Beleks fangs seemed to almost freeze in mid-air. Soren grabbed for his dagger, his arms still mobile from the elbows. Everything seemed to be in slow motion except for him. He struggled to orient his hand to a position where he could grab the dagger, but his pinned shoulders made it almost impossible. The belek's fangs grew ever closer as he forced his hand into the hilt and pulled the dagger free from its sheath. He twisted the handle in his fingers pointing the blade up and pushed it up into the belek's belly, then pulled it toward his face, spilling the beast's warm guts down upon himself.

Its eyes widened in shock as the pain registered, and for the briefest of moments Soren thought that it would strike one final blow to kill its killer, but the damage done was too severe and its heavy body slumped down on top of him. It gave out a prolonged, exhausted gasp before its body relaxed and life escaped it.

Alys's voice filled his ears. She was over him, barely visible past the belek's body, pulling at the carcass, but its weight was too much for her to budge. The world returned to normal as though Soren had been violently ripped from one place and hurled roughly into another where everything happened more quickly and more loudly. He felt as though he had plunged into a pool of misery. He burned with exhaustion and pain. Voices created a confused cacophony that startled him. His breathing slowed and became difficult, all the more so with the belek's bulk pressing down on his chest. His head lolled as he fought to remain awake.

He realised that the belek had sunk its fangs into his shoulder as it had collapsed, but the pain was becoming only a faint, muffled feeling, damped by his exhaustion like the way the snow seemed to muffle the sound. There were more people about him now, appearing as no more than shadows in the pale light. The skeletal shapes of the branches of bare trees etched their way across the blindingly white sky. He remembered the feeling of the belek's body being jostled on top of him, and then nothing.

Chapter 23

A QUICK RECOVERY

He awoke in a bed of crisp white sheets with a feeling of comfort so intense he did not want to move or change a thing. It took a moment for the memories of what went before to make themselves known. He pushed them to the back of his mind and sat up to make a fuller examination of his surroundings. A man who was not much older than Soren sat on a wooden chair by the window. He was staring idly out of it, a look of extreme boredom on his face. Soren cleared his throat as he propped himself up in the bed on his elbows. A tightness and pain in his left shoulder reminded him of the wound.

'Oh! You're awake!' the man said. With that he bolted out of the room, unceremoniously slamming the door behind him.

Soren sat, puzzled by the behaviour for a few minutes, until there was a commotion at the door and Captain Jarod walked in.

'It was all that I could do to keep the Princess and her ladies out, I don't imagine you need them fussing over you right now,' he said.

'No, thank you, the peace and quiet is nice,' Soren replied. He still felt a little disoriented and was also unsure of how long he had been asleep.

'I won't be able to hold them off for ever mind, but I should be able to give you an hour or two more at least,' he said. His face broke into a smile, the first Soren had seen on it. 'I wanted to thank you for what you did. It was the bravest thing I have seen, and when hunting belek is your main occupation, you witness a great deal of bravery. I'm sure stories of you killing a belek with only a dagger are already on their way back to Brixen. What I want to thank you for though, is saving her Highness's life. It was careless of me not to notice she frightened one of the younger nobles into switching places with her, and if she had been hurt? Well, I've heard what the inside of Brixen dungeon is like, and I've no desire to see it first hand.'

'She was all right then?' Soren asked.

'Yes, we got to you just as you killed the belek. In truth I thought you were already dead. There is a reason we use such a long spear to kill them, few get as close as you did and live. I hope it doesn't set a new precedent though, the last thing I need is hordes of clueless nobles wanting to kill a belek with a dagger.' He chuckled. The relief at having avoided a near disaster seemed to have relaxed his usually rigid countenance.

'What happened? How did it get around behind you?' Soren asked.

'It didn't. There were two, which is unusual. Ordinarily they stay in their own territories, only meeting with others when the mating season begins, which won't start until the thaw is well and truly under way, three or four weeks away at the very least, I should think. Lord Aratha took the other and is suitably pleased with himself, but I don't think there will be very much talk about that! Before I go, I wanted to give you this.' Jarod reached over and handed Soren a small medallion hanging from a fine silver chain. It was a small silver disc, with a clear gemstone at its centre that had the faintest of blue hues. There was an inscription in finely engraved letters around the edge of one side. 'It's the amulet of a royal huntsman,' said Jarod. 'The inscription is a blessing intended to keep the wearer safe and the stone is a telastar, which is also supposed to keep the wearer safe from harm. I'll leave you in peace now, and thank you again.'

He left Soren to stare at the beautiful little trinket, alone with his thoughts. He tried to recall all of the detail of the incident. As he delved back into his memory, the pieces began to come back to him. The cold, the stench of blood, the red splatter on the snow, steaming in the wintry air. The sound of the belek, its growl, the crunch of its paws on the snow, the pained screams of his horse.

He remembered the blue glow on the belek's fur. He would have thought it a figment of his imagination were it not for the fact that he had seen it once before, surrounding a freshly activated drone in the training hall at the Academy. That time he had discounted it, but now? He remembered the feeling of sickness and the way everything around him slowed, while he had not. He remembered the exhaustion afterward, and that he still felt. He thought of what Master Dornish had said to him about the ability enjoyed by the bannerets of old; had Soren experienced the Moment that he had spoken of?

He did not have long to dwell on this however, as Jarod's promised two hours proved to be a gross over estimation. Alys and her ladies whirled into the room, creating a not entirely unpleasant fuss. Ordinarily he did not like being the centre of attention, but he found that he did not mind this type of attention so much.

Soren was always surprised by the dichotomy in Alys; part of her wanted to fence, race the ice and hunt belek, and part of her was as girly as the most delicate of her ladies. It took him some time to convince them that he was perfectly all right. The wound on his shoulder had not been as deep as he had feared, and it had been expertly cleaned and dressed while he slept. Other than a very vague discomfort, he barely noticed it so long as he did not move too quickly. It did amuse him, however, that Alys's ladies looked at him with the same air of adoration that they had hitherto reserved for Jarod. Ruripathian women seemed to view belek scars in a similar fashion to the way duelling scars were regarded in the south. He wondered what Alessandra would think of them, the remembrance of her making him oddly uncomfortable in Alys' presence.

He did not accompany the hunt again. Although he felt up to it, Alys had made him promise that he would rest until they left the summer palace. 'Anyway,' she had told him, 'it would be greedy to kill more than one belek on your first hunt.'

He only agreed to remain at the Palace on the condition that she did the same, although both of them knew that Jarod would not be so careless a second time.

The remainder of the trip was a mixed success. Two more belek were killed before they departed and sadly also three members of the hunting party. Most of the hunters went home without a kill, but with a story that would soon be abuzz around the principality.

When Soren returned to the city, there was only one topic of conversation on people's lips; the brave young southerner who had slain a belek with only a dagger. Those in the know also whispered that he had saved Princess Alys in the process. This had been kept discretely out of most of the gossip though, to spare Alys from her father's anger, but more importantly to spare Captain Jarod, who had not really been at fault but would likely pay a severe price nonetheless if word of the incident were to reach the Prince's ear.

A state funeral had been held for Chancellor Marin, which had by all accounts been a solemn affair. Amero had represented Ostia and consoled with the Prince over the loss of one of his most trusted advisors and oldest friends. More importantly, no suspicion was cast upon the Ostians. It seemed that Chancellor Marin had had a history of heart trouble, and an incident such as this had been feared, if not expected, for some time. It had all worked out perfectly to the advantage of Ostia. What was more, rid of Marin's influence, the Prince was leaning more heavily on his other counsellors, who, it seemed, were far more favourable to Amero's propositions.

The night of their return, a small banquet was held to welcome them back. The seating arrangements were very much the same as they had been at the first banquet, Soren on one side of the Princess, a disgruntled Captain Varrisher on the other. Where before all the female attention had been directed at Varrisher, now it was to Soren. Varrisher was a man who enjoyed being the centre

of attention, and was now very clearly on the outside looking in.
Soren did not so much enjoy the attention he was receiving as the
absence of it that Varrisher was experiencing.

Soren did however enjoy the new found respect he was being
treated with by the other men at the table.

'Have you ever considered coming to our Academy here in
Brixen to study?' asked a heavily built man in his early forties. He
had an impossibly well sculpted moustache, thick in the centre
and curving into fine upward pointing tips. He sat with a martial bearing in an immaculate grey uniform and wore the insignia
that designated him as a Banneret of the Grey, an accolade that
immediately commanded respect. Soren replied that it had not
occurred to him, but that it was certainly an interesting idea.

'We fight with a slightly different technique, but it is easily a
match for your southern style when properly executed. Regardless, it's never any harm to study things from a different perspective,' he said.

Soren was about to respond when Varrisher interjected.

'Southern swordsmen seem to be more interested in dagger
play than proper swordsmanship. I'm sure he would have little
interest in our northern ways,' he said, with a slight sneer in his
voice. His comment was intended to encourage Soren to say something that could be considered an insult, and he recognised the
fact at once. He took a short pause before responding. He did not
want to be drawn into offending the Ruripathians but likewise he
was not going to be condescended to by Varrisher, who was clearly
smarting at the lack of attention he was receiving.

'I assure you that I'm more than capable with sword as well as
dagger. What's more, I'm always open to learning new styles and
techniques. Perhaps you would oblige me with a demonstration?'
Soren replied evenly.

The heavy-set banneret guffawed and banged his fist on the
table. 'Excellent, a friendly duel then! Shall we call it for noon
tomorrow? I would suggest tonight, but I wouldn't want you to
spoil your dinners!'

Soren immediately agreed that this would be perfect, and Varrisher was left with no choice but to agree also. Soren felt that

he had turned Varrisher's sniping comment to his own advantage with satisfaction. Out of the corner of his eye he could see that Amero was watching him, his brow slightly furrowed. He really misses nothing, Soren thought.

The conversation quickly moved on from the sensation that was the impending duel between Soren and Captain Varrisher, although Soren did catch ladies at the table eyeing him with regard on more than one occasion, which made him feel slightly awkward.

'You should consider studying here you know,' Alys said. 'If a treaty is successfully concluded then there would be no reason not to, what with you being a personal friend of the Princess and all.' She let the comment hang in the air between them for a moment before continuing. 'I do hope a treaty is concluded. With Chancellor Marin gone, I worry. He was such a moderating influence on the council. So many of my father's advisers are firebrands, who would happily go to war for honour, glory and the ever-desired warm water port.'

Her comment caught Soren by surprise. Surely she must have it wrong?

'But, if we had a warm water port,' she said, 'what ever would Captain Varrisher do with himself, with no ice gauntlet to run!'

Soren chuckled, but Varrisher glowered at his plate. Perhaps he was coming to the determination that his one year at the Academy and dozen or so skirmishes with pirates might not be enough to defeat Soren.

Chapter 24

A SHOW OF STRENGTH

V arrisher had been correct when he had said that there was an excellent fencing hall in the Palace. It was long and high ceilinged, with polished wooden floors and was decorated with all sorts of martial artefacts, banners, swords and suchlike. A reasonable crowd had gathered, most of those who were in regular attendance at the court and some that Soren did not recognise. The moustached banneret whose name Soren could not remember was at the front, clearly looking forward to a good display of swordsmanship. All the ladies of court were there also, looking on giddily.

The moustached banneret had appointed himself as the referee for the duel and quickly ran through the rules of what he repeatedly referred to as a friendly exhibition bout. In consideration of this, Soren would be allowed to use a straight, southern blade, while Captain Varrisher would be using a Ruripathian backsword. The match would be to three touches.

The two duellists spent a few minutes loosening up and then with a cursory shake of hands, they began.

Right from the off, Soren knew he had a serious advantage. After Master Dornish had given him the Ruripathian swords, he had practised against them for hours despite his tiredness and Dornish's recommendation to rest. Varrisher was no slouch; Soren had to give him that much credit. Against many Academy students, he would have held his own. If he had stayed on at the Ruripathian Academy and graduated, he would probably have made quite a good swordsman. As it was, for Soren he was little more than fodder.

As Soren would have expected, Varrisher was flashy. He attacked quickly with sweeping cuts and a loud 'ha!' each time he did. He saw himself as being the daring, swashbuckling type, and was eager for others to see him in the same light. Showboating didn't bother Soren. It was the lack of respect that necessarily accompanied it that did. Soren wasn't some scurvy ridden little pirate who barely knew the pointy end of a sword from the blunt one and he was determined that Varrisher would learn this sooner rather than later.

The attack was not challenging at all but Soren decided to play along for the time being, letting it appear that Varrisher was putting him under far more pressure than he actually was. He seemed to have plenty of time to consider his course, a trait that he was now beginning to think of as having something to do with the ability Dornish had spoken of, the Moment. Varrisher smiled as he heard the sighs from the ladies in attendance each time he attacked. Soren sighed too, but for an entirely different reason.

At the end of one of Varrisher's attacks, which had been growing in flamboyance commensurate with his building confidence, Soren quickly stepped inside his reach and with a flick of his wrist touched Varrisher gently with the button on the tip of his sword, six times. So smooth was the attack that it appeared as though all six strikes were one movement.

The moustached banneret gasped loudly in astonishment and it was clear from his reaction that there were not many present that had understood what Soren had done. The bout was reset after each touch, so the six touches only counted for one. What he had done however was to strike Varrisher precisely in each of the six main killing targets from groin to throat before Varrisher had even had the chance to draw breath. It was a difficult thing to do with that level of precision slowly against a dummy, but to do it at that speed against a moving opponent was something else entirely.

As they reset, Soren could hear the moustached banneret whispering animatedly to those behind him as he explained the significance of what they had all just seen. Soren was pleased that he had managed it with so little effort. It proved to him that all the hours of training and study had been worthwhile. He caught a glimpse of a smile on Amero's face, which pleased him. He had idolised Amero as a youth and it was as satisfying to earn his approval as it was to score a touch on his opponent. The banneret restarted the match and this time Varrisher waited for Soren to come to him. He had learned a harsh and somewhat embarrassing lesson already and clearly had no desire for another.

Soren moved smoothly toward him and feinted quickly left and right. Varrisher moved to cover him but in his confusion Soren simply reached forward and touched him squarely on the heart with the button on his sword tip. Varrisher's face twisted with anger. The ease with which Soren had scored his second touch was something of an anti climax, and also made it look as though Soren was toying with Varrisher. Which he was.

Varrisher's brow furrowed as the duel was reset. He was clearly determined to make more of a go at it this time. In all probability he had conceded defeat in his mind, but would at least try to ensure it was not so easy the final time. He made a couple of tentative attacks that Soren parried away with ease. He was happy to make more of a show of it this time, as he felt that he had proved his point. He replied with a couple of half-hearted attacks that were flashier than he would usually be, but he was starting to enjoy himself. He received another few attacks, noticing that Varrisher was not making nearly as much noise now when he attacked, and responded flamboyantly. When he made his winning touch however, there was nothing showy. It was precise, and fast. Likely faster than anything Varrisher had ever seen.

Just as Soren relaxed, Varrisher struck him on the left shoulder. In Soren's view it had come just a fraction too late for it to be passed off as an accident. What was more, it connected just where he had been wounded by the belek. The pain flared through him like a flame, and without thinking he stepped forward and smashed his fist and the pommel of his sword into Varrisher's face. Varrisher dropped to the ground, his hands pressed to his face that was bleeding prodigiously.

'Perhaps you should stick to your boats,' Soren said with an edge to his voice.

There had been several gasps from the crowd, but Soren did not take much notice of them until his anger abated.

'That's quite enough, I think!' said the moustached banneret. He looked sternly at Soren, but knew well enough that Varrisher was guilty of a late blow and cheap shot which combined with the look on Soren's face was enough to convince him not to take the matter any farther. Two servants rushed to help Varrisher, who was still on the ground bleeding.

Soren turned to leave and was quickly followed by Amero and Emeric. He had known Alys was there, but had not looked for her reaction. As he walked out of the room, there was some muted applause, but the duel had not ended quite the way he had hoped.

'Not a pretty ending,' Amero said, when they were out of ear-shot. 'Nonetheless, it served its purpose. A show of strength, and that we aren't unwilling to sully our hands if necessary. All in all not a bad result really, when I think about it.'

Amero happily announced at lunch the next day that a treaty had been signed and that they would be leaving immediately.

He had just sent his baggage down with the servants to the carriages and was checking his quarters to make sure he had not left anything behind when there was a knock at his door. It was Alys.

She held two bundles in her arms, one large, wrapped tightly in linen, the other small and square, wrapped tightly in some kind of oilcloth.

'I am sorry that you are leaving so soon. I have enjoyed meeting you so much. I shall be lonely without you. And with you saving my life and all, well, it's all a bit overwhelming really.' She paused and looked down at her feet before continuing. 'I brought you your belek cloak,' she said and handed him the larger bundle.

'I'm sorry, Alys, I don't have anything for you!'

'My life is all the gift that I need or want! You broke your sword saving me, and I never thanked you. I hope this will be enough.' She handed him the smaller object, its weight taking Soren by surprise. It was a metal ingot. 'It's Telastrian steel, the very finest grade. My father keeps it back for diplomatic gifts, and rewards and such. There should be more than enough for a sword and dagger. I hope you can find a smith worthy enough to work it. I'm only sorry I didn't have time to have it forged, but I understand that such a thing cannot be rushed.'

She stepped forward, kissed Soren gently on the cheek and then was gone. He looked out for her every moment until they left, but he did not see her anywhere. And so his great northern adventure was over.

PART II

Chapter 25

THE RETURN TO RIVER HOUSE

The sea journey home was slightly longer than the outward one due to having to beat against the wind, zigzagging back and forth as they inched their way south. He was glad to get back to the Academy and to his own room, rather than the vomit scented cabin he had occupied for the sea voyage.

Term had not yet begun when he got back; there were still two weeks of the vacation remaining. The Academy was quiet, but not empty. All of the staff were there, as were the students who had graduated the year before and had been offered a place in the Collegium. It would be one of those students against whom Soren would be competing for the place in the Competition, which would be a focus for him this year.

The Collegium was a very different experience to the standard three years of the Academy and one that Soren eagerly looked forward to. While the Academy in itself taught on a wide range of topics that would be advantageous in the future lives of its students, the Collegium focused on one thing only, swordplay. Although only one year of study was required to earn one's colours and the title of Banneret of the Blue, some stayed there for years, studying and training to perfect their swordsmanship. They would travel to other Academies and serve in the military, but would still remain part of the Academy, with furthering their studies being their primary motivation for all they did.

Although his room in River House bore none of the luxury of his accommodation in Brixen, it was a pleasure compared to his cabin on the ship. Added to this was the fact that there was something comforting about being home. It still felt odd calling somewhere 'home', but home it was and it felt that way now too. He opened his trunk and removed the belek cloak that he had carefully folded and placed in it. He had not worn it home for fear of soiling it, most particularly by vomiting on it while at sea, although it would have provided a welcome shield against the chilly sea breezes.

He held it out in front of him and the thick fur felt deep and silky on his hands. The belek's curved fangs had been polished to a high sheen and crafted into the cloak's fasteners. It had been lined with blue silk, the colour of Ostenheim and the Academy. It was a nice touch that made Soren feel a little nostalgic for Brixen, and more importantly, Alys. He draped the cloak over his shoulders. It was heavy and very, very warm. Wearing it felt like being trapped in a cosy world of comfort and luxury. He noticed that thankfully none of the belek's scent remained on it. He took it off and carefully folded it once more before turning to the second of the two gifts he had been given in Brixen, the ingot of Telastrian steel.

It had been wrapped in oiled paper that left the steel with a damp sheen, but this did not mask its majesty. Its surface was embossed with the royal arms of Ruripathia and the steel was a deep grey with swirling patterns of differing darkness giving it an almost translucent appearance. It was almost the colour of the belek's fur, but when the light caught it in a certain way, it gave the briefest glimpse of a lightening blue sheen. He wondered where he should get the sword made, and when it occurred to him that there was only one, easy answer to that question for steel of this quality, the more pressing question was where he would find the money to get it done.

With his unpacking finished, Soren went into the common room and took brief pleasure in sitting on one of the couches that had been previously always been claimed by adepti in the year above him. The pleasure was short lived though, as he found River House to suddenly be quite depressing, what with it being empty. Three former River Housemen had joined the Collegium, but they all lived in apartments in the front building overlooking Old

Square now. Where there usually was noise, laughter and chatter, there was only silence, which was disquieting.

As term hadn't started yet, there were no restrictions on leaving campus, so he could come and go as he pleased, for the next two weeks at least. He decided to take a walk around the city, so donning his blue doublet, he left the Academy and walked up the Duke's Road. He crossed over the Westway River by Blackwater Bridge and stopped. There was something about being in Crossways that still made him uncomfortable, even just standing there thinking about it made him uncomfortable. It would be busy and he didn't feel like pushing his way through the crowds, but his reluctance stemmed from the deep-rooted fear he had of running the risk of a beating from the City Watch. Of course that was a ridiculous thought now. In his Academy blues, their scrutiny would be directed elsewhere. It irked him and he told himself that he really needed to get over these obsolete feelings. Nonetheless, he turned right after the bridge and walked along by the river towards the docks, avoiding the square. As he walked down the gently sloping street to the docks, the smell of the city was replaced by the smells of the sea, salty air, fish and the smells of all the exotic goods that were shipped through the city.

He let his mind drift as he wandered through the streets. The sounds and the bustle were strangely cathartic. He was not entirely surprised however, when he found himself standing outside the tavern where Alessandra worked, the Sail and Sword. He went in. Early in the day, it always seemed to be quiet, but there was something about the relaxed atmosphere that was anticipatory of busier times to come that he enjoyed. He certainly preferred that to a packed crowd.

He stood in the centre of the room feeling slightly awkward as he looked around to see if he could catch a glimpse of Alessandra, but he could not. He felt a twinge of disappointment and considered leaving, but realised that it would look odd. Already the barkeeper was looking at him with a quizzical expression, so he went over and ordered a mug of ale.

He sat by the window nursing the mug for a while, not really feeling like drinking it. He idly watched the coming and going of people, dockworkers, traders, merchants, and occasionally one or two that were unmistakably sell-swords. They all had a relaxed, watchful air about them, and scars, more often than not. They had a quiet confidence in themselves and a comfort in their surroundings that suggested they were happy to deal with whatever came their way, devils may care. There was something about their attitude that appealed to Soren. It was a far cry from scavenging and cowering in the gutter. They had no ties, a life of complete freedom where no one but their chosen employer got to tell them what to do, and only then for the duration of the contract they chose. They probably weren't particularly wealthy, or owners of great estates, but they certainly didn't lead dull lives.

When he returned to the Academy late that afternoon, there was a note pinned to his door. It was from Master Dornish's adjutant, and requested that Soren present himself to the Master of the Academy at the first convenient opportunity, no appointment necessary.

Dornish was clearly enjoying the peace and quiet of the Academy out of term. There was a far more relaxed atmosphere around his office and everything was being done at a slower pace.

'Welcome back, Adeptus,' said Dornish warmly. 'I trust your journey to the North was worthwhile.' He placed his hand on some papers on his desk and continued. 'I have here your application for the Competition. Are you serious about going for the Academy's place?'

'I am,' Soren replied.

Dornish studied him closely for a moment before continuing. 'Good! Ordinarily I would try and talk an adeptus into withdrawing his application. It only draws out the selection process and inevitably they fail to win the spot. You, however, I feel are different. That's not to say you won't be at a disadvantage to the Collegium candidates. They will have far more time to train, not to mention a little more experience. As you may or may not know, each member of the Collegium has a personal tutor assigned to him. For the duration of your involvement in the Competition, I am assigning you to Master Bryn. Your classes with him will take place outside of the hours of your other classes.'

Soren nodded and Dornish's face took on a more serious expression.

'I am allowing you to compete for selection because we both know how very good you are and how much better you can be with the appropriate guidance and effort. Do not let that make you complacent. There are many very good swordsmen in the Collegium, all of whom will be working very hard to win the right to represent this Academy, and this city. You will have to beat each of them, and they will sell their dreams dearly, mark my word. Master Bryn is on campus, and I would recommend that you seek him out and make the most of the next two weeks before term starts.'

Chapter 26

MORE THAN A PRETTY FACE?

'Drones are all well and good, but disarming two or three of them at a time is little more than a parlour trick. A man has his instincts and sometimes, pure luck, which can often be enough to dodge or parry a blow that would have a drone. Now, take your guard!' said Bryn.

They were in one of the private salons in Front House that were used for the Collegium. It had a high ceiling and wooden floors, and was in many respects a miniature of the training halls, but was equipped purely for fencing, with mirrors lining the walls, giving the room a feeling of being larger.

While he had watched Bryn perform demonstrations in the past, and had even sparred against him as part of his examinations, it was only now that the true level of the man's skill became evident. He had always been something of an enigma at the Academy. He had a short and undistinguished career on the duelling circuit before he had returned to the Academy to teach. He lacked the swaggering ostentation that had won Amero so many of his fans, but his movements were precise and technically perfect. He attacked with an almost mechanical rhythm that was at once mesmerizing and deadly, and an intensity as though each point was for his life.

Initially Soren fell back into a steady defence, allowing Bryn to dictate the pace and direction of the duel. The sound of real blades clashing and sliding against each other was far more satisfying than the dull feeling in a practice sword. It was the first time that Soren had been in what seemed like a 'real' fight with a master, and more than once the thought flashed through Soren's mind that he might ultimately be outclassed.

He needn't have been worried though. Bryn was very good, but could not best Soren. Despite not having the speed to beat him outright, Bryn's technical proficiency was greater, and Soren found, with satisfaction, that he had learned something new, or improved slightly, with each training session.

Soren was fast and he knew it. It frustrated Bryn that even his most perfectly executed attacks could not find their way home. At times he was even faster, but he could not explain why. He was never slow; not since the day he duelled dal Dardi had he experienced that. His speed advantage did seem to vary though. Some days he was fast and on others his speed was such that it surprised even him. Why, was the great mystery. He had also not experienced anything like the intensity he had when he killed the belek on any other occasion. That added even more confusion to his understanding of what it was that set him apart from the others.

<hr />

He was going out for one of his now regular post lunch walks through the city a few days before the beginning of term when a large black carriage rattled past him and turned into the Academy. When it stopped, Ranph stumbled out, stretching his back and walking stiffly as he stepped away from the carriage. He spotted Soren.

'Back from your adventures in the North I see!' he said. 'Are the women there really as beautiful as they say?'

Soren was not surprised that this was the first question Ranph asked him. To say he had a roving eye was something of an understatement. 'Well, if blonde is to your taste!'

'Always! I need a drink, let's go into the city while they stow my things,' said Ranph.

'I was just heading to the Sail and Sword as it happens,' said Soren.

'Drinking alone? You?' He paused for a moment, the look of surprise on his face changing to a smile. 'Ah, no, the barmaid! I recall you giving her the glad eye last term, how could I forget! Come on then, let's see if she still looks as good,' said Ranph.

They walked slowly back toward the Sail and Sword, Soren recounting his tale of the belek hunt. Ranph had spent the vacation running his family estate. His father had gone south with a regiment of foot to put an end to a border dispute with the Principalities of Auracia to the south. They had stopped their usual practice of fighting one another and were going through a period of national unity, taking the opportunity to try to expand their borders by flexing their collective muscle.

Soren felt a rush of excitement as they entered the Sail and Sword. Alessandra was standing behind the bar, working the ale tap.

'Two mugs of ale please!' Ranph said.

'Hello, back for the new term already?' she asked as she reached for two empty mugs.

'Not at all, back early just to see you!' Ranph replied flirtatiously.

'Aw that's very sweet of you! Here you go, a shilling please,' she said.

They went back to one of the usual Academy booths, with habit overriding practicality as one of the servants was scraping the ash out of the fireplace beside them, with loud scraping noises irritating Soren and making conversation difficult.

'No wine today, Ranph?' Soren asked.

'Gods no, I've had enough wine to last me quite some time. Last year's vintage was awful and father made the decision to sell on our reserves of the good stuff to cover the bad year. Which means we've had to drink this year's slop ourselves. No, it's ale for me for the time being at least.'

'Alessandra is looking well,' Soren said idly, but hoping that something would come from the comment.

'She always looks well. Just ask her out, stop being such a wimp,' said Ranph.

Soren put down his mug and looked over to the bar.

'Fine, I will,' he said.

Ranph raised his eyebrows, and then his cup in salute when he realised that Soren was being serious. Soren stood up and walked purposefully to the bar. For some reason the image that was burned on his mind was that of the belek as it stared him in the face.

'Finished already?' asked Alessandra.

'No, I, well, I was wondering if you might like to go for a drink some night, when you aren't working,' he said.

She seemed completely taken off guard. The usual cheeky casualness with which she deflected requests such as this was gone. 'Well, I work every night,' she replied.

'Maybe I could walk you home after then?' he said, grasping for anything other than outright rejection.

'Maybe,' she said awkwardly, trying to seem distracted with the mugs she was stacking.

Deflated, Soren returned to the booth, where Ranph had an uncomfortable look on his face.

'Well?' he asked, cringing.

Soren just shook his head. Ranph nodded.

'Nothing another few ales won't fix!' he said hopefully.

Soren sighed. 'I'm going to go home, I have some things to do before training in the morning.' There was a sound of despondency in his voice.

Ranph looked at him closely and realised there was no point pressing the issue. He looked away then, and over toward the bar. Alessandra was staring over at them, but quickly looked away when she saw Ranph looking back at her. He smiled to himself while Soren stared into his empty mug. Perhaps all was not lost just yet. They left the tavern, Soren shyly saying goodbye and Alessandra trying to avoid his gaze.

—◆◆◆—

Soren did not want to ever return to the Sail and Sword, but when his other classmates started returning it became impossible not to do so without letting his reason be known. Ranph was discreet enough and would not mention his refusal, and had given Soren space since then, not trying to pressure him into going into the city. When the others returned it was a different story though. They all wanted to share their summer tales and hear about Soren's adventures in the snowy North. The Sail and Sword was the obvious place to do that.

He felt a little sheepish going in, not knowing how to react when he saw Alessandra. A few months before he would never have thought he had a chance with a girl like that, but life had changed so much so quickly, anything seemed possible now. It was this sense of optimism that had led him to hope, and it was this hope that led to him feeling so disappointed.

He recounted his adventure in Ruripathia, again and again, leaving out one obvious part, but gradually embellished the rest with each telling, despite it not being needed and without really meaning to. Each night, it was the same story but a larger audience. Some of the others had vaguely interesting tales to tell, but Soren could never really pay much attention to them. All he could think of was Alessandra, and all he could do was concentrate on not staring at her when his own tale was finished.

Jost and Henn made regular exclamations of their envy. Their own summers had been mundane by comparison, with rural life on their family estates seeming very dull after the activity of the city. The more he heard of how little the others had been up to, the more he began to realise how lucky he had been in getting to go north with Amero.

With term due to begin the following day and the restrictions that would place on their leaving the campus, a larger group than normal had gone into the city for drinks. Students would be welcomed back with several days of very hard training to shake the summer cobwebs off so the evening was far from a riotous party. No one wanted to be the worse for wear over the next few days, and then have to spend the rest of the year climbing back through the class standings. The mood was convivial; there was a lot of joking, laughing and shouting, but not a great deal of drinking, to the landlord's chagrin. They stayed until closing time, the stories of what each student had gotten up to over the vacation keeping them entertained all evening.

Gradually the students began to return to the Academy, and Soren's group was among the last to go. As Soren was walking toward the door, he heard a voice call his name. He turned to see Alessandra standing by the bar, a small purse clutched in her hands and a nervous, hopeful expression on her face.

'Do you want to walk me home then?' she asked.

'Well, yes, of course,' replied Soren with surprise, his face involuntarily breaking into a smile.

They left the tavern, walking out into the dark night. The air was cooler than it had been and Alessandra tightened her shrug around herself. Since returning from Ruripathia, Soren had thought it very warm, although he did notice that the evenings had begun to take on an autumn chill.

'Why did you ask me?' he said after they had been walking in silence for a few minutes. 'I didn't think you liked me.'

She smiled, but continued to look forward. 'I don't know. I suppose I've been watching you, and you didn't seem like the others. Not so full of it! Like you have nothing to prove. It's nice.'

They both laughed, the ice finally broken. They chatted and laughed for what seemed to be an age. It seemed odd to Soren that she would live so far away from where she worked, but he did not mind. The conversation flowed freely and without end. When she had first asked him, Soren had wondered what they would talk about, and had felt something like panic in his gut. After the first laugh however, his worries had been allayed. Just like Alys, they seemed to laugh at the same thing, to have similar dreams.

They were both orphans. Her mother had died in childbirth, and her father had been a small merchant. He had gone off with a trading caravan to the east one spring, and had never returned. She had been left with her uncle and aunt and as the years went by they came to the sad conclusion that he was never going to return. Soren felt a pang of sadness for her, even though he had never known either of his parents. It must have been harder to have known him, and then lost him.

Soren had been completely honest with her, telling her how he had been thrown out of the Cathedral orphanage at fourteen to make room for younger children. He said it matter of factly. It had only been fair, they had looked after him for more than a decade, and at fourteen you were considered old enough to fend for yourself on the streets. She had listened sympathetically, but he tried not to labour on his deprived youth, which even he found depressing. He tried to put emphasis on the life that was ahead of him now, all the fantastic opportunities that had been opened up to him, through a stroke of luck and the generosity of the Count of Moreno.

He hadn't really been paying attention to where they were going as they talked, and was thus surprised when he looked up to see that he was standing back in front of the Sail and Sword.

'What are we doing here?' he asked incredulously.

'This is where I live,' she said, with a smile.

'But?'

'Take no mind of it. I told you I didn't think you seemed like the rest. I just wanted to make sure!' she said. She rested her hand against the doorknob, but paused before she opened it. 'I know it gets tougher to get out of the Academy in the evening once term starts, but will you call on me when you can?'

'Yes, of course,' said Soren. With that she opened the door and disappeared inside. He felt as though his heart was going to leap from his chest.

Chapter 27

THE PICNIC

Soren had missed the first week of term the previous year, so he had no idea what to expect from the first week back that all of the other students seemed to hold in such dread. He was not too worried about it though, as he had been training hard with Bryn twice a day, and then spending an hour or two in the evenings with the drones since he had gotten back. He had been keeping careful track of any symptom that could be attributed to the special ability that Dornish had suggested he might have. He began to suspect that it had something to do with how he perceived time. On any occasion where it seemed that something was moving more slowly than Soren felt it ought to be, he paid particular attention. The effect seemed to be stronger when he fought the drones, less so when he trained with Ranph or Bryn, but Soren felt that it was always present to some degree. It was never so strong as it had been in the final moments of his fight with the belek. He did not understand what was going on, or if indeed he was just imagining it all because Master Dornish had put the idea in his head.

He found it both frustrating and exciting. If it was true he had something that set him apart from all others, that thought was more than a little intoxicating. There was something very appealing to him about having something in common with the heroic bannerets of the past. He also wondered, if indeed he did have the ability, what other benefits there were to be enjoyed.

Despite the two weeks of hard work, the first few days back at the Academy were a mix of painful limbs, strenuous exercise, and a ravenous appetite to allow the body to repair itself from its exertions. When the end of the week approached, he was almost too tired to leave his bed, but he was determined to do something with his day off as a reward for all the hard work and in order to spend some time with Alessandra. The weather was still fine, although the autumn chill in the air was becoming ever more pronounced, particularly in the mornings and evenings, so he had decided to take Alessandra on a picnic.

He had approached the issue coyly with Ranph, who was envied for courting some of the most beautiful young ladies in Ostenheim's society. Ranph had teased him mercilessly, but Soren had prepared himself for that, and had reckoned that the advice would be worth it. Ranph's suggestion had been to take her on a picnic to one of the Breakers' Islands. They were a small archipelago of islands in Ostenheim Bay that were sheltered from the sea by a series of reefs that were a danger to shipping at low tides and during stormy weather.

In times past, ne'er do wells from the city that were no better than common pirates had used false signals to lure unsuspecting ships onto the reefs, and then scavenged the cargoes that washed up on the small beaches of the islands. The Empire had stamped these activities out long before the Mage Wars, and one of the remaining landmarks from those days was the great lighthouse that stood on one of the islands as a warning about the reefs and to direct safe passage into the harbour. The largest mage lamp in existence sat at the top of the lighthouse, and its light had not dimmed an iota in hundreds of years. They said the lighthouse would crumble into the sea long before the brilliance of the lamp was diminished.

Ranph regaled him with a story of how he had taken lady something-or-other to one specific island, and that she had been putty in his hands as a result. The story also included the finely equipped family barge he had used to get there, the team of servants who had rowed it, and the staff at his town house who had prepared a sumptuous picnic. Soren could see immediately several issues in transposing this suggestion to his own needs with less than modest resources.

Nonetheless, it was better than any of the ideas he could come up with himself. After investigating the possibilities and expense of hiring a small rowboat for the day, he came to the conclusion that he could just manage to scrape together enough money from his small allowance to hire the boat, and the food he could sneak out of the dining hall. He had a note sent to Alessandra, who responded right away. Her enthusiasm was obvious from her note, and she outlined at length, in what was approaching being a written stream of consciousness, what she would bring in the picnic basket, the responsibility for which she made her own.

The reply came as something of a relief to Soren, both her pleasure at the thought of spending the day with him and also that she was taking charge of the picnic basket, something that Soren had briefly put his mind to, but had come to no satisfactory decisions on.

He hired one of the small rowboats that were available at the slip in Oldtown and collected her from the pleasure boat docks that were a brisk row across the busy inner harbour, which left him with a sheen of sweat on his brow. She was waiting for him, a basket in hand on the dock side, looking beautiful and attracting admiring glances from every man that went past her. He held the boat steady for her as she stepped down from the dock, feeling an enormous sense of pride as she looked at him with a trepidatious smile for reassurance as she cautiously climbed into the boat.

'So, what's our destination then?' she asked, as they pushed off and Soren broke into a steady stroke.

'That's a surprise,' Soren replied mirthfully, as he tried to concentrate on their course, weaving between wherries and lighters that darted back and forth between docks and ships. He was able to keep up a brisk pace, almost matching the boatmen who plied the waters on a daily basis.

He breathed a sigh of relief as the traffic eased when they passed between the two great towers that guarded the entrance to the inner harbour and out into the open anchorage in the bay. He was beginning to tire though; despite all of his training, he still found the rowing to be hard physical work. He wished he had been able to afford to hire a boatman as well as the boat, as those heading out to the islands ordinarily would. Having access to a private barge and crew would be even nicer. Alessandra sat comfortably in the stern of the small boat, idly curling her hair as she watched the bustle of the harbour traffic slipping by. Occasionally she would cast Soren a coy look, and for a moment the burn in his arms would seem to fade.

The boatman had warned him that the row was longer than it appeared, but Soren had presumed that he had exaggerated in the hope of earning the fare as well as the rental. It was indeed farther than it appeared from the shore though, and Soren was grateful when they finally reached the sandy beach of the island he intended for their afternoon.

It was a small island, but consisted of a dozen or so trees and a small patch of grass and a sheltered beach, just large enough for a picnic. He helped Alessandra out and then hauled the boat halfway up the pebbly shore before tying it to a nearby tree. As Alessandra spread a rug which she had taken from her basket on the grass, Soren took the bottle of Blackwater wine that Ranph had given him out of its hiding place in the bottom of the boat. Ranph had told him that it was good, so it was with a smile on his face that he presented the bottle to her. Her jaw dropped when she spotted it.

'Where did you get that?' she asked.

'I have my sources,' Soren replied, trying to sound as mysterious and well connected as he could, the latter of which, it struck him, wasn't all that far from the truth in this instance.

'We keep a couple of bottles of this at the tavern, but no one ever drinks it because it's too expensive! You are really spoiling me today!' she said.

They exchanged slightly awkward small talk for the first few minutes, commenting on how lucky they were with the weather that day, and how it was nice to be away from the chaos of the city, but soon their conversation once again slipped in to the same easy flow that it had the night he walked her home.

She had filled the picnic basket with all sorts of treats, pilfered, she had said mischievously, from the pantry of the Sail and Sword. There were slices of delicious pastry pies with various fillings, grapes, apples and oranges, and a pie of custard and lemon that Soren thought was one of the nicest things he had ever eaten, even nicer than the desserts in Brixen. It was all washed down with a fruit cordial that Alessandra had brought, and the bottle of Blackwater wine which, even to Soren's unrefined palate, was quite superb.

The day seemed to slip by dreamily, in the light haze of the wine and easy conversation. They lay beside one another on the rug, chatting and laughing bathed in the warm sunlight. Soren wished the moment could go on forever.

Chapter 28

A GRATEFUL NATION

S oren always felt awkward in his full dress uniform, and despite
having worn it several times now, he doubted he would ever
feel completely comfortable in it. This occasion was one of the
many ceremonial functions that Academy students were obliged
to attend as a mark of respect. Ranph's father was being awarded
the Grand Cross and several of his officers and men were being
given lesser awards for bravery in what had been far more than
the small border dispute that Ranph had casually referred to it as.

Seemingly quite a major action had been fought in one of the
more strategically important southern passes on the border where
Count Bragadin's regiment had been dispatched. It appeared
that they had been outnumbered and caught by surprise, but had
fought tenaciously and had turned back the attackers from the
Confederation of Free Principalities of Auracia. The Grand Cross
was the highest award that could be given to a citizen of Ostenheim, noble or commoner and required Count Bragadin's presence to receive it from, as was the tradition, both the Duke and
Grand Bishop, who were the nominal heads of the Order of the
Grand Cross.

Ranph had seemed on edge since the announcement was
made. At first Soren had wondered why, but was then reminded
of the evening he had saved him from attack. There were many
things that Soren did not understand about Ostenheim, most of
which had never had any cause to affect him when he had lived in
the orphanage or on the street. He had understood the dangers
of the rivalry between various street gangs, and that these rivalries

seemed to work their way up through society to some degree. Organised crime and occasionally violence between the guilds was as much as he had ever witnessed but it appeared to him that wherever there was power to be had, people would fight over it, even aristocrats.

Ranph asked Soren to stay close by him for the duration of the ceremony. He explained that it was not likely that anything would happen, but just in case. He did not elaborate on what 'anything' might be, which bothered Soren. He knew his friend was probably not able to elaborate, but it would have been nice to have an idea of what to look out for.

The ceremony consisted of a triumph through the city gates and a march down Northgate Road with an honour guard to Crossways and the Cathedral. The Academy students would line the steps of the Cathedral to honour the recipients of the awards. The banners of the swordsmen receiving their awards fluttered proudly from flag poles at the top of the steps. That of Ranph's father took pride of place in the centre, a little higher than the others. It was a pleasant affair, but Soren took Ranph's comments seriously and he was not able to relax.

As it transpired, nothing happened. The honour guard entered the Cathedral while the students remained in their positions outside. A modest crowd had gathered, perhaps not as large as one would expect for the award of the Grand Cross, but the size and significance of the battle had clearly been played down for whatever reason, and none of the men receiving awards would have been known to the citizens, with Count Bragadin being the only likely exception.

When the ceremony was finished, the awardees all left, with the Duke being hurried to his awaiting carriage by his personal bodyguard of half a dozen men. After the nervous energy of expecting trouble, Soren felt somewhat deflated when the event ended with no incident. Ranph had clearly been more worried than he had wished to appear and Soren doubted that any threat he spoke of had been imagined. When the son of one of the wealthiest and most powerful men in the world feared for his safety, despite being well able to take care of himself, Soren realised that there were forces at work in Ostia that were beyond his awareness or ability to influence.

Nevertheless, Count Bragadin and his retinue returned to their townhouse, and Soren, Ranph and the other students returned to the Academy safely.

———————◆•••◆•————————

In the days since their picnic on the island, Soren had found it difficult to think of much else. He had seen Alessandra a number of times since, but only briefly. Their respective responsibilities had kept them from another outing like the picnic. It had been the perfect day. In class he daydreamed of her, the sound of her voice, the way she laughed, the smell of her hair. In practice he imagined she was watching him, and he pushed himself to ever more flamboyant swordplay. His skill and speed with a sword was all that he had to offer her. With no money, land or titles, it was all he had to set himself apart from all those who he knew had far more to offer than he ever would. As long as it was not enough to support himself, how could he ever contemplate being able to keep a girl like Alessandra?

When he was in a normal practice class, this ostentation was fine. By now there was not another student in his class who could match him. It was different in his private lessons with Master Bryn.

Bryn had long since acknowledged Soren's skill. Master Dornish had always made it clear that Bryn's evaluations of him had been exemplary. Although each of their duels in training were close, Soren was beginning to come out on top by ever greater margins. When he introduced unnecessary flourishes into his swordplay, it enraged Bryn, who would hurl abuse at him for being a popinjay and for the dangerous openings they left. Soren knew they were there, knew the danger existed, but was also certain that he could get away with them. Bryn knew it too. In point of fact, every time he did try to exploit one of the openings, Soren easily parried and countered, further angering Bryn.

Bryn was an angry fighter. He had a flawless technique, but there was a deep-rooted anger in every attack he made, as though each time he struck, it was not his opponent he saw, but some other person or event. It intrigued Soren, but he was well aware that it was unlikely that he would ever find out its cause.

He made to leave the salon at the end of the evening's practice, a spring in his step as he was going down to the Sail and Sword to see Alessandra.

'Soren!' Bryn shouted. The towel he was using to wipe the perspiration from his face muffled his voice somewhat. Soren paused, his hand hovering over the door handle. Bryn stared over at him, his face hard, the towel held just below his face. 'One day you will meet a man who is at least your match. On that day, do not let your arrogance kill you.' He returned to wiping his face and neck as Soren left the salon.

As he knew that it was likely Alessandra would be busy again this evening, he brought Ranph along for company. She was, as he suspected, rushed off her feet and only had time to give him a warm smile as he passed by the bar with Ranph to take possession of the booth by the fire. A convoy had arrived the previous week and its sailors were still in coin enough to pack out every tavern around the harbour. It was great for business, but it meant that Soren would not get to spend time with Alessandra for some days yet.

She always got a lot of attention from the patrons at the bar and this gnawed at Soren. He knew that there was nothing he could do about it and for the most part he pushed it from his mind. Most of her admirers were men of little means and would have even less to offer her than Soren did. The regulars never bothered him, former sailors and stevedores on their guild pensions with nothing better to do, but the crowd for the past few days was different. Merchants with money were in town, and they were spending it readily.

There was one man in particular that stood out, one that Soren could not ignore and put down to just being another example of him being overly sensitive to the inadequacy of his own means. He was a grown man and he could not stand on his own two feet, let alone provide for a girl like Alessandra and that chafed at him. Until he graduated, he was still a nobody with no more to show for himself than he had when living on the street. His position was entirely dependent on Amero's continued goodwill and generosity. His livelihood and success after graduating would almost certainly also be dependent on Amero.

At first Soren had thought the man to be Captain Varrisher, but he was mistaken in this. He was just a prosperous looking merchant who dressed similarly and held himself with the same overconfident swagger. He looked a little too wealthy to be in a place like the Sail and Sword though. From his finely tailored clothes with silver thread embroidery, Soren would have thought him more comfortable in one of the expensive inns elsewhere in the city. From the way he watched Alessandra though, it was clear why he was there.

'How can I ever hope to compete with the likes of him?' Soren said idly. 'What do I have to offer her?'

'Well, you can cross good looks, charm and talent off the list for starters!' replied Ranph, hoping to lighten the mood. He did not succeed.

Soren continued to watch the merchant as he tried to make conversation with Alessandra every time she passed near. He wished that he had the money to be able to take her out regularly, or to get her something that would show her how much she meant to him. Then it occurred to him that perhaps he had something already.

———◦•※•◦———

The award ceremony at the Cathedral was not the only formal occasion for Soren that term. He also had his own, in the form of his initiation into the Blades Society. Only the other Blades were present, and several of the masters who had been Blades in their student days. He was given a fine platinum badge of crossed swords and a perfect sapphire set in the centre, the same shade of blue as the city's.

It was a moment of enormous pride for him. He had achieved this on his own with his own skill and hard work. No amount of influence from the Count of Moreno could have won him this place. It was reserved for merit alone and was proof of his acceptance by his peers.

Chapter 29

A QUESTIONABLE OPPORTUNITY

Soren slipped out of the Academy early and stopped at a silver-smith's shop on his way to the Sail and Sword. He had Alessandra's name engraved on the reverse of the huntsman's amulet he had been given in Ruripathia. Aside from the block of Telastrian steel that would not have made an attractive gift to anyone other than a swordsman, it was the only thing of value that he owned.

The prosperous looking merchant was there again when Soren arrived. He regularly bought rounds for the other sailors at the bar. His sailors, Soren assumed. As he had been on the previous night, he was propped up against the bar, joking with Alessandra every time she was there, watching her hawkishly when she was not. He was the focus of attention at the bar, the type of man who was friends with everyone. Money was the key. Without it, charm was useless. It was the only way he could keep Alessandra, to show her that he would be able to give her a good life. As he watched the merchant another man caught his eye and a solution to his problem formed in his mind.

'Mr Braggock?' Soren asked.

'Just Braggock, lad,' he replied, his face breaking into a smile that did not seem to suit him.

'You mentioned before that you might have some work. I'm a student at the Academy,' said Soren.

'I did indeed. What's your name then?'

'Soren.'

'Soren?' asked Braggock.

'Yes, just Soren.'

'Fair enough. I'll tell you what, Soren, come back to me in a day or two, and I should have something for you. The work pays well, lad, but I'm not going to lie to you, it's dangerous,' said Braggock.

'I know how to handle myself. I'll see you here in two days then.'

Braggock turned back to his drink at the bar and Soren cast a look to Alessandra, who was still laughing with the merchant, although he thought he caught her give him an unusual look. He waited for some time to talk to Alessandra, to give her the gift, but as was always the case these days, the tavern was busy and she could not afford him anything more than a warm smile.

It grew late and he could not remain there any longer. On his way out, he gave the small paper packet that he had put the amulet in to her uncle, the tavern keeper, and asked that he give it to her, which he said he would. He left the tavern and walked out onto the street. The air had more of a chill in it than he had noticed recently, the bite making him think fleetingly of Ruripathia.

He had only gone a few paces up the street when he heard a voice calling his name. He turned to see Alessandra standing by the door.

'Going already?' she asked, smiling.

'Your rich merchant friend seems to be keeping you occupied. I need to get back to the Academy to train,' he said.

'Oh, don't be like that. You know I have to be nice to the customers. My uncle would tan my hide if I wasn't,' she replied, detecting the sulky tone in his voice.

'Well, I need to go,' he said.

'Will you come tomorrow?' she asked hopefully. 'I promise that I'll have some time for you tomorrow.'

'I'll try,' he replied. He turned again to walk away, but she called out to him again.

'Promise me you'll stay away from that man you were talking to. He's bad news.'

'I'll see you tomorrow,' he said, ignoring her request, before walking on into the darkness of the night.

He did not go back to the Sail and Sword the next night. Instead he spent it with Bryn in the salon, channelling his frustration into each attack, discarding his flourishes for determined thrusts. He tried desperately to find a way to consciously bring on the Gift, the Moment, or whatever it was, but it seemed that the harder he focussed on it, the more nebulous that it became. He felt that the Gift was influencing him, but he could never clearly identify how much, and no matter how hard he reached for it, he could not bring on the Moment, if that was in fact what he had experienced when fighting the belek.

He attacked relentlessly, without rest or fatigue, constantly willing on his ability to envelop him completely, so that he could demonstrate to Bryn exactly how good he could be, and in some way prove to himself that he was enough for Alessandra. His determination was such that he had even earned a grudging nod of approval from Bryn as he left to return to his room.

Chapter 30

DELIVERING THE PACKAGE

He returned to the tavern the next night to keep his appointment with Braggock. When he arrived, Alessandra was not yet there, but Braggock was.

'Ah, Soren. I had wondered if you would show, but I see I worried unnecessarily. Come, we have much to discuss,' he said. He gestured to one of the more secluded booths, and nodded to the barman to bring more drinks.

They sat, and Soren felt a growing sense of unease. Not only of the possible mistake he had made in meeting with Braggock, but also for fear of being seen with this man by Alessandra. The confident determination with which he had set out to make this arrangement was fleeing him, but it was too late to turn back now.

'Now, my lad, down to business. There is a package being delivered from one of the ships in the outer harbour to my associate on the docks two nights from tonight. He will need an escort to ensure he gets home safely with it. Are you up to it?'

Soren responded in the affirmative, but with a degree of hesitation that he did his best to conceal from Braggock. The barbarian dressed in the fashion of a citizen of the Duchy, but his manner was still that of a plainsman. It both made him fit in and seem out of place at the same time, which unsettled Soren.

'There shouldn't be any killing involved, but you might have to frighten off a thug or two chancing his arm. All the same, I'd bring a set of blades if I were you. A fright is all most of them need, and the glimpse of steel is usually enough to take care of that. If it

comes to it though, do you have the stomach to draw some blood?'
asked Braggock.

Soren nodded, keeping his face a mask.

'Good. Forty crowns for you, shouldn't take more than an
hour. Half now and half when you're done.'

Soren nearly inhaled the ale he was drinking. Forty crowns was
more than a dockworker would make in a month. What could be
of such value? Then it occurred to him. Dream seed; the zom-
bie maker. The slums were littered with addicts, who lived only
to breath in the sickly sweet fumes it gave off when burned. They
wandered about all day, like zombies, searching for their next fix.
It was also said to be popular among the aristocracy, although
the purer, more expensive form they enjoyed had fewer of the
unpleasant side effects experienced by the poor. It was imported
from the south, one of the many far off lands that Soren was only
vaguely aware of. Doctors could import it by special licence; otherwise it was highly illegal.

'Agreed,' Soren said, his mind snapping firm to the decision.

'Meet him by the steps on the slip in Oldtown at sundown. Give
him this to identify yourself.' He handed Soren a small metal disc,
not much bigger than a florin coin with some symbols etched onto
both sides. 'My associate will be looking out for you. Wear dark
clothes and the best of luck to you,' Braggock said, with that smile
that looked out of place on his face.

There was still no sign of Alessandra, so Soren left with a mix of
relief and disappointment swirling in his gut. Relief that she had
not seen him with Braggock, disappointment that he had not seen
her. He passed the side door of the tavern that led to the residence
above and heard the squeak of hinges.

'I got the evening off,' said a voice from the darkness that made
Soren jump.

He turned to see Alessandra standing in the doorway.

'I'm sorry about the other night,' he replied. 'It's just that
merchant. How can I compete with him, all his money and fine
clothes?'

'Silly boy!' she said, stepping forward and cupping his face in
her hands. He noticed she was wearing the pendant he had given

her. 'Money is nice, but it isn't everything. I love the amulet you gave me, it's absolutely beautiful, but I would far rather you had given it to me yourself. It's the meaning behind it that matters, not the value. I'd trade it in a heartbeat if it meant being able to spend more time with you, but we are so busy, and I have to do what my Uncle asks of me. He's been so good to me since father left and he desperately needs the help. There's nothing to be jealous about though. I like you because you're different to all the others, the merchant included.' She cast a nervous glance over her shoulder and then looked back to Soren. 'My uncle will be busy in the tavern tonight. Will you come in?' she said, and then with a brazen look in her eye and a cheeky smile on her mouth, 'I'll show you how little you have to be jealous about.'

194

Chapter 31

A FRIEND IN NEED

Soren was sitting on one of the more comfortable couches in the common room of River House idly flipping through a book on cavalry tactics that he was finding it difficult to engage with when there was a commotion at the door. He looked up to see Ranph enter the room, red faced and flustered.

'My house is on fire!' he said.

Soren immediately thought that he was talking about Stornado, which, while certainly unpleasant was not likely to have put Ranph into the state that he was in. It had not been long since Ranph's father had been awarded the Grand Cross, and he was still in the city attending to his affairs. The cogs of Soren's mind turned slowly that lazy afternoon, but he quickly enough came to the realisation that it was not Stornado that Ranph was talking about. He bounced to his feet and made off after Ranph who had already turned and left, grabbing a random sword from the rack of 'old beaters' in the hallway as he left.

The Academy and the wealthy area of Highgarden were of particular convenience to one another, either by coincidence or design, and it was not long before the pair reached Ranph's family's town house at a brisk pace. On another day, it would easily have been one of the finest houses in Ostenheim. On this day however, smoke billowed from its many windows that almost concealed the flickering orange glow behind.

Intrigued by the activity of two of the better-known students at the Academy, several others had followed to see what all the fuss was about. As a group, they all stood mouth agape at the magnificent mansion that was not long for the world.

It occurred to Soren how Ranph would react a moment before it happened. He reached out to put an impeding hand on his shoulder only a fraction of a second too late and it slipped off ineffectively as Ranph rushed forward, through the great doors, and disappeared into the smoke. Soren delayed for a second before cursing and following after him.

He had not been in the house before so its layout was a mystery to him. To add to the confusion, there was smoke starting to fill the corridor and the sound of flames eating away at whatever they touched. He kicked open each door he passed, peering in without breaking his stride until he came to one that was already open. With his knuckles white on the hilt of his sword, he rushed in.

Ranph stood statue still staring across the room. Soren moved further into the room, which appeared to be a study and followed Ranph's stare. There were two men dead on the floor and one collapsed into a leather chair, also dead. The man in the chair was Ranph's father, Rikard dal Bragadin, Banneret of the Blue and the Grand Cross, Count Elector of Ostenheim, Lord of the County of Bragadin. There was something tragic and heroic about the scene. The two dead men had clearly fallen before him, and he was covered in many wounds, his clothes sodden with his own blood. His sword hung limply in his half open hand and his eyes stared out into oblivion. His mouth was still set with the same determination that Soren had remembered as he had walked past them in to the Cathedral. Ranph stood dumbfounded and the smoke was slowly but visibly beginning to thicken.

Soren grabbed Ranph by the shoulders and turned him to face him.

'You can mourn him later, we have to go! Now!' he shouted at Ranph, whose face was frozen with despair. His eyes were glassy, either from grief or from the smoke, Soren could not tell. He didn't react so Soren grabbed him and shoved him out. As an after thought he ducked back into the office and took the rapier from the former Lord Bragadin's hand. Ranph should have his father's sword, Soren thought.

He rushed back out into the hallway where the smoke made it almost impossible to see, expecting to find Ranph standing there still dumbfounded. Instead he found Ranph sitting on the floor, clutching his stomach with both hands. There were three men lurking in the smoke, the orange glint of flame on steel visible at their hands.

There was no time to ask questions, or to identify friend from foe. Soren merely reacted. He reacted as he had a thousand times before in training, but this time with the indignant rage of someone who has been wronged. He screamed at them with a fury that visibly shook them and rushed at the men, spinning as he entered their midst. The two swords he held sliced through the smoke, leaving clear little trails in the air behind them. Two of the men began their drop to the floor as he stepped toward the third who had had the presence of mind to step back when he had seen Soren coming at them. As he raised his sword, it appeared to Soren to slow. He could see that it was wet with blood that began to form a drip on the lower edge.

He drove both lengths of his blades through the man's chest. He gasped and spluttered and Soren could feel the tug on the swords as the man's weight began to drop on them. He whipped them out quickly and booted the body out of the way as it fell. He turned to see if there were any other enemies to be dealt with, but there were none. The flames which had been rippling slowly and sensuously through the air resumed their earlier aggressive lapping at the walls. He felt lightheaded and the taste of smoke in his mouth was joined by the bitter tang of bile. He only now noticed the biting sting of the smoke on his eyes, the burning in his throat and lungs and an overwhelming feeling of exhaustion.

He didn't have time to inspect Ranph's wounds, but he was determined that two Bragadins would not die in that house on that day. Taking the swords in one hand, he grabbed Ranph around the waist and hoisted him onto his shoulder, and fled the inferno.

He had little time to unwind from the attack on Ranph's house before he had to embark on his own task for the barbarian. He had been utterly exhausted by the experience. He thought hard about how the final assassin's sword had seemed to slow. It moved faster than the belek had, but more slowly than it should have normally. It seemed as though the Gift had been stronger than normal, but not strong enough to be the Moment. It was all so confusing though, and he could never tell if he was trying to attribute explanations to things that needed none.

Ranph was safely in the infirmary and there was nothing more that Soren could do for him. He tried to push his concerns for his friend from his head and prepared for his job. He borrowed a sword and dagger from the arms cabinet in the salon where he trained with Bryn. Borrow was perhaps the wrong choice of word, as he had to force the lock, but managed to do so without causing any damage that a little careful bending of metal would not conceal. He would have taken one of the beaters from the rack in River House, but they were as they were named, old, beaten up and not to be relied upon if there was a better option.

Alessandra had certainly allayed his concerns about his lack of money, but he had made the commitment and did not think Braddock was the type of man who would take to being let down with friendly aplomb. He resolved that the money would go into the poor box at the Cathedral. After that he would be done with it.

The smuggler was waiting for him as planned. Soren felt slightly ridiculous discretely passing over the chit Braggock had given him to confirm their identities, and this sense of the ridiculous was added to by the smuggler's garb that could not be more clichéd if it had been intended. A long dark cloak covered him completely, with its hood casting a shadow over his face. The only colour he bore was the brace of fat leather satchels, a faded brown, which were slung over his shoulder. If Soren were to draw a picture of a smuggler, this man would have been it. He constantly had to remind himself that this was not a game that he was playing.

He made to introduce himself to the smuggler who gruffly told him to be quiet. In silence, they made their way out of Oldtown and down the street into the city proper. The smuggler insisted on taking back streets and tight alleys through Docks, clearly concerned that they would be approached by the City Watch and arrested if they were out in the open. It felt to Soren as though they were inviting as much trouble as they were avoiding, and this suspicion was confirmed when two figures loomed out of the darkness in the lane ahead of them.

'Get rid of them,' said the smuggler, before they had even moved.

They approached and the first of them, a scrawny looking wretch in garish clothes, the type often favoured by thugs to suggest wealth or reputation, drew a knife and spoke.

'Hand over the package and we'll let you live,' he said.

'I don't think so,' replied Soren. He pushed back his cloak to reveal the hilt of his sword.

The thug smiled. 'Anyone can strap a sword to his waist and act tough! Just hand over the package and save us all a lot of unpleasantness.' He became more menacing and the second thug, taller and more heavily built than his colleague, revealed the club that he was carrying. The scrawny thug watched Soren, his eyes bright, revealing a cunning that would not otherwise have been attributed to him. His lips curved slightly in a smile as he nodded to his colleague who approached. 'Fine then, we'll do it the hard way,' he said, a smile still on his face.

The mage lamp on the street at the end of the alley flickered gently. Soren waited until the second man was close; the fool was taking his time with what he clearly thought was an easy kill. The smuggler had not budged from where he stood behind Soren, his faith blindly placed in an unknown swordsman's skills.

Soren reckoned that a non-fatal splash of blood would be enough to scare the thugs off. In one movement he drew his sword and flicked the tip across the large thug's chest. His eyes widened in surprise. Blood bubbled from the corners of his mouth as he dropped to the ground.

The depth of the wound was as much of a surprise to Soren as it was to the others. He had only intended to draw blood, but had cut all the way through muscle and bone and into the thug's lungs. His control should be better than that. It was only as he berated himself for the sloppiness of his stroke that he realised things seemed slower than they should. The speed was similar to that he had experienced at Ranph's house. Slower than normal, but not as slow as time had seemed when he killed the belek.

The scrawny thug in the false finery roared in anger, but his voice was dull and the roar was long and drawn out. He came at Soren with his dagger. There was no mistaking his intention; he meant to kill. Without thinking, Soren lashed out with his rapier, slashing its tip through the thug's throat, tearing it open.

He gasped and tried to speak, but his destroyed throat allowed no more than a rasping whisper. He dropped his dagger and pressed his hands to the wound, as though trying to put everything back in place and hold it all together. 'Don't you know who I…' Then his face relaxed and his eyes lost their focus. His last exhale spluttered from his throat rather than his mouth.

Soren had killed the scrawny thug in less time than it had taken for him to even think of doing it. It was as though his body had identified a threat and destroyed it without him ever needing to consciously make a decision. He had not intended to kill the larger of the two at all and yet that was what he had done. The whole episode had been done with in only a few seconds and it was taking his brain longer than that to make sense of it all. Still somewhat bemused, he turned back to the smuggler, his bloodied sword still in his hand.

'Are you ready to continue?' he asked.

'Gods alive, I've never seen anything happen so fast,' the smuggler said, his mouth agape.

Chapter 32

CHOOSE YOUR FRIENDS WISELY, BUT YOUR ENEMIES?

Forty crowns was a huge sum of money to Soren. The street child inside of him grew giddy at the thought of so much, but there was just something about the way that he had earned it that tainted it. The fact that they were violent criminals made him feel a little less sullied by the experience. That he had not intended to kill them at all did worry him though. His physical action had gone beyond what he had intended to do, almost as though he could not control his own body. He did not think he had been in the Moment, the experience had not felt nearly so extreme as that in Ruripathia. It was however, as with the time when Ranph's father had been killed, noticeably different to the way he normally felt.

There was no satisfaction that he had done something worthwhile, as there had been when he killed Chancellor Marin. It felt as though he was squandering the opportunities that he had been given. He could not shake the feeling off and resolved that any work he took from then on would have to have a higher, more honourable purpose. Killing for coin was a last resort, for when a swordsman had no other alternatives. Soren was a long way from that situation.

He had arranged to meet Braggock at another tavern, no longer wishing to risk being seen with him by Alessandra, and it was here that he sat, waiting for the barbarian.

'You bloody fool,' a voice rasped out of the darkness. 'I've just heard what you did. You can forget about getting the rest of your money.' Braggock slipped out of the shadows into the booth beside Soren. 'If you've any sense you'll get out of the city fast, although if I had any sense I'd kill you myself and hope that it would make amends.'

Soren raised his eyebrows to indicate the foolishness of such a course of action, but nonetheless he felt a sinking feeling in his gut.

'Why? What went wrong? The courier arrived safely as agreed,' said Soren. Of its own accord he found his hand tightening around the hilt of the dagger he wore at his waist.

'You killed Don Abelard's nephew, his sister's boy,' said Braggock.

Soren recognised that the strained quality to his voice was from fear and tension rather than anger. He also recognised the name.

'My associate's already dead. I'm leaving town now. I'd already be gone if I'd heard what happened any sooner but I only just found out myself. All you had to do was scare them off, you fucking idiot!'

Everyone in Ostenheim knew who Don Abelard was. He controlled almost all of the illegal activity in the city and its surrounds, or received a tributary cut from that which he was not directly involved in. In truth, Soren had assumed that indirectly it would have been him that he was working for. It appeared however that Braggock had created this little venture on the side and had attempted to get it through without paying a percentage. As though this were not bad enough, one of Abelard's many relatives was now rotting on the cobbles of a back alley. He wondered briefly which of the two men he had killed that it had been, but it was clearly the scrawny one in the gold embroidered doublet.

'The best thing you could do now is disappear!' said Braggock, and with that the barbarian stood and took his own advice.

He collapsed onto the cot in his room, the soft mattress momentarily easing the tension in his body. He jumped up with a start at a knock on the door and opened it cautiously, dagger in hand. It was an Under Cadet.

'Master Dornish wishes to see you immediately,' he said.

Soren felt every part the naughty schoolboy as he knocked on the door to Master Dornish's office. It was imposing and decorated with ancient looking wood panelling. The somewhat ornate decorations on the wood betrayed its original function as the door to the study of the head of the city's Library of Mages.

'Soren,' Dornish said, his face grim.

Soren didn't reply. He was still uncertain as to why he had been summoned, and how much the Master knew, if anything at all. It was however becoming clear from his demeanour that the summons and Soren's concerns were directly related.

'A broken lock on an arms cabinet in the salon where you train. A sword and dagger missing. Two corpses in a backstreet killed with surgical precision, and finally, every thug on the streets of Ostenheim looking for a student of the Academy who is believed to have killed, I won't say murdered although that is what is being said, a nephew of the largest figure in the city's underworld. I hear the reward is two hundred crowns. A hefty price indeed. Regretfully, all of these little clues lead inexorably to you,' said Dornish.

Lying flashed through Soren's mind, but it was not in his nature and it would have been pointless anyway.

'Yes, I did it,' said Soren.

'I won't ask why, it isn't really important. What is important is that you have made every student in this Academy a target for any thug that fancies his chances of making some easy money and that is something I will have a very hard time forgiving,' said Dornish. He paused, resting his chin on his hand. His brow furrowed, then relaxed. 'Nonetheless, you are still a student here and your safety is also my responsibility.'

There was a cursory knock on the door and Amero swept into the room, his cloak billowing behind him. He removed his gloves and sat down without a word, before looking up at Soren, his face breaking into a half smile.

'Got yourself into a spot of bother I hear!' he said. 'I rather expected you'd knocked up some tavern wench whose father was banging on the Academy doors, but word of this is spreading like wildfire! This is a proper spot you've got yourself in!'

It relieved Soren that Amero did not seem to be angry, but the fact that he was there at all brought home how serious a situation he was in.

'That Soren needs to disappear is a given,' Dornish said. 'How we go about that is another matter.' Dornish paused again for a moment in silent contemplation before continuing. 'It will mean missing the Competition. A shame, but unavoidable.'

Soren had not even thought of the Competition. A ticket to a future of fame and fortune and he had thrown it away for forty crowns, only twenty of which he had actually got.

'I would suggest the east,' said Dornish abruptly. 'A garrison commander on the frontier is a former apprentice of mine. We shall send you to him. It will be worthwhile experience anyway. Return to your rooms and pack what you will need. I will prepare the necessary letters of introduction and we will have you on your way before nightfall.'

'Does it mean that I have to drop out of the Academy?' Soren asked, a hint of fear entering his voice for the first time.

Dornish scratched his chin thoughtfully for a moment before speaking. 'No. You've easily surpassed the standard required to graduate. I shall pass you so you will be eligible to return to the Collegium next year. By then this matter will have hopefully blown over. Criminals are killed with such frequency in this city that I expect other matters will be occupying their attention by then. Now go.'

Both Soren and Amero left Dornish's office and were walking across the courtyard when a thought jumped into Soren's mind.

'There's a favour I need,' he said.

'Name it!' Amero replied.

'There's a girl. She works at the Sail and Sword. Her name is Alessandra. Can you go to her, and explain what has happened. Perhaps it would be best if you didn't reveal all the details of why I've had to go. Just let her know that it couldn't be helped and that I'll be back as soon as I can,' Soren said. He thought about adding to tell her that he loved her, he certainly felt as though he did, but for some reason he found he could not admit it in front of Amero.

'The Sail and Sword. Alessandra. Consider it done,' Amero replied. They had reached the centre of the courtyard where they parted, Amero headed out the gate to where his carriage was waiting, while Soren went back to his room to pack his things.

Chapter 33

THE WILDS OF THE EAST

T he lights and smells of the city seemed like nothing more
than a dream by the time he arrived at Fort Laed. It had
taken a full week to reach, and it was the farthest outpost
properly garrisoned by the Duchy. After they had passed out of the
river lands, the scenery had become uninteresting and repetitive.
Flat plains stretched as far as the eye could see. On a particularly
clear day Soren thought at times he could just make out the peaks
of the mountains far away to the north, but for the most part, there
was rarely even a tree to break the monotony of the seemingly endless miles of grassland.

The fort was beyond what was considered to be the borders, or
marches, of the Duchy. In the distant past a busy trade road to the
east had passed through the region, but merchants from the far
eastern empires were rare at best since the old Saludorian Empire
had fallen.

The fort itself was far from being an impressive affair. The last
building he had seen made entirely from stone had been East-
march Castle, but that was several days to the west and still well
within the borders of the Duchy. Although there was a stone hall
in one corner of the rectangular area enclosed by the wooden
palisade, it was roughly constructed and if anything, less imposing
than the other wooden buildings in the compound.

The arrival of the carriage in the compound caused something
of a stir. It was clear that contact with the city was not that fre-
quent. After disembarking, Soren asked a soldier who was collecting the mail package from the carriage where the commanding

officer was. The man struggled with the bulging canvas parcel as he gestured to what was little more than a shed on the left hand side of the muddy square in the centre of the fort. It was certainly a far cry from the Academy.

He stumbled his way through the churned mud, his legs stiff from the cramped inactivity of sitting in carriages for so long. He knocked at the door and was instructed to enter by a curt and gravelly voice.

'I am Banneret Soren, recently of the Academy. Master Dornish provided me with these letters of introduction.' He took a parcel of papers from his doublet and handed them to the commanding officer who stood opposite him on the other side of a desk. His face was weathered and had gone several days unshaven. The combination made him look several years older than Soren suspected he actually was. He wore a dark blue doublet trimmed with the mustard colour of the Duke's Legion of the Eastern Marches that was so faded the different colours were barely discernable. He took the papers suspiciously and broke the blue wax seal. He read through them for a moment before speaking.

'I am Banneret Weston dal Vecho, Colonel, the Duke's Legion of the Eastern March, commander of Fort Laed,' said the officer formally. 'Dornish says you aren't completely green and that you are to remain here under my command until he sends word for you to return to the Academy. He hopes this will be in time for the start of the next academic year.' He raised an eyebrow as he read and Soren could tell that he was wondering what it was that had precipitated Soren's unexpected arrival. 'I hope for your sake that is the case and you are better than the other spoiled brats that occasionally come out here seeking experience. They don't tend to last long. Speak to the quartermaster in the next building to the right. He will give you your necessaries and see you squared away.'

'Thank you, Colonel,' said Soren. As Soren turned to leave, dal Vecho spoke again.

'We're very shorthanded here, and the barbarians are acting up more than usual. As an Academy graduate you're going to be leading men sooner than you might have thought, so prepare yourself for that.'

Soren nodded, saluted and left.

The quartermaster was gruff and unfriendly, but efficient all the same. Soren had not known what to expect. The marches were often somewhere young graduates of the Academy who were from less influential families would go to get some experience in the hope of getting promotion to postings closer to home. Otherwise it was not somewhere an ambitious swordsman would be inclined to spend a great deal of time.

He was given two uniforms, a plain but functional sword and a variety of other items that would serve him during his stay in the east. After signing for the items and being told he would be expected to return them all as soon as his service was finished, the quartermaster's assistant took him to the officers' barracks.

Each officer was afforded the luxury of his own room in a long single story bunkhouse, which the quartermaster's assistant informed him was mainly due to the shortage of officers, and, he added with a smirk, the frequency with which they were killed. The assistant left Soren to stow away his things, but he was not left to his own devices for long.

He had barely finished organising his things, much in the same fashion as he had in the Academy, when a trooper knocked at his door with orders for Soren to attend on the Colonel at once. He left what he was doing and followed the trooper, hoping to make a good impression with promptness if nothing else. The trooper led him back across the muddy yard and back to Colonel dal Vecho's office. When they arrived, he opened the door and gestured for Soren to enter. It seemed that they did not stand on ceremony in the marches. Nonetheless, Soren saluted when he entered.

'Ah, Banneret Soren, I know you haven't had much time to set-tle in, but a report has just come in of a raid on a farmstead a few hours away. I'm sending out a patrol that will be commanded by Lieutenant Dalvi. I want you get a feel for the job and the lie of the land. The next time you go out, it will likely be you in command, so learn as much as you can. I have given you a field commission of Cornet. The legion is a light cavalry regiment, so I hope you are comfortable in the saddle! If you've got questions, ask Lieutenant Dalvi, he knows what he's about,' said dal Vecho.

Despite his trepidation, Soren found himself to be enjoying the
patrol. While he loved the Academy and the life that he had there,
the patrol had a quality to it that was missing from there. This was
real. The sense of exhilaration that it gave him went some way to
easing the concern he had at the very real possibility that he would
never be able to go back to the city, or the Academy, at all.

The patrol consisted of twenty men and two officers, Lieutenant Dalvi and himself. Dalvi was considerably older than Soren
but had a face that made it difficult to determine exactly how old
he was. It was tanned and lined, but he could have been beyond
middle age or just weather beaten. He didn't say much, nothing
more than the occasional command to the sergeants who rode
directly behind them. His head scanned constantly from left to
right, his steely grey eyes squinting into the bright, early summer's
day as he searched for anything out of place. It was unusual for
an officer not to have been to the Academy, but it was clear that
when dal Vecho had not referred to the Lieutenant as Banneret,
it had not been an oversight. Unusual, but, as Soren was quickly
learning, the rules on the marches were very different to those in
Ostenheim.

Soren still knew virtually nothing about the patrol beyond
what the Colonel had already told him. A little after midday they
stopped at a small farmstead. It was two small wooden buildings
and a corral, a tiny dot on what seemed like an endless plain. The
officers and sergeants dismounted and approached one of the
buildings and were greeted by the man who exited it.

'Lieutenant Dalvi!' he said happily. He gestured to a table and
chairs by the door that had been laid out with rough wooden cups.
'Am I happy to see you,' he added, as they sat. 'Caroline! They're
here!' he yelled as an after thought.

A moment later a stout woman that perhaps had once been
pretty, but now showed the wear of a frontier lifestyle, came out of
the building. She carried a heavy pitcher and after heaving it up

to the table began filling the cups with lemon water. Soren stared idly at the corral that contained half a dozen horses.

'Magnificent, aren't they!' the man said, following Soren's gaze.

'Thomas, this is Banneret Cornet Soren, just joined us from the west, as punishment for a variety of misdeeds, no doubt!' Lieutenant Dalvi said.

Soren cast him a half glance. 'They are magnificent indeed,' he said, returning his attention to the horses. 'They remind me of Ruripathian destriers.'

'You've a good eye. There's a fair amount of Ruripathian in them, but these are my own breed. Just as strong, just as brave, but these fellows are faster and will run all day. When I have a good stock I'll start selling them to the Duke. He'll have a cavalry to beat anything the Ruripathians can send against him!'

'Well, hopefully the days of war with Ruripathia are far behind us,' Soren replied

'Ha!' said Thomas. 'That day will never come.'

'Thomas is a veteran of the last war,' Dalvi said, between mouthfuls of lemon water.

'Aye. I saw how the Ruripathian cavalry operate first hand. Well, I used my veteran's pension to buy some captured horses, and came out here to put them to stud. It's the perfect place. You can run them for hours on end in every direction. Perfect but for the barbarians that is.' He cast a glance over his shoulder. 'I suppose that's why you're here.'

'A prospector said he saw smoke on the horizon and reported it to us at the fort,' Dalvi replied.

'The smoke had faded out by noon yesterday. It's the Androv stead I reckon. There's nothing else out there,' Thomas added glumly. 'I was going to ride out and check, but the lads are still young and Caroline won't let me go more than an hour or two from the stead on my own.' He said it with shame in his voice, but everyone knew that it would have made no difference to what they would no doubt find.

'Thank you for the drinks, Thomas,' said Lieutenant Dalvi. 'It's my plan to overnight there and stop by here on our way back tomorrow, but my advice to you now would be to pack up your family as quickly as you can and head to Fort Laed until we are sure the area is safe again. There are too few of us on this patrol to chase them down and offer you protection also.'

'Aye, you're right. I need to go to the fort for some supplies anyway. Good luck to you!' said Thomas.

The patrol mounted quickly and before long the farmstead was fading into the distance.

Chapter 34

THE DISTANT OUTPOST

'I grew up on the marches,' Dalvi said abruptly, an hour or so after they had left the farmstead. 'It was nicer back then, before the barbarian tribes moved down from the hills in the north. First they started raiding in the summer, now they seem to be attacking whenever they want. As the frontier stretches ever farther to the east, we just can't keep them from raiding settlements. The Duke won't send us more men, beyond volunteers. And who would volunteer for danger and hardship out here when there is a nice comfortable life in the city, with parades and balls and fancy uniforms? Who indeed?' He cast a glance at Soren with a smile on his face. 'What did you do anyway?' Dalvi asked. 'Sleep with the wrong noble's daughter?'

Soren did not like Dalvi's assumption that he was a privileged and indolent idler. 'I killed the wrong man,' Soren replied, with as much chill in his voice as he could muster. He did not want anyone here thinking he was a spoiled rich boy. His statement had the effect of killing the conversation for the remainder of the journey.

———◆◆◆◆———

There was little left at the Androv stead bar a scorched patch on the ground and some charred wood. The sergeants barked commands and the troopers fanned out searching the surrounds as Dalvi and Soren surveyed the remains.

'What would these people have had that is worth doing this over?' Soren asked.

'The prospectors to the north would have silver and gems, but these people? Very little,' said Dalvi. 'Androv was a cattleman. They must have taken his stock, no more than a few dozen or so. Barely worth the effort. They haven't caused this type of destruction before. Androv wasn't the type to fight back, so I doubt if he provoked them. He wouldn't have put his family at risk.'

One of the sergeants called out so they walked over to him.

'Two sets of remains, sir,' the sergeant said.

'Thank you, sergeant. Have them buried, but keep searching. Androv had three children so there should be five in total. I want to give them a proper burial.'

The sergeant left to go about his duties.

'Surely the cattle must have been spread out over a large area. Couldn't they have just driven them off without interfering here?' Soren asked.

'Perhaps, but they didn't. I doubt if we'll catch any of them either,' Dalvi replied. 'They just bleed off into the plains as though they were never here after a raid. Nonetheless, it calls for a change of plan. Androv had daughters. If we don't find any more bodies, perhaps we'll still find them alive. I'm going to send a rider back to Fort Laed with a message to send more troops. We need to go out in force and give these barbarians a bloody nose, dissuade them from doing this kind of thing again for a while. In the meantime the rest of us will go south. There is a small trading post and the shell of an outpost a few hours away that we haven't been able to man. We'll base ourselves there for a day or two and see if we can pick up any scent of the barbarian trail. We can go after them when the reinforcements arrive.'

The outpost had been built the previous year, in answer to the settlers who were ever pushing the frontier further to the east. It was too small to be called a fort, being nothing more than a log palisade reaching about ten feet in height, enclosing an area large enough to contain a modest horse corral and three small wooden buildings. The plan had been to occupy it for a few weeks a year, and to serve as a stopping off point for passing patrols. There was one building outside the walls, a ramshackle affair that looked as though its original shape had received more than one ill-planned extension. One day this would probably be a major fort, like Laed, and a thriving frontier town, but for now it was still only a remote statement of the Duchy's expansionist plans.

The killing of the Androvs and their still missing daughters had put a dark mood over the patrol. They had the men set about making the outpost ready for occupation, while Soren and Lieutenant Dalvi went to speak to the occupant of the small shack beside the outpost.

As they bowed their heads to get through the too-small doorway, Soren thought of the great merchant palaces in Ostenheim and how far removed this was from it.

'Hello there?' called Dalvi.

A man in a grubby ensemble of what was once city finery appeared from behind a cabinet of oddities.

'Hello, gentlemen, how might I be of assistance?' he asked. 'Ah, legion men!' he added after taking in their uniforms.

'I am Lieutenant Dalvi. I haven't met you before.'

'No, I'm Morris. I just bought this concession. A pleasure to meet you,' said the trader.

Soren had seen his kind slumped against walls in the city with a bottle. Traders who had made and lost fortunes but had run to the end of their nerves and fallen on hard times.

'A farmstead a few hours to the north was destroyed and its herd was driven off. Have you seen anything, or heard anything from passing traders?' Dalvi asked.

'Nothing as yet, but it might explain why no one has passed this way for several days,' Morris said.

Dalvi appraised him for a moment, his brow furrowing when it became clear to him that he would not learn anything from this man.

'Do many people pass this way?' Dalvi asked, giving it one final try.

'A few, the number has been growing. One day in the not so distant future I expect this post to be a regular final stop for merchants heading to the east, and the first port of call in the Duchy for those heading in the other direction!' said Morris cheerfully.

Soren thought that Morris was deluding himself. Regular trade with the east was unlikely to be passing through here in either of their lifetimes.

'We will be occupying the outpost for a few days until we have a clearer picture of any threat in the area. I expect you will inform me immediately if you become aware of anything at all,' said Dalvi.

'Of course, Lieutenant,' said Morris. He smiled obsequiously and bowed as they made their way out.

They left the building and walked back to the fort and to the hut that Lieutenant Dalvi had designated as the officers' quarters. Dalvi shuffled in and sat down wearily hoisting his feet up onto the table. He lit a thin twist of tobacco and inhaled deeply, billowing smoke out of his nostrils as he stared into nothing.

'Well, he was a pretty revolting creature. I wouldn't be surprised if he is as eager to be of assistance to the barbarians as he is to us. I know that type. They come out here when they've lost everything else and drink themselves to death inside a year. From the smell of him, Mr Morris might not even last that long!

'I want to take some heads before these bastards get back into the hills,' said Dalvi. 'I want you to take two men and patrol east. Five or six hours should be enough. Take Sergeant Smit, he'll see you right. I'll go south. We'll leave at first light tomorrow, but be sure to be back before nightfall. I'll leave the rest of the men here to get the outpost in order. I want to find their trail before it goes cold and be ready to go when the reinforcements get here. Then we will hunt them down. Now, get some rest.'

There was venom in his voice whenever he referred to the barbarians, and Soren was a little surprised that he was pursuing it with such determination. At this point the barbarians were probably long gone with their bounty, and perhaps the unlucky Androv girls, who Soren doubted would ever be seen again.

———◆+◆◆+◆———

Scouting parties were not necessary. Neither was chasing the barbarians. The barbarians came to them. A sentry raised the alarm
shortly before dawn. The sky was a cold murky blue hinting that
the sun was not long from breaking the distant horizon when a
lone rider approached the walls of the small garrison. The sentries watched him ride in, not concerned by the threat posed by a
single man, but curious as to his intentions nonetheless. He threw
a brown sack high into the air and over the wooden palisade, land-
ing in the yard with a dull thud.

Soren groggily roused himself from his pallet in the hut at the
sound of the alarm and stumbled outside into the pale light to
be greeted by the ghostly shapes of the men's tents in the enclosure. Dalvi had gotten outside before him, and was sounding the
all clear, as the guard in the small tower on the northeast corner
shouted down that the rider was galloping away.

Dalvi approached the sack and poked it with the tip of his
sword. Satisfied that it posed no danger, he used the tip to pull the
material back from its contents. Although the object that rolled
out was bloodied and disfigured, it was clearly the head of the
rider that had been sent back to Fort Laed the previous day.

Dalvi looked at it with a frown.

'I only hope that Thomas took my advice and headed to Laed
with his family,' he said grimly. 'I think we can forget about any
help coming. Under the circumstances it is best if we break camp
and return to Laed also. I'm beginning to suspect that the attack
on the Androv stead was intended to draw us out here. Perhaps
they've decided that they want more than a few slaves and some
cattle.'

Chapter 35

UNWELCOME VISITORS

It took less than an hour for the men to break camp and get ready to leave, their haste added to by the fear that all the men, even the seasoned campaigners, felt at the prospect of being slaughtered by the barbarians. Dalvi gave the men a very brief inspection before they all mounted. He had his hand raised to give the command to open the gate when the lone sentry remaining on the rampart, about to climb down to join the column, called out the alarm. Soren could feel his heart drop and there was a collective groan from the men.

'To arms! Man the ramparts!' yelled Dalvi.

In response, the sergeants started barking orders. The horses had to be corralled again, travelling kit had to be stowed and the men had to fit out for combat.

Dalvi beckoned for Soren to follow him as he clambered up the ladder to the rampart. Soren followed him, and once he had hauled himself up onto the narrow walkway he found himself looking down over the trader's shack, and out onto the plain. A large body of horsemen and several wagons moving slowly toward the fort broke the otherwise featureless grassland.

'I suppose it would be too much to hope for it to be a trading caravan?' Soren said, without much conviction.

Dalvi just nodded. 'We have an hour, maybe two before they get here. I've never seen that many on the move before. More than one tribe must have united for the season's raiding. They're not in any hurry either. With our dispatch rider dead, they know we're cut off.'

'Do we have time to make a run for it?' Soren asked. He did not have any hope for the fact, but felt the question should be asked nonetheless.

'Look behind you,' Dalvi replied.

Soren turned and looked to the west. A smaller, but still large group of horsemen were approaching from that direction.

'Surrounded then,' Soren said.

'They're masters of the ambush. They're jumping merchants, prospectors and caravans as soon as they're old enough to walk. An outpost like this is no challenge for them. I'm sure they'll love to go home with our colours and the tale of slaughtering soldiers rather than just women and children,' said Dalvi.

Arrows that were stored in wax-sealed barrels were passed out among the men, the majority of whom were on the rampart trying to improve the meagre protections it afforded. Soren watched the slow progress of the advancing barbarian raiding party until it halted just out of arrow shot. One of the troopers tried a shot, but as Soren expected, it fell short by a dozen or so paces. Some of the barbarians shouted something in a language that Soren did not understand, but you rarely need to understand a language to recognise an insult.

The group that had approached from the west had skirted around the fort and joined with the main body of the barbarians at the front of the outpost. Enclosed within the walls, there was only one way out for the troop, and that was through the barbarians.

That they were in no hurry to attack was clear. The only question was why they waited. There was plenty of food in the fort. The patrols always carried more than they needed in case of emergency and it seemed unlikely that the barbarians would want to embark on a siege when they had such an obvious advantage in numbers. Dalvi's description of the usual tactic employed by the barbarians spoke against a siege also. They attack, they grab everything they can carry away, they disappear. Simple and effective.

The day dragged on, and still nothing happened. In all the excitement of their approach, no one had thought to bring the merchant into the fort, but nothing had been seen of him, so they assumed that he had hidden away somewhere in his shack.

The tension in the fort visibly increased. Soren made slow circuits around the ramparts with Dalvi, who offered encouraging words to the men. Despite this everyone was on edge. The barbarians had set up a large fire, and while most of them remained in fighting array, a group were huddled around it. Dalvi and Soren stared out at them, waiting and wondering.

As they watched, Soren felt strange suddenly. An electric tingling ran through him. It reminded him of how he had felt in the presence of the belek, but the feeling was far more intense now. While it was not an entirely unpleasant feeling, it was unsettling.

Storm clouds had begun to gather on the horizon, rolling down from the unseen mountains in the north. Great, heavy, dark clouds covering the blue sky like a blanket. While the weather in the marches was known to change quickly, there was something unusual about it this time. Dalvi and Soren watched as the group that had gathered by the fire began what looked like a ritual of some form.

'What are they doing?' Soren asked.

'Magic. We may have outlawed it but the barbarians haven't. They always defer to their shaman before an attack. I wouldn't worry about it though; it's little more than a parlour trick to frighten their enemies. I've yet to see anything that comes close to the descriptions of the magic done in the days of the Empire. When it's done they'll attack,' Dalvi replied.

They brought a bound man into view. It was the merchant. How they had managed to take him from his shack without being noticed was anyone's guess. They pulled him to his knees, and the one who appeared to be officiating stepped forward, staring directly at the forty odd frightened eyes on the rampart. He pulled a large knife from his belt and pushed it into the merchant's back until its tip protruded from the front of his chest after having cut through his heart. For a moment nobody moved an inch, entranced by the horror of the ritual sacrifice that they had just witnessed. After a few moments, the shaman became animated and starting leaping about the place shouting and screaming. As soon as he did, Soren felt like he was about to burst with energy. His entire body tingled and he felt the pressing urge to run, jump and throw things about, anything to burn off the excess energy. It was all that he could do to stop himself from jumping down from the ramparts and attacking the barbarians single handed.

The clouds had brought a premature darkness to the day, such that no one had noticed that the day had in fact worn on and night was fast approaching. Smaller campfires lit up in the gloom, surrounding the fort. It appeared the attack would wait until the following day. Soren was unsure if this was a blessing or a curse. None of the men, he concluded, had experienced this type of fighting. Small skirmishes on open ground was all they knew. Now though, they were trapped inside this ill kept fort and surrounded by a large hostile force.

Added to his already touchy state of mind, the energy coursing through him burned at his veins and pushed him to the point where he wanted to grab the nearest man and beat him to a pulp. He took a deep breath and tried to calm himself, but it was to no avail. This was far stronger than anything he had experienced before though, even with the belek's hot breath on his face and its drool dripping into his eyes. He took another breath, but it was becoming too much to bear.

They stayed in battle array all that night, pairing up with another man and taking turns to sleep. Soren slept feverishly, his slumber tormented by vivid dreams that woke him in sweats. He tried to conceal this for fear that the men might think that he was afraid. He was, but not to a degree that would cause that type of behaviour. Despite his fitful sleep, when dawn finally broke, he did not feel at all tired.

The barbarians had brought back their picketing troops, and reformed in front of the fort. With a guttural cry that seemed to resonate across the plain, they moved forward, beginning their attack before any of the men had time to break their fast.

'Ready arrows!' Soren had shouted without even thinking, the command training given at the Academy rushing back into his mind, the practicalities of what had seemed a pleasant diversion from the classroom now all too evident.

'Loose!'

The sound of a dozen bowstrings thrumming was far less impressive than the hundreds or even thousands he had imagined commanding when training on the drill square, but seeing as he had never heard it for real, perhaps this was as impressive as it got. The arrows whistled through the air, most punching noiselessly into the turf, with only one or two hitting a barbarian shield. None took a life. One of the men vomited over the rampart, the futility of the volley of arrows pushing his terror to the point where he could no longer contain it.

'Loose!' Soren shouted once again. The second volley had much the same effect as the first. The arrows were too few and spaced apart to provide any real threat at this distance. The barbarians continued on relentlessly.

'Save the rest of the arrows until the men can make aimed shots,' said a voice behind him. Dalvi stood behind him looking down grimly. The barbarians had formed a wall of shields in front of them, wide discs daubed in a variety of colours. Soren wondered briefly if they represented different barbarian tribes, the way the different noble houses of Ostenheim had different colours and banners.

'They haven't got anything to tackle the walls,' Soren said.

'No, you're right,' Dalvi replied, a hint of puzzlement in his voice. None of the barbarians carried ladders, rams or anything else that could tackle the wooden palisade at the front of the fort.

Just as the shield wall reached the trader's shack, two men ran out from the rear rank with flaming torches in their hands. The dry timber from which the shack was constructed took the flame up eagerly and it was only a few seconds before thick black smoke was billowing up from the opposite side.

'I don't see what that will achieve,' Dalvi said, with a grunt. The shield wall had halted its advance. As flames began to leap skyward and reach around the shack with their consuming embrace, Soren felt a tug, not at his body, but at his very being. The burning sensation in his body that he had managed to force into the background returned with a renewed vigour. A breeze began to blow.

The flames, which had stabbed skyward, were now leaning toward the fort, and its wooden palisade. The wind increased steadily and the flames crept ever closer as more of the shack became engulfed in flame. Soren felt his skin tingle with energy.

'How the hell are they doing that?' wondered Dalvi aloud. 'Bloody magic. I've never seen them use it for anything more than tricks to try to frighten their enemies. But blowing up the wind like that? The flames are going to set the palisade on fire. Pull the men back from that part of the rampart.'

Sergeant Smit reacted immediately, barking out his orders.

'I won't have them using their filthy murder magic on any of my men,' Dalvi said to Soren. 'We fight to the very last breath, Cornet. No man is to be taken alive. Do you understand?'

Soren watched the sap leak out of the backs of the wooden posts as the flames began to lick the palisade. His eyes stung from the first wisps of smoke to reach them.

'I understand, Lieutenant,' said Soren.

The posts began to blacken and smoke as the fire charred it, grasping for a hold on the young timber, until finally they ignited. The men watched them burn, transfixed on what seemed like the countdown to their deaths.

'I'll take some men down into the courtyard to hold them back for as long as we can. You stay up here on the wall and keep the men up here firing into them,' said Dalvi.

One of the posts exploded in a loud crack and shower of sparks. The barbarians let out a throaty cheer and began banging their shields with their weapons.

'To the end, lads, no one to be taken alive,' Smit shouted. While most of the men were quiet with fear, Smit seemed to be invigorated by the situation.

It took what seemed like an eternity for the wooden wall to finally collapse; all the while the men watched in silence, both those on the inside and outside of the walls. The small fort was filled with a tangy black smoke that clawed at the throats and bit at the eyes of those trapped inside. When the wall did finally give way in a crashing shower of sparks, Soren saw the barbarians move forward through a fleeting window in the thick smoke. They banged whatever weapon they had, ranging from clubs to axes to swords, against the back of their shields, creating a rhythmic thrumming that Soren was surprised to find quite intimidating.

Somewhere in the midst of all the smoke Soren heard Smit yelling for the bowmen to fire. He fought down a sense of panic that he could feel stirring in his gut. He was virtually blinded by the smoke, and all he could hear was the sound of the banging getting ever closer. The thrum of bowstrings and the sound of arrows whistling into the air brought him to his senses. He drew his sword and looked around, trying to make some sense of the unfolding scene through the smoke.

The banging was supplemented by bloodcurdling screams and war cries and somewhere in the midst of it all he could hear Lieutenant Dalvi forming the men up to receive the oncoming barbarians. Mixed through with this was Smit barking orders to the men firing from the ramparts. It quickly occurred to Soren that this was his first battle, and he wasn't doing anything other than stumbling around in the smoke and trying not to wet his britches. He would have taken a deep breath to steady himself, but the air was still chokingly full of smoke. All the energy that he had been filled with had manifested itself in a jittery nervousness that was proving to be useless at best and at worst threatened to overwhelm the wall he had built in his mind to keep back the fear of dying.

In all of the smoke, in all of the confusion, in all of the panic, a thought made itself known to him through all the chaos, or rather a memory. The memory was of all the days that he had woken on the street, so hungry that if he did not eat that day, he would probably not wake up on the one following. It had happened many times, and the memory of it now was calming. Despite all the opportunities that had fallen in his lap, all the comforts and luck that had come his way, he was still the same, still able to struggle through a day of adversity and still be living at the end of it. The thought gave him comfort. The thought directed the energy into a more positive form. His grip on his sword became firmer and he tried to clear some of the smoke from his face.

There wasn't much he could do from the ramparts other than give the men words of encouragement, or point out targets for them to aim for when the smoke cleared enough to see them. Despite their best efforts, Soren could only confidently say three barbarians had fallen to their arrows.

The fire had all but consumed the trader's shack and the volume of smoke blowing into the fort began to decrease, allowing a clearer picture of the scene below. Lieutenant Dalvi had clustered a small group of men as close to the breach in the wooden wall as the flames allowed. By doing so he also prevented the barbarians from using their greater numbers to their advantage. Despite this, things were not going well. Two troopers lay in the dirt and the barbarians pressed forward with relentless determination. Soren's men fired down from the ramparts, but all they hit were the shields the rear ranks of barbarians held up over their heads to protect themselves. If they fired at the front row they would hit their own troops, who were few enough as it was.

Dalvi cast a glance up to the ramparts, his face for the first time showing desperation. His eyes met Soren's for the briefest moment before he plunged into the fighting alongside his men.

'Smit!' Soren shouted. 'Form up the men, we're useless up here, let's at least die where we can do some good!' Soren led the way, rushing into the melee, which was gradually pushing back from the breach, allowing more of the barbarians join in the fighting. As he rushed toward the enemy, everything around him began to slow. He welcomed and embraced the feeling as all of the anxious and turbulent energy he had felt tormented by since the arrival of the shaman flooded into him and focussed itself into a fine point. Then the Moment took over with a strength and intensity that he would not have imagined possible.

Chapter 36

THE PURSUIT

Soren woke slowly, each sense returning grudgingly. First came smell, or what was left of it. His nose and throat burned and all he could smell was acrid smoke. Taste followed, but that was much the same. His mouth was bone dry, and smoke was all he could taste. He opened his eyes, the light stabbing at them causing his pupils to contract with painful speed. They were red and sore around the edges, and dry from the smoke. It was the worst Soren had ever felt, worse even than being cold and hungry on the street. He tried to make a sound but his dry throat wouldn't let him. He tried to move and every joint and muscle in his body screamed in pain, so he relaxed and stayed still, just concentrating on breathing, which in itself was uncomfortable.

He became aware of movement around him but could not make out who it was. The barbarians most likely. Imminent death still awaited him. Voices also, but his ears felt clogged so he could not make them out. He lay still, trying to will his eyes to remain open a crack, and waited for death to come. He felt a boot nudge him.

'Sergeant, this one's alive!' a voice called out.

There were more sounds of movement and the harsh cracks of light in Soren's eyes were shaded. He hesitantly opened them a little more. Two men in trooper's uniforms stood over him. One held out a water canteen. The water washed whatever debris covered his lips into his mouth and was foul with the bitter taste of smoke and the metallic tang of blood. He could feel his throat soften as the water touched it and the relief was immeasurable.

'Thank you,' he said, although it was more of a croak and sounded unintelligible even to his ears. He took more of the water, and gradually the foul tastes faded away. He took a deep breath and coughed heavily. The soldiers helped him to his knees as his lungs purged themselves of smoke.

He looked up, his eyes gradually becoming accustomed to the harsh light. Sergeant Smit stood there.

'Glad to see you still breathing, sir!' said Smit. He had never called Soren sir before. The other two troopers left, and Smit offered a steadying hand as Soren struggled to his feet.

'Likewise. I really can't remember much after we came down from the wall. Lieutenant Dalvi, where is he?' asked Soren.

Smit shook his head. 'Only six of us survived. Dalvi was dead by the time I got down from the wall. The rest of us would be too, if it weren't for you. Fairly scared the piss out of those barbarians so you did. After you killed a score of them they weren't so hungry for a fight, but they kept coming at us. They were even more afraid of their witch doctor than they were of you. Colonel dal Vecho turned up somewhere in the middle of it, and the barbarians ran. Left their wagons, and a couple of unfortunates that they must have picked up along the way. No sign of the Androv girls though. They were pretty young lasses; they'd fetch a high price as slaves, enough to make the entire trip worthwhile for the barbarians I'd say. Colonel dal Vecho left Fort Laed as soon as Thomas and his family arrived, so we have him to thank for the help arriving.

'The Colonel wants to talk to you if you feel up to it. They brought the apothecary with them, you might want to see him first by the looks of you though,' said Smit.

Soren was chewing the leaves the apothecary gave him when the Colonel was finally free to see him. At first the leaves seemed to do nothing, but gradually the pain he felt in every limb seemed less severe, until it was little more than a dull ache.

'I'm glad you're still with us, Cornet,' said dal Vecho. 'It's always a disappointment to lose a promising officer so early in his career. It's a shame about Lieutenant Dalvi though, he will be difficult to replace. Sergeant Smit has nothing but praise for your conduct. He served under me in the North, and I know his praise is not easily earned. I'm giving you a field promotion to lieutenant. Reports have been coming in from all along the frontier of barbarian attacks. The attack on the Androv stead was sadly not an isolated incident. Tomorrow we'll be riding out to hunt the rest of them down. We will not be letting these raids go unpunished. I've already sent my dispatches back to Ostenheim and you are mentioned favourably in them, but your work isn't done yet. Rest up now, because you'll be needed when we ride out in the morning.'

Soren felt like death warmed up the next day. A bucket of cold water had happily revealed that none of the blood that had covered him was his, but it did little to alleviate the stiffness, aches or pain. He knew that the Moment had taken him over the day before, it was the Gift, but many times stronger and the strain it had placed on his body was immense. He could not work out where the Gift ended and where the Moment began or if indeed there was a clearly defined line between them.

He was as certain as he could be that he had experienced the Gift at a stronger level before; with the belek, when Ranph's father had been killed and when he had killed the two thugs in Ostenheim. Of those experiences only the incident with the belek had been nearly as intense as the one at the outpost. While he had lost control against the thugs, he could still at least remember everything that had happened. He had put it down to not knowing his own strength or simply sloppy swordsmanship, but this time he had lost control to such an extent that he had no memory of the experience at all. It unnerved him that this could happen at all, and it frustrated him that each time he felt as though he was beginning to grasp a basic understanding of this ability he seemed to have, something happened that rubbished his theories.

From the bits and pieces Smit had mentioned, and from the hushed mutters of the men, it seemed as though the result had been truly terrifying. While in the Moment, killing seemed to be the easiest thing in the world. As terrifying as it was for others, the fact that he could not seem to control it terrified him also.

————•◦•◦•————

Colonel dal Vecho had brought out almost the full strength of the Legion and it was quite a sight. Pennants fluttered at the tips of lances and the martial sounds of a large number of men marching to war filled the air, even if it was still only a few hundred men. It was far more in keeping with Soren's dreams of military splendour than the small patrol had been. They didn't move quite as fast as the patrol had, but with luck the barbarians would be slowed by their wounded.

Dal Vecho had sent scouts to shadow the barbarians so their direction was being constantly reported to them. They had reported that the barbarians were near at hand, but to Soren's surprise, he realised that he already knew this. The strange tingling sensation of energy dancing across his skin and through his body that he had felt when the shaman had arrived at the outpost had returned and had been growing stronger. He recognised it now though and the connection between the two had to be more than a coincidence. Perhaps the intensity of the Moment as he had experienced it at the outpost had something to do with the shaman also.

Once cold, stiff and tired muscles began to warm, their strength returned and any discomfort faded entirely. By the time the dust cloud the barbarian's flight kicked into the air became visible, Soren had shaken off all the soreness and fatigue that had blighted him earlier in the day. He felt relaxed, rested and ready to fight again.

'Lieutenant Soren!' shouted Colonel dal Vecho. Soren spurred his horse to a canter until he reached the front of the column.

'Sir!' he said.

'Lieutenant, take Sergeant Smit and first squadron and lead the vanguard ahead. Catch them and slow them down. We shall follow in hard behind you,' said dal Vecho.

'Yes, sir!' Soren replied. He could not help himself but smile at the prospect. He wheeled his horse around and relayed the order to Smit, who barked his commands at first squadron, thirty troopers, who peeled off the main column and reformed at the side of the main formation of men.

Soren was quickly becoming accustomed to the fact that the army was in reality run by the sergeants. Once Smit knew what his general orders were, he took care of the minutiae, leaving Soren to feel like something of a figurehead. The curious glances he got from the troopers pleased him though. They all knew the tale of what he had done at the outpost, and all wanted to see first hand. The older troopers because they did not believe it, the younger ones because they were in awe.

On Smit's command, the squadron broke into a trot and then to a canter that pulled them away from the main column. From the front, Soren found himself constantly looking back, trying hard to keep a smile from his face at the sight of thirty troopers with shining metal breastplates and lances with their squadron colours fluttering at the tip. As he watched them, he wished that he had had the opportunity to have his own banner made before he had left the city. It would have been nice to be able to ride into battle under his own colours, as was now his right. Nonetheless, the dreams of a street urchin were a reality.

The barbarians spotted them before they had covered half the distance between the column and them. They tried to increase their pace, but it was to no avail. Several of their horses towed litters behind them with wounded men strapped to them, while others carried two men. Smit roared at the top of his lungs for them to increase to a gallop, which they did instantly. After the episode with dal Dardi and being thrown from his horse, he had never particularly enjoyed the riding classes at the Academy, but now for the first time he could see the appeal in being a competent horseman. There was something exhilarating about the thundering of the hooves, the wind tearing at his hair and clothes, and the prospect of glory in battle.

They were within a hundred paces when the barbarians finally accepted that fleeing would no longer serve. The shaman gesticulated furiously to the men as they formed into a defensive wall to receive the cavalry charge. Everything started to slow for Soren. At first it seemed as though the gallop was slowing and the rhythmic thrum of the horses' hooves dropped in tempo. The intensity of the feeling of energy had been building as they got closer and Soren felt certain that the Moment was not far from taking hold of him.

The troopers formed into a wedge, and Soren slipped into its side, drawing his sword and allowing the lancers lead the charge into the enemy. Soren looked about him, at the troopers who were all staring intently at their foe. He noticed the sense of relaxed composure that had enveloped him as all the sense of haste and exigency disappeared. As they galloped on into the enemy, Soren felt the world around him continue to slow. He focussed on staying in control of how the ability took hold, to remain aware of what was happening around him. It felt as though he was submerged in water that exerted pressure all over his body, trying to force its way in.

The charge hit the poorly arranged barbarian wall with a crash of metal, wood and screams. The weight of the charge pushed into the line and Soren was in the midst of the barbarians. A barbarian swung his axe at Soren's thigh. Soren watched it coming toward him, realising that despite his best efforts to control it, the Gift was affecting him with greater force. He moved his leg out of the way and lashed out with his sword, slashing through the barbarian's throat. Blood sprayed from the wound, each droplet slowly floating through the air. An angry roar sounded slurred to his other side. A barbarian, a friend or relative of the man he had just killed, came at him, his movement seeming slow. Soren revelled in the time he had to play with as the man swung a crudely sharpened sword at him.

Soren reached out and slipped the length of his sword into the man's armpit, unprotected as it was by the thick leather armour he wore, angling the blade so it ran through his vitals. In an effortless gesture he batted the barbarian's sword away with the back of his free hand. He had pulled his own sword free again with a twist to ensure the wound was mortal before the man even had time to realise that he had been struck.

It came as something of a relief that he was able to remain aware of what was going on, but his body reacted so quickly that it seemed to be almost detached from his mind, as though it was acting on instinct rather than conscious control. He still felt the pressure on him and had to focus to prevent it overcoming him completely. He scanned the crowd and spotted the shaman on the other side of the melee, screaming at his men.

In one of his hands was a mass of blonde hair, in the other was a curved knife; the same one he had used to murder the trader at the outpost. Soren could not see what the hair was attached to, but he was willing to bet that it was one of the Androv girls. He slipped down from his horse and began to force his way through the press toward the shaman.

The shaman stared at him with wild eyes, and at this proximity Soren could feel the energy crackling through his body. The girl was on her knees at the shaman's feet and wide eyed with terror. The shaman extended his hand in Soren's direction and spat some guttural words at him. A strange feeling passed over Soren, as though he was being enveloped in a warm mist. It felt as though his very being was tugged at, but the force could not pull it free. As quickly as it had begun, the feeling passed. It made him pause for a moment, but when he continued toward the shaman, the look of shock on the man's face was profound. He stood mouth agape for a moment before hastily returning his attention to the girl. He drew back his knife to full stretch, ready for the downward blow. Soren took two fast steps forward and ran his sword through the shaman's gullet. The shaman was wide eyed, his pain matched by his amazement at the speed with which Soren had moved. As his life ebbed away, so too did the energy in Soren. The world gradually returned to normal speed, and all the strength left his body.

He dropped to his knees sucking in deep gasps of air as quickly as he could. He could see that Colonel dal Vecho had arrived with the remainder of the column, and all that really remained was to slaughter the last few barbarians. In what he thought a great irony, he found himself slipping into the arms of the girl he had just saved, too exhausted to complete his rescue.

Chapter 37

HOME AGAIN

At his age, seven months had seemed like a lifetime. What had started as one large raid grew into a season of crazed barbarians urged on by their shamans raiding in large numbers ever deeper into the new territories being settled by the Duchy. The smoke from their fires could even be seen from Fort Laed at times, as the barbarians grew ever more daring, drunk on the power of their shamans, hungry for slaughter and whatever wealth they could plunder from the settlers. The like of it had never been seen before, and it was not conducive to encourage new settlement. The work had been exhausting and exhilarating and the opportunity to lead men into danger on a daily basis had moulded Soren into a competent cavalry commander.

Soren sat on his horse as it slowly trotted toward Ostenheim, which was becoming an ever-larger feature on the landscape. His time beyond the marches had been thrilling and had been an invaluable experience, not to mention improving his horseman-ship immeasurably. Nonetheless he was glad to be returning home to his friends, to the Academy and most importantly to Alessandra.

The first scent of sea air set Soren's heart racing. It was a smell that had characterised his entire life and he had not felt its absence until it returned, and greeted him like an old friend, filling him with a happiness and excitement that surprised him. Finally he was home.

He slouched comfortably in the saddle as he approached the city, with the confidence of a man who has seen death, who has delivered it and who has avoided its grasp many times. He had several days of dark stubble on his face that showed the potential to become a thick beard if it were not soon attended to. His wide brimmed hat with its white feather did not look as fine as it once had, his britches were dusty and his boots were worn, but he was an officer of the Duchy returning home from war and it felt fine indeed.

For some reason he had expected things to have changed during his absence. They hadn't. The city remained the same, a bustling hive of activity. As he rode through the main gate, down toward Crossways, he felt incredibly proud of the faded and thread-bare Legion doublet that he still wore. As an officer of the Duchy, people looked at him with respect, doffed their hats and occasion-ally a woman would curtsey. All for a street urchin. He drank in the sights and smells of the city as his tired horse took the last steps across the Blackwater Bridge into Highgarden and finally to the ornate gates of the Academy. It felt odd to have a place that he considered home, but it was a good feeling.

It was his plan to drop off his baggage, pay a courtesy call on Master Dornish and then go straight to the Sail and Sword to see Alessandra. He had intended to write so many times, but even now he didn't feel comfortable expressing himself with the writ-ten word, and there had never really been the time anyway. The thought of seeing her in so short a time made him feel giddy.

Term had already begun several weeks before and it was early in the day, so those of his classmates that had returned for the Col-legium would be in lessons. He was glad of it, as running into any of them would only have further delayed his reunion with Ales-sandra. He left his horse and baggage with a porter and skipped up the steps to Master Dornish's study. Dornish's adjutant led him straight in, where the old master sat behind his desk tugging at his moustache as he scrutinised some roughly drawn diagrams of fighting positions. He looked up and a smile broke across his face.

'It's good to see you, lad!' He stood and came around to the front of the desk and clapped Soren on the shoulder. 'You cer-tainly look more wise to the ways of the world now! I hope for your own sake that is the case anyway!'

Soren smiled, feeling slightly uncomfortable. 'I hope so too.'

'Happily the cause of your departure is firmly in the past. I don't think it will cause you any more trouble. Abelard Contanto was able to make the claim that the perpetrators were killed; there were two as I understand it. When it was made clear to him that if he persisted in hunting down a student at the Academy also, every banneret in the city would consider him and anyone who worked for him as little more than sport. I have had his assurance that the matter is settled.'

'That's something of a relief,' said Soren.

'It goes without saying that this caused a great deal of fuss, and you are very lucky to have had the support that you did. It will not be available to you a second time however. You might keep that in mind when seeking employment in the future.'

'I understand, sir. I'll do my best to be more discerning in future. I am glad to be back though,' said Soren.

'And it's good to have you back, Soren. When we are done here my adjutant will show you to your new quarters in the Collegium. I've appointed Banneret of the Blue, Gustav Caravello as your master for the year. He's a fine swordsman, is a former soldier and has studied many exotic fighting styles. You will learn much from him,' said Dornish, as he returned to his leather chair.

'I've been following your exploits in the east with some interest you know. I can't say I expected you to return as a brevet captain though, but from the reports of your conduct it is not entirely surprising. The siege of Fort Faraway, as the people have taken to calling it, was quite the talk of the town for several weeks after the reports of it reached us. So too was the young swordsman who defended it single handedly!' He let out one of his barking, incredulous laughs. 'I wouldn't let it go to your head though, if I were you!'

'I'll try to take it with a pinch of salt, sir,' Soren replied, a little surprised by what he had been told.

'This is for you. There wasn't time to give it to you before you left,' said Dornish. He took a rectangular wooden box from a drawer in the desk and slid it across the top to Soren. He picked it up and opened it. Inside was a tightly rolled piece of parchment bound with a piece of dark blue ribbon and sealed with dark blue wax bearing the crests of the Academy and the Duchy.

'Congratulations, Banneret Soren. Always remember that your learning never ends, this only signifies the beginning of your journey to becoming a master swordsman. You may take that certificate to the Hall of Bannerets and have your own banner emblazoned. Now, I think you have an overdue appointment with a bath. We can talk more at mess. It's good to have you back safely, lad,' said Dornish.

It was not seemly for a gentleman to run through the streets, even less so for a banneret, so he forced himself to walk, albeit at a brisk pace. The thought made him smile. Although he had been graduated early and had been using the title during his time in the east, as was his right, there was something uplifting about having the parchment in his possession, of it all being official. Banneret Soren. Perhaps some day he would be able to add a 'dal something' to the end of it. It reminded him of the block of royal grade Telastrian steel wrapped in grease-cloth at the bottom of his trunk. His ill-gotten gains would not tarnish it by paying for its smithing into a sword. They would be dropped into the poor box at a church as soon as he had the opportunity. He would have to find the money elsewhere. There was also the matter of having his banner made. He would have to start thinking of elements he would like to be incorporated into the design. Perhaps Alessandra would have some suggestions.

Despite not taking very long, it felt as though it had taken an eternity to reach the Sail and Sword. What he found there caused his jaw to drop. There was a gap on the street frontage like a missing tooth. Where once the Sail and Sword had stood, there was now nothing more than a charred remain. A low fence had been erected in front of it, so it was clear that it had burned down some time before. He hopped over the fence and wandered around in the ash. From recent habit he looked for charred bone fragments, but saw none. Perhaps no one had died in this fire. It almost seemed too much to hope for.

What had happened to Alessandra?

He left and turned back toward Highgarden, heading to Amero's town house. He hoped that he would be there and expected that he would be. Amero was not known for spending much time out of the city at his country estates

He was recognised by the servant who led him into the palatial house and to the drawing room. Despite the wealth of his neighbours, Amero's house was by far the most impressive on that street. He was now head of one of the oldest and wealthiest families of the Duchy. Many of his ancestors, and most recently his grandfather, had been elected as Dukes of Ostenheim. His wealth was said to be enormous and that was confirmed by his town house. There was one question about him that had never truly been answered. With such wealth why would he bother with duelling in the arena? It certainly was not the financial reward that most were drawn to it for that attracted him. The joy of perfecting his art said some; to further inflate his ego said others, usually those who disliked him. Whatever the reason, it had made him hugely popular with the ordinary people of the city.

Soren waited for some time before Amero breezed into the room with his usual alacrity. He was finely dressed as always, but not entirely in the peacock-ish fashion of many young aristocrats, particularly those who had not bothered with an Academy education, foregoing its hardships for an indolent lifestyle of idleness and luxury. His entire dress and poise suggested that he was as ready for a fight as he was a social engagement.

'Banneret Soren! Well, the hero returns from the East. I'm sure you will be delighted to know that I have heard your name being mentioned more than once at court. It seems that my faith in your potential has proved well placed!'

'Thank you, my Lord. I wanted to call on you promptly after returning. I am glad to see you well. I wondered though, if you might recall the girl I asked you to take the message to before I travelled east?' said Soren.

'The girl?' Amero asked, as he sat down. 'Oh yes, the girl. Emeric took her the message as requested. That's the last I heard of it though. Why?'

'I'm looking for her. I haven't been able to find her yet. The Sail and Sword was burned to the ground,' said Soren.

'Burned to the ground? I hadn't heard, but I'm afraid I can't help you. Anyhow, don't you think you were setting your sights a little low there? You're a banneret now and have already won yourself a little fame in the east. There are wealthy ladies in society who you would have eating out of your hand. You have advanced in the world, and wealth will follow, but allying yourself with the right families is important. A well considered marriage, perhaps to the daughter of a grand burgess or a minor aristocrat, would do your career the world of good. If you wish to take your place in my retinue, better things will be expected of you.'

'Perhaps, my Lord. Right now I just want to find out what has happened to her,' said Soren.

He returned to the Academy, deciding to eat while he tried to work out what his next step in finding Alessandra would be. He was walking across the quad when a high-pitched voice rang out through the air.

'Look, look! It's the hero of Fort Faraway!' A chorus of decidedly lower pitched laughing followed it.

Even in falsetto, Soren recognised the voice as Ranph's. Soren awkwardly exchanged pleasantries with Ranph and the others with him for a few minutes, all the while hoping to steer the conversation elsewhere. He deflected the questions that would require lengthy answers before finally asking for a word alone with Ranph.

He explained quickly how he had gone looking for Alessandra and how that had resulted. He asked Ranph to find out what he could. Ranph agreed without hesitation, but it took a moment of uncomfortable silence before he realised that Soren wanted him to do it right away. He hurried away when he did, leaving Soren to fret, not really knowing how to make the time pass until Ranph returned.

He spent the time finding the small room that would be his for the year, which was situated in the front building of the Academy. It overlooked the Old Square, and Soren sat on the edge of his bed, staring out the window for any sign of Ranph returning. The day faded into evening, and evening quickly into night. Mage lamps created orange tinged pools of light around the square, giving it a warm, welcoming feeling. He began to wonder what could be keeping Ranph so long. Finally fatigue got the better of him and he collapsed back on the bed into a deep sleep.

He awoke to the sound of the door to his room opening. Ranph was standing at the end of his bed by the time he managed to open his eyes. It was morning and the room was bright.

'Did you find her?' he asked groggily, squinting at Ranph's silhouette.

'After a fashion. Get washed up and I will meet you at the dining hall,' Ranph replied.

They sat at the top table in the dining hall, which was reserved for bannerets, usually members of the Collegium but occasionally also a visiting banneret from another city-state, but the privilege of being there was lost on Soren. All he wanted, all he could think about was what Ranph had to tell him.

'I know where she is,' Ranph said solemnly.

Soren's heart leapt. 'Where? Tell me! I'll go at once.' He blurted the sentence out, only then noticing the ominous tone in Ranph's voice. 'Is she all right?'

'Yes, she's fine. Look, Soren, she's a tavern girl. I know what your background is, but please believe that I am saying this to you as your friend. You're a banneret now. If you want to get serious about a girl, there are plenty of nobles that would be delighted to marry a daughter off to a famous young banneret. Hells, I'd even marry you to my own sister, if she wasn't such a harridan. I wouldn't wish her on my worst enemy!' He chuckled, but it sounded forced.

'My point is though, if you want to get ahead in society, it's the only option. I mean, if you wanted to take her as your mistress, that would be fine, but I know you and I know that's not what you want. You need to forget about her Soren, for your own sake.'

Soren could feel his anger rising. The same anger he had felt when he thought of the Androvs being slaughtered and their daughters being taken as slaves. He pushed it away as quickly as it entered his mind; it had use in battle, but had no place here, among friends. Ranph was only trying to help. Nonetheless, when Soren spoke his voice was cold and flat.

'Just tell me where she is,' he said.

Ranph frowned and let out a sigh.

'Fine. If you're sure that's what you want, I'll take you,' he said.

Chapter 38

AN UNEXPECTED DISCOVERY

Ranph led Soren out of the Academy and down the hill into Oldtown, not to Docks or Crossways as he had expected. Oldtown was a fashionable area and had been for many years, where the wealthy younger members of society would take apartments. It was the original site of the city before it had grown to its current size and it was an expensive area to live, second only to Highgarden, where many of Oldtown's residents would ultimately live when they settled down.

They walked in silence until they reached a well-maintained building with an ornate door.

'How can she afford to live here?' Soren asked, his surprise overshadowing any inquiring thoughts.

'She's called Bevrielle now,' Ranph said. He gave out the information with great reluctance.

Soren's heart dropped. It had been racing ever since Ranph had told him that he knew where she was, but now it slowed. A wave of nausea swept over him and took a firm hold of his gut. The only women that changed their name were whores.

'Do you still want to go in?' Ranph asked.

'Why didn't you tell me before?' Soren asked, choking down anger.

'You wouldn't have believed me. But now you can see for yourself. It's early, so she probably isn't entertaining any clients yet. We can call on her,' he said, reaching for the doorbell.

'Wait,' Soren said, the cold edge returned to his voice. He stared at his feet for a few moments, his brain fuddled with confusion.

How could she have become a whore? What could have happened while he was away? He reached for the doorbell cord and gave it two firm tugs.

'Wait for me here. I won't be long,' said Soren.

A maid opened the door.

'How can I help you, sir?'

'I'm here to see Madame Bevrielle,' replied Soren.

'Of course, sir. It's a little early, but if you'd like to come through I shall let the lady know you are here.'

He sneered at the use of the word 'lady', and cast a look at Ranph as he stepped through the doorway, oblivious to the fact that the shocked look on Ranph's face was due to the dark expression on his own.

The maid led him into a comfortable sitting room, scented with lady's perfume, and another heavier, muskier scent; the residue of dream seed smoke. The apartment was not quite what he would have expected of a whore, but he had never seen the inside of a brothel before, so he had nothing to gauge it by.

'A fine apartment,' he said. His knuckles were white on the hilt of his sword as he struggled to contain the anger that was welling within him.

'Yes, my Lady has taken the bottom two floors of the building. It suits her very nicely. If you'll excuse me, sir, I shall go and tell her that you are here.'

He nodded his acquiescence and watched her leave the room. He thought about sitting, but he was too uneasy to sit, and stared out of the window into the harbour as he tried to think of anything that would not make him angry. He waited for some time.

'I'm so sorry to keep you waiting, sir, but I was not expecting any callers at this hour,' said a lady's voice. It was one that Soren recognised instantly.

He turned to face her and she stopped in her tracks, her mouth open with surprise.

'I see you missed me!' he said brightly, forcing a smile to his face, his hands beginning to shake with anger.

'Soren, I...' Her voice faltered, the look of surprise completely taking over her face.

'You took to whoring very quickly. I was gone less than a year,' he said, his tone still bright, incredulous, but now betraying a hint of the cold hard anger which was coursing through him.

She walked further into the room and sat down on one of the plush chairs. For a moment Soren wanted nothing more than to forgive her, to take her in his arms, to just hold her and breathe her in. She looked exquisite, beautiful, fresh, just as he remembered. Now though, she was dressed in the finest clothes money could buy, her hair styled in the noble fashion and her face ever so carefully made up, just enough to accentuate her features, but not so heavy as to stand out. It was gilding to an already beautiful lily, but the effect was such that it was overpowering.

'You just left,' she said, her voice quiet, uncertain, sad.

'I just left?' Soren said.

'Yes,' she replied, firmer now. 'You just left. Without a word, without a note. Nothing. You just left me.' Her words were edged with anger now; she almost spat the last sentence at him. Her brazenness astounded and infuriated him. His heart jumped up and down in his chest as it pounded away angrily.

'I sent word. I sent word to let you know that I had to leave the city suddenly.'

'Oh yes, I got a message all right. The Don's men came looking for a barbarian and his sell sword. It was clear enough that it was you they were after! After that it was pretty obvious that you'd run off. I even went to your noble patron to see if he knew where you were,' she said.

Soren's thundering course of anger came to an abrupt halt, as though he had run at full pace into a brick wall.

'Amero dal Moreno?' he asked, his voice the one now sounding uncertain.

'Oh yes, the great Amero. Where else do you think I got all these wonderful things?' she said, gesturing around her, her voice loaded with spite.

This revelation was too profound for Soren to take in. Anger once again replaced his uncertainty.

'I told you I loved you. You should have waited. He knew where I was. He would have told you what had happened and where I'd gone,' said Soren.

'All he told me was that he had no idea where you'd gone. There was trouble, and you'd disappeared, but I'd already worked that much out for myself. You could have been dead for all I knew, but I reckoned the Don's men wouldn't have come around if they had caught you. So I thought you'd just gone. And to think I'd have gone with you if you'd only asked.' She snorted in disdain at her own words.

'And because of that you started whoring yourself to the high-est bidder. I thought you were more than that, but now I see they were right about you,' Soren said, sneering again.

'I had nothing else left to me,' she said, standing as she did, her voice choked with anger. 'Now get out. I won't have you com-ing in to my own house insulting me. Just be satisfied that you're the only man to have had me for free. Now get out!'

The intensity of her words shocked him. 'Of course, my Lady,' he said, aping a bow. 'I wouldn't want to interrupt the service to your paying customers!'

He turned on his heel and stormed out, too focussed on his anger to see the tears welling in Alessandra's eyes.

Ranph had known better than to speak to him, or to follow him, so by the time Soren got to a tavern he was alone. He ordered two men out of a dark booth at the back of the tavern, and once they saw the sword at his waist they did as he demanded. He sat and began to drink and the drink lubricated the raging thoughts in his head.

Amero had lied to her. That was the one inexorable fact. But why? Did it change anything? She was still a whore. High class or not, she was sullied. He would never have anything to do with her. There was always something else, some other option, some other way to survive. He had been on the streets with nothing. Other boys and girls had taken to it for a few pennies, but he never had. He could never forgive Alessandra for doing what she had done, but why had Amero behaved as he had?

After several more pitchers of ale he decided that he would find out for himself.

He pounded on the door of Amero's townhouse until a servant opened it. He pushed his way in, shouting for Amero. Emeric appeared in the hallway, dressed in his dark and well fitted britches and doublet. As always, he looked like he was ready for a fight. As always, he looked as though he would welcome one. He gave Soren an inquisitive look and then nodded his bald head toward a door to Soren's left. Soren strode up to it and slammed it open. He was faced with the naked back of a giggling young woman who was sitting on Amero's lap, obscuring him, the lower part of her dress covering them both.

'My Lord, I would speak with you!' he said, his words slurred rather than authoritative as he had intended. The woman looked back at him with a petulant and irritated expression. Amero's face appeared from behind one of her breasts.

'Why don't you go upstairs, Lucy, I'll be along in a moment,' he said to her gently.

'Yes, my Lord.' She giggled, kissing him seductively before bunching her dishevelled clothes up around her and left the room, casting Soren a filthy look as she went.

'This better be good, Soren,' he said, exasperated as he buttoned up his shirt.

'You didn't give her the message,' Soren said quietly, his voice full of anger.

'What?' Amero asked, his voice still exasperated before he realised what Soren meant. 'Oh, her. Come now, she's a tavern wench. What's the difficulty?'

'In point of fact she's a whore. At least she is now. Why didn't you give her the message?'

'Soren, I fully expected you to have forgotten about her by now. In truth I thought I was doing you a favour. In point of fact,' he said, mimicking Soren, 'I still think I have done you a favour!

You're a banneret. Have some bloody sense! A girl like that is no good for you!'

'I loved her,' Soren replied, his words slurred.

'Find a woman of quality to love,' Amero said angrily. 'You'll thank me for it later. Anyhow, you can still rut the wench if you want, it'll just cost you a few crowns now! Your allowance will stretch to it I should think!'

'Don't say that!' Soren screamed at him, tears streaming down his face.

'You uppity little bastard! How dare you come in here and bark at me!'

In a pique of anger Soren reached for his sword. He felt a strong hand grip his sword arm and prevent him from drawing it.

'Don't be a bloody fool, lad,' Emeric whispered in his ear.

Amero cast a wild glance at his own sword, sitting in its wooden mount on his desk before looking back to Soren.

'So that's how it is. You'd throw it all away for a whore. You bloody little fool. Well, if that's what you're after, then you've got it. I'm finished with you. Emeric, throw this piece of gutter trash back where it belongs.'

Emeric gripped Soren more forcefully and pulled him back toward the front door. Addled with booze, Soren didn't resist.

A bucket of cold water brought him partially to his senses. He was sitting on the street outside Amero's house. Emeric dropped the bucket and sat beside him.

'Well, you've gone and spoiled it, lad. I don't think I've ever seen the boss quite that angry. Still, you got further down the track than I did. Some of us just aren't meant to reach the top, no matter how much skill and luck we have. You've done all right though. You've made a bit of a name for yourself in the right circles, you're a banneret now, and that title can never be taken away from you, so you'll be able to stand on your own feet from here. But to throw

it all away over a girl?' He chuckled. 'My temper was my problem, that and I killed a count's son in a duel at the Academy, but
that one followed the other.' He paused, becoming reticent. 'She
was a bloody mess when she arrived here you know. She'd been
raped. More than once the physician said. Beaten too. Her uncle
hadn't been paying his protection money to the local gang, and
they made an example of him. They killed him, burned his tavern
to the ground, and, well... She came to Amero as a last resort. He
had tried to get her into bed the previous time she had come calling looking for you, but she was only interested in you. He'd said
that he felt responsible and guilty about the way you had treated
her and that he would help her if she ever needed it. So this was
where she came when she did.'

Perhaps it was the alcohol, but Soren felt as though he was in
some terrible nightmare, where misery was being piled upon misery and he could not wake up from it.

'She has the face of an angel though; thank the Gods that wasn't
permanently damaged. A face like that is worth something. One
thing my Lord is good at is seeing value in folk, as well you should
know. So he patched her up and set her up. After what she'd been
through she seemed agreeable enough to it. It's a better life than
she might have had. Now she passes back any amorous whispers
her well-heeled clients let slip that might be of use. You might not
like the way the world turns, but there's not much people like you
and I can do to change it. You're best off accepting that and getting on with it. Find yourself a rich wife and forget about this one.
Good luck, Soren; be a clever lad and take my advice to heart. If
I see you here again, I'll kill you. Don't think for a second that I
can't manage it. You've a trick or two to learn yet! Now, off with
you!'

Chapter 39

A CHANGE OF DIRECTION

He skipped lessons the next day. Soren had been so caught up in things that he had not even thought to introduce himself to his new tutor. There was no doubt that he was starting off on the wrong foot, but it was the farthest thing from his mind. He found a tavern that opened early, one that catered for dockers that worked through the night. They were a tough crowd, and after several hours of drinking he ended up in a fight with one. He couldn't remember why when he came to several hours later in an alley outside the tavern, or even what the man looked like. He stumbled back to the Academy, bruised, bloodied and still drunk.

He sat in the dining hall the next morning trying to force some food down, but after the previous day's excess it was a struggle. His head was still a tangle of conflicting thoughts and emotions. He could not understand how Amero could have played him so cheaply and he could not forgive him for it. He could also not forgive himself for having judged Alessandra so quickly. He thought of trying to apologise to her, but he had no idea how he could even begin to make amends for the things he had said to her.

His train of thought was broken by the appearance of Jost at the far end of the hall. Like Ranph, he had also chosen to return to study at the Collegium. Soren watched him as he collected his breakfast and made his way up to the top table. As he drew near, Soren adjusted his things in expectation of Jost sitting down next to him, as he had done hundreds of times before.

Instead of sitting down next to him, Jost continued past and sat with some others who had been in Ancelot House before moving to the Collegium. When Soren tried to catch his eye, Jost looked away awkwardly. It made sense though, all of Amero's friends, and anyone who wanted to be Amero's friend would now treat Soren like a pariah. He just hadn't expected it to happen so quickly.

Jost's behaviour had upset Soren more than he would have cared to admit as he made his way to the salon where his class was due to be held that morning.

'So, you've finally decided to appear. Your absence makes little difference to me; I am paid regardless. It is only you that loses out,' said the man. He paused for a moment before shutting his book and standing. 'I am Banneret of the Blue, Gustav Caravello. Master Dornish has appointed me as your instructor. Take a practice blade and we shall begin.'

There was something about the man's casual, arrogant air that instantly irritated Soren. Hungover, he was not much in the mood for company. Less so for social niceties. He picked up a blade, but despite his rising temper, his mind felt clogged and his reactions felt slow.

Caravello came at him quickly with perfectly executed attacks, but even in his befuddled state Soren had little trouble parrying them or stepping out of their way. Caravello attacked again, and again after, increasing the intensity each time. Still Soren managed to find it within himself to defend against them, eventually drawing the slightest hint of frustration from Caravello's face.

'You are fast, of that there is no question. While your technique is functional, it is far from good. We have a great deal of work to do. Were it not for your speed, I doubt you would even have graduated!' he said, with a sneer.

Soren did not rise to the bait, but inside he raged. Soren stormed out while Caravello was mid sentence. He had heard enough of the man's prattling.

———— ◆•✕•◆ ————

Ranph found Soren in an expensive tavern in Highgarden, more expensive than he could afford, but the one closest to the Academy. After his brief session with Caravello, the thought of spending at least another year at the Academy did not seem so appealing. What was the point of spending another year shut away from the real world when he knew that he could already fight more than well enough for war? He saw no reason to delay leaving the Academy to become a soldier now that he was no longer obligated to Amero's service. All the more so when it seemed that for the first time in more than a decade the city was going to war, with the barbarian tribes.

Ranph sat with him in silence for half an hour, although it felt like longer. It took him that long to throw caution to the wind, as he was confident that there was nothing he could say that would be well received.

'Bad day?' he asked.

'I'm leaving the Academy,' Soren said.

A stunned silence followed. It could not have been longer than the initial silence, although it felt as though it were.

'Not the answer I was expecting,' Ranph replied, trying to sound cheery.

'I'm going to re-join the army, see if I can get posted back to the frontier.'

'I'm sure there will be plenty of fighting left when we finish at the Collegium. Master swordsmen are highly sought after,' said Ranph, hoping to inject some reason into the conversation.

'I'm no longer under the sponsorship of the Count of Moreno,' said Soren. 'I can't afford to stay here any longer. I have to stand on my own two feet.'

'I'd heard about your spat with him,' said Ranph. 'It's been doing the rounds of the rumour mill. But if it's money that's your worry, I can—'

'No,' said Soren, more abruptly than he had intended. 'Thank you, Ranph, but no. It's time that I strike out on my own. I've learnt all I need to know for killing. There's nothing that prancing ponce Caravello can teach me that's worth a damn on the battle-field. I was fooling myself with all the things I thought I would have, a family, a home, a place in the world. Now I know what my path is. My mind's made up. I'm going to leave tomorrow.'

———◆·❉·◆———

'I'm sorry you have come to this decision, but it is not for me to try to persuade you otherwise. Just know that the issue of fees and lodging should not trouble you. The Academy can always afford to keep on promising students who cannot afford it on their own,' said Dornish.

'You've heard then,' replied Soren.

'Of course, there is little that happens involving my students that I do not hear. I would have thought that you of all people would have realised that by now! Irrespective of that, there are also other opportunities available to you now that you are a banneret. There are many young men looking for private tuition to assist in their admission here. That can pay very well, more than enough to keep you in comfort while you remain in the Collegium. The time spent here will be invaluable in discovering the intricacies and full potential of your gift. I would also welcome the opportunity to work with you and learn more about it. I would prevail upon you once again to reconsider.'

Soren smiled grimly. 'I just feel that I've learned all that will be of benefit for me in the army. A career as a duellist doesn't appeal to me anymore and I have no interest in teaching. I want to get back out of the city, where things are really happening.'

'I understand,' said Dornish. 'I know how hard it can be as a young man to sit by when great events are going on. I sometimes feel the pull myself, even now. Just know that there will always be a place for you here should you ever choose to resume your studies.'

———◆◆◆◆———

He bought a good set of blades from a reputable, but not famed swordsmith in the city before returning to the Academy to scrounge travelling rations from the dining hall and pack his things. Having not risen until well after noon, it was dark by the time he finally left the Academy, much as he had first entered it. Alone, in the middle of the night, and with no idea of what lay ahead of him.

Chapter 40

A RETURN TO THE EAST

F ort Laed was very different in appearance from the last time
he had passed through. Where it had been a sleepy, somewhat run down outpost the previous time he had arrived, it
was now a hive of activity, being the supply hub for a major army
in the field rather than just supporting a handful of patrols. He
didn't recognise any faces as he walked his horse across the parade
ground, but as he approached the commandery, a subaltern recognised the rank insignia on his worn doublet and rushed forward
to take his horse.

Colonel dal Vecho looked up from a stack of papers and his
harried face relaxed somewhat, but didn't quite manage to break
into a smile.

'Banneret Soren! It is good to see you. I assume from your doublet you wish to return to duty?'

'Yes, sir. That is what I was hoping to do,' Soren replied.

'Excellent. I'll assign you back to the Legion. It is short of officers but was attached to the main army to provide skirmishers
and scouts.' He reached for a piece of paper and scribbled on it
before sliding it across the desk to Soren. 'The army headed north
four days ago after reports that a large barbarian force was moving south in the direction of the fort. My latest report says they
have been bivouacked for two days now, so they are only two days
march away. You would probably like to rest first, but they should
be reachable by nightfall for one man on horseback if you were
of a mind to leave now. A marching army is never a hard thing to
follow!'

'Thank you, sir. I'll leave immediately,' replied Soren.

———————◆◆◆◆◆———————

Colonel dal Vecho had not been exaggerating in his advice. The army had left a wide brown scar on the plain twisting away to the northern horizon. He pushed on at a hard pace and was pleased to sight campfires in the distance as darkness began to fall. He passed the pickets after only a few moments delay while the less than alert guards tried to confirm his identity. With directions it did not take him long to find the General's tent. It was large and partitioned into several sections with thick cloth screens. Beyond the entrance, there was a large area with a camp table in the centre. It had been laid out for campaigning, and judging by the maps that were spread out all over it, it appeared that contact had been made with the enemy.

'Can I help you?' It was less a question than a challenge. Soren recognised the lieutenant who stood up from where he had been sitting in the corner as having been an adeptus at the Academy when he was in his first year.

'I have orders and am reporting for duty, Lieutenant,' Soren answered, holding out the papers Colonel dal Vecho had given him. The lieutenant's eyes widened a little when he saw the crossed swords on Soren's collar and realised that the scruffy man standing before him was a superior officer.

'Yes, of course, thank you, Captain.' He took the papers and scanned them quickly. 'The General has retired for the night, but I can direct you to your unit. These orders make you senior officer of the Legion, so you will be required to attend the staff briefing tomorrow morning at bugle call. I shall send an orderly with you to take you to your men.'

Soren was surprised that the rank of captain would put him in command of the Legion. The losses taken while he had been back in the city must have been very heavy. It took a moment for the orderly to appear and then he briskly led Soren through the camp. It was the first time Soren had seen a full army on campaign, but it was much like a smaller patrol camp, with each unit building a cooking fire and erecting its tents around it. Hundreds of units had set up their small communes all across the plain, their fires twinkling in the darkening evening.

'That's the Legion's bivouac just there,' said the orderly, pointing and clearly eager to return to his own fire as quickly as possible.

Soren thanked him and walked up to the fire. There weren't many of them there. From the time that he had left the frontier, the Legion had been under constant attack by the barbarians. It had taken its toll, but hearing the reports in the city and seeing the effect were very different things. There had been over five hundred men in the regiment when he had joined them almost a year before, now there were less than half that, and he was the senior officer. He looked around but did not see many faces that he recognised. Seemingly most of the men that he had known had been killed or invalided, but he should still have known a few. He was about to give up the search and read his orders to the assembled men when he spotted Sergeant Smit.

'Smit!' Soren shouted. The recognition made him feel at ease. Smit glanced up, a puzzled look on his face for a moment before it broke into an approximation of a smile.

'Captain! Good to see you.' He stood and gestured for Soren to sit by the fire. There was none of the formality that would be expected in any of the other regiments. Soren sat and looked around. He didn't recognise the other men.

'How many are there in the regiment now?'

'A little more than two hundred. We were having a hard time of it out here before the army arrived,' said Smit. 'Not long after you left, there was another surge of activity and it cost us dear every time we drove the war parties back. Of the few of us that survived Faraway, I'm the only one left, and you now too.'

'I'm sorry it's been so hard,' said Soren, trying to be considerate.

'Well, with luck this army will put an end to it. The barbarian army is camped over yonder.' He gestured out into the darkness.

'We came upon them the day before yesterday and have been sat here ever since.'

'A full army?' said Soren. The barbarians never formed war parties larger than a few hundred men, and even parties that large were a thing of recent times. 'How many?'

'Don't know, sir, but it's a full army all right. Some of our lads have been scouting. They said it was more barbarians than they had ever seen before, ten times over. None of them seem to be able to come up with an exact number though. Every time they come back from a mission, they seem to be a bit confused. It's odd; they're good, steady lads. Makes me think back to that strange wind that blew up before Faraway and that bloody shaman.

'It has the officers in a right state though. They won't order an attack until they've a better idea of what we're dealing with. Don't know how much longer the lads will be able to stick just sitting here waiting though.

'At any rate, you've had a long journey. I 'spect you've a mind to get your head down. I'll show you where you can bed down for the night,' said Smit.

The journey had been fuelled by his excitement at getting back to the front, but now that he had reached his destination the energy had fizzled out quickly and he could think of nothing more attractive than a warm blanket.

———◆◈◆———

He woke with a start. Pulled from a deep sleep it took him some time to remember where he was, and a few moments more to take in his surroundings. His brain still echoed with the dream he had been dragged from. He had dreamt of Alessandra, in a world where everything had gone right for them. It was the type of dream he did not want to wake from and he was left with a profound sense of loss and disappointment as reality replaced imagination. He found it difficult to think of his last conversation with her, but he found there was often little else on his mind, other than perhaps

Amero. Those thoughts brought the intense anger he felt over the way Amero had used him and Alessandra both, to suit himself with no consideration for them.

A voice had woken him, distant but still loud. He had to concentrate to make out what was being said, but he quickly realised that the shouting was in the barbarian language. He dressed quickly and left the tent. Smit and a few others were sitting around a recently re-lit fire, drinking from steaming mugs and chatting in muted tones.

'Good morning, sir!' said Smit. 'Care for some coffee?'

'What's all that racket?' asked Soren, ignoring the offer of coffee.

'That's the giant. He's been doing that every morning since we arrived. He walks over, just beyond arrow shot, and shouts abuse at us like that. He keeps it up for an hour or two and then heads home. A few of us thought about going over to shut him up, but he's bloody massive and the order was given that no one's to go near him.'

'Oh. I might go and have a look then,' Soren said absently.

He walked through the camp at a relaxed pace, his mind already set on a course of action. All around him he could see the effect that the barbarian's taunts had on morale. Men visibly cringed with each new outburst, a mixture of shame at their inaction and fear. There could be no doubt that they believed that when the battle was finally underway, many of them would meet their end on the enormous barbarian's axe. By the time he reached the camp's pickets, the guards were engrossed in a completely irrelevant argument, grabbing onto anything to take their minds from the gigantic barbarian. He was several paces past them before they even noticed that he had gone by. One of them called out to him, but Soren dismissed him with a wave. He couldn't explain why he was doing what he was doing, other than it was something to occupy his mind for a little while, to distract him from his thoughts of Alessandra.

He had covered about half the distance between the camp and the barbarian before the barbarian noticed him. He continued shouting, but now instead of addressing the camp generally, his insults were hurled directly at Soren. Soren continued to walk toward him at a casual stroll, until he was almost within range of the gobs of spit flying from the barbarian's mouth. All the while he could feel an ever increasing tingling energy dancing across the surface of his skin.

The barbarian was truly huge. Soren was tall, but the barbarian was taller than him by more than a head. His blonde hair was long, dirty and matted, but his armour was clean and well maintained. So was the edge on the massive axe that he rested his hand on.

The content of the barbarian's ranting must have changed, as a large number of barbarians began to gather at the crest of the hill to watch. The giant turned to face his compatriots and shouted to them, gesturing to Soren. Whatever he said caused them to laugh, which rankled with Soren. He felt a flash of anger.

'Get on with it you stinking sack of shit. You know what I'm here for!' he said.

The barbarian turned back to look at him, and screamed something at Soren. His eyes bulged with manic fury and a deluge of spit flew from his mouth. In one quick movement he lifted his axe and swung it in a great arc at Soren. With his massive shoulders he hefted the axe as though it was weightless. Soren ducked and drew his sword. The barbarian swung the axe back with barely a pause, twisting the head so the blade was facing the direction of travel, which drew a great cheer from the barbarian onlookers. His bulk hid Soren's movement from the crowd. As he ducked and twisted out of the way of the axe, he whipped his sword across the giant's belly. The razor sharp blade parted the toughened leather armour as easily as it opened the guts underneath. The barbarian groaned in pain as his abdomen twisted with the momentum of the axe and opened the wound even farther. Soren stepped back and watched with grim satisfaction as the barbarian dropped to his knees and let go of his axe to try and hold his guts in his belly.

Soren braced himself for the wave of exhaustion that would follow. He had known from the tingling feeling on his skin that whatever forces affected his gift were strong.

The barbarian crowd had gone deadly silent, unsure of what had happened. Soren took the man's head from his shoulders with a quick stroke of his sword to clear up their confusion. Before it hit the ground he turned to walk back toward his own lines, hopeful that he would reach them before the Gift faded and the fatigue arrived.

What he saw when he had turned surprised him. The entire army had gathered at the pickets to watch the fight, but had remained silent the whole time as they were certain Soren would be killed. Now they were jubilant. The barbarian champion was dead and their morale spilled over. As a single body they spontaneously began to charge toward him, and toward the barbarians.

The barbarians, who were silenced by the death of their champion, began to murmur. Soren looked at them as their shock turned to confusion. Some of them were armed, while others were not. Some had not even bothered to don their armour to watch their champion kill a Duchy man. Now they were faced with the entire Duchy army charging across the field at them. Soren stood still as the body of men reached him and passed by, all eager for their own share of the glory that morning. Realising that they were in full attack, the barbarians began to turn and run back to their camp. Some were too stunned to move, and they were cut down where they stood. Soren watched as the Duchy troops disappeared over the hill and down into the barbarian camp.

A slaughter sounds very differently to a battle, and it was most definitely a slaughter that Soren could hear. Spirals of dark smoke started to rise up into the air. A group of finely uniformed horsemen galloped up to Soren. A portly man with grey hair in a doublet liberally embroidered with gold thread pushed to the front.

'What is going on here, Captain?' he said.

'I believe the barbarian army is being routed, my Lord Colonel,' said Soren.

The colonel of cavalry looked at the large headless corpse on the ground behind Soren.

'Fine work,' he said, before spurring his horse to a gallop toward the barbarian camp with his aides and adjutants following hotly after him.

Chapter 41

AN UNWANTED HERO

It was late in the evening before the Duchy army was brought back to any semblance of order. Soren had spent the afternoon half-heartedly looking around the remains of the barbarian camp for any booty that was worth having. A few coins and rings were all he had found, but they would fetch a few florins that just about made the effort worthwhile. There were too many greedy hands to make a fortune on the battlefield though. He had returned to his tent as the afternoon dimmed into evening to see how many of the old frontier regiment had survived the carnage. They straggled in over the course of the early evening. Most made it back. It seemed that Duchy casualties had been remarkably light. An adjutant arrived shortly after with a summons to see the General.

He knew the way to the General's tent, but the adjutant led him there nonetheless, keen, it seemed, to ensure that he arrived. He was bustled into the tent, through the antechamber he had been in before, into a separate room at the back.

'Banneret Captain Soren, sir!' said the adjutant.

'Thank you, Lieutenant. You may go,' said the General. He looked up from his papers and turned one of the lamps to cast more light on Soren. He studied Soren for a moment before speaking.

'It was a nice piece of work today, killing that barbarian. I expect you are here anticipating some sort of reward or decoration, but I'm afraid that isn't the case. I gave express orders that no one was to fight that man. His morning rants may have been bad for morale, but not half so bad as my entire army watching one of their officers being butchered. You were lucky and the result was good for us, but if you were killed it could quite easily have been this camp that was a looted and burnt wreck,' he said.

Soren felt his confident bluster fade to apprehension.

'Now I have to decide what to do with you, my lad.' He leaned back in his chair and laced his fingers in front of his face.

Soren opened his mouth, but was cut short.

'I didn't tell you to speak!' said the General, raising his voice and showing an undertone of anger for the first time. 'On one hand you have disobeyed an order and placed my entire army in jeopardy. On the other, you are the man that killed the barbarian champion and that rallied my demoralized army to victory. My reports will inevitably have to make more of the latter than the former, and you will no doubt win some recognition for your "heroism". I understand that you have already had a taste of fame at Fort Faraway. It occurs to me that perhaps you are a whore for fame, but no matter.' His words had become more of a stream of consciousness than a lecture. 'Needless to say I am displeased with you, but your actions have made it impossible for me to censure you in the way that I would wish. So instead I have to come up with something else, which is exactly what I've done.

'We've learned a surprising number of things in the past few hours. Members of the Intelligenciers have been interviewing prisoners all afternoon and continue to do so as we speak. They have come upon an answer for the barbarian invasions. It seems that a new cabal of shamans have taken power in the barbarian lands, and their magic has allowed them to unite the tribes. Not all of the tribes are happy with this, or happy with contributing troops and supplies to this shaman's army. They're just too afraid of him to do anything about it. We have corroborated intelligence that suggests if the head shaman were to be killed, the tribes would fragment and once again be reduced to seasonal raiding and be little more than an irritation.' He paused again and studied Soren, waiting for him to take the hint before continuing. 'I understand you have some experience dealing with the barbarians,' said General Kastor.

'Yes, sir, I spent the past season with the Legion,' replied Soren.

'And in this time did you manage to learn any of the barbarian tongue?'

'A little, sir,' said Soren. 'But no more than to ask a few basic questions.'

'It's a shame that you don't have more, but I'm sure what you have will come in useful. When you are in the barbarian city that is. I have had my adjutant prepare some maps that should allow you to find it without any difficulty. I want you to infiltrate the city, find this shaman, and kill him. If you succeed you will have performed a valuable service for the Duchy. If you fail you will be dead and will have learned an important lesson in hubris.'

'The latter seems more likely than the former,' said Soren, knowing that he really didn't have any choice in the matter.

'It does, but such is the price for patriotic service sometimes. See my adjutant on the way out to get your instructions and official orders.'

Once Soren had gone, General Kastor took one last look at the letter that he had received only the day before. The letter had been sealed with wax that bore no marking, which meant only one thing to the General. It had warned him of the coming of a young officer and requested that he did everything in his power to ensure that the officer did not return to the city. Satisfied that he had sent Soren to his death, he held the letter over the flame of his candle until it caught light and did not drop it onto the drip tray of the candle holder until it had burned all the way to his fingers. It would be a nice bonus if he actually managed to kill the shaman, he thought.

Navigating across the featureless plain was second nature to Soren after the time he had already spent in the east. The summer he had spent there had largely been about not getting lost and he had been reasonably successful at it. He did not hurry, although he was very eager for the whole experience to be done with one way or the other.

On horseback he quickly began to catch up with the small groups of barbarians who were struggling to make their way back north. He gave them a wide berth. He was not concerned about being discovered, but he suspected that his horse would make him an attractive target for a robbery, which was a complication that he did not need.

It took four days to reach the barbarian city, which was not at all what he had expected. Instead of a mud smeared wattle fence surrounding a shanty of thatched roofs, there was a proper stone wall, and tiled roofs. The wall was not nearly as tall as those surrounding any of the cities in the Duchy, but it was solidly built and well maintained and more than enough to provide an obstacle to an attacker without heavy siege equipment. It was nestled at the foot of a hill with a river running along its western wall. From his distant vantage point Soren could see that there was a steady passage of traffic in and out of the main gate, and there was little in the way of security. It was likely that nearly all of the men of fighting age had been with the army that had been defeated.

As he surveyed the city, his eyes stung from lack of sleep. He had trouble sleeping on the way north and the result was that his fatigue had built to a point where he was beginning to be concerned that it might become a problem. Nonetheless he wanted to get the job over with as quickly as possible. The longer he stayed in or near the city, the more likely he was to be engaged in conversation. Despite having a very basic grasp of their language, he had no desire to be caught out over that. He got rid of his horse a short distance away and then made his way toward the city gates on foot.

Soren watched and waited for a larger group to accumulate at the gate before attempting to enter the city. The barbarian clothes he wore and the days of travel lent him enough of a disguise to appear no different to any of the other survivors who were arriving in dribs and drabs. The inside of the city proved as much a surprise as the outside. He didn't really know what he had truly expected, but he imagined something along the lines of a poor Duchy farming village but on a much larger scale. Here things were very different. Instead of the mud streets covered with pot-holes and filth, there was a wooden boardwalk raised above the level of the ground. Most of the buildings were of stone, and many had slate roofs, although there were some that were thatched. The stereotypical barbarians that Soren had expected were present in large numbers, roughly dressed, with long hair and beards. There was another class though, in finer clothes, wearing valuable gold jewellery and who looked well washed. They even gave Soren a wide berth, treating him with the contempt a citizen of the Duchy might show a barbarian. He allowed himself a private smile as he walked deeper into the city.

It was not as large as Ostenheim, but no city was in his experience. Even Brixen had been smaller. Despite this, its population must have numbered into the tens of thousands, far more than he had expected. After a little while he entered a large open area that was paved with irregularly shaped stones. It contained a large number of bedraggled looking men, either beggars, or more likely survivors from the army with nowhere else to go, as well as others who were passing briskly through. The bedraggled men huddled in groups around the square, some sleeping and some sitting sombrely with no purpose. Soren fitted in well with them. He sat down a short distance from one such group and put his head down on the ground. He was exhausted and despite the circumstances, no sooner than it touched the cold, wet stone, he was asleep.

It was dark when he awoke. There were many small fires scattered across the square. Although it was hard to tell in the darkness, it seemed that there were more men on the square than there had been when he had arrived. They sat around their fires in small groups, huddled around its meagre warmth. Soren took a few moments to take in his surroundings. No one took any notice of him. He was just one of many new faces there, not particularly welcome, and completely ignored.

His first task was to discover where the shaman was. A rough description of the temple he based himself in had been elicited from the prisoners. The most straightforward thing to do seemed to be to walk around until he found a building that fit the description. He also wondered if he would be able to feel an increasing energy when he got closer, as he had the previous times he had been near a shaman. The Intelligenciers told him that the shaman never left this building other than to preside over religious ceremonies.

The biggest danger to him was that someone would try to engage him in conversation. The more he thought about the whole situation, the more convinced he became that the General did not expect him to return. He certainly didn't seem to care one way or the other. Soren was determined to kill the shaman and then to disappear. He had no intention of dying here.

It was cold and he didn't feel like sleeping any longer, so he began his search through the streets of the barbarian city. He felt a growing excitement inside, the danger and thrill of his mission were almost intoxicating and he felt himself eagerly anticipating the kill.

The building was not hard to find, but he hadn't expected that it would be. It had been remarkably well described, and the energy that ran through him as he drew near was unmistakable, just as he had hoped would be the case.

He walked past it as innocuously as possible, taking in as much detail as he could and then circled around behind it. He had determined to carry out his task immediately. He had no desire to remain in the city any longer than he had to as the chances of being discovered grew with each minute he spent there. Neither had he any desire to spend another night on the street. It brought back too many unpleasant memories, and he could not rent a room in an inn because he could not speak the language well enough.

After an hour or so of observing the building from various vantage points, it was clear to him that as with the walls of the city, security was lax. There were a few armed men about, but they were inattentive and appeared bored. They weren't expecting problems. Why would they?

Chapter 42

THE LURE OF POWER

He shambled up to the main entrance of the building. The guard took his time in noticing him. It was dark and either very late or very early in the day, so Soren did not expect him to be overly alert. He barked something at Soren in barbarian, the meaning of which was obvious enough. As he got closer, the man reached out and shoved him. Soren cut his throat with a quick slash of his dagger and shoved the body back into the darkness of the doorway. Now came the difficult part. The building was large and he had no idea where the shaman would be. It had occurred to him in a fleeting moment on the journey north that the easiest thing would be to move methodically through the building as quietly as possible, killing everyone he came across, but that seemed both excessive and to invite disaster. He would have to employ stealth and hope he could find and eliminate his target quietly.

The doorway led through to a large high ceilinged hall with the sharp taste of smoke in the air. It was empty other than for furniture, with several doors leading out of it. At the far end of the hall there was a raised wooden platform with a wood and leather chair on it, what seemed to be a throne of some sort. There was a door behind the platform, which Soren approached. He pressed his ear to its surface and listened carefully, trying to quiet his own breathing. When he was satisfied that there were no sounds coming from behind it, he gently opened it. The short corridor behind it was dark and led to a stairwell. It grew darker as he went, forcing him to slow his pace to a hesitant crawl. He had to reach out with a hand to feel for the steps in front of him as the inky darkness seemed to grow thicker. He would have loved a mage lamp, but the darkness was as much his ally as it was his enemy.

The steps led up to a passageway that was faintly lit by moonlight entering from unseen windows recessed into the thick walls on one side. Doors lined the other side of the passageway, which terminated in a large double door at its far end. From the layout of the floor below he reckoned on there being either a large room or a continuation of the corridor on the other side, so this was where he determined to try first. He slipped down the passageway as quietly as he could and once again pressed his ear to the door. There was sound coming from the other side, low and muffled. It was impossible to tell how far from the door its source was, or how many people were making it. He took his dagger in his left hand and drew his sword before grasping the door handle with a free finger and turning it slowly, his heart on edge as he prayed for it to turn silently. His prayers were answered as the well-oiled mechanism turned without sound and the pressure of the door against his shoulder released as it inched open.

To his relief it was also dark on the other side of the door. Every grain of his being jumped into life. Energy flooded over him as though a gust of cold wind had blown through the opened door. He felt light headed for a moment and had to take a deep breath to steady himself. He had to fight back a brief feeling of nausea before continuing. He slipped through the doorway and quickly saw the source of the sound.

The shaman had his back to him, kneeling on a large bed in the centre of the room. It was dark, but Soren was able to make out his naked shoulders, and the legs of the woman that were wrapped around him. The room was silent but for the sound of his deep breaths and her shallow moans. Soren's heart was racing as he approached. He was not going to take any chances, so he struck quickly with his dagger, plunging it into the man's back, between his ribs and into his heart. He pulled the blade free with a twist and felt blood spill over his hand. The man gasped slightly but uttered no other sound. He tried to turn to see his attacker, but shock had taken him and he tumbled sideways from the bed.

With the man out of the way his eyes met those of the woman. She appeared a little older then he had expected, but was undeniably attractive. What really caught his attention were the markings all over her body. Dark blue swirls and symbols snaked over her pale flesh, covering her slender body from head to toe. In the darkness, they seemed to twist and writhe on her flesh. It was then that Soren became aware that there was no interruption in the energy around him. Could he have been wrong about the shaman being the source of the odd feeling he had experienced each time he had encountered one? No. It was her, not the man. She looked at him with a lustful and challenging stare. She parted her legs further and touched her upper lip with the tip of her tongue. Soren could feel his hands begin to shake, not just with the arousal of the beautiful, naked body in front of him, but with the intoxicating and inebriating effect of the energy that swirled around him and through him, like the woman's tattoos, which almost seemed to be alive on her skin.

He felt strong, like he could run a hundred miles and tear a city's walls down with his bare hands. He focussed hard to resist the embrace of the Moment. He felt as though he was being pushed toward it by an unstoppable force, but he also desired it on some fundamental level despite his reason dictating that he resist with all his will. He knew that to allow himself to slip into the Moment now could mean his death. On both of the previous occasions, he had fallen unconscious as soon as it had ended. If that were to happen here, it would mean capture, most likely torture and then execution. He had to fight to stay in control and to prevent himself from going from the Gift into the Moment.

The temptations on offer threatened to overwhelm his senses. He wanted her more than he had ever wanted a woman. More than even Alessandra, who now seemed worthless. It was primal and fundamental desire. Her mouth twisted slightly, the corners turning up in a triumphant and anticipatory smile. With constant access to her energy he would be undefeatable. In an instant he knew that with her at his side he could conquer an army, could conquer the world. He felt that without her he would not be able to go on, not even for another moment. She reached down between her legs with one hand and beckoned him toward her with the other. She said something that he did not understand, but her voice was low, husky and filled with lust. He felt his heart race and his resolve seeping away. All he could think of was the power, and what it would feel like to be between her legs. As though he had tasted of it before, he knew that the pleasure would be exquisite. The joys of dream seed would be but a passing fancy compared to the ecstasy of a moment with her.

Like a glass dropped on the pavement, the spell was smashed in an instant. He didn't know how or why, but suddenly he was free of her and she knew it. The lust and seduction left her eyes and were replaced with surprise.

He took her throat out with a flick of his sword. She gagged loudly, and grasped her throat with both hands, blood, dark and oily streaming from between her fingers. Soren felt as though some-one who had been holding him up, weightless, had just dropped him. In an hour or two he knew he would be too exhausted to move. He ran her through the chest to be sure the job was done, turned and began to run.

The kill had been quiet enough to get out of the building with-out incident. It was still dark, but dawn could not be far off, and the bodies would surely be discovered at daybreak, if not sooner. He also expected that there must have been others who would be sensitive to the disruption in the power that had been emanating from her as he had been. His sole concern was to get as far from the city as he could before the discovery was made and the fatigue became too much for him to bear.

<hr/>

The sun was making its presence known but still below the western horizon when he felt that he could go no further. The sky was a pale blue and its serenity distracted him momentarily from the pain. He felt as though he had not slept in a year. Every single one of his muscles burned as though they had been doused in pitch and set alight. He could only dream of the sweet relief of being back in her presence, of how she could have made him feel. He cursed himself for having killed her; forsaking the joy he could have known had he let her live. Then, despite the brightening of the sky, he collapsed to the ground, unable to go any further.

Chapter 43

THE REWARD OF FOLLY

It was daylight when he woke. The sun was high in the sky and he felt confused and disorientated. He had no idea how long he had been asleep, but he felt even worse than before, if such were possible. His lips were dry and cracked, and it felt like his tongue was stuck to the back of his throat when he tried to swallow. The skin on his face felt tight and sore to the touch. It seemed he had been lying there for some time. It took a moment for him to recall what brought him to be there and he sat up with a start.

The plains seemed almost endless from where he was, the horizon disappearing into the haze. He looked around but could see no sign of the barbarian city and was pleased that he had managed to put in so much distance before collapsing. He had no idea where he was, and he had no idea if he was being hunted, but it stood to reason that if he hadn't been found while he was asleep, then it was likely that he was out of harm's way. Perhaps the barbarians had been telling the truth when they said they were as eager for the shaman's death as anyone. The thought of the shaman made his heart jump. The temptation of the power she had presented still sent a shudder through his body. For the first time he could empathise with the dream seed addicts that wandered around the streets of Ostenheim. At least he had managed to destroy the source of his temptation.

He got to his feet and could feel every muscle in his body protest. The bottom of his feet stung when he put weight on them, and he could not remember ever having felt quite this bad. Clearly the years of good living had made him soft, he thought, which made him laugh painfully. He looked up to the sun and tried to take a rough bearing from it. It was high, which made it difficult to be sure, but he satisfied himself that south was where he thought it was and headed in that direction.

As he walked he began to chastise himself about the way in which he had carried out his mission. He had been in such a rush to carry it out he hadn't given proper thought to what would come after, and how best to make his escape. He had no water, and no idea of where to get any. It was likely that he would not get any until he re-joined the army, if he actually managed to find them again, an eventuality he was beginning to doubt.

Seconds stretched to minutes and minutes stretched to hours as he walked, ever more slowly. His throat was so dry that he could not swallow any more, and his tongue felt as though it had doubled in size. His eyes itched and burned at the same time, but when he rubbed them the burning doubled and his vision blurred. His lips cracked when he smiled at the thought that this was all down to his own stupidity. Instead of taking his time and planning properly, he had succumbed to his own arrogance. Now he was going to die of thirst on the endless dusty plains. It would be a foolish death for a deserving fool.

He walked until he collapsed with exhaustion that night, and was amazed when he awoke the next day. How he had survived through the cold of the night was anyone's guess, but he had, so he struggled to his feet and continued to walk. At this point he didn't even know where he was going, but walking seemed better than just lying down on the featureless plain and waiting for death to come.

The sun was beginning to sink toward the horizon when he spotted a short, stunted tree in the distance. It was the only feature on the otherwise barren plain, so for no reason other than that, he walked toward it. It took him some time to get there, shambling along with barely enough energy to lift his feet. When he did, he slumped to the ground and shuffled under its meagre shade. It was as good a place as any to die.

As he leaned back against the gnarled trunk he watched the leaves moving gently in the breeze. Where their edges touched the sky, there was the faintest of blue tinges. It was strange, yet familiar. A trick of the light he thought, or perhaps he was hallucinating. He let his mind drift. He thought of the snowy north. He had liked the peacefulness of the snow-blanketed woods. It would have been nice to see them again. He thought of Alys and of the belek. He wondered what she was doing now. It was a shame he had never had the opportunity to wear his cloak. It was just too damned warm in the south for the heavy fur. He thought of Alessandra, and the way he had reacted when he found out what she had become. He wished more than anything that he had apologised for the way he behaved before he had left, but there was nothing that could be done about that now. The thought caused him pain, but what she had become caused him more. And Amero. He had caused it all. He didn't even want to think of him.

His rambling train of thought came to an abrupt halt. His mind suddenly felt clearer. Where for so many hours there had been only a disorientated stream of consciousness and a primal desire to survive, there was now focus. He didn't feel quite as tired as he had. His eyes flicked to the leaves as his mind demanded an answer to his sudden feeling of wellbeing. The blue tinge was still there, but his eyes were no longer foggy and ranging in and out of focus. His sight was sharp once more and the tinge was, if anything, even clearer. He reached out with his hand to touch it and felt the faintest, almost imperceptible tingle at his fingertips. Warmth spread through his hand, which had been numb with cold the second before. The tinge fluctuated ever so slightly, and understanding came to him like a light being turned on in a darkened room.

As the clarity continued to return to his train of thought, he could recall the times that he had seen the blue glow before, the belek standing out foremost in his mind. He considered that to have been the first time he had experienced the Moment. He had noticed the glow just before he had entered it and now it seemed that he could see it again. He had discounted it on those previous occasions as a figment of his imagination, and perhaps this time it was also, but unlike the previous times, it was not a fleeting glimpse; the glow remained.

The warmth it had bestowed on his cold, tired fingers continued to spread down his arm toward his shoulder. He looked elsewhere for the blue glow, but the tree was the only feature for miles
around and he could not see anything on the short, scrubby grass
that covered the plains.

He toyed with the glow, which stuck to his finger as he slowly
drew it away from the leaf until it stretched and pulled away as
though it was syrup. His head felt so much clearer that he was sure
he was not imagining it. The tingle was unmistakeable and the
glow did not go away, it was definitely there. What was more, there
could be little doubt in his mind that it was responsible for, or at
least connected to, his increasing feeling of well being. Considering that he had seen the blue glow prior to entering the Moment
on previous occasions, did that also mean that it was responsible
for causing the Moment? Was this blue glow the manifestation of
the energy that caused the Gift of Grace, that fuelled the Moment?

He thought over what he knew of the history of the old bannerets, but there was so little that was of any use to him now. The
old stories and legends had made them out to have exceptional
speed and strength that allowed them to achieve feats far beyond
those of a normal man. He would have discounted the stories as
nothing more than fairy tales were it not for Master Dornish having lent them credence when he suggested that Soren too might
have these exceptional abilities. Now they started to make sense. If
this blue glow was indeed an energy source that he could draw on
to enhance his speed and strength, then perhaps they were true.

He did not know enough about what the Gift of Grace was, nor
how it had come about to work out how it related to the energy,
but it made sense that the Gift was what had allowed the early
bannerets to make use of this energy. The Order of the Bannerets had been created by the mages, an elite bodyguard to protect
them, presumably in times of vulnerability, although the reason
was never mentioned in any of the histories he had read. So much
of the documentation had been destroyed or lost to the passage of
time; perhaps it would never be known.

Once bestowed with the Gift, the bannerets could experience
the Moment, but that was all either he, or seemingly also Master

Dornish could find out about it. To Soren, it seemed he was influenced by the Gift almost all the time, although it did wax and wane in intensity. Then there was the Moment, which it seemed allowed him to push beyond all physical limitations.

One glaring question remained. If it was the mages that bestowed the original bannerets with their ability, the Gift of Grace, how did he come by it? There were no mages left; they had been wiped out in the Mage Wars centuries before. The practice of magic had been illegal and mercilessly rooted out ever since. To his knowledge there was no one alive in Ostia, or any of the other states of the Middle Sea, who could perform anything more than a parlour trick. There had been the shaman of course, but he had experienced the Moment before ever coming into contact with them. Indeed, when he thought on it, he had been exhibiting signs of the Gift since his late teens.

The mages, their society had been known as the College of Mages, had grown arrogant and drunk on power. They had thought themselves beyond the laws of men and had delved into ever darker magics as, in their megalomania, they sought out more power. Eventually their dark acts became too much to bear and the Empire, and even their own bodyguards, the bannerets, turned on them. The wars lasted for years, but in the end the mages were defeated and any survivors were hunted to extinction, by the bannerets.

With the mages gone, there was no longer anyone to imbue future bannerets with the Gift of Grace. They, like their former masters, were gone from the world in only a generation. There was an irony in that, Soren thought. The concept of bannerets continued however, until the present day, but those with the right to bear their own banner no longer had any skills beyond those earned through countless hours of training. That was until Soren, it seemed.

It appeared that the Gift of Grace had been simmering away in the background without Soren ever really noticing it until he had started to look for something out of the ordinary. Now that his body was being pushed to the very brink of survival, the Gift was taking a more prominent role to ensure that he did not die. All the parts of his mind that dealt with it subconsciously were being opened to him. It was the only explanation that he could come to. Did it mean that he would see this blue glow everywhere the energy existed from now on? Where did the energy come from and where else did it gather? There were so many more questions that Soren had, but on his limited information and his only limited experience, they would have to remain unanswered, at least for the time being.

While he still felt hungry and thirsty, his body felt stronger, no longer on the verge of failing. Now that he was presented with the energy right in front of him, it seemed like a good opportunity to experiment with it. He needed to know if the Moment was something that would happen of its own accord, or if he would be able to influence its coming. He already reckoned that he could stave it off through will alone, he had discovered as much when he killed the shaman. Could he likewise bring it on?

He focussed his mind on the blue glow, willing it into himself. He felt a flush of warmth across his body, but neither the sensation of the Gift gaining in strength, nor the Moment. Perhaps there was not enough energy here, gathered around that lonely little tree. Perhaps this simply wasn't the way to do it. He tried once more, but the result was the same. He did, however, feel a little stronger.

He sat under the tree for some time, allowing his body to recuperate further. Despite feeling better than he had, he was still desperately thirsty and his stomach felt as though it was twisting itself into knots. As he sat there he continued to try to reason out the aspects of his gift. It did not appear that he was drawing energy from the tree, merely from around it. Perhaps the energy gathered where there were living things. Perhaps it leaked out of those living things and accumulated around it. It was purely speculation, but it seemed to make sense. He looked at his hand. There too was the faintest of blue tinges. How had he never noticed this before? He pulled back his sleeve. All of his bare skin had it.

It was clear now that despite his expectations, he was not going to die under that tree. The energy was giving him strength and in spite of his hunger and thirst, it was enough for him to carry on.

He got up, and began to walk.

Chapter 44

AN UNEXPECTED FACE

His mind was so full of thoughts that time passed quickly as he continued his trek home. He was hungry and thirsty all of the time, almost to the point of mania, but it didn't seem to have any serious negative effect on him. His clothes were looser on him, but it was clear to him at this point that he was not going to starve. He could absorb enough energy to keep him alive.

Finally he found a river. After sating his thirst, he began to follow it downstream. He had not gone more than twenty paces before he vomited up the water he had just drunk. After so long without anything to eat or drink, he had gorged himself and paid the penalty. He drank again, this time a more measured amount, and then continued on his way.

Eventually he came upon a village. The guards gave him inquiring and not entirely friendly looks. He was still wearing his barbarian's garb and combined with many days of rough living, he was quite certain that he did not look like the type of person a sleepy rural village would want visiting.

He went to the magistracy, and after some effort, convinced the guards and the magistrate's clerk to allow him an audience with the resident magistrate. A great deal more convincing was needed to make the magistrate believe that Soren was in fact an officer of the Duchy, but eventually his accent, manners, and rhetoric was enough to win the magistrate over. He agreed to allow Soren free passage on the next carriage back to Ostenheim, and board and lodging until it left.

When he arrived in Ostenheim many days later, he looked little better than he had when he arrived at the village. The magistrate's generosity had extended only so far, and Soren was still wearing the same barbarian clothing he had worn since starting his mission.

He wasn't really sure what to do initially. He was no longer a student at the Academy and for the first time it struck him that he was in fact homeless once again. After wandering for a little while trying to work out what to do next, he decided to head to the city barracks. It had occurred to him that he should report in to be debriefed. It amused him to think of how surprised the General would be when he turned up. On his wanderings he discovered from overheard street gossip that General Kastor and his army had returned a week previously to great acclaim. It appeared the tribes had turned on themselves after their defeat on the plains and their leader had been killed. Their coalition had disintegrated and as such they were not expected to be more than a minor annoyance during the raiding seasons once again.

After convincing the sentries that he was a banneret and an officer, something he seemed to be doing a lot of, one of them reluctantly agreed to escort him into the barracks. He reported to the officer of the day who did not know what to do with him. He sent an orderly away with a note and told Soren to sit and wait. Sitting in the dim light he realised how tired he was. He drifted in and out of sleep jolting himself awake each time he felt his head dropping. He spotted the orderly whispering to the officer of the day. He had completely missed him coming back into the room. The officer of the day cleared his throat.

'Banneret Captain, General Kastor will see you now. The orderly will take you to his offices,' he said, visibly disdainful of Soren's appearance.

Soren followed the orderly up several flights of stairs and through a labyrinth of corridors before finally reaching the General's offices, a route that did not seem to be the most direct. He was whisked through the anteroom by the adjutant into the General's office. It was spacious and luxurious as was befitting the current hero of the Duchy. The General sat on the opposite side of his desk, framed by a large window that opened out onto a balcony overlooking the city. He was in his shirtsleeves with his dress doublet sitting on a stand beside his desk.

'Well, you look a sorry state. I must admit that yours is a face I did not expect to see again. I got word that you had carried out your mission, but then my agents lost track of you. When you didn't re-join the army, I assumed you were rotting somewhere out on the plains!' he said.

'Happily not the case, General,' Soren replied.

'So I see. Well, to business then. Thinking you were dead, the death of the barbarian shaman had a bit of spin put on it. It was thought it would be better for morale in the city if the people thought the barbarians had turned on each other after their catastrophic defeat and are no longer a threat, which is pretty much the case now anyway. So, you won't get any credit for that I'm afraid. You'll be rewarded of course, I promised you that. You'll be given the Duke's Cross for slaying the barbarian champion, so count yourself lucky.'

Soren's eyes flitted over to the General's doublet where a Duke's Cross sat amongst a host of other awards, including the Grand Cross. The red and white jewels on the Duke's Cross must have been worth a small fortune. If nothing else, he could sell it if he ever needed the money.

'We'll come up with something flattering for the official citation; you won't have to worry about that. I think that satisfies my part of the bargain.'

The adjutant returned to the office and handed the General a sealed envelope. He took it and rapped it against his knuckles and smiled.

'Your discharge papers. I had the adjutant prepare them when I heard you had returned. It's honourable of course,' he said, with an insincere smile.

This took Soren aback. Since his break with Amero, he had planned for a career in the military. It seemed to be his best chance for advancement. He had done everything that had been asked of him, and barring that one incident when he killed the barbarian champion, he had not done anything wrong. Why was he being discharged?

'Don't look so shocked, Banneret. You have your strengths and your uses, but they aren't best suited to the regular army. Now that you've returned, I'm confident that I can find a better use for your ability to kill and survive. Placing you outside of the army makes you all the more,' he paused for thought, 'flexible! There's trouble in the city, and that trouble sometimes needs dealing with outside of official channels.

'You'll be on half pay and officially on the reserve list. You can call yourself Captain, Banneret of the Duke's Cross, whatever you like. In the meantime, you can do as you choose. I shall call on you from time to time to take care of the things that need taking care of. Half pay will keep you alive, but not much more, so feel free to supplement your income. Low profile and not too illegal is preferable. By preferable I mean required.' He quickly spotted the look of indignation that appeared on Soren's face. 'Required if you wish to have any future in this city, or this entire Duchy, if you take my meaning.' He seemed satisfied with the look of resignation that replaced it. 'Good. Here are your papers. You will be contacted with details of your award ceremony. Any other questions?'

'Am I not already too well known for the kind of work you have in mind for me?' Soren asked. He was not entirely happy with being railroaded into being what he knew would be no more than an in-house assassin. It was not at all what he had hoped for, and certainly not how he saw himself spending his career.

The General let out an incredulous laugh. 'Come now, hero of Fort Faraway, slayer of the barbarian giant? I'd be surprised if more than a dozen people on the street even remember either of those events. The routing of the barbarian army was the talk of the town, as was I, for a few days, and perhaps we will continue to be spoken about with less frequency for a few more weeks to come and then something else will happen and this will all be relegated to a book of histories. Then there will be another battle or tragedy, and then another and so on. Heroes might live long in books, but they live short in the memories of the citizens, not many of whom can read. Such is the way of the world. I'm sorry if it shatters any illusions of fame and glory you may have held, but I assure you that you won't have any difficulties passing through the city unnoticed. Maintain a low profile from here on and it will be plain sailing. My adjutant will sign a chit for you to pick up your back pay from the commissary. So, until needs must I call on you again, fare well!'

After Soren left, the General called on his adjutant once more. As the lieutenant entered the room, the General finished sealing the note he had just written, in red wax but not with his own signet. He used only a flat, round shape to press down on the wax, devoid of any sigil, betraying no clue as to the author of the note.

'Deliver this to the Count of Amero,' he said. 'Personally.'

PART III

Chapter 45

AN ENTREPRENEUR, OF SORTS

W ith money in his pocket Soren's first order of business was to find somewhere to live. He had wanted to live in Highgarden ever since he had first been there. While grand mansions and parks dominated the area, there was a fashionable shopping district opposite the entrance to the Academy where many younger, single gentlemen kept apartments. It did not take Soren long to discover that they were far beyond his price range and he would need to be a little more humble in his choice of accommodation.

Oldtown would have been the next obvious choice but with Alessandra living there, he did not want to set foot beyond the walls of the old district. That ruled out the west of the city. Docks was where he had spent a great deal of his childhood and he had no desire to return to living there. The artisans' district on the east bank of the Eastway River was a bustling hive of activity with craftsmen and merchants plying their trades. Soren wanted somewhere a little quieter than that, which left one of the quarters around Crossways. The four quarters were named after the principle building that occupied them. The northeast was Cathedral, home to the eponymous building, among others. The southeast was Guilds, where the Great Guilds' Hall and most of the guild chapter houses were located. The southwest was Bankers, where the Great Exchange was situated, as well as the houses of the city's banks, moneylenders and counting houses. The northwest was Barons after the great domed Barons' Hall where the Council of Nobles met. Each quarter was also home to many of the city's inhabitants.

He felt that Barons was where he was most likely to find something that suited his requirements.

He had never rented a property before and he wasn't entirely sure of how to go about it. He walked around the quarters for a little while and soon became aware of signs advertising properties for rent. They were usually one floor of a building above a shop, although some of the buildings were purely apartments. He chose one in Barons that was above a bakery and across the street from a small tavern. The convenient access to prepared food was a prerequisite, as he did not know how to cook anything he would wish to eat.

The apartment was sparsely furnished, but it was more than adequate for Soren's needs. It was on the second floor of a six-storey terrace with a small metal balcony beneath three windows that looked down over the street. Access was by way of a doorway to the side of the bakery that led to a communal stairway up to each floor. The baker, whose family had been there for generations, owned the building. There were three rooms, a bedroom, a living area and a kitchen. The rent seemed reasonable to Soren, and his half pay would just cover it. Despite the tavern opposite the bakery, it was a quiet street and that suited Soren nicely. The back of the apartment overlooked a yard that was surrounded on all sides by the block of terraced buildings. It was accessed by three narrow alleyways and Soren was confident he could climb the back wall if needs be, which would give him the comfort of more than one way to get into his home, and also out of it. It also contained a small, fully functional water closet next to bedroom, which was a luxury he had not expected, but was glad of all the same.

With his rent covered he could put his mind to more material needs. He had his trunk sent over from storage at the Academy. What had filled his tiny room at the Academy was barely a drop in the ocean in his new apartment. All of his clothes took up a tiny portion of his closet and wardrobe. With the expanses of bare walls he could begin to understand why people wasted their money on art, but it still wasn't an extravagance he could afford to take.

The only extravagance he was willing to take was at the bottom of his trunk. It was the small cloth-wrapped block of Telastrian steel that Princess Alys had given to him. He picked it up and the heavy solid block was oddly comforting in his hands. He had no idea how much it would cost to convert it into a sword and dagger, but his back pay and the various bits of booty he had gathered up during his times in the east added up to a not inconsiderable sum. He also wanted to have to have his banner made up, but he had still not had time to think of a design. He would have to rely on the Emblazoners of Arms to suggest something appropriate.

He was enjoying being back in the city. Its sights, sounds and smells, while familiar to him seemed new and vibrant, but comforting at the same time. He walked briskly down the narrow streets to the Blackwater Road and turned left toward Crossways. He dodged his way through the crowds around the market stalls and continued on down Merchantsway to the artisans' district. In the Academy, all of the students talked of owning a sword made by one man. His name was Carlujko and his workshop was just off the Merchantsway, the road that ran east from the Crossways, through the city and then on toward the frontier. It was said that his swords were surpassed only by the legendary blade 'Adparatus', the sword of Saludor, the first emperor. It was to Carlujko's studio that Soren was headed.

Soren had not been sure what to expect, but he was a little surprised by the size of the workshop. It was far bigger than he would have thought. It was clearly a prosperous business, but that was hardly surprising considering Carlujko's reputation. Men came from all over the world to have a blade forged by him. He went inside to the reception room. A young man in a smith's apron sat behind a desk with a bored expression on his face. He became more alert when Soren entered the room.

'My name is Nicolo, smith's apprentice, sir. How may I help you?' he asked.

'I'd like to have a sword made,' replied Soren.

'Well then, you've come to the right place. If you'd like to take a seat I'll take your details, and put together a quote for you!'

Soren sat. 'I had hoped to speak with Master Carlujko.'

'Oh, I'm afraid that isn't possible. The Maestro is far too busy with his work,' said the apprentice.

'I very much wish to speak with him personally. Perhaps if you show him this, he might make himself available,' said Soren. He placed the wrapped block of steel on the table.

The young man looked at Soren quizzically and then, with a resigned look, he reached forward and opened the oilcloth wrapping. At first his face remained impassive, but when his eyes fell on the Ruripathian Royal Insignia, they widened with surprise.

'This is what you wish your sword to be forged from?' he asked. Soren nodded.

'I've never actually seen Telastrian steel of this grade before. I recognise the mark of course, but even the Maestro has only forged from this grade of Telastrian steel a handful of times. If you'd like to wait here, I shall see if I can interrupt him,' said the apprentice.

He quickly locked a drawer in his desk and disappeared through a curtained door. Soren smiled with satisfaction and crossed his hands on his lap. Small victories like this never failed to please him. He could hear the muffled sound of hammering from the back of the building stop. A few moments later a bald man, who appeared to be toward the end of middle age appeared through the doorway.

'I am Carlujko, may I ask to whom I have the pleasure of speaking?'

Soren stood but did not offer his hand. He was a banneret after all, and this man was only a tradesman, despite his skill and reputation. 'Banneret of the Duke's Cross Soren, Captain of the Duke's Legion of the Eastern March.'

'Welcome to my establishment, Banneret. Please sit,' said Carlujko. Soren did and Carlujko sat also, turning Soren's block of steel over in his hands.

'This is perhaps the finest piece of steel I have ever held. I realise I am prying, but I cannot help myself but ask how you came to possess it.'

'I was on a diplomatic mission to Ruripathia some time ago, the steel was a gift from the Royal Court,' said Soren.

'A generous gift indeed! I can tell you that from the size and weight of this block there is enough steel here to make both a sword and dagger blade of more or less the standard length. There is plenty of room for customisation though, taper, point of balance and so forth. If you have any preferences these can of course be accommodated. While I am always eager to have the opportunity to work on steel of this quality, I do require some latitude with the minutiae of the design. It is what gives my work its signature. If I were to follow my client's requests to the letter, it would be their blade, rather than mine, if you follow me.'

'I have no difficulty with that, Maestro, your reputation speaks for itself,' Soren replied.

'Excellent. Hilt design is all that remains to be discussed. Again I like to be able to make my own judgements in this regard, but I do like to agree on the general design with my client before beginning so as to ensure it will meet its functional requirements.' He reached to a small bookshelf behind the desk and withdrew a well worn folder full of sheets of loose paper.

'I have drawings here of my previous work, which you can go through for ideas. I am sure an experienced swordsman like you will have some of your own specific requirements and these of course can be accommodated. I would say this however. For a fighting weapon, the poorer the skill of the wielder, the more elaborate the hilt. For steel of this quality, I would suggest something austere but bold, beautiful but not ostentatious. I pride myself in being able to visualise what I like to consider the perfect match for each piece of steel,' said Carlujko, with infectious enthusiasm. He very clearly took great joy in what he did. He took a sheet of paper and a piece of charcoal from a drawer in the desk and began to sketch. It took only a moment for the image to take shape.

The pommel was disc shaped with rounded concave sides. A long slender cross guard that flared at the ends protected the handle. A knuckle guard curved back from the cross guard toward the pommel but stopped just short of touching it. The only concessions to artistry were the two curved arms that reached an inch up the blade and framed it with an ellipse, but even this afforded the hand extra protection. It was simple, but there was something elegantly beautiful about it. Carlujko sketched out half a dozen pictures of his idea from every angle. As he drew, he talked through his reasoning, and Soren knew this was the right man to make his sword.

'This is a true fighting design. Not too elaborate, but with just enough flair to make it an individual. I believe there will be enough steel to make the hilt. To pair the blade I have in mind with a hilt of any lesser metal would simply be a crime. Now, I'm sure you would like a quote. The steel is difficult to work, but the design is not so complicated. You'd be amazed how many people want hilts that cost ten times more than the blade!' He chuckled. 'The beauty of your sword is in its steel. I think five hundred crowns should cover it. That will buy you something your grandchildren and their grandchildren will wield with pride!'

Soren swallowed hard. He had been paid eighty crowns in back pay and he got thirty a month on half pay, but much of that was taken up by rent. He would need to find well paying work and fast.

'Ordinarily I have a waiting list of two years, but I honestly will not be able to restrain myself from working this steel for that long, so I will begin as soon as I have finished my current piece, which will only require another ten hours or so of work. I would expect your sword to require roughly two hundred hours of work, say six weeks from today to be on the safe side. I will require a ten per cent deposit.'

'Thank you, Maestro.' He counted out fifty crowns, almost the sum total of his wealth, and left them on the table.

'Very good, I shall see you in six weeks,' said Carlujko, with an anticipatory smile.

In one instant he had gone from being reasonably well off, to facing an impending debt if he wanted his sword. It was feasible for a swordsman to make that kind of money in six weeks, but a sword was a prerequisite, and needless to say he didn't have one. He had left the one he purchased before returning to the army in the east behind at the camp and had long since discarded the barbarian weapons he had used to kill the shaman.

He pondered the quandary all of the way to his apartment. When he arrived, there was a note waiting for him. It was sealed but there was no imprint on the red wax. It seemed the General did not intend to let him rest for long.

Chapter 46

CLOAK AND DAGGER

T he cloak and dagger aspect of the summons and the meeting seemed a little ridiculous at first. He always seemed to find it difficult to absorb the fact that he was living a life of importance, rather than just surviving on the street. He wondered if that would ever change.

He was not altogether happy at having been forced into a role as an assassin, even if it was in the service of the Duke, but now that General Kastor had discharged him from the army, a military career was no longer open to him. He could have refused Kastor; he had after all already undertaken one suicide mission. It seemed a little much to expect more from him, but he could not see any other viable options if he alienated the General and through him whomever of the Duke's court was assigned the responsibility of security and counter-espionage within the city. Too many doors would be closed to him if he did. Joining a family retinue was the only other alternative, but the opportunities were slim there also. No family associated with Amero would have anything to do with him. To any others, he would just be a blow in with no proven record of loyalty. He knew that Ranph would always employ him, but that would only serve to put him back in a situation where he was reliant on another's goodwill to earn his livelihood. He was determined that he would stand on his own two feet, and if being an assassin was the only way he could do that for the time being, then he was all right with that. Eventually, another opportunity would pass his way, but until that time, at least his work would be of importance in keeping the city secure from those powerful enough to cause serious unrest.

He was to meet his contact by the campanile of the Cathedral just off Crossways Square. The contact would identify himself to Soren and give him instructions. He left his apartment a little earlier than was necessary, and stopped at a pawnshop on one of the small streets off the Crossways. He bought a cheap but serviceable sword and dagger, probably an old army issue and certainly not a banneret's weapon, before continuing on to the Campanile. In keeping with the clandestine nature of the meeting he ensured that he arrived before the appointed time, and surveyed the location from all directions. It was probably a little pointless, but he felt inclined to do so nonetheless. He might as well start forming cautious habits early.

It was early evening and there were fair sized crowds moving past the Campanile. It had the usual bustle and noise of a busy city street and seemed as good a place as any for a meeting that did not desire undue attention. He approached the Campanile trying not to appear as though he was looking for someone. He felt a hand on his arm and warm breath against his neck.

'Abelard Contanto, Anton Spiro, Tanto dal Trevison. Repeat them to me. Quietly,' said an unfamiliar voice.

Soren repeated the list of names. He recognised each one of them. Abelard Contanto's name was one he was all too uncomfortably familiar with. He was known to be the leading figure in Ostenheim's underworld. He passed himself off as a wealthy merchant, but everyone knew what he really was. He was just too powerful to touch by legal means. A magistrate had launched a campaign to investigate him several years before, but had been found dead in a drug den not long after, seemingly of a self-administered overdose. The rumours were that his body was also badly bruised, not a side effect of the narcotic that killed him. He had also placed a two hundred crown bounty on Soren's head for the killing of his nephew, despite not knowing that it was Soren specifically. Killing Contanto would be as much a service to himself as to the General.

Grand Burgess Anton Spiro was the head of the Congress of Guilds. His presence was understandable. As figurehead of the guilds, he wielded considerable power and it was common knowledge that he had a poor working relationship with the Duke. On his word, all of the members of the various guilds in city would down tools. It was a vast amount of power for a commoner to wield.

Tanto dal Trevison was the head of one of the oldest noble families of Ostia. His grandfather had been Duke, which ruled him out of eligibility for the office but he remained an elector count and one of the wealthiest and most powerful men in the Duchy. He was also the First Lord of the Council of Nobles, a position of considerable influence, but one of inheritance rather than one of personal merit. His mind raced with the possibilities of conspiracies as he repeated the names.

'An account has been opened in your name in the Austorgas' Bank. There are fifty crowns in it for expenses. On confirmation of each successful completion, a further two hundred will be deposited. The task is to be completed by the Feast of Eilet.' With that the man disappeared into the crowd. Soren had not even seen his face.

He stood by the Campanile for some time unmoving, trying to assimilate the information he had been given and the task before him. Which should he go for first? His mind was racing, but he fought to keep a leash on it. His ordeal on the plains was still far too fresh in his mind to allow him to plunge in recklessly. Killing them would not be difficult. The only challenge for him would be getting away. All of the men were high profile, and all of them would have bodyguards.

He turned and walked back to Crossways and looked across it to the Guilds' Hall. Most of the guilds had smaller private houses scattered through the guild district, but they all contributed to this one, a majestic tribute to their wealth and power. Anton Spiro would be somewhere within. He would most likely keep a home in Highgarden, which Soren would need to find, as it might be a suitable location for Spiro's assassination. The Barons' Hall was to his right, but the council was not in session and would not be until after the Feast of Eilet. He would have to find dal Trevison elsewhere.

Abelard Contanto would be first. Despite Dornish's assurances and what the General had said to him about short memories, Soren had killed Contanto's nephew, and he could not dismiss the potential threat to him that existed so long as Contanto lived. With Contanto dead, this threat would be gone, and he would be able to move about without having to look over his shoulder ever again. He would need to move more quickly with this kill, as he didn't want to spend too much time hanging around places that he might be recognised. Perhaps he was being paranoid, but even still he was not willing to take the risk.

His overriding concern was not to cause too much of a mess. He was confident that he could deal with any number of guards, but slaughtering dozens of men to get to one target was far from ideal. The quieter the better, as it would allow him to get away cleanly to prepare for the next kill. Having to lie low for several weeks, or even worse, having to leave the city because the Watch were looking for him would be a disaster. There would have to be no witnesses.

As he expected Contanto was not difficult to locate. Soren spotted him for the first time walking down a street in Docks. He was chatting in friendly terms with some of the business owners as he passed. Most, if not all of them were paying as much protection as they could afford without it shutting down their business, yet they greeted him with a smile and a handshake. He had four men with him, all large and rough looking. They were something of a cliché, but Soren supposed that the mean look was as much of a deterrent as actual violence.

He followed them for an hour or so as Contanto continued his route before returning to a building beside a warehouse in Docks. He remained there for the rest of the day, which Soren spent on the rooftop of a small merchant's offices on the other side of the street. Boredom was his worst enemy as absolutely nothing of any interest happened. A few men came and went, most of them tough looking individuals, a few less so, some well dressed, others not so. He found himself trying to work out what each of them was in relation to Contanto's crime empire, but realised it was a distraction that might cause him to miss something of importance and tried to stop.

It was well after dark when Contanto left, escorted by a different group of goons. He lived in an older part of the city, that had once been the exclusive suburb of Oldtown, but now was on the fringes of Highgarden and would certainly not be considered to be part of it by the more elitist of citizens, but then again, neither would Contanto. It was a fine and solidly built house though with a pleasant garden and a very visible security presence. Soren didn't know if Contanto's family lived here with him, but if they did, it could create an unpleasant complication.

That night, Soren slipped into the building in Docks that Contanto had spent the day in. A roof window posed little challenge to his pry bar. Slowly and methodically, he worked his way around each floor, inspecting every room, corridor and closet as he built a map of the entire building in his head. The most obvious room to be Contanto's office was on the second floor. There was nothing else of any significance on that floor, just the office that occupied over half of its space and two small guardrooms, along with a corridor that ran along the front of the building, allowing access to those rooms and overlooking the street. There was a stairwell at either end of the corridor.

The office contained a large dark wooden desk and several comfortable leather chairs. The walls were lined with filing cabinets, filled with thousands of pages of numbers. There wasn't any ideal hiding place, but there were windows at the back through which he could effect his escape if necessary. He examined the desk more closely. There was generous space underneath it; just enough to hide in, but it still wasn't ideal. He did discover a small loaded crossbow tucked away there and a red pull cord. It disappeared down underneath the lush carpet, and Soren could barely contain the urge to pull on it to see what would happen. He expected that it was an alarm of some description. He had not encountered anyone in the building thus far, but he would have been surprised if there were no night watchmen lurking around somewhere. Probably asleep on the lower floor, although with Contanto's reputation, Soren didn't like their chances if they were caught sleeping on the job.

He continued his stalking of Contanto for several days until he was sure of the crime boss's routine. He was quickly learning that there was something about all men that when identified, made them easy to kill. Despite living a life under the constant threat of a violent death, even Contanto left gaps in his security. He was always heavily guarded, but he was a thug of the old school. He liked to be present when his rivals, or someone who had betrayed him was being beaten or killed. He liked to randomly inspect his gambling dens and brothels and even from time to time the legal businesses that his organisation extorted.

There would be many opportunities to get to him, but there was a balance to be found between ease of access and discretion. Contanto would be harder to get to quietly, but Soren found he was relishing the challenge. It might also mean a slightly higher death toll, but all of those men knew the job they were doing and whom they were working for; there would be no innocent blood spilled. So long as the numbers did not get out of control, too much attention should not be an issue. The death toll around Contanto would be less of a concern to the Watch due to the nature of the men he was killing. A crime den full of corpses would be less of a problem than a similarly filled mansion in Highgarden.

And so it was that Soren decided to kill Abelard Contanto in his office, his own sanctuary, his own fortress. It was as much a statement of his belief in his own ability as it was the most logical choice. Then he would slip into the warren of streets in Docks, hopefully to disappear.

Chapter 47

THE DANGEROUS AND THE POWERFUL

One of his brothels and two of his drug dens were reporting reduced takings. His first thought was always that someone was trying to take advantage of their position of trust. It was costly to replace the operator of one of his businesses, so he liked to be sure. Swift action was needed though, or it would send the wrong message to the other businesses. There was no such thing as a quiet life, he thought. They would have to be visited regularly to let them know that he was watching. If his suspicions were confirmed, the culprit would be dealt with harshly and held up as an example to dissuade others from similar behaviour.

He was always glad to get back to his office after his morning inspections. It was a cool sanctuary, sheltered from the heat and noise of the city, where he could be alone with his thoughts and make the decisions that would keep his empire running, and more importantly, him at its head. He closed the door with a click behind him and walked to the comfortable leather chair behind his desk. He sat and allowed his body to sink into the plush leather padding. He would never cease to appreciate the simple pleasures that life offered. As he sat looking idly out of the window with his back to the door, it clicked again. He swivelled his chair around to look at the door and instinctively slipped his hand beneath the desk and tugged on the alarm cord that was hidden there. There was a tall man standing where a moment before there had been nothing. He was draped in a dark hooded cloak that partially obscured his face. The hilts of the pair of blades at his waist were not obscured.

He surreptitiously tugged the cord one last time before moving his hand to the crossbow. 'I think it safe to assume you've killed my guards, so all that remains is to discuss what you want,' he said. His voice was sharp and assertive. Contanto had faced death many times before, but come out on top and he refused to be afraid of it.

The cloaked man remained silent.

'It's like that then.' He paused a moment and sighed. 'What did I do? Kill someone close to you? Put your family out of business?' He had tilted the gimballed crossbow and pointed it at the intruder. He intended to kill the man regardless, but he would like to know what had brought him here, and if there were more people that would need killing, to ensure that this irritating interruption was not repeated.

The front of his desk was false wood, being little more than a paper screen. He had spent hours firing bolts at targets all around his office, at first entirely in preparation for a situation such as this, then because he found it diverting and enjoyable. In a moment the bolt's deadly toxin would be coursing its way through the intruder's veins, but first he wanted to know why he was here. Still the man said nothing. It was disappointing, but that was often the way of things. The man reached to the hilt of his sword and began to draw it, the hood falling back from his face a little. He was young, younger than Contanto would have expected, but his eyes were old, old and hard. He had seen eyes like that before. The man meant to kill him and he would do it without hesitation or mercy.

They had toyed with one another for long enough. He clicked the hair trigger on the crossbow and was comforted by the thrum of the bowstring and the release of tension in the small weapon that accompanied it. His expectation was such that it took a split second to realise that there had not been any sound of the paper being punctured, nor of the man reacting to being hit. That split second was all it took for the man to move across the room. He was freakishly fast.

Contanto looked around for something, anything that might influence what was to come. Had he been over confident? He let out a slight gasp as the intruder's blade pierced his chest. He couldn't quite believe that anyone would have the audacity or ability to actually manage to kill him. It wasn't quite as painful as he was expecting either, but perhaps that was just the shock. Then it was done.

Soren left by the front door as innocuously as anyone could. He walked briskly away discarding his dark cloak and quickly blending into the crowd. His heart was racing with excitement. It was a perfectly executed kill. He wondered briefly if he should try to send word to the General, but decided it was unnecessary. Word would spread quickly that Contanto was dead but what would follow that, he could only guess. With the head of the city's underworld dead, there would be chaos and internecine warfare amongst the criminal gangs.

He spent two hours on a circuit around the city, looping around and backtracking several times until he was certain that no one could be following him. Then, and only then did he return to his apartment.

'Ruripathian scouting parties seen crossing the border! Farmers reporting their livestock being rustled. Outrages and atrocities being committed all along the border!'

Despite the noise on the square, the crier somehow managed to raise his voice above it allowing himself to be clearly heard even from fifty yards. The news disappointed Soren. After all of their efforts, it seemed that relations with Ruripathia had disintegrated regardless. Something occurred to him, it was a familiar thought, almost like déjà vu, but he couldn't quite work out what it was. Something someone had said to him, but he couldn't remember whom. He was struggling with the memory, trying to dig through the jumble in his mind. It had been about Chancellor Marin not being what he was supposed to be. Nevertheless, he had other matters to attend to. Grand Burgess Anton Spiro walked out of the Guilds' Hall onto the square with his two minders, and this required Soren's full concentration.

He was greeted by several traders, much like Contanto had been, but with a noticeably different atmosphere. The greetings seemed genuine, not rooted in fear. Soren had not been able to discern any notable pattern in Spiro's behaviour. Every day was different. His house was in Highgarden, and he was married with two children, one of whom was preparing to enter the Academy. Soren had no desire to kill Spiro in front of his children no matter what the reasons for his assassination, so the house was out. He worked long days but was never far from his minders. It looked as though the Seafarers' Guild had provided them. They had the tough weathered appearance of sailors. They were big, mean looking men but Soren was willing to bet that they were more brawn and aggression than ability. For angry merchants and guild members, they were more than enough of a deterrent but they would amount to no more than an inconvenience to Soren. The greatest threat they represented was escaping to raise the alarm.

The Guilds' Hall was enormous and given the time frame within which Soren had to complete the assassination, he really didn't have the luxury of being able to acquaint himself with the layout.

He had divided the available time evenly between the three targets, which in reflection might have been mistake. He felt he had spent longer then necessary in preparation for Contanto's assassination and had not taken into consideration the fact that one of the other ones might require more time. The imposition of this novice error was making itself known to him now. It narrowed the options in terms of locations, but as he had discovered, every man left an opening, it was just a case of finding it in the time he had.

The street was busy, just as Soren had hoped. Crowds were vital for the success of his plan. Spiro walked down the street every morning on his way to the Guilds' Hall. For three mornings Soren had been watching him, from the point that his bodyguards collected him from his house, and walked with him down to the hall. It was the only consistent element in Spiro's daily routine that Soren had been able to identify.

The street was always busy at this time of the morning. It was neither too wide nor too narrow, and there were a multitude of alleyways leading away from it, any of which would facilitate a good escape. It would be a brazen killing, in full view of the crowds and the bodyguards and would cause quite a fuss. It was this fuss that he hoped would allow him to melt into the crowd and disappear. If it went wrong it would be a disaster, but Soren found the prospect thrilling nonetheless.

He lurked at the entrance of one of the side alleys waiting for Spiro and his men to appear at the end of the street. He had been at the house when Spiro left, but had rushed on ahead to be ready for them. In the crowd his sword would be useless so the dagger would be the best choice. Something with a smaller hilt would have been better, but he had not got the money spare to buy a stiletto. The wound it would cause might not have been severe enough either. He would only have one chance so he needed to be sure that his equipment would do what was required.

He spotted the larger of Spiro's two bodyguards first, and then focussed in on Spiro himself who followed shortly behind. Most people moved out of the way as soon as they saw Spiro and his men, but there were enough who didn't to cause some bustling and jostling. It meant the bodyguards were a little farther from Spiro than they should have been. Not by much, but just enough.

Soren stepped out from the alleyway and walked toward the approaching men. He slipped seamlessly between the moving people around him and readied his dagger. The bodyguards drew closer and he fought the urge to look at them, forcing himself to stare toward some imagined purpose at the far end of the street. He was between the guards before they noticed him, not that they paid him very much attention anyway. As Soren bumped against

Spiro, one of them gave him a gentle shove away. But the bodyguard was too late and it was already done.

'Excuse me,' he said, and sidestepped out of the way before walking quickly toward the nearest laneway. He had sharpened the blade to a wicked edge. It cut so smoothly that it would be seconds before any pain was felt. He had slipped it between Spiro's ribs, into his heart and given it just enough of a twist to ensure the wound would not close. Spiro would take three, maybe four steps before the catastrophic loss of blood would cause him to drop to the ground and die. Perhaps he would have enough time to realise what had happened to him, but perhaps not. Either way, Soren was halfway down the alleyway before the body hit the ground.

His heart was racing and it was a struggle to maintain his composure, as it always was after a kill. Walking calmly away from the scene of an assassination was perhaps the most difficult part of the whole undertaking. There were shouts from the street behind him, and a scream. If the bodyguards had more than a shared brain cell, which judging by their appearance and demeanour may not have been the case, they would by now have connected him to the fact that their boss was lying on the ground in a pool of blood. Working out where he had gone would be more difficult for them. The fog of confusion and panic was an invaluable tool.

Chapter 48

THE BLACK CARPET

O nce the excitement of the kill faded, Soren found he was always left with a sense of disappointment and emptiness. He had bought a small mage lamp in a dealer's shop in the artisans' district a few days before and he held it now as he sat on the edge of his bed. He waved his hand over the glow in the centre of the glass sphere that was framed by two flat metal cylinders top and bottom which were connected by metal rods. It was not the brightest mage lamp he had ever seen. Either it was so old it was nearing the end of its usefulness or it had never been a good one to begin with. There had been no more made since the outlawing of the practice of sorcery, so the value of one even as dim as this was still high. He studied the lamp in search of the blue fringing, but he was not sure if he could see anything. He had come to think that magic was the key, or at least some sort of magical energy, but he had not seen the blue glow since the day on the plains, no matter how hard he tried.

He had bought the mage lamp to continue experimenting with the Gift. He was still no closer to understanding how it worked than he was that day and he had no desire to starve himself just to see if that would bring on the same experience. He reasoned that the mage lamp was a concentration of magical energy, so he hoped it might, if held close enough and long enough, bring on a mild form of the feelings that he had when near the shaman. It didn't.

He had been trying it most evenings since he had moved into the apartment, but the result was always the same. He was becoming frustrated by the fact that he had no control over when, where or how strong the Gift of Grace affected him. He knew he should be grateful for what he had. The Gift was always influencing him and even at its most unnoticeable it gave him the speed and strength that he took for granted, but that gave him the edge over all others.

The fact that he knew there was so much more if only he could just learn to call on it was maddening though. He threw the mage lamp onto his bed and went to the window. He looked down on the street and the sight of people passing by reminded him of how lonely he was. He thought of Alessandra, as he still often did. He missed not just the fact that she was no longer in his life, but also the idea of her being in his life.

To make matters worse Ranph was not in the city. He had returned to manage his family's estate on the shore of Blackwater Lake. As head of his family, that was his duty now. Henn, Jost and his other acquaintances from River House valued the favour of the Count of Moreno above their friendship with Soren, and as a result would have nothing to do with him.

He thought of Alessandra again, involuntarily as his mind drifted, whoring in the finery of her apartments in Oldtown. Thoughts like that popped into his head for no apparent reason at the most random of times and they always hurt. Frustrated and lonely, he decided to go out. He knew that he ought to be scouting his next target, Tanto dal Trevison, but he really could not put his mind to it so he thought there was little point in trying to force the issue.

He wandered through the streets without any thought or purpose. There was usually something comforting about the sense of familiarity they provided, but tonight he couldn't seem to find the peace that it brought. He walked for hours, until the night had well and truly arrived. Certain parts of the city never slept, and it was in one of these areas that he found himself. There were bars, brothels and gambling dens; the types of places once overseen by Abelard Contanto but that were now enjoying an independence that was unlikely to last long.

He had not really been thinking about it, but his wanderings had been taking him toward one place. It was a duelling club that

he had become aware of some time previously. Not one that set
its competitors on the road to competing in the city's arenas, but
one which might well lead to floating face down in the harbour
the following morning. He had his blades with him of course; no
self-respecting banneret would be seen out of doors without them.

This form of duelling was highly illegal, and every few months
the city crier would announce that the Watch had closed one of
the clubs down. There were never any arrests of course, the clubs
were frequented by aristocrats, merchant princes and criminals,
not to mention that the competitors were usually bannerets, alleg-
edly the finest men the city had to offer.

Occasionally someone who had not studied at the Academy
would try their luck, most often a thug or a bruiser who over esti-
mated his abilities. They tended to end up providing whatever types
of marine life that could survive in the filthy harbour with a meal.

He stood for several minutes watching the door to the club.
Cloaked people would stop and knock at the door and an inspection slot would open. A moment later the person would either be
admitted or they would move away, their night's entertainment
refused them. Entering would mark a step down for him. Bannerets tended not to resort to this until there were no other options,
or they had a drug addiction to feed. The money to be made was
not fantastic compared to what a banneret could earn, but it was
better than nothing for those that either could not find choicer
work or for those that could no longer expect any better. Soren
didn't need the money though. He was looking for something
entirely different.

He knocked at the door and waited for the inspection hole to
open. It rasped open and a pair of eyes regarded him suspiciously.

'What do you want?' asked the man on the other side.

'To come in,' Soren replied, smiling. He pushed back his cloak
to reveal the hilts of his blades and the purse at his belt. The eyes
stared at them for a moment and then the inspection slot shut.
The door opened and the man who owned the eyes gestured for
Soren to enter.

'This way, sir, the bar is down the stairs. I hope you enjoy your
evening,' he said, smiling to reveal a set of filthy teeth.

Soren walked in and made his way down the steps. As he went, the sounds of raucous shouts and the clashing of steel became audible with increasing volume.

He came to the end of the steps and out into a large cellar room. It was lit with large mage lamps and despite the subterranean location, it was very bright. There was a small bar with a disinterested tender to the left, and a large crowd of men gathered in front of him. He couldn't see beyond them, but from the noise it was obvious to him what was going on. He walked to the bar.

'Who do I need to speak to?' Soren asked.

The bartender took one look at the hilts of his blades and nodded to a man standing quietly to one side of the crowd. Soren made his way over.

'The barman said to speak to you,' said Soren.

'Did he now. And why did he do that?' the man replied.

'I'm here to duel.'

'Are you now.' He appraised Soren with a little more interest and his eyes drifted down to the hilts of his blades. 'Well, are you ready to go tonight?'

'Yes.'

'Good, what's your name?' the man asked.

'Soren.'

The man looked at him questioningly, expecting more. 'Just Soren then,' he said, after a moment. 'I am Mateo. Are you a banneret?'

'Does it matter?' Soren asked.

'Well, the bookmaker will need to know one way or the other. I have no objections to putting a normal person into the duels, but obviously your chances for victory are significantly smaller if you're not,' Mateo replied.

'Yes, I am a banneret,' Soren said.

'Good. I'll put you in at the end. So until then, relax, enjoy the duels, place a bet or two, and I'll call on you when it's time.'

He watched the next few duels with interest. The competitors were older men for the most part, many carrying that air of men who have seen war, as well as carrying the scars that come with it, although these could have been the dividends of a life on the underground duelling scene he supposed. That was the major difference between the clubs and the arena, sharp blades and three blood drawing wounds here compared to dulled edges and three touches in the arena, where blood was occasional and not a requirement. 'To the death' was rarely seen in the arena, but on occasion it was known to happen. Here it was no problem if one of the blood drawing wounds resulted in death. In fact, killing was actively encouraged. Bets would be placed not just on the result of the duel, but if would be won by blood or death.

They fought on a strip of black, painted on the floor and affectionately known as the 'black carpet'. It was twenty paces or so long, and only a few paces wide. The restricted space would take a little adjustment, but Soren didn't foresee it as being a problem. He wondered what the penalty would be for stepping off the carpet, as no one seemed to break the rule. Perhaps it was the duellist's last vestige of honour in a life that had reached the lowest ebb that made them adhere to this one rule, but it seemed to be the only one that there was.

Punching, elbows and knees were all part and parcel of the black carpet. That didn't bother Soren though. He had always found the formal duelling at the Academy restrictive and stuffy, the strict rules being a poor reflection of real fighting. This would be far closer to the reality of combat, which was fitting, as it was quite likely that someone would die on the black carpet that night.

'You're next. Are you ready?' Mateo asked.

'Yes,' Soren replied, as he removed his cloak. He was wearing the neat black fighting doublet and britches he had on earlier in the day, which were perfectly suited for fighting. They had been purchased while he was still under the patronage of Amero, so were of particularly fine quality, and perfectly tailored for him. They were clearly expensive and Soren could see that questioning expression on Mateo's face again. It was not uncommon for bored young aristocrats to find their way onto the black carpet in search of a little excitement. It was less common for them to be of a level of skill high enough to win.

Soren drew his sword and dagger and took off his sword belt. He handed the belt and cloak to Mateo. 'Would you mind holding these for me while I fight?'

'Not at all,' Mateo said, taking the items and gesturing for Soren to make his way to the carpet. He focussed his mind on trying to enhance the Gift. This did nothing. He tried to mingle his concentration on his upcoming duel with what he should try next. He stepped onto the black paint, which had some sort of grit mixed through it to increase grip. It would restrict sliding movements, but when he saw the dried blood present on it from the earlier bouts, he realised it was designed to prevent slipping on wet blood. The choice of the colour black was also obvious. It was to hide the bloodstains.

His opponent was much older, with close-cropped grey hair and a few days' worth of stubble. His clothes were functional but of a lesser quality than Soren's and his face bore a number of fine pink scars. The man took his guard in a workmanlike fashion and Mateo shouted for them to begin.

His opponent shuffled forward quite smoothly, but from the start Soren could see that his technique was less polished and less disciplined than freshly graduated swordsmen. That did not mean he would not be a dangerous opponent however, perhaps quite the opposite.

He tried to imagine everything in the room covered in the blue glow, hoping that if he pictured it hard enough, it would actually appear. He tried to imagine it enveloping him, filling him with warmth and energy. And then, like a deep breath of cool, fresh air, it appeared. It was around everything, the mage lamps, the crowd, his opponent. Almost as suddenly as it had appeared, it went, but the effect remained. It felt as though his heart had slowed, while his limbs felt light and energized. The noise of the crowd seemed to fade into the distance and his opponent seemed to slow.

He smiled at his success. If he could do it once, he could do it again.

The man attacked with three strikes that followed one another with reasonable fluidity, but which Soren parried with both sword and dagger, their blades clashing and sparking, much to the delight of the on-looking crowd. His counter attack was almost as instantaneous as his decision to make it. Soren countered with a thrust of his sword. It flashed in the lamplight three times, its tip contacting with flesh without interruption from the man's sword or dagger. The crowd gasped, and Soren stepped back to survey his handiwork. What he saw shocked him.

He had intended to cut the man three times in that attack; just enough to draw blood from three wounds and end the duel, but no more. Unlike in more formal duels, on the black carpet a duel was not re-set after a scoring touch. It continued on uninterrupted until there was a victor. The man had dropped to his knees in an ever increasing pool of his own blood. His clothes were rent in three places, each revealing a perfectly executed killing strike.

Killing the man did not bother him in the least; any man who came before his blade was either there by choice or by necessity. What shocked him was that on this occasion he had only intended to wound the man. His skill was such that his sword should have carried out his intentions perfectly. At what stage had he lost that control? It was the incident with Contanto's nephew all over again.

A clap on his back pulled him from his thoughts.

'You certainly like to make a big first impression. Faco there was a fine blade, but you made him look like he'd never held a sword in his life before. You do know that only three draws of blood are needed to win?' asked Mateo. He paused for a second, but when no response appeared forthcoming, he continued. 'Your prize purse is ten crowns. If you want to come this way I will settle with you.'

He led Soren over to a table in the corner with a strongbox on it. Two large men stood nearby, and eyed Soren apprehensively. They were clearly there to guard it, but after having seen Soren fight, he could see in their eyes that they doubted their ability to stop him should he choose to take it.

Mateo pulled a stool from under the table and sat. 'Please, sit. Can I get you a drink?'

Before Soren could answer Mateo had called to the barman to bring a bottle of wine. Soren sat on a stool opposite him. Mateo took a small key from his jacket pocket and opened the strongbox. He took a leather pouch and placed it on the table in front of Soren, the coins within clinking quietly.

'Ten crowns and your things are just there. One of the boys will clean your blades for you if you wish, but you bannerets always seem to want to take care of that kind of thing for yourselves. Can we expect to see you here again?' Mateo asked.

Soren took the purse from the table and pocketed it. He thought it would be wise to appear to need the money more than he did; at the very least it would keep Mateo guessing as to his reasons for being there. He didn't want the man to know more about him than was absolutely necessary.

'Perhaps,' Soren replied. 'But ten crowns is not enough.'

Mateo smiled wolfishly. 'Well, now that we know what you are capable of, we can weigh the odds accordingly. I can assure you that the purses will only get larger, particularly if you can repeat that kind of performance.'

'That won't be a problem,' Soren replied.

'Excellent. When can I expect you then?'

'The night after tomorrow,' Soren said, before getting up and leaving. He felt dirty when he exited out onto the street, but he couldn't deny the thrill that the duel had given him. Measuring himself and his skill against another man and to prove himself better was addictive. More importantly, he had finally learned how to call on his gift whenever he chose. He was an urchin from the gutter and now he felt as though there was not a man who could stand before him. He pulled his cloak up over his head and walked briskly out into the darkness.

Chapter 49

A MAN OF NO MORALS

Tanto dal Trevison was an Elector Count. While Spiro and Contanto were both at least equally as powerful in their own ways, they were self-made men. Dal Trevison had been born to his power and wealth, and while no more powerful or dangerous than the other two men, killing a noble had altogether more dangerous connotations. It was breaking the unwritten rule of the city; only noblemen could kill other noblemen, which they often did in duels of honour. The assassination of any noble would draw attention. The assassination of one so powerful as dal Trevison would draw a great deal of it.

Dal Trevison had visited a brothel on every evening that Soren had followed him. It was not an unusual thing for aristocrats to visit prostitutes and no one would give the fact a second thought, but Soren would have expected a man with dal Trevison's wealth to keep a mistress, or even a personal harem, rather than to use normal brothels. They were all very high-class brothels, but brothels nonetheless. It made him want to get the job over with quickly, nauseating him to think that some night he might follow the man to Alessandra's apartments in Oldtown.

As with the others, Tanto dal Trevison kept a personal bodyguard with him. His bodyguards would be of a different calibre to those employed by the others though. A man of dal Trevison's position attracted a large number of court followers. He would have lesser nobles and the younger sons of greater nobles joining his retinue in the hope of advancement. He would also be a man who would, like Amero dal Moreno, sponsor promising young fighters at the Academy. What it meant was that his bodyguards would certainly be bannerets, and most likely very good ones.

He recalled a tenet from one of his classes at the Academy, that the best way to win a fight is to avoid it altogether. It was not an approach that had ever made sense to him before, but it seemed to be appropriate to his present needs, so he made his plans accordingly. He was quite sure that the bodyguards would not be in the room with dal Trevison when he was with the prostitute. That would be the time to kill him. The only question that remained was how to get in there also.

Soren had always seen the rooftops as being an ally. In a city as old and crowded as Ostenheim, buildings tended to grow upward, the only direction usually available to them. The result was that the roofs of the city were almost as much of a warren of nooks and crannies as the alleyways below. There were half roofs and extensions everywhere, hiding places, forgotten windows and blocked up doorways to balconies that no longer existed.

Soren made his way onto the roof of the brothel and took his bearings. Like most of the buildings in the city the roof was of dark orange, ridged terracotta tiles. The tiles stopped short of the front of the building leaving a small flat roof that had a round table with four chairs around it, and a large plant in a pot with big, wide rubbery looking leaves. The prostitutes must come up here to relax when they are not working, Soren thought. It was actually a nice spot, peaceful high over the city. The building was tall enough that Soren could just glimpse the sea over the roofs of the city, with the sun setting on the horizon. He suddenly felt like an intruder, invading the unfortunate women's small sanctuary.

There was a trap door in the corner of the roof. He went over to it and knelt down beside it. He listened carefully for several moments before gently lifting it open. There was a flight of rough wooden steps leading down into a darkened corridor. He silently descended the steps and into the corridor. He drew his dagger; the sword would be useless in such a confined environment, and quietly advanced.

The top floor seemed to be small bedrooms, where either the girls or the staff lived, but it was certainly not where business was conducted. The corridor was quite shabby; it had not been decorated for some time and was not nearly luxurious enough for entertaining customers. He made his way down one floor and the décor changed significantly. Instead of unvarnished floorboards, there was deep, plush, scarlet carpet. Expensive looking paintings lined the walls, and there was so much gilt that Soren wondered if it crossed the line from classy to gaudy. From the sounds coming from behind some of the doors he could tell that he had descended to a level on which the brothel's business was conducted.

Identifying what room dal Trevison was in was the only obstacle left. The working practice of the brothel would help to some extent; the girls placed a red tassel over the door handle of any room that was in use. Only one of the rooms on this floor had a tassel on the door, but Soren knew from a previous scouting visit that the higher profile clients were entertained on the lower floors. They didn't want to be fatigued from climbing up too many stairs.

He made his way down to the next floor, which was the last one above the ground floor. It was here that he thought it most likely that he would find dal Trevison. There were eight doors lining the corridor, and three of them had tassels on their handles. Taking his chances, he reached for the handle on the first door, and opened it slightly.

'This one's taken, can't you see!' said a young woman in a state of undress, standing by a bed occupied by a man that was not dal Trevison. He had not opened the door enough to reveal his face and he had decided to wear a mask on this job so he would be unrecognisable if seen. On the other missions, a mask was either inappropriate or not needed, as there would be no witnesses alive to identify him. On this job, there was a likelihood that he would be seen by one, or several of the courtesans. They were innocents, and he had no desire to kill any of them. He hoped the mask would make this possible, but being seen wearing one before completing his task would cause the alarm to be raised and destroy any chance of him successfully carrying it out. He closed the door quickly with a mumbled apology and moved on to the next door. What he saw when he opened the door left him mouth agape in surprise.

Surprise subsided quickly to an uncomfortable amusement. In his investigation he had heard rumours of dal Trevison's tastes, but the forewarning was still not enough to prepare him for the ridiculous scene before him. Dal Trevison was strapped to a wooden frame, arms and legs outstretched. A courtesan stood next to him with a light whip in her hands. His entry caused her to pause in what she had been doing, and she cast him a stern gaze.

'What is it? What's going on?' said dal Trevison. He was strapped to the frame belly first, and the restraints prevented him from turning his head far enough to see what was going on behind him. He strained at the leather straps and his frustration was evident as he twitched and twisted, the wooden frame creaking in protest.

'Get out! Can't you see we're busy!' screeched the courtesan.

Soren couldn't help but chuckle at the sight. It was not a very fearsome introduction, but was completely unavoidable, and he hoped his appearance would be menacing enough despite this. He pushed back the folds of his cloak to reveal his blades, which had the desired effect of shutting the courtesan up.

'If you remain very quiet, you may survive this night,' Soren said to her, as menacingly as he could, although he felt its effect was diminished by his earlier levity.

'Who the hell do you think you are bursting in here like this? Do you know who I am? Do you have any idea what I can have done to you for interrupting me like this?' said dal Trevison furiously. He continued to rage, spittle flying from the corners of his mouth as he twisted and jerked against the leather restraints. The pasty white skin of his back was streaked with pink lines where the courtesan had been flogging him. She had retreated to a corner of the room where she had adopted the foetal position and was whimpering in terror, her earlier bravado now well and truly gone. Soren suppressed another laugh as he returned his stare to dal Trevison, who at that moment was perhaps the most ridiculous looking man he had ever seen. He stepped forward and spoke, interrupting dal Trevison's stream of vitriol.

'I know who you are,' said Soren, in a low throaty voice, 'and that is the reason I am here.' In a smooth movement he stabbed

dal Trevison through the ribs, just where the blade would punc-
ture the heart and cause a swift death, more than he deserved.
From what he had heard, dal Trevison liked to reciprocate the
treatment he was receiving, but with far more vigour.

'You can start screaming in five minutes,' Soren said to the
cowering woman, 'any sooner than that and I will be back for you.'
As an afterthought he threw her a purse containing five crowns,
more than she would have earned from dal Trevison, before turning and leaving the room.

Chapter 50

A SLIPPERY SLOPE?

'Welcome back, sir. Mister Mateo told me to keep an eye out for you tonight!' said the doorman. He beckoned for Soren to enter the club from the doorway. 'Good luck with your duel, sir,' he added as Soren passed him.

The doorman's obsequiousness sickened Soren almost as much as his bad teeth. He went down the stairs and quickly spotted Mateo standing by the table with the strongbox, talking to two men in particularly fine clothing. Now that he thought of it, there were a number of notably well dressed people there, even more so than on the last night. Soren hoped they were not there on the back of word of his duel on the previous occasion. Mateo spotted him and hurried over.

'You're here! Excellent! I was beginning to worry that you would not come. Your purse for tonight will be fifty crowns. As I'm sure you can see, word of your duel has generated quite a bit of interest in high society.' He seemed a little nervous tonight in contrast to his relaxed and confident manner on the previous night. 'There will be a few duels before yours, but yours is the main event of the evening. Needless to say there are some very important people here; this night could prove very beneficial to both of us. I hope you've brought your best.'

'You don't need to worry about that,' Soren replied. He was slightly irked at having to wait for his duel again. Ever since leaving his apartment he had been anticipating the action like a hungry man awaiting a gourmet meal. 'Is there somewhere private that I can wait?'

'Yes, of course, this way,' Mateo said. He led Soren to a small room behind the bar. It was far from luxurious, being little more than a storage closet containing a single stool, but it suited Soren. His primary concern was to be away from the gawking looks of the people that had gathered in the cellar that night. The room was damp, musty and dark, so he sat back and closed his eyes. His mind drifted to Alessandra. It always did when the darkness came. He tried to force his mind to other thoughts, but it was impossible to blot her out, or the hurt and anger that thoughts of her brought.

A knock on the door brought him back to his senses. He had no idea how long he had been resting in the small room, but apparently it had been long enough. The barman peered in and Soren followed him out into the cellar that played host to the duelling club.

The previously rowdy crowd quieted as he walked toward the black carpet, led out by Mateo. It made him uncomfortable to know that every eye in the room was on him, but he maintained as blank a face as he could, something that resembled a scowl, but not so much that it would seem forced. He was uncertain how much people would know about him, but the crowd was larger, and a significant percentage looked very wealthy. As with all things in the city, the underground duelling dens varied in their level of sophistication and class. This one would only have been somewhere in the middle of the scale. It was better than the rougher places that had little more than brawls calling themselves duels and would rarely if ever see a true swordsman, but it was not a top tier venue that attracted the wealthiest of citizens. This evening, many of the spectators looked decidedly out of place in their finery. He tried to ignore them as he took his place at the end of the carpet, but it made him wonder how Amero had coped with the thousands of spectators in the Amphitheatre.

Mateo launched into a speech that Soren didn't pay any attention to. He looked at the man at the other end of the black carpet. After the last night, there would be no element of surprise available to Soren. After that display, he wondered what kind of man would put himself forward for this duel. Was he there by choice? It didn't matter. It was not Soren's intention to kill this man, although that had also been the case on the last night when he had killed. The fact unnerved him a little, but he was aware of it and forewarned was forearmed.

The man was again much older than Soren. This club seemed to attract a certain down on their luck type of swordsman. He was dressed in worn but well fitted duelling clothes, and his blades looked well maintained with a keen edge. The condition of a banneret's weapons was often a better indicator of his mettle than his appearance. His face was firm and his eyes showed no fear. He looked like a man that had faced many hard fights, but had come through them on top. What would bring a man like that to a club like this? Could it have been the thrill of combat? The same thing that had brought Soren there?

Mateo had finished his introductions, so it was time to begin. They both saluted and it began. Soren fought off his initial urge to try to tap into the energy in the room. He was hesitant as a result of the death of his previous opponent. The killing had been uncontrollable, as though his body were entirely detached from his mind and was operating purely on instinct. Some detachment made for the best swordplay though. While the mind commanded the body, it was separated from the pain and fatigue signals that the body would ordinarily send back. The Gift seemed to have prevented him from sending a stop command back to his body though, and this bothered Soren.

Without any effort on his part, the Gift of Grace gave him an almost constant advantage in speed and strength. He reasoned that his perception of time was probably affected when he was in this state, although for him this was what was normal, and if there was any effect on how he saw things, it was not enough for him to notice. He had come to think of this as his 'state of grace'. He could not forget however, the occasion when he fought dal Dardi and the state of grace had seemed to desert him completely, something he still had no explanation for.

The initial excitement in the crowd seemed to be waning quickly. After two or three exchanges there were more disappointed mutterings than excited gasps. Soren decided it was time to take the initiative. As he had on the previous night, he pictured the blue glow in his mind, and focussed all of his concentration on it. Distracted, he allowed a gap in his defence, which even with his superior speed he was unable to completely close in time. His opponent's blade glanced from a parry and was deflected across his upper arm, neatly slicing through his shirt and flicking a little blood into the air. The man's face betrayed the slightest hint of a smile as he backed away to recompose himself. He thought he had Soren's measure. There was some tittering in the crowd and Soren felt a flash of anger. He forced himself to ignore the laughter and the pain in his arm, shutting out the world around him, focussing on his mental image of the blue glow surrounding everything. With his mind concentrated on this image and concept, everything suddenly became illuminated with the ethereal blue glow. His purpose achieved, he let his concentration return to his opponent, and the glow disappeared. It had been enough though, that fleeting connection with it. He felt the energy course through his body. His opponent's movements slowed and Soren could not suppress a smile.

He lunged forward with speed that elicited a shocked gasp from the onlookers. In a smooth movement he neatly pushed aside the other man's guard with his dagger and cut three times with his sword. The increase in speed had surprised even him to some extent, and he fought to focus on not killing the man. Only wound him, he thought.

The duel was over almost as soon as Soren had drawn on the energy. He breathed a sigh of relief as he saw that the man was still standing before him. His sword and dagger dropped from his hands, which hovered over the three diagonal wounds on his gut. He looked at Soren with a mixture of surprise and disbelief. It was an expression that Soren was becoming familiar with. There was something of a stunned silence in the room that gradually gave over to excited whispering and then applause. Soren looked at the man and began to smile, but his mirth was replaced with sick realisation. Blood bubbled from the man's mouth, and his dark clothes had concealed the fact that blood had been running down his body. It was now beginning to pool on the floor. He gasped once, a raspy, gurgling sound before dropping to his knees and then falling over on his side. The fall exposed the three deep rents in his abdomen, one of which went all the way to the spine. Soren looked at the blade of his sword, half of which glistened with ruby red blood. Full applause broke out and Soren turned and bowed, trying to supress the wave of panic that was flooding over him. He couldn't control it. Whenever he used it, his opponents would die. Could he learn to control it, as he had learned to unleash it?

He felt in limbo, not really sure what to do next. Mateo beckoned to him, and he was relieved to move away from the spotlight. The crowd parted to let him through, women applauding him and men clapping him on the back. He wondered how much Mateo had made from the duel. It was clear that the fifty crowns he had offered Soren was a bargain for him, but Soren had no idea the duel would draw so many aristocrats so he hadn't thought to drive a harder bargain. Perhaps his prowess with a blade would allow him to renegotiate the terms, but that was a little too ruthless, even for him.

Mateo was standing by his small table with the strongbox flanked by his two guards.

'The man of the moment!' said Mateo in an overly familiar way. 'Another excellent result, well done!' He pushed a fat coin purse across the table to Soren. 'After tonight it will be harder to find you an opponent. You're the man to beat now, and the reward will be big for anyone willing to take the chance. That will attract someone to the challenge sooner or later, but for now, I don't have anything more for you. I'm not one for sending notes, so if you call in here to see me in a week, I expect I'll have something for you then.'

Soren nodded and took the purse. He was already beginning to feel woozy and wanted to get out of the cellar as quickly as possible. He had achieved most of what he had set out to in coming to the black carpet. He now knew how to draw on the energy, and he expected, by extension, also the Moment, although he had not yet tried this. He was no closer to controlling it, and the thought of piling up a stack of corpses while he tried to learn how was not appealing to him. He had already decided that he would not be returning.

As he left, there were two men watching him closely, but fighting off the fatigue that was falling heavily on him, Soren did not notice them.

Chapter 51

A FRESH START

Soren awoke the next morning to the sound of something being pushed under his door. At first he thought that it was another call from General Kastor and he was surprised to find that the thought filled him with dread. He picked up what proved to be a small letter, and noticed that there was a sigil pressed into the red sealing wax holding it closed. He broke it open and took out the note contained within. It was a request for a meeting that afternoon. There was little detail; if anything the tone of the note was rather cryptic. It simply asked for him to meet with the author, one Banneret of the Blue dal Dragonet, at the Bannerets' Hall.

He was unsure of how to react. The note did not ask for a reply so it seemed he was just to turn up if he so chose. It occurred to him that he had little to lose and in any event he was curious.

<hr />

He stood in the vestibule of the Bannerets' Hall waiting for the porter to bring him to his meeting. The Bannerets' Hall provided a continuing point of contact for graduates of the Academy. It was a club of sorts, containing lounges, dining rooms, meeting rooms and accommodation where bannerets could stay when they visited the city. As a banneret, Soren was automatically a member, although he had never before actually visited the building. He had been intending to for some time, as it also housed the Emblazoner of Banners, who would make up Soren's banner if and when he got around to having it done.

The porter returned and brought Soren to one of the private meeting rooms that were available for the use of members. There were two men sitting at a table that dominated the centre of the room, smoking and sipping at what appeared to be whiskies. They both stood when Soren entered the room.

'Pleased to meet you, Swordsman,' said the taller of the two men. He extended his hand to Soren. 'I am Rudigar dal Dragonet, Banneret of the Blue. I'm very glad you decided to come. I have a proposition for you.'

Soren took his hand, a firm handshake. A proposition then. He wondered what it might be.

'We have been tasked with putting together a bodyguard for a member of the high aristocracy. We need good swordsmen who are discreet and aren't shy of killing when it's needed. We feel that you would be suitable for a place on that bodyguard. The pay will be excellent, and we know that you are well trained for the job. The instructors at the Academy speak very highly of your skill, and Master Dornish spoke very strongly of your suitability for the position. As a matter of fact, he actively encouraged us to seek you out. In any event, the initial contract is only short term, until the current unrest that has been building in the city of late has subsided, but if you impress, further opportunities exist,' said dal Dragonet.

It seemed that Soren's clandestine work for General Kastor and whoever gave him his orders had been worthwhile. By putting his head down and getting on with things without complaining, it seemed that he had indeed opened doors to better opportunities.

'I don't need an answer right now, but I will need it soon. By tomorrow at the latest. We feel that the matter is time sensitive and want to get the process in motion as soon as is possible,' said dal Dragonet.

Time sensitive. It seemed to Soren that the aristocrat in question must be in fear for his life. Perhaps the forces that Soren had been working against had employed assassins of their own to strike back against the Duke. He was pleased to have been considered for the work. He found the idea of protecting lives considerably more palatable than taking them.

'Come to this address when you have decided,' dal Dragonet added. He handed Soren a stiff white card with raised black lettering. 'I cannot emphasise enough what a good opportunity this is for you.' He stood and clicked his heels together making a staccato bow of his head before sitting again. It was the salute of a banneret and a mark of respect, but also a gesture that indicated the meeting was over.

———•◦••◦•———

Dal Dragonet watched Soren leave the room, and took another sip of whisky as the door closed. When it had, the other man spoke for the first time.

'Do you really think he's suitable?' he asked.

'I do,' replied dal Dragonet, without hesitation.

'But you found him in a black carpet duelling club,' said the other man. 'Is that really the type of person we want?'

'That may be the case, but I have made my enquiries and I am confident that he's a perfect fit. I've never heard Dornish singing anyone's praises so strongly, and he has battlefield experience, as well as two duelling kills. I think he will do quite nicely.'

———•◦••◦•———

It was no surprise to Soren that the address dal Dragonet had given him was a house in Highgarden. He watched it from across the street for some time, something holding him back from going straight in. He wasn't sure what it was, but it was hard to fight down. He realised that he was on a precipice, and in real danger of becoming something that he did not want to be. If he did not take this job, it seemed likely that he would remain in the shadows as an assassin, which was a life he did not want.

When he approached the black iron gates that fronted the house, an attendant appeared from the small gatehouse and brought him through. The driveway was wide and circular, designed to allow carriages entry and exit without the need to turn, and was surrounded perfectly manicured lawns. The wealth in the city never failed to amaze him, no matter how many times he was exposed to it. At the door to the house, Soren was handed over to a butler, who led him to a small waiting room.

He only had to wait for a moment before a man emerged from another room. He wore a military uniform, but not one that would have been practical on the battlefield. It was tightly fitted and sported an abundance of brass buttons and gold braid.

'I am Lord Dragonet's aide de camp. If you'd like to come this way please,' he said. He brought Soren into the room he had just emerged from, which was a small office, and then through to another room, which was much larger. Dal Dragonet lounged in a leather armchair on the far side of a large desk covered with dark green leather.

'Banneret Soren!' he said. 'I'm glad you decided to take me up on the offer. Please sit.' He gestured to a chair opposite the desk.

As he sat, Soren became aware of the other man who had been with Dal Dragonet at the Bannerets' Hall standing by the fireplace to the left. There was no fire, and the light from the large window in the left wall had lost much of its brilliance by the time it got there, leaving him somewhat in shadow.

'I am correct in assuming that you are here to accept my offer?' Dal Dragonet asked.

'You are,' Soren replied.

'Excellent. Now, I'm sure you are eager to hear what the job is. As you may or may not know, I am equerry to the Duke. With the growing unrest in the city, some of us in the Duke's circle have become concerned that the Duke may be at greater risk of an act of violence when moving about the city. As a result, we have decided to put together a bodyguard for him, of somewhat different character to his official one. There won't be any fancy uniforms or highly polished boots. We want tried and tested men who will be able to get the job done when things get tough.

'A little background will be necessary for you to adequately carry out your duties, and it of course goes without saying that all you see, hear and do in the execution of your duties will be kept in the utmost confidence, on your oath as a banneret.

'We fear there is a faction within the city that seeks to strike at the Duke. With the growing tensions on the northern border, war with Ruripathia seems inevitable. This kind of thing always stirs up a population, for better or for worse, so we are going to have to be extra vigilant. The Duke has enemies within the city and we must do all we can to ensure they do not get to him,' said dal Dragonet.

Soren presumed that the men he had already killed numbered among these enemies, but for some reason there was a nagging concern beginning to form in his mind. 'General Kastor made it clear that there was unrest in the city and it's starting to become quite noticeable. I'm just very grateful that you've chosen me for this new role.'

Dal Dragonet's brow furrowed for a moment. 'Kastor? Oh yes, of course, the general who broke up the barbarian incursions into the marches. But to return to matters at hand, any ordinary man could decide to strike at the Duke, so you must be alert at all times, and be ready to kill quickly and without hesitation to protect the Duke's life. What I am saying is, if in doubt, strike. We can clean up any unpleasant mistakes afterward. The Duke's safety is paramount. Do I make myself clear?'

'Perfectly, my Lord,' replied Soren. He was a little puzzled by dal Dragonet's reaction to the mention of General Kastor. Had it not been him that recommended him for this appointment? Was dal Dragonet so concerned over security that he would obfuscate any details that were not directly pertinent despite Soren's steadfast service to date? His fledgling concern grew a little stronger.

'We don't want you to be all spit and polish. We want to send a message that the new bodyguards are not just for show, that you will take the gloves off and get your hands dirty without hesitation. However, you will be representing the Duke, and certain standards need to be maintained. On your way out, speak with my aide and he will arrange for you to be suitably attired.' He started to write on a piece of paper, and then held a stick of red wax over the flame of a candle, dripping the melted wax onto the bottom of the page. He pressed his signet ring into the soft wax and slid it across his desk to Soren.

'Take this letter to the Commander of the Guard at the Palace. You will be quartered there, and you will take your orders directly from me, or the Duke. His safety is my sole concern, so in the event of a conflict of orders, I will expect you to follow my command, even if it means doing so discretely so as not to incur the Duke's wrath.'

Soren took the letter and spent several uncomfortable minutes in dal Dragonet's aide's office as he fussed around him with a measuring tape. The job was an opportunity to break with the life it appeared he was going to lead in the shadowy service of the General, whose fidelity he was now not so sure of. His first order of business upon leaving the house would be to clear the account at Austorgas' Bank and then collect his blades from Carlujko's. There was little packing to be done in his apartment, which was unfortunately already paid up to the end of the month and he could be reporting to the Palace that evening.

Chapter 52

A THING OF BEAUTY

The teller at Austorgas' was suspicious of Soren from the start, but was even more so when he saw the balance in the account that Soren was seeking to close. It took several minutes of the teller conferring with his supervisor and comparing forms and signatures before he returned, grudgingly satisfied that Soren was the right person and had the authority to make the withdrawal. He was paid a part of the sum in a bill of exchange, which would satisfy the bill at Carlujko's and the rest in cash which would be a good sum to live on until his pay at the Palace started to come through.

With a feeling of cheerful excitement, he walked across the city to Carlujko's. When he arrived he was brought directly to a small room that was laid out to display weapons to their prospective owners. He waited for a few minutes before Carlujko bustled into the room carrying a long package wrapped in oilcloth.

'Good afternoon, sir, I trust you are well!' Carlujko said. He didn't extend a hand to shake, which was proper etiquette when addressing a banneret. Instead he placed the package down on the red felt covered table against the wall. He unwrapped it with what was almost reverence, revealing the physical manifestation of the sketch that Soren had seen the last time he had been there.

The steel glistened with an oily sheen and the lines of the blade were perfect in every respect. The pommel was a perfect disc with a slightly concave surface and the quillions of the crossguard flared at their curved ends. The knuckle guard curved back elegantly from the cross guard, stopping by the pommel, but not connecting to it, its end mirroring the curved edge of the pommel. The entire hilt, while simple in its physical design, was covered with beautifully elaborate etching that appeared black on the surface of the steel. The dagger was a smaller copy of the sword, the etching on its hilt slightly less elaborate, but it was still the perfect match for the sword. Carlujko gestured for him to pick the sword up.

He did, and instantly it felt perfect. The balance was better than any other sword he had ever held. It felt as though his hand had merged with the grip and the sword became an extension of his arm. There was no movement or pressure points, and he had to resist the urge to swing it in the confined space of the room. Carlujko smiled with satisfaction as he watched Soren's reaction to the weapons.

'How is the balance?' he asked, in a manner that suggested he already knew what the answer would be.

'Perfect,' Soren replied distractedly.

'And the grip? How does it feel?'

'Perfect,' Soren said, a smile breaking out on his face as he looked at Carlujko.

Carlujko returned the smile with satisfaction. It was clearly a scene he was accustomed to witnessing.

'Telastrian steel is hard to work, but when it has been properly forged, it is second to none. It won't rust, it will hold its edge far better than ordinary steel and it will give far more flex when it is required! All in all, I feel comfortable stating that these are two of the finest blades I have ever created. The hilts, as we discussed, are simple but elegant, reflective of truly great swordsmanship, I think. Those blades will serve you well, and your son, and his son. They are a truly magnificent possession, and utterly lethal weapons. All that remains is the fee we agreed,' said Carlujko. If anything, his smile was broader at this point.

———◆+◎+◆———

As always seemed to be the case with new experiences, Soren approached the Palace with a degree of trepidation. All of his belongings had fit quite easily in his campaign pack, and he had slung his blades over his shoulder in the oilcloth covering. He would have to have scabbards and a suspension made for them soon. He would probably be able to make do with an old one until he found the time to do so.

After passing the guards at the gates to the Palace, he went to the guardhouse and reported in. He was expected there and an orderly brought him to his quarters. He had thought he was destined for a bunk in a barracks room, as there was a full regiment stationed between the Palace and the older castle on the cliff overlooking the bay below, but he was brought directly into the Palace itself.

The interiors of some of the buildings at the Academy had been magnificent and he had been in one or two very impressive mansions, dal Dragonet's standing out, but none of them came close to the splendour of the Palace, not even the palace in Brixen could match it. The walls and ceilings were a mix of intricate white plasterwork and gilt, while the walls were lined with massive portraits of former dukes and notables of the Duchy. The Palace was enormous, and for the briefest of moments, Soren thought that his quarters were going to be unbelievably luxurious.

As the guard led him through the Palace and up several flights of stairs, his expectation began to build, and it seemed as though he had landed himself a very cushy number.

'These are the Duke's personal apartments,' said the guard, gesturing to ornate double doors in a corridor. He didn't stop however, instead continuing down the hall to a door that was camouflaged into the plasterwork of the wall and was barely visible. He opened it with a discrete handle, and went through. The décor on the other side of the door was non-existent. It appeared to be part of the warren of service corridors that often existed, invisible in the houses of the rich. He stopped at one of the unadorned doors that lined the corridor.

'This is your room. Once you've settled, report back to the guard house.'

The room reminded him of the one he had in his first year at the Academy. It was spartan, utilitarian and small. It didn't bother him though. He sat on the bed and began to unpack his belongings. It was then that he noticed a brown paper parcel on the floor beside the chair and small table. He opened it to find that it contained several suits of clothes, those that he had been measured for by dal Dragonet's aide. They were not particularly stylish, but they were about what he expected from what dal Dragonet had said. He changed into one of them and then unwrapped his blades.

Every time he looked at them, their austere beauty struck him. They were the weapons of a warrior, not some dandy who strutted self-importantly around the city. Yet despite that there was something captivating about them. He strapped his old suspension on around his waist and put the blades into the scabbards. They were not a perfect fit, a thumbs width of the blade showed above the neck, but they would do for the time being. He would have something made for them as soon as he possibly could.

The clothes fit as well as any clothes he had worn before, and they suited him, he thought, with satisfaction. He checked himself over quickly, and then returned to the guardhouse by the way he had come.

Chapter 53

A PLACE AT COURT

'**B**anneret Captain Soren, pleased to meet you. I'm Edwart dal Gawan, Banneret of the Blue.'

He was dressed in the dark blue uniform of an infantry officer, but he wore no rank or regimental insignia. He had the slightly fairer complexion of those who come from the northern parts of Ostia and was clean shaven, contrary to the prevailing fashion at the time. He gestured to a chair and Soren sat.

'I've been tasked with the command of the Duke's new bodyguard,' said dal Gawan. 'Our duties are simple. We will be with the Duke at all times when he is outside of the Palace compound. While he is at the Palace, the responsibility for his safety will rest with the Guard, leaving us to our own devices. I fear overcoming boredom may become our greatest challenge, so I intend to put together a rigorous training regime for us, but otherwise you will be free to enjoy life here, which I think you will,' he said, with a smile.

Soren's first meeting with his new commander was promising. While he was an aristocrat, he had outlined his extensive résumé of operational experience and coupled with his brusque military manner it was obvious that he had spent as much time on drill squares as he had on ballroom dance floors.

He found the first few days of life at the Palace to be tedious as dal Gawan had hinted they might be. There seemed to be a banquet or a ball almost every night, and as a banneret, and a member of the Duke's retinue he was expected to be present. He had never felt comfortable with high society, even though at some level it represented the life he was striving to live. He hadn't grown up with these people, didn't know them and didn't much care for the things that they seemed to enjoy doing. He had quickly noticed, while at the Academy, that a bond existed between those who had grown up in the same circle that could never be fully achieved by a blow-in like Soren. As a result, he knew he would always be an outsider to some degree.

It seemed that the other members of the new bodyguard were of a similar mind. With the exception of dal Gawan, none of them were members of the nobility. They were all men who were lucky enough to get into the Academy, and from there had worked hard and fought to carve out their career. They were all older than him, and for most of them this was the pinnacle of their career.

Dal Gawan was the only one of them that truly belonged there. He was an aristocrat, but nobody could criticise his credentials. Being a Banneret of the Blue was testimony to his ability. When he had introduced himself, Soren felt a vague pang of regret that he had chosen not to remain at the Academy and complete his studies. He supposed there was always the possibility of returning there to complete the training at a later date.

While Soren and the others sat at their table at the banquets, not really talking, dal Gawan moved between the groups of other aristocrats, chatting, dancing and fully taking part in the evening. It occurred to Soren that they must have seemed like outcasts, but he had never enjoyed this kind of activity after its initial novelty value wore off and he did not expect that to change.

The Duke was always the centre of attention at these gatherings. It occurred to him that he had never actually seen the Duke before, other than in profile on one side of a one crown coin. He had assumed that he would be an older man, probably corpulent and decrepit, but in actuality he was a young man, as the numismatic depiction suggested, not much over thirty, and in good physical condition. He was still unmarried and was clearly considered attractive by the noble ladies of the Duchy. He came from one of the preeminent families of the Duchy, the elector counts, and had been elected as duke a decade or so before. It surprised Soren that such a young man would have been elected, but he did not pretend that he even began to understand the complex political machinations of the Duchy. All he knew was that once the scion of a family had served as a duke, no member of that family could be eligible for election for the next two generations. The system was designed to ensure that no one family could establish itself as a ruling dynasty and it had been successful in this aim since the founding of the Duchy, the better part of a thousand years before.

At the second banquet he attended, Soren had spotted Amero. In such company he had known that it was only a matter of time before their paths crossed once again, but it had put him into a black mood for the rest of the evening nonetheless. Amero spotted him and held Soren's gaze with no expression on his face for a moment before he returned to laughing with his companions. Soren looked around to see if Emeric was there. Amero's lap dog never strayed far from his master. It occurred to him that the same could now be said for him, but in the service of the Duke.

It came as a relief when the call finally came for them to escort the Duke out in to the city. The Duke rode in his carriage, with two of his New Guard as they were now being called, while the rest, including Soren, followed behind. The Duke was headed to the Cathedral. Despite having spent his childhood in a Cathedral orphanage, the religious liturgies taught had never established themselves in Soren's memory and he had never actually been inside the Cathedral itself. It seemed likely that a declaration of war against Ruripathia was coming any day, and the Duke wanted a blessing on any future military endeavours.

The carriages rattled along the cobbles of the streets with forerunners clearing the way until they passed out of the tight streets, and the rows of tall buildings fell away to the vast open space of Crossways. The square was, as always, crowded. For the first time Soren felt a twinge of apprehension at the prospect of the job ahead. In a wide-open space, with large crowds, there were any number of ways someone could attack the Duke. By bow from a rooftop would be impossible to head off; all they could hope to do was provide an adequate screen, which would mean that one of the bodyguards would take the arrow. That wasn't a solution Soren found particularly attractive but he supposed that was part of the job.

A direct attack would be easier to deal with. It would be easier to spot, and Soren was comfortable that no one would get past him. He hadn't seen much of the other members of the New Guard yet, other than a little in practice sparring sessions, but they all seemed to be well able to handle themselves. You could never tell though, not until the true test came.

They took position around the carriage and waited for the Duke to exit. One of his attendants exited first, then the Duke and another of his aides. Soren scanned the crowd, his eyes moving slowly back and forth. Their arrival was generating little, if any interest. People kept about their business, some casting a brief glance at the ornate carriage. As the Duke walked toward the Cathedral and up its steps, Soren and the New Guard walked with him in a loose ring around him and his attendants.

Weapons were forbidden in the Cathedral, which made the bodyguard all but useless. Those that followed the rules often left themselves vulnerable, and Soren knew that if he were planning to assassinate the Duke, he would wait inside the Cathedral, with all the weapons necessary to complete the job. Screened off from too many eyes, there were plenty of places to hide in wait; it really was a very attractive option for a potential assassin. The only question that remained was if anyone was blasphemous enough to shed blood in the Cathedral. It wouldn't have been a problem for him.

He actually gasped in awe when he went into the Cathedral. It was the largest enclosed space he had ever been in. The training hall at the Academy had been vast, its ceiling was dizzyingly high and every sound echoed around it when it was empty. The Cathedral was at least twice the size, if not more. But where the training hall had been austere and functional, the Cathedral was magnificent. Great banners hung from poles sticking out from the walls running down either side of the nave, which led to the altar at the front, some one hundred paces distant. The banners were those of heroes of Ostenheim, there as a mark of respect to honour their service to the city. Soren wondered if his as yet unmade banner would ever hang there. When he looked to the ceiling, he felt a little dizzy, so high above him were its graceful vaults.

Dal Gawan told them to wait by the doors, close to their weapons, which in one sense was comforting to Soren, but in another, it bothered him that they would be too far from the Duke to be of any use to him. It wouldn't do his career any good to have the Duke assassinated on their first proper day out.

In the end he need not have worried. The Duke conferred with the Lord Bishop for half an hour, prayed for about the same length of time, and then they were all back in their carriages returning to the Palace. Soren felt a mixture of relief and disappointment that nothing of interest had occurred. Hopefully it would not be so long until their next outing, because until then it would be little more than vapid parties, banquets and boredom.

The relationship between the members of the New Guard began to thaw with the passage of time. It took a few days, but gradually they all came to the conclusion that they were all outsiders there, all there to do a specific job, and they were all more than qualified. The initial efforts to maintain a tough, distant air dissipated and the chat at their table behind the Duke's became more congenial. Technically they were not on duty during the parties, where there were enough guards to put off any would be assassin. Nonetheless they were all aware of how important their jobs were and how good an opportunity they had, and with this in mind, they could never fully relax or consider themselves completely off duty. All of them carried at least their daggers and none took more than furtive sips of wine, their eyes always keen, their expressions always alert.

Soren felt physically ill when he saw Alessandra come into the banqueting hall one evening on the arm of an elderly aristocrat. He was stuffed into an immaculate military uniform, and his hair and moustache were clearly dyed. The lines on his face betrayed his age though. She looked radiant, as she always had. The already bright room seemed to brighten with her presence. He looked away as soon as he saw her and felt himself shrinking into his seat. He didn't want her to see him. The next time he saw her, he wanted to have been ennobled, wealthy, a great hero and famous swordsman. Not just a journeyman on retainer.

Chapter 54

A CHANCE ENCOUNTER

The Duke was something of an incompetent romantic. He was said to be skilled in governance, and respected by the counts and merchants of the Duchy, but when it came to women, he was useless, even by Soren's standards. He made Soren look like a veritable lothario. The Duke was being pressured both by his advisors and family members to marry. He was already old to be single at his station in life and by all accounts his mother was keen to ensure that their branch of the family continued into the next generation. As such, she regularly arranged for him to lunch with various eligible young ladies of the Duchy. There were constant rumours as to who his potential bride might be and each time he was seen talking with an eligible young lady, the flames of these rumours were fanned once more. Other rumours were less kind about the Duke, and were intended to be injurious to his rule.

On this afternoon, he was walking in his garden with the daughter of the count of somewhere or other. Soren didn't bother trying to keep track of who they were any more. Soren was with him, maintaining a respectful distance, for what it was worth. There was no danger of eavesdropping as the conversation between them was stilted to the point of being non-existent. It was so uncomfortable that Soren actually felt embarrassed for the Duke.

The gardens were laid out in geometric patterns, with bleached gravel paths between them. It was very restful and an enjoyable way to spend an afternoon. It required constant maintenance and at any time there were four or five gardeners tending to the carefully shaped trees and bushes. They were instructed to keep their distance which Soren expected did not make for the most efficient work practices, as they had to keep moving from area to area to keep out of the Duke's way.

He walked slowly behind the couple, a few yards back, with his hands resting on the hilts of his blades. It was difficult to keep up concentration under the circumstances. Other than the young lady, the gardeners were the only other people visible. To keep his mind active, he started imagining scenarios where each of the gardeners was an assassin. He imagined what they would do to remain outside suspicion until they were ready to make their attack.

He ran through dozens of scenarios, deciding how he would react to each of them. If he was honest with himself, he would have acknowledged that he was bored at the Palace. He had not known what to expect, but in the two weeks he had been there, the Duke had only left the grounds on that one occasion to go to the Cathedral. Otherwise, it was all meetings, balls and banquets. Soren enjoyed being around beautiful women as much as anyone, but Amero and Alessandra were there regularly, which made him uncomfortable. He was beginning to feel as though he was not achieving anything useful, and allowing his abilities to go to waste.

Palace gossip seemed to be more up to date than the news announced by the crier on Crossways everyday, and it seemed that war with Ruripathia was only days away. He thought of Alys with regret. It seemed stupid to be going to war with them, when the potential for friendship was there. He wondered how things had gone so wrong. He had a nagging doubt about the killing of Chancellor Marin, but he could not reconcile in his head what Amero would gain if it had not been done in the best interest of the Duchy. His grandfather had been a duke, so he was ineligible.

The General had ordered him to assassinate three of the most powerful men in Ostenheim, but surely those orders had to have come from the Palace. They were supposedly all men whose power represented a threat to the Duke, but what dal Dragonet had said sowed seeds of doubt in his mind about that. Of course there was no one he could ask. His role in the killings, if they were indeed an attack against the Duke's reign, however unwitting, was something he did not wish to have discovered.

Something beyond his understanding was going on, and he was beginning to feel that he had played a role in it without his consent. That bothered him greatly.

The Duke's stroll with the young lady ended, leaving Soren to escort him back to his apartments. They walked in silence initially, the Duke's tension palpable. Eventually he broke the silence.

'That really didn't go at all as I had intended,' he said.

'It rarely does, sir, in my experience,' Soren replied, giving what he hoped came across as a fraternal and conciliatory grimace.

———◆◆◆———

The Duke was speaking at the Barons' Hall, at the opening ceremony of the Council of Nobles' term. During the summer and harvest months, most of the nobles would be away on their estates. With the drawing in of winter, they congregated in the city for the six months that their assembly sat. Soren wasn't exactly sure what it was they did, only the elector counts had a say in the Ducal elections, and once elected the Duke had supreme authority over the Duchy, but he supposed there were other issues in which their input would be required. The edicts that were read out by the city criers at the beginning of each week had their origins in the debates there.

They went out in a procession of two carriages with forerunners clearing the streets ahead of them as usual. Soren stared out of the window of the carriage he was in as it rattled over the cobbled streets, constantly looking for any potential threat.

The city was in a high state of agitation, and it was clear that the majority of the debate at the House of Nobles would be concerned with the Ruripathian transgressions on the border. Their chief speaker was dead, which was Soren's doing and there was a lack of political unity and direction as a result. It was the Duke's hope that he could address the issue and inject some stability with his opening speech. The guilds remained a problem for him however. With Spiro dead, they had been vying with each other to have their candidate fill the vacancy. The problem was exacerbated by the fact that the obvious successors to Grand Burgess Spiro, those next in the hierarchy of the Congress of Guilds, had also been killed around the time that Spiro had. With no clear successor, chaos had descended on the guilds. Violence had already erupted more than once, with several men dead as a result of the last incident. He had heard that the City Watch were becoming increasingly alarmed.

With the increase in random acts of crime, the Watch were under siege. Parts of the city had become no go areas in a matter of days as violence erupted between the criminal gangs. They too had experienced the killings of several of their higher ranking members. With no clear-cut order of succession, there was an intense and violent power struggle spilling over into the streets. While the guild members tended to restrict their violence to broken bones and cracked heads, the criminal gangs were killing with reckless abandon.

Dal Gawan kept a small office at the Palace where he worked when he was not accompanying the Duke or training with the New Guard. He had called Soren in for unknown reasons, so Soren felt a little apprehensive as he entered the room.

'Soren, thank you for coming. I don't have much time, so I'll be brief. You're efficiency and discretion have caught the Duke's eye, and he has singled you out for praise. He asked me to make you a small award, so I have given you the rest of the day off and a small financial reward.' He slid a small coin pouch across his desk. 'Be back to barracks by eight bells if you would.'

Ten crowns was a tidy sum and the acknowledgement of his work by the Duke was a huge reward in itself. If he continued to gain the Duke's favour he would do very well indeed. He made straight for the artisans' district to find a scabbard and suspension that would better fit his sword. He could have one made up, but that would add to the expense and there would be a very good selection to choose from amongst the leatherworking shops there anyway. On campaign they tended not to last long, so he really didn't see the sense in commissioning one especially and putting himself through that additional expense.

As he walked across the city, he felt good about himself. The approbation of the Duke had far more of an effect on his spirits than he thought it would, and it seemed to give reason to the evenings sitting uncomfortably at balls and the boredom of waiting around the Palace. For the first time it occurred to him that the job was not just about actually keeping the Duke safe, but it was equally about making him feel that he was safe.

He purchased a medium tan coloured scabbard, sheath and suspension at the third leather workers that he visited. It was plain, but of good quality and solid workmanship and he felt it was a worthy accompaniment to his sword.

His last task for the day was to pay a call to the Bannerets' Hall, where the Emblazoners of Banners kept their office. He still had no idea what he would have on his banner, but had more or less decided to allow the emblazoners to guide him on the matter. He had been putting off having it made for some time, but now that he was part of the Duke's retinue, not having one had become somewhat conspicuous.

In keeping with custom, the banner would be white, with whatever design he settled on embroidered onto it. Had he completed his studies at the Collegium he would have been entitled to have a blue banner, the colour of Ostenheim and the Academy.

After some thought and discussion with the emblazoner who had been assigned to him, he decided on two belek, standing rampant on either side of a sword, a representation of his greatly prized Telastrian steel blade. The belek had also seemed like an appropriate choice. Having hunted them, killed one and having nearly been killed by it himself, he felt he had more of a connection with them than any of the other beasts, real or mythical, that the emblazoner had suggested.

The chosen colour of the design could not be changed at a future date, so he chose a silver thread for the bulk of the embroidery, which he felt would stand out equally well on either the white cloth he was currently entitled to, or the blue of a Collegium graduate. He had decided that he would return to the Academy to complete his studies as soon as his commitments to the New Guard were satisfied, or as now seemed to be most likely, when the impending war with Ruripathia was over.

The only features of his design not in silver were the tongue, teeth and eyes of the belek, all of which he wanted emphasised, the tongue a brilliant red, the teeth white and the cold blue eyes the shade of a clear winter sky.

The process of having the banner designed and made was free, a gift from the city to those that would serve her. The emblazoner ensured him it would be delivered to him at the Palace as soon as it was ready.

With his errands all complete, he decided to treat himself to a mug of ale and a pie before returning to the barracks. It would pale in comparison to the food he was becoming used to at the Palace, but there was something about ale and pie's simplicity that appealed to him. It was hearty eating and not too rich, like many of the delicacies served up to him at the Palace. He had a plain palate, and after years of scavenging for every meal, even the simplest of fare seemed like a feast.

He chose a tavern on his way back toward the Palace that placed it at the edge of Oldtown, on the street one would take if going from the centre of the city to Oldtown. Soren would turn right once he crossed the bridge over the Westway river and go up the hill toward Highgarden and the Palace, rather than left through the gate in the old city wall and into Oldtown.

He sat by the window and let his mind drift as he stared out over the street and the river beyond. Barges plied their way up and down the river. They were long and flat to allow them under the bridges while still maintaining good cargo capacity and were towed by teams of horses that walked along the bank of the river when they were outside of the city walls. Once they reached the city, the barges were connected to a series of cogs and chains that dragged them up and down the river. The cogs were turned by teams of horses in tow-houses at various intervals along the river as there was not the space on the riverbank for a towpath as there was outside of the city. They brought goods and trade up and down the river. The Westway went as far as the Blackwater to the north, while the Eastway River on the other side of the city was navigable by the barges all the way to the Silver Hills in the North East, nearly as far as barbarian territory.

He received his food and didn't waste a moment in starting. The pastry was thick, crusty and rich, and the ale was sweet and bitter at the same time. As he ate, he watched a noblewoman and her two attendants walk by with a number of packages. The attendants were clearly overloaded and struggling, and one of them dropped a package on the ground. As she struggled to retrieve it, she managed to drop the rest that she was carrying.

Soren could not help but let out a chuckle at the comedy of the moment. Square and cylindrical boxes tumbled across the cobbled street, and the noblewoman turned to scold her servant. She was dressed in a fine scarlet and gold silk cloak with a hood that had concealed all but a few dark curls. As she turned however, he could see her face. It was Alessandra. His heart jumped into his throat, and the mouthful of pie nearly choked him. She looked exquisitely beautiful. She had been at several of the Duke's balls, but the ballroom was enormous and she had never been closer to him than a dozen paces. Now though, little more than the length of an arm and a pane of glass separated them. The glass was warped, which gave his view a slightly surreal appearance. His heart raced and he felt a tightness in his chest as he watched her turn.

Her view passed over the alehouse window as she turned; to Soren it seemed as though she moved in slow motion. Almost like when the Gift was strong. Perhaps it was. As her view passed by him, he saw her eyes widen. Where a moment before there had been exasperation, now there was uncertainty. She looked back to where he sat and their eyes met. He didn't know what to do. Their gaze locked for an instant, which felt like an eternity. There was a sadness on her face and he didn't know how to react. Part of him wanted to go out onto the street and take her into his arms, but he couldn't do that. He was too ashamed of the way he had behaved. All he felt was pain. She gave a sad smile that almost broke Soren's heart. All he could do was stare. She turned back and began helping her attendant gather up the packages, the chastisement that had been on her lips now well and truly gone. Then she was also gone. It felt to Soren that part of him was gone too.

The bill for his ale and pie arrived. It was far higher than he expected, far higher than it should be, even in a reasonably nice alehouse such as this. He didn't quibble over the price though; all he wanted was to get out of there, into the open air. It felt as though he was suffocating.

Chapter 55

THE DUKE'S BODYGUARD

S oren sat in the antechamber to dal Dragonet's office at the
Palace. The walls were paper-thin though, and sitting next to
it, he could hear the conversation on the other side.

'It's been a month since the last shipment got through,' said a
voice.

'And what are our reserves like?' said another, which Soren
thought to be dal Dragonets.

'Fine for now, my Lord, but we are entirely reliant on the supplies coming down river. Not a single grain ship has come into
the Ostsea since before the feast of Eilet. The merchant's are well
aware of this, and already the price for basic foodstuffs has gone
up fourfold. Needless to say there has been a knock on effect on
the sentiment of the populace!'

'Not what we need right now,' said dal Dragonet. 'Thank you
for bringing this to my attention. I will discuss it with the Duke
immediately. For now, start to release grain from our reserves to
keep prices from going any higher. I want to be kept updated on
how the situation progresses.'

The official making the report came out of the office and dal
Dragonet's secretary went in.

'Banneret Soren is here for you, my Lord.'

'Thank you. Send word for Admiral dal Assegar to attend on
me at the soonest possible time. Show the Banneret in,' said dal
Dragonet.

Soren walked into the office. Dal Dragonet did not even look
up from the pile of papers he was going through. The burden of

work on the man had increased enormously in recent days, and the strain was beginning to show on him.

'There is a demonstration in Crossways Square. It's been going on since daybreak and shows no sign of abating. We have decided that it will be necessary for the Duke to address the crowd himself. Banneret dal Gawan is away attending to family matters, so I'm putting you in charge of the bodyguard for the day. Are you willing to take on the responsibility?'

It was an opportunity that was not likely to come a second time, so Soren accepted.

There was some urgency to their task, and the Duke's departure had been delayed as long as possible to allow for adequate security to be put in place. As it was there had not been time to recall any of the members of the New Guard who were off duty and about the city somewhere. Including dal Dragonet, there would be six of them to protect the Duke. They were going on horse back, as the Duke wanted to be able to get to the steps of the Cathedral without drawing undue attention, and to make his address from there.

They rode out, cloaked and unidentifiable, at a brisk pace through Highgarden, slowing only when they crossed the river and entered the narrower and more crowded streets of the centre of the city. There was little to arouse Soren's suspicion, and they arrived at the square with nothing to cause him concern. What they found when they got there was a different matter however. A man was already addressing the gathered protestors, who were silent and attentive. There was something eerie about them, so many people so completely silent. The man had a firm hold on them. It was Amero.

They carefully drew closer to hear what he was saying. The Duke decided not to press on in and make his appearance, but rather wait a little longer to gauge the sentiment. When dealing with large and angry crowds, care was always appropriate.

By the time he had finished speaking, the crowd seemed calmed and slowly began to disperse. On the face of it, every thing Amero said seemed to be in support of the Duke, but there was an underlying tone to it hinting that the Duke was weak and not capable of dealing with times of difficulty, but that it was not really his fault, he was simply not up to the job. As they rode away from the square, the Duke said one thing to dal Dragonet.

'That man is dangerous.'

They began their return journey to the Palace the same way they had come, a slightly longer route north out of the square and then west to the river, so they could avoid having to pass directly through the square and risk recognition. There had been too much vitriol in the mob that day to make it worthwhile for the Duke to take the chance. It was a bad state of affairs when the leader of a city could not pass through it as he chose without fear of assault.

As they rode back, Soren tried to be aware of everything that was going on around him. There was something nagging at him though, in the back of his mind. There had been a man in the crowd who he had seen looking at them one too many times for it to be coincidence. Perhaps it was nothing.

As they passed through a narrow street with high, balconied buildings lining either side, he heard a dull grunt from one of the other men in the New Guard. He turned to see the man looking down at his chest. The thick stubby shaft of a crossbow bolt stuck from the centre of it. He took hold of it with one hand as though he was going to try to pull it out. His face held an expression of incredulity as blood began to bubble from the corners of his mouth. He reached graspingly for the hilt of his sword with his other hand in an automatic but futile response to danger, before toppling off his horse.

It had taken a fraction of a second for what was happening to register with Soren.

'Ambush!' he yelled at the top of his voice, while he drew his sword. He took a deep breath and focussed on the energy. Everything flashed blue for an instant, the glow disappearing as soon as he directed his thoughts elsewhere. The world around him slowed perceptibly.

There were bowmen on two of the balconies above them. One was reloading while the other had just loosed a bolt. Soren watched as it flew through the air, its tip and tail oscillating while its centre remained still. It was on a direct trajectory toward the Duke, appearing to Soren as though it was trying to force its way through a viscous liquid rather than air. It drew ever closer as all around him was chaos. The Duke had seen it too; his face was frozen with resigned terror. Soren reached out with his sword, and with an upward flick of his wrist he lopped the steel tip off the bolt, and with the following downward flick, he batted it to the ground with the flat of the blade. The look of terror on the Duke's face was replaced with one of astonishment.

The others had gathered their wits quickly. They were professionals and the surprise of the attack would not affect them for long. They had returned fire with their own small bows and already one of the two attacking crossbowmen had been brought down. There were also men coming at them from the front and behind at street level, and the New Guard were wading into them with their horses. Two of them had also closed in around the Duke to protect him.

Comfortable in the knowledge that the other bodyguards were handling things, Soren took a second to survey the situation. As soon as the surprise had subsided, the real threat had passed. Now it was nothing more than a mop up. He backed his horse up to bring himself closer to the Duke. Out of the corner of his eye he spotted a man in a black hooded cloak at the end of the street. By the time he looked directly, the man was gone. He had an uncomfortable sense of recognition in his stomach. He was sure that it had been Emeric.

⚊⚫✳⚫⚊

Soren was finding himself at dal Dragonet's office more and more frequently. He was not particularly bothered by the fact, thus far it had usually signalled good news. The aide led him into the office as usual and dal Dragonet gestured for him to sit down. He looked agitated as he set a sheaf of papers down on the side of his desk.

'I'm moving you from the New Guard,' he said.

Soren's mouth opened in surprise but before he could speak, dal Dragonet continued.

'After the attack the other day, the Duke has requested that you be made his personal bodyguard. I agree with his reasoning, so you will be moved to that detail immediately. It's clear now that the threat we perceived to the Duke wasn't a paranoid fantasy. Be vigilant. Where the Duke goes, you go. His life is your responsibility now, and I needn't warn you of the consequences should we fail. You will need to know something else now also. We received word that the Ruripathians crossed the border in force last week and invested Northmarch castle. Part of their army went right past it and marched straight into Baelin. Word of this hasn't reached the populace yet, but the news will be no more than a day or two behind our messengers. We have mobilised the army, and called up the reserves. The Duke needs to be ready to declare war and march as soon as word reaches the people on the street. His position is tenuous. A coup is as likely right now as another assassination attempt. Our enemies are within as well as without.'

Chapter 56

THE DRUMS OF WAR

There was something stirring about marching to war, and as soon as Soren found out that he would be going the excitement occupied most of his thoughts. The morning they rode out of the city, Soren had pride of place at the head of the army beside the Duke. His banner had arrived just in time and it was with great pride that he watched it flutter in the air at the end of his lance, just beneath that of the Duke, which was his privilege to carry.

An honour guard of five thousand men had been chosen for a procession through the city before they joined with the main body of the army that was camped outside the walls. The streets were lined with people as they passed through the city, from the Palace through Highgarden down to Crossways and then out of the North Gate. Alessandra was there; standing with other well dressed ladies in an enclosure at the side of the road that had been cordoned off for them. Beautifully dressed and catching the eye of every soldier that filed past her, his eyes were the only ones she met. It angered him that after all that had passed between them she could still have such an overwhelming effect on him with nothing more than a gaze. There was a sadness in her eyes, but Soren refused to allow himself to be baited by it. He hardened his jaw and directed his gaze ahead, like a good soldier. He hated himself for doing it, but he could no longer admit how much he loved her, even to himself. It simply hurt too much.

Soren loved being in an army encampment, the activity and the order of it all. There was no time to be wasted however, and as the honour guard passed through the camp, parts of it were being packed up as the men waited to fall in behind them and join the march. The army was so large that many of the men would be sleeping where their tents were that night, not having to pack and begin the march until the following morning. It made the army he had been part of in the east look like a small scouting force.

They only marched for a few hours before they camped for the night. Soren was a little surprised when they came upon the Duke's compound, already set up over a small rise in the road. A party had ridden on ahead to set it up so that it was all ready for him when they arrived. Considering the eagerness that all of the senior officers had been speaking with when talking about joining with the enemy at the earliest possible opportunity, Soren had expected that there would be several long forced marches in the early days of the advance. It surprised him to see that this army was going to be moving so slowly. It seemed that these officers were of a different calibre to those that had led the army in the east, all pomp and ceremony but no grit.

They dined that night with a full silver service, fine wines and crystal goblets. The officers then all retired to their personal tents, while the army was settling in around them. Privileged aristocrats ran this army, and it made Soren uneasy to think what would happen when they were finally engaged in battle.

The food was good, and he could appreciate that; he would never turn his nose up at a meal no matter how inappropriate he might consider its trimmings. He was thankful that the Duke had dedicated tasters though. The days when a full belly was worth the risk of being poisoned were well and truly behind him. He sat to the Duke's right and to all intents and purposes was one of the privileged men that sat around the table despite never feeling like one. The only difference was that he was the only man at the table who was armed. Even dal Dragonet had surrendered his weapons as a gesture to the others, one or more of whom it was feared could be part of the conspiracy against the Duke. General Kastor was not there; he was in command of a division somewhere to the rear and hadn't made it to the officers' enclosure in time for supper. That, at least, was one threat avoided. He determined there and then that whatever unwitting role he had played in aiding the conspiracy, he would play a very conscious and determined role in pulling it apart and seeing that its perpetrators suffered the full consequences of their treachery.

After supper, Soren was relieved by dal Gawan. While he slept, the New Guard would watch over the Duke. He strolled out amongst the tents in the fresh evening air. Officers stood around communal fires, smoking twists of tobacco and laughing and joking. Most of them would never have been to war before. They would all be well-trained swordsmen, having had to pass through the Academy, which in most cases was a formality of their station in life, but they would lack the experience that combat brought.

Near the edge of the officers' camp and where the neatly laid out grid pattern of the army's camp began, there was a small cluster of tents that were of a very different character to the rest. When he heard the first feminine voice, he smiled to himself. Where an army marched, a coterie of camp followers tagged along. They would be wives and sweethearts of the soldiers, some welcome, some not so, and enterprising whores who were willing to endure the privations of the road to earn a little extra money. Before the war was over, he fully expected that some of the wives and sweethearts would end up as whores, and some of the whores would end up as wives and sweethearts. Such was the way of war.

He slept well that night, which was not something he did often. It confirmed in his mind that he was best suited to a martial lifestyle. He enjoyed the hard living and plain requirements. Being the Duke's personal bodyguard was as high as a swordsman could hope to rise at such a young age, but it was largely boredom and struggling to look the part in a world that he had once coveted, but now realised he was completely unsuited to. He had been a fool, dreaming and wishing of having a place in high society. When the war was over and the conspiracy dealt with, he determined to resign from the Duke's service. He would return to the Academy and complete his studies, and after that there was always plenty of mercenary work to be had. It was in combat that he felt most alive, as though that was his place in life.

Waking to the sounds of a military camp coming to life was a cheering thing for him. It was a world he understood and felt comfortable in. He could act with authority here, not concerned that he was committing some faux pas that would mark him out as a social pariah.

'We break camp at ten bells, Banneret Soren,' an adjutant called to him, when he walked out of his tent.

Ten bells, Soren thought with surprise. It was only six. In his experience, an army's camp would be broken with the army on the move by eight bells at the latest. He shrugged and waved a response to the adjutant, who smiled at the acknowledgment. In the Palace he was ignored like part of the furnishings. In the camp of an army he was a man of authority. He liked that.

He made his way to the tent where they had eaten supper the night before in the hope of scrounging up some breakfast. What he found made him smile. The cooks had clearly been up at the appropriate waking time for an army, and the table was fully laid out in anticipation of the arrival of the earliest rising of the officers. As Soren was the first, he had his choice of the freshly cooked food. He over-ate a little, spending longer at the table than he would have were it not for the fact he had four hours to kill before the army would be getting under way.

He returned to his tent and checked his kit, then rechecked it, and then oiled the blades of his sword and dagger. Eventually when ten bells came, he was waiting outside the Duke's tent. Calling it a tent was somewhat deceptive, as it was more like a portable mansion, with thick carpets and heavy furniture that would be packed up and loaded onto carts to be taken to the next camp location.

There was more activity in the command tent than he would have expected and it didn't seem as though anyone was in a hurry to move. Although he had no role in the command hierarchy, as the Duke's personal bodyguard, he had access to all areas. He wandered into the tent, passing the sentries with a cursory nod. Dal Dragonet leaned on the campaign table, his arms wide and his head hanging low.

'We shall go out and meet them on the field of honour!' barked a noble in a pristine uniform.

'You don't understand, my Lord,' dal Dragonet replied, his head still hanging down, his voice sounding strained. 'The army is not fully assembled, and we will be unable to meet them with sufficient force to stop them. We should retreat to the walls of the city where we will be able to form up the army in full strength and fight on reasonably favourable ground.'

Soren turned to one of the adjutants waiting in the background. 'What's going on?' he asked.

'The scouts that came in overnight have reported that the Ruripathian army is less than a day to the north. Our pickets have already spotted some of their foraging parties. It seems like they really got the jump on us.'

'Rubbish!' barked another of the officers, drawing Soren's attention back to the conversation at the table. 'We cannot be seen to be running from the enemy. They have advanced far enough into our territory. Not one step further!' This was met with resounding acclaim from the other officers. All men with trumped up notions of honour and no experience of war. Dal Dragonet's was the only voice of reason, but he was not being listened to.

'We shall send them yelping back to their frozen wasteland like the dogs they are!' added another officer, which was received with another chorus of cheers.

Soren had had about as much as he could stomach, so went back outside. He looked north and wondered just how far away the Ruripathian army was. It was impressive that they had marched so far so quickly, but it was entirely possible that the Ostian scouts had been slow in reporting their crossing the border, and that they had been moving south for longer than had been thought.

Dal Dragonet walked quickly from the tent and when he spotted Soren he walked over to him. 'The army is to march to engage the Ruripathians. You saw most of what happened in there. Gods help us!'

———◆◆◆———

Unlike on the march from the city, the Duke and his retinue were to make up the rear guard of the advance into battle. Each of the division commanders had gone to join their regiments so his camp was relatively quiet. The army was to advance in battle order and it took some time for the divisions to spread out in line abreast. It was late afternoon before they finally got under way and despite the apparent foolishness of their advance, it was a magnificent sight to behold, thousands of men in blue tunics, lined up in ranks underneath their different coloured regimental banners.

When the army finally began to move off, the Duke's camp looked very much as it had that morning, with no real preparation for the advance having been undertaken. The only concession that dal Dragonet had been able to win from the Duke was the agreement that he would remain well behind the line and in relative safety. It was expected that battle would be met early the next day, so the decision was made to remain where they were for the night, and to continue on at dawn. If they moved quickly, they should re-join the army before it engaged.

Chapter 57

THE FINAL INTRIGUE

The afternoon had become early evening when a carriage appeared on the road from the city. The Duke was resting in his tent and Soren's hands went instinctively to the hilts of his blades. He watched the carriage make its way toward the camp until finally it arrived. He was a little touchy about security, only having four men of the New Guard, a few dozen soldiers and the men of the Duke's retinue, who were of no fighting value with him. The arrival of the carriage concerned him.

When Alessandra stepped out of it, he could not help but feel that this was a complication that he did not need. His mind bubbled with reasons for her being there, one of the aristocratic officers having hired her services being toward the top of the list. She caught his gaze, took a deep breath and approached him.

'I need to talk with you,' she said uncomfortably.

'What could you possibly need to say to me, now of all times?'

'The war is what makes it all the more pressing. I had to speak with you before the fighting starts. I received this letter yesterday evening and set out at first light. I didn't expect to happen upon you so soon to be honest,' she said. She held up a letter with a broken red wax seal. He was torn between not wanting to talk to her and desperately wanting to talk to her. He allowed his curiosity over the letter to sway his decision.

'I don't know what it is you need to say. I'll listen, but be quick, I have duties to attend to,' he said. He gestured for her to walk alongside him.

'This letter. It's from our patron, Lord Amero.' She placed a bitter emphasis on the words 'our patron'.

'What did he have to say?' Soren asked.

'He told me the truth, for once. He told me why you disappeared that summer, why you had to go. He apologised for what he did,' she said.

Soren let out a sarcastic laugh. 'Finally it seems he's discovered a conscience.' It gave him pause for thought. It just didn't seem likely.

'I felt that I had to come to set things between us to rights, before the fighting started, in case... I couldn't leave this unsaid. After you disappeared I went to him to find out where you were. He said that you'd just gone. That he had no idea where. I was upset, and he was kind. He said that he felt bad for what had happened and that if I ever needed help I had but to ask. A few weeks later, the Don's thugs came around. My uncle hadn't been paying his protection money. They killed him and my aunt and burned the tavern to the ground. I managed to get away. I was so afraid and confused. I had nowhere to go and no one to help me. I remembered what he said, so I went to see him. I thought he might find me a job as a maid or something. Well, you know how that ended up.' She smiled bitterly. 'I didn't think I'd ever see you again. I really didn't. But I never stopped loving you.'

Soren's brain was racing furiously to answer an amorphous question that was floating around in his mind. In Soren's time of knowing him, Amero had never done anything positive for another person unless it was a consequence of his own selfish plans. What had changed? Soren looked at Alessandra, studying her closely. She seemed confused by his scrutiny. What was her role in this? Was she part of something that she wasn't aware of also? What did Amero have to gain by playing with his head like this?

The impact of her words was like a kick to the stomach and he was finding it hard to think clearly. His love for her was so intense that resisting it made it feel as though his heart was being crushed in his chest. He did not doubt the sincerity of her words. He could hear the heartfelt honesty in her voice. He wanted to believe her more than anything in the world, and he did. But something was amiss, and he could not shake that feeling off. Why had Amero waited until now to send the letter? He was being played again and he could not allow it to happen.

Soren began walking quickly toward the Duke's tent, breaking into a run as he went and leaving Alessandra standing where she was in confusion. He pulled the door flaps apart and looked in, his heart dropping.

'Alarm!' He shouted at the top of his voice. Two guards rushed to him, while others made for their arms around the small camp. Soren turned to one of them, whose face had paled at the sight. 'Get word to Lord Dragonet. The Duke is assassinated.'

The guard nodded and left, leaving Soren to look back on the scene before him. The far panel of the tent had been cut, allowing a blade of light into the otherwise dull tent. Two attendants lay dead on the ground; there was no sign of a struggle, indicating the speed with which they had been killed. The Duke sat on a chair beside his morning table, his head lolling back with his throat open to his backbone. An assassin who had killed three men in such silence was a skilled professional who would be long gone. Or he could be one of the men in the camp, disguised and unidentifiable.

The tent had the tangy metallic stink of blood. Soren turned and stepped away from the tent. His eyes met Alessandra's. Her face was pale and shocked. Her role in the assassination had been unknown to her; looking at her he was sure of that. He gestured with his head to her carriage.

'Go now. Quickly. Get what you need, leave the city and don't come back. You are part of this now, knowingly or not and you'll pay for it with your life if you stay,' he said, his voice flattened by complete and utter defeat.

'What about you? Come with me, we can escape together,' she said hopefully. 'Please.'

'This lies at my feet. I have to stay. I'll come and find you if I can. Now go, quickly!' he said. She nodded solemnly, tears welling in her eyes, but she did as he said and walked to the carriage. As she stepped up into it and shut the door behind her, Soren rushed forward. He reached through the window and took her face in both hands. He kissed her. He could feel her tears on his cheek. He pulled back.

'Drive on!' he shouted to the carriage driver. As it jolted to a start he let go of her and stepped back off the running board. As he did, he spoke to here one last time.

'I love you.'

Chapter 58

AN UNWANTED REUNION

Dal Dragonet came galloping into the camp with five men. He dismounted and walked quickly to where Soren was sitting on the ground, cross legged and completely dejected. He cast a glance at Soren but continued past and into the Duke's tent. He emerged a few moments later with a grave look on his face. The five men who had ridden in with him had gathered outside the entrance and they parted to let him pass.

He knelt down beside Soren and looked at him intently. He made to say something, and then stopped. He shook his head and stood, turning to his men.

'Pull down his banner and bring it to me,' he said, 'and arrest the Banneret.'

Soren didn't struggle. He slipped his sword and dagger from their scabbards and handed them, hilt first, to dal Dragonet.

'I don't know what part you played in this, if any, but he was killed on your watch. At best you've failed in your duty.' He sighed deeply. 'I'm disappointed in you. What else is there to say?'

One of the men brought Soren's banner to dal Dragonet. He held it in his hands and looked at it gravely before looking back to Soren.

'I've never had to do this before,' he said, with a pained look. With that he took his dagger from his belt and roughly cut through the crumpled banner several times before handing it to Soren. No more needed to be said. Soren's banner was torn asunder by one of his peers, signalling his dishonour and damning him for it.

Dal Dragonet turned back to his men. 'Hold him under guard and send for a gaol wagon and an ambulance from the city.'

———◆·◆·◆———

The gaol wagon did not have any windows so it was only the sound of the wheels clattering on cobbles that let him know that he was back in the city. He was less afraid of his fate than disappointed in himself for having allowed Amero to so easily get the better of him. It was beyond doubt now that Amero had been behind it all and that his seemingly good act of telling Alessandra the truth was in fact another one of his manipulative schemes.

There were so many pieces that fitted together now. Princess Alys had said that Chancellor Marin was against a war, and yet they had killed him for the stated reason of securing peace. Dal Dragonet had not been familiar with General Kastor, whose orders now seemed to have been designed to stir the people up against the Duke. He must also have been involved in the plot. That unrest gave Amero the opportunity to take the stage and once again become the champion of the people. He had seen Emeric the day of the attempted assassination in the city, he was sure of that now, although at the time he had not been. It all seemed to make sense but for one thing. Amero could not become Duke by having the old one assassinated. There would still have to be an election, and Amero's family would not be eligible to run for another generation. Nevertheless, whatever his motivations, it was done, and at his whims, Soren had been made and undone.

He was hauled out of the wagon in the courtyard of the old castle, which sat on top of the cliff over-looking the bay. The sun was setting, and although it hurt his eyes after the darkness of the wagon, he watched it and took pause in its beauty, not knowing if he would ever see such a sight again. He was shackled at wrist and ankle and shoved unceremoniously forward by his guards. From the courtyard it was into the castle and down into the dungeons. They led him through a labyrinth of passages before stopping by one of the heavy oak doors that lined it. They took off his shackles, shoved him into the small room that lay on the other side of the door. He tensed as he waited for the inevitable sound of the thick wooden door slamming shut.

Time lost all meaning in the small, dark room. He was not sure how many times a day he was being fed, so counting meals was useless. After six or seven he had lost count anyway. It was difficult to discern between the meals he had, those he dreamt of and then to remember how many there were. Life blurred into one big void.

The door opened and a mage lamp cast an orange light into his small room. He looked up, but even that dim light pierced his eyes painfully. He looked back to the corner of his cell and tried to watch what was going on at the doorway from the corner of his eye. A large person stood framed in the doorway, larger than his usual gaoler. He stepped in, realising the effect the light from the lamp was having on Soren's eyes and shielded it behind his back.

'You're a sorry sight, lad. A sorry sight indeed. Shoulda taken my advice when you could! Now get up, you're coming with me.'

Soren struggled to his feet and looked at Emeric, who gestured for him to walk out into the passageway. He had not gone more than a few yards before his legs ached and he felt as though his calves were going to cramp. He stumbled on with Emeric and the gaoler as his eyes gradually became accustomed to the light, dim though it was.

They brought him to a guardroom that contained several mage lamps and was thus brighter than anything he had experienced in some time. He had to shield his eyes as the gaoler shoved him into the room, and onto a short stool.

'Well, well, you're looking worse for wear indeed.'

Soren recognised the voice immediately. 'What do you want Amero? Come to gloat?'

'Not at all, and it's "Your Grace" now, I feel the appropriate honorifics are important to maintain the proper respect,' he said.

Soren barked out a short laugh, as much a consequence of the fluid in his lungs as his disdain. 'How did you manage to wrangle that? How many aristocrats did you have Emeric kill for you?'

Amero looked at Soren with a smile on his lips for a moment before continuing. 'After Duke dal Tanosa was murdered by Ruripathian assassins, the army was sadly routed during a day long engagement with the Ruripathian army near a town called Sharn-home. But before that, when news of the Duke's untimely death and of an impending battle reached the city, an emergency election was held. Pietr dal Lloedale was elected as Duke, being head of the most senior eligible family. He rode north to join the army and led our forces at Sharnhome, but sadly he fell in battle, as did the heads and heirs of several of the other senior elector families. It was a grim day for the Duchy, but not one from which we could not recover. In the absence of enough elector counts or enough readily identifiable candidates for Duke, I offered myself up as interim ruler.

'I bought a little time with a peace delegation while I regrouped the army and counter attacked. This caught the Ruripathians entirely by surprise and I am happy to say that we defeated them utterly. When I returned to the city, I was naturally amazed to discover that the people were calling for my investiture as Duke by popular acclaim. After much soul searching, I acceded to their demands,' said Amero.

'And how was it that you managed to catch the Ruripathians so completely by surprise?' Soren asked.

Amero smiled and leaned back languidly in his chair, which, Soren noted, looked far too comfortable for the guardroom. He paused thoughtfully for a moment and gestured to Emeric with his eyes. Emeric shoved the gaoler out of the guardroom and closed the door behind him.

'Because they weren't expecting it of course. They do still teach about the value of the element of surprise at the Academy do they not? It may also have had something to do with the fact that it was an express breach of the agreement I made with the Ruripathians on our visit there. I give them Baelin, the warm water port they so desperately want, an easy victory in the field and they agree to peace and return to their own borders. They had no real stomach for a hard fought war, which I assured them they would have if they tried to go beyond the limits of our agreement, which happily they did not. Of course, all of that wouldn't be quite enough to get me elected Duke, now would it. I would need to pull off something a bit more impressive!

'Half the army was loyal to me, under the command of General Kastor, or Marshal Kastor dal Cadena as he is now. They managed to get lost during the night advance toward Sharnhome and by the time they found their way back to the rest of the army, the battle was well and truly lost. They did the only sensible thing and withdrew. A shame really, as had they been there, we would almost certainly have won. Nevertheless, with those troops and the survivors from the battle, I was able to cobble together an army. We fell on the Ruripathians as they were marching home. It was a magnificent victory, and one that I was able to take full credit for. Who better to lead Ostia than their saviour in their hour of need? When I retake Baelin and bring the war to Ruripathian territory, sending word of victory after victory home, the people will be confident that their choice was the correct one, a unified and confident voice in support of my confirmation as Duke. A voice far too strong for any noble to question with trifling issues such as legality.

'You're a clever lad, Soren; it's one of the things I always liked about you. I'm sure you can put the pieces together now, why everything that was done was done. The only thing I hadn't counted on was how much you liked that bloody girl! At first I had hoped your skills would be added to my plans. But after your little tantrum I feared you might become a problem. Try to kill me, or some such mischief. So, I had Kastor send you off on a suicide mission. Problem solved, or so I thought, and then you turn up in the city a half starved husk. Still you looked better then than you do now! With you alive and back in the city, we thought you could be useful again. We needed the city's civic leaders killed off, so we had you take care of a few of them. The unrest it created would help make dal Tanosa unpopular, and leave the people looking for a figure to unite behind. Me. The nobles fear nothing half as much as the popular voice. When that voice is united, it is a fearsome thing indeed.

'Why all the killing, you might ask. Well, even my wealth is not limitless, and it very quickly becomes more cost effective to kill people rather than to keep paying them off. Curiously aristocrats seem to be easier to keep a grip on, which is convenient as killing them is a damn sight harder. An unsavoury gambling debt, a cata-mite, a pretty whore.' His voice trailed off as he saw Soren's eyes widen and his jaw tighten.

'Ah, yes, everybody had their role to play, large or small, even your little strumpet. I have to admit, it came as something of a shock when dal Tanosa made you his personal bodyguard!' He chuckled. 'It took several hours of brainstorming to come up with a solution, as we didn't think we'd be able to get anywhere near him while you were protecting him. In the end the answer was right under our noses, as well you know. She knew nothing of our plans, for what it's worth. Just another unwitting piece on the board. A concept I think you should be familiar with by now.

'Well, enough of this. Now to my reason for bringing you here. I had my plans, and I've used people when and where necessary, but that doesn't change the fact I've always been fond of you, Soren. I'm only sorry that this story will end for you on the heads-man's block, but that's the way of things sometimes,' said Amero.

He stood and walked to the door and turned. 'Goodbye Soren, I do not think that we shall see one another again.'

Chapter 59

A DEBT SETTLED

He had no idea of when his execution was to be carried out. Each time the door to his cell opened, he waited to be bundled out to wherever it was to be done. Crossways perhaps, in front of a huge crowd baying for his blood, or more discretely in the courtyard of the castle, where the military executions were usually carried out. Most likely it would be the latter. As far as he could tell he hadn't been found guilty of any crime and execution was an unlikely punishment for not having been able to stop the assassination. It seemed that Amero wanted him out of the way and that his execution would be extra-judicial.

When the day finally came, he met it with reserved acceptance. He prayed that Alessandra had gotten away. As long as she had managed that, he could accept his fate. It pained him to realise that it was unlikely he would ever find out, one way or the other. The fact that Amero had not mentioned her capture, imprisonment or execution gave him hope, however.

His hands were tightly bound behind his back. They pulled a hood over his head as they dragged him from the cell. He realised that it was an act of mercy, whether they knew it or not. After so long in the darkness, candlelight would be painful to his eyes. Sunlight would likely blind him, not that it would matter much.

Down the corridor, up some steps, another corridor and more steps and then out into fresh air. All the while a strong pair of hands gripped onto his upper arms guiding him toward his impending death. He sucked in a deep lungful of the fresh sea air. How wonderful it was. He smiled to himself beneath the hood. He had had an incredible run. Once it had been unlikely that he would live past his teens on the streets. Instead he had rubbed shoulders with the finest society had to offer, he had been instrumental in the affairs of great nations and he had been one of the finest swordsmen who had ever lived. And he had known a love, one second of which made all the other achievements seem worthless. He was ready.

It seemed that he was to be executed in Crossways as they were bundling him into a wagon. He would have preferred the castle courtyard, there would be some shame in dying as a public spectacle, but so be it.

The wagon jerked to a start and the wheels rattled on the cobbles. It stopped at the castle gate for a brief, muffled conversation before starting off again and he could feel it angle down the hill toward the city. He tried to absorb every sensation, the sound of the wheels on the cobbles, the creaking of the suspension and the jostling motion of the wagon. Each experience was amongst his last, and he wanted to drink it all in, to imagine he was sharing each one with Alessandra.

Finally the wagon came to a complete halt, and he was pulled down onto the ground. The hood was pulled from his head and he squinted around, looking for the scaffold. It took a moment to focus, and when he did, it was not a scaffold he saw, nor an executioner. Instead he saw a jetty, and Ranph. He let out a crazy, desperate laugh.

'Ranph! What's going on?'

'I told you I wouldn't forget,' he said, a sad smile on his face. 'I'm sorry it took so long, but I've been having my own problems. I expect my estates to be declared forfeit any day now. Despite his power, Amero hasn't been having it all his own way in clearing out the old families, but he is getting there. As soon as I'm done here I'll be heading home to Bragadin to get my sisters, and from there, on out of the Duchy. You needn't fret; my family have adequate resources in other cities that will ensure we won't go hungry! I couldn't just leave you here to be executed though!'

'So what now?' Soren asked.

'The wherry there will take you out to a ship in the harbour which will sail as soon as you set foot aboard,' said Ranph.

'Where to?' Soren asked.

'Auracia. I hear that it's nice there at this time of year,' Ranph said sardonically.

'I can't thank you enough, Ranph. You've been a better friend than I could have ever asked for.'

'Don't get all gooey on me. Let's just call it even, shall we?' Ranph replied, with a smile.

'Did you hear anything about Alessandra?'

'She fled the city. She sent a maid to find me with a message, to let you know she was safe,' Ranph said.

Soren breathed a sigh of relief. 'Any idea of where she went?'

'Auracia,' Ranph replied, breaking into a wider smile. 'Now enough with the questions, we both need to be going.' He offered his hand, which Soren took, and shook firmly.

'Good luck, Ranph. I hope our paths cross again in happier times,' said Soren.

'I do also,' he said, before turning and walking to a waiting horse.

⸻⸺◆•◆◆•◆⸺⸻

Soren walked quickly down the jetty and hopped into the wherry.

'Pull away now, quick as you can,' he said to the boatman. He sat down in the small boat and looked nervously around him. Each stroke away from the shore was one closer to safety. He looked into the bilge and saw an oddly shaped bundle, wrapped in a familiar blue material. He reached for it and gasped with surprise when he realised it was his belek cloak. It was wrapped around his Telastrian sword and dagger. His heart jumped and he looked up and around. Standing on the now distant dock stood a tall man. He was dressed in black and was completely bald, and had only moments before been standing out of sight, unseen but watching.

⸻⸺◆•◆◆•◆⸺⸻

The ship's sails dropped from their booms as soon as the passenger clambered aboard. Emeric watched it sail away until it dropped under the horizon and disappeared from sight. He smiled a wry smile and ran a hand over his bald head as he made his way back to the Palace, and back to the service that he so rarely broke faith with.

AUTHOR BIOGRAPHY

Duncan is a writer of fantasy novels and short stories. He has a Masters Degree in History and when not writing he enjoys reading history, particularly the medieval and renaissance periods.

He doesn't live anywhere particularly exotic, and when not writing, he enjoys cycling, skiing and windsurfing.

duncanmhamilton.com

Made in the USA
Coppell, TX
04 November 2019